The Ashes of Home

Other work by Ian S. Bott

Science fiction

Ghosts of Innocence

Master assassin Shayla Carver has killed many times. That's what assassins do, nothing to lose sleep over, but this mission is different ... she's never killed a whole planet before.

Tiamat's Nest

The virtual world comes alive and reaches out into the real world with deadly results. University professor and devout technophobe, Charles Hawthorne, confronts technology full on to end the hidden threat to humanity.

Non-fiction

The Critique Survival Guide

Even amongst friends a detailed critique can be hard to take, but blunt and honest critiques are a necessary growth pain for any writer. Venturing into the anonymous jungle of online critique groups in search of tough love is both terrifying and exponentially rewarding. *The Critique Survival Guide* shares practical tips for surviving - and thriving on - the harshest of critiquing experiences.

The Ashes of Home

Ian S. Bott

Dark Sky Press

Copyright © 2018 by Ian S. Bott

Published by Dark Sky Press,
an imprint of Ian S. Bott, Writer and Artist

Visit our website at www.iansbott.com

Book Design by Jim Bisakowski
Cover illustration by Ian S. Bott

ISBN 978-0-9937242-5-1

Printed in the United States of America
First Edition: March 2018
10 9 8 7 6 5 4 3 2 1

To readers who enjoyed my first book
and gave me the encouragement to keep going,
I hope you find this a fitting continuation of Shayla's story.

Chapter 1

'Hope springs eternal' the ancient saying goes, but you need more than hope on your side when death comes knocking. Shayla Carver, master assassin (retired) and first governor of the Freeworld of Eloon, enjoyed more security than any ordinary paranoid could possibly hope for.

Any *ordinary* paranoid would be dead by now.

Official security measures handled casual bounty hunters and the merely competent. Shayla survived the serious threats through her own senses and training.

Tonight, returning to her quarters on the top floor of the Governor's Residence, her airways clamped shut at the first salt-sweet taste on her tongue. Years of hazardous experience identified the airborne drug immediately. Peritax. A small dose would knock her out in seconds.

Ambushed! In my own fucking bedchamber! Shayla pushed aside the annoyance. Questions of who and how could wait. The first priority was survival.

Time slowed as Shayla's mind kicked into overdrive. The thump of her heartbeat doled out the seconds of her life. Peritax was not a poison, it would just leave her helpless. It dispersed and broke down quickly, which meant someone was nearby to release it and to finish the job. Whatever that might be.

Shayla stumbled forward a couple of steps, feigning the effects of the drug. With a flicker of her eyes she mapped the room's few furnishings in readiness for combat. The texture of plain floorboards through thin slippers reassured her of her footing. Around the bed, an oasis of light beckoned.

Two figures appeared to one side in servants' robes. Barras and Gingallia? She almost gasped at the shock of betrayal, but these surely couldn't be her servants. Head bowed, Shayla tracked the imposters' movements from the corners of her eyes. One behind Shayla cut off her escape; the other glided between her and the doors leading out to the balcony and the sitting room to her right, the only other ways out of her suite.

Anyone else?

Shayla's lungs screamed for release. To draw a breath. *A breath would mean death. Hah! I'm a poet!* The irrational thought flitted through her mind on butterfly wings of madness. *Focus!* She was losing her fight against the drug just from that small taste.

Her hand crept to the hilt of the knife under her robes. She stilled the movement and instead stumbled another step towards the bed. She couldn't fight these two. If the drug didn't take her, anoxia would.

Another step.

The figures closed in behind her.

Shayla flopped towards the bed, buying herself a few precious moments. As she pitched forwards her legs folded under her, then she launched herself across the bed. She rolled, outstretched hand reaching for a concealed button under the edge of the headboard. Mid-roll, she glimpsed upside-down a face in the shadows of a hood. It *looked* like Barras, but Shayla noted nose plugs, a tiny breathing unit clamped between thin stretched lips, and eyes filled with hate.

A razor line of blue fire bisected the space she'd just vacated. Holy Space, a rapier shimmerblade!

Her groping fingers found the hidden button. The bed collapsed behind Shayla, halved effortlessly by the shimmerblade. Tall windows ahead of her flew open and she continued her motion, hurdling the waist-high sill out into a seventy foot drop.

Shayla forced the dregs of tainted air from her mouth and drew in a deep, clean draught from the night rushing past her face. A moment later, her feet connected with the broad eaves overhanging her bedroom windows. She hung upside-down in the grip of an artificial grav field and drew her own blade, watching the lit window for signs of movement.

If at least one of her attackers leaned out of the window to see where she'd gone, she'd soon have one less to deal with.

No such luck.

First one, then the other, flew through the opening, too fast and out of Shayla's reach. They landed on the eaves back to back in fighting crouches. The nearer one saw Shayla and signaled to his companion, who also turned to face her.

The Barras lookalike (traitor or imposter?) swung his rapier. Shayla's own blade flashed blue and met it with a jarring wrench.

A shimmerblade was a rare and fearsome weapon, highly prized by undercover agents as a weapon of stealth. When activated, the vibrating crystalline edge could shear through anything less than military grade vehicle armor—or another shimmerblade. But when two such blades clashed, the results were random and potentially catastrophic.

Shayla's knife hand went numb with the impact. She barely managed to keep her grip on the hilt as she stumbled back against the wall. Shaken, she blinked away sudden vertigo at the sight of the ground hanging impossibly above her head, but at least she'd braced herself for the shock. She'd activated her shimmerblade at the last moment and caught her opponent by surprise. The jolt threw him backwards and one foot found the edge of the eaves. He was now half out of the edge of the grav field, and conflicting forces led his reflexes astray. He lost his balance. The planet's natural gravity reclaimed him and he fell, shrieking, into the night.

The remaining assassin reached into her robes. Her hood had slipped, revealing a perfect likeness of Gingallia, one of Shayla's senior personal servants.

Shayla backed carefully along the eaves, feeling her way over the joists and decorative moldings adorning the roof line. The wall at her side turned a corner. She glanced upward over her shoulder to where the balustrade of her bedroom balcony hung a few feet above her head. 'Gingallia' followed her gaze, and Shayla knew she'd spotted the guards lining the balcony, weapons ready, alerted by the alarm triggered when Shayla used her escape route. Bard Jovin, Shayla's guard captain, took up a position just out of sight of her attacker.

Shayla thought she saw a flicker of calculation in the imposter's eyes. *She knows she can't get off a shot before getting blown away.*

'Gingallia's' hand emerged slowly from her robes. Instead of the needle gun Shayla had been expecting, she held a thermal grenade. Her thumb pressed the arming trigger, which rapidly pulsed orange. Shayla noted white knuckles gripping the slim cylinder.

Shayla sheathed her knife and calmly asked, "Dead switch?"

'Gingallia' nodded.

"So if you get shot," Shayla said clearly, so the guards a few feet away could hear her, "we all die."

Shayla continued her careful tread along the eaves. She was now alongside the balcony. She could do with taking this one alive, but killers who got this close all came prepared to die. On the other hand, there was one thing the real professionals prized even beyond life.

She glanced up once more and caught the eye of Bard Jovin, who gave a nod. Returning her attention to 'Gingallia', Shayla said, "I am your target. You're a professional. You know you're not walking away from this, but you can keep your reputation intact if you minimize collateral damage."

The assassin's eyes hardened.

Crap, she's not buying it. "While I'm standing meek as a dove, at least let the guards retreat to safety before you finish this."

Her voice was calm and conversational even as she leaped for the balcony, rolling to compensate for the sudden reversal of gravity. From the corner of her eye she saw the assassin's feet leave the eaves.

Good man! Bard, quick on the uptake, had killed the grav field the moment Shayla jumped. As she landed, Shayla grabbed the nearest guards and shoved them towards the open doors leading into her quarters.

"Inside!" the captain roared, dragging more guards to safety.

Behind Shayla the night blazed. Stone slabs under her feet bucked and sagged. She scrambled for a grip on subsiding masonry. Her feet paddled lava.

Shayla dug her fingers into the widening crack where the last slab was parting company with the wall. She gathered her legs under her to catapult herself to safety.

Too late.

There was no time for fear. Even as Shayla lost her battle with gravity, her mind was casting for options. The collapsing balcony offered no leverage. The protruding lip above lay just out of reach. A firm hand grasped her forearm. She relinquished her handhold and let the slab slide past her to join the cascade of glowing debris tumbling into darkness.

She grabbed the uniformed arm with her free hand as her body slammed into the wall. She dangled for a few moments while she caught her breath.

The wall radiated blistering heat.

She glanced up at her rescuer and almost lost her grip. "Bard," she gasped.

The captain grimaced with the good half of his face. The other half, a charred mask, gazed at her with sightless eye.

———•————

Hours later, with sleep a long forgotten prospect, Shayla stood in the doorway watching firefly cinders from the far edge of the balcony drip away into the night. The clean-up crew had long gone. The only sound nearby was the occasional brittle clink of heat-shocked stone.

Three guards dead. Men I knew. Men I trusted with my life. How have I served them?

And two more badly burned.

Bard had not wanted to leave her side. He'd threatened the medic who'd tried to sedate him. Only when Shayla palmed the medipen and administered it herself did he allow himself to be led away.

Peritax. She wondered at the choice of weapon.

They wanted me alive. Why?

Helpless rage knotted her stomach. Attacks on her life she knew how to deal with, she'd had enough practice, but this had touched other lives too. Collateral damage. It could have been worse, she tried to reassure herself. She'd counted on that momentary hesitation while the assassin processed Shayla's words, and the balcony had shielded them from the worst of the flash.

The building below her looked a mess, but that was just superficial. Beneath the decorative facade of her residence was an armored shell.

Prudent. Not paranoid.

The physical damage would be repaired, but some things could not be set right.

———•————

Sweat rolled down Shayla's cheeks and flew from the end of her nose as she whipped the heavy stave to counter the training dummy's blows. Her morning training routine had turned into a full blooded outlet for the fury that still threatened to drown her. The walls of the dojo faded into shadows dancing in the single overhead light.

Parry high ... parry low ... counter ... damn! She barely blocked the vicious swipe that would have cut her off at the knees. She recovered and countered again, this time finding one of the targets on the dummy's torso.

She blinked sweat from her eyes and glanced at the machine's scoreboard. *Level twenty-eight? Space alive!* She poked the 'pause' switch before the dummy came back to life again. She'd never pushed past twenty-six before.

Shayla whirled at the sound of a cough behind her. The tip of her stave came to rest half an inch from the bridge of a freckled nose. Hazel eyes, only slightly widened, gazed steadily back.

"You sent for me?"

Shayla calmed her breathing. "Simone. You shouldn't take me by surprise."

"I've never managed to surprise you before." Simone's voice held an edge of reproach.

Shayla hesitated, acknowledging the truth in her servant's words. She sighed. "I'm getting too old for this."

"Forty-one? Barely into your prime."

Shayla searched Simone's face for signs of mockery. Her servant wore her sixty-plus years well. "Death stalks me. It ages me."

"You are the child of your past."

But I want to rebuild, not bring ruin. She sighed again and shook her head. "We have some cleaning up to do." *Firenzi assassins in my own residence!* She swallowed the anger that surfaced once more. *My guard is slipping. They got too close this time.*

"The bodies have been recovered," Simone said.

"And ...?"

"One was holding the grenade. That one will yield no secrets. The other has been removed to a secure place for ... *appropriate* examination."

Shayla caught the emphasis in Simone's voice and knew that her most trusted servant understood the implications. These attackers could not have gotten into her residence with any ordinary disguise. They had to be using the Firenzi implants, a mimetic technology which

Shayla had also used in her undercover life and which she still found useful from time to time.

"The owners will want some reassurance." Simone's voice held just a hint of expectation.

"Yes." Shayla cursed under her breath. Damn, but she was slow this morning. "I'll need to arrange a *private* conference."

The subcutaneous implants were a jealously guarded secret. One which Shayla was as eager to keep as her former Firenzi masters. And she could do without antagonizing any more enemies than she already had.

Chapter 2

Cobra scowled out of the window of the one-room cabin as he broke the communications link. Through a gap in the trees, mist rose where a torrent from the spring melt thundered unseen to the valley below. Out of long habit, his gaze flitted along the skyline to the places where hidden defenses kept watch on the world outside.

His features showed no emotion as he stood to face the only other occupant of the sparsely furnished room. Cobra noted beads of perspiration on the smooth walnut skin of the man's face. Even his fuzz of wiry black hair showed a damp sheen that had nothing to do with ambient temperature. And although he held himself rigidly at attention, his fingers clenched and twisted at his side.

You damned well should be nervous! Aloud Cobra said "That was too close. She almost died."

"She has always proved herself more than competent to deal with any threat."

True enough, but this was a delicate stage of the game. No fuckups allowed. Cobra's scowl deepened. He picked up an antique hunting knife from the table at his side, and scratched a few geometric patterns in the worn tabletop while he thought. "I assume you had intelligence on this attempt?"

The other man swallowed, and nodded.

"You are supposed to notify me of any credible threat."

"We ... I ... underestimated the severity."

Cobra let the silence lengthen. When it was clear that no excuses or further explanations were forthcoming, he grunted and laid the knife back on the table. The other man's acceptance of accountability had just saved his life.

Cobra strode over to a closet that stood across from the window, and pulled out a ready-packed haversack. "Well, Mongoose, what have you learned from this latest incident?"

"Her enemies are getting creative."

"And, so?"

"I must be doubly vigilant."

"True enough. But what does that mean for us?"

Mongoose frowned, then a thin smile crept across his lips. "More pressure. She'll be ready to jump when the time is right."

Cobra turned to the mirror hanging on the wall above a small hand basin. Light streaming through the armored plastic picked out complex patterns in his braided hair. "The kettle is coming to a boil," he whispered. "Time for our tame guard to dupe Milady's house guests."

He gazed deep into his own eyes, aware of the web of scar tissue and pale synthetic skin running from the bridge of his nose to the angle of his jaw. *And what did I learn from that encounter?* His finger absently traced the lines of the scar, reliving the hectic chase across the skies of Magentis seven years past, when he'd tried to bring down Shayla and the Emperor. The chase that had ended in disaster, the ruin of his plans, and a crash from which he'd been lucky to escape alive. *I learned the true meaning of dedication.*

Evading the clumsy security services closing in on his downed cruiser had been easy. Living through the years since had been the hard part. Once a high-ranking member of the Insurrection, he was now little more than an outcast. Shayla had fooled him. She'd fooled them all, but *he'd* been entrusted with handling her mission on Magentis when her personal agenda had suddenly and so spectacularly diverged from their own.

Now he was exiled to this spitball of an outworld. Waiting, collecting information, passing messages. Just one link in the Insurrection's intelligence network. No longer on active field duty.

Dedication! To rebuild a network of trusted contacts. And to subvert the Insurrection's intelligence and long reach to his own means.

He picked up a pair of clippers and set to work on his tight-woven hair, leaving only a thick stubble covering his scalp.

Cobra noted his companion's questioning gaze as his butchered braids fell to the floor.

"So, it is time?"

"It is time," Cobra said. "You will have to manage events from here now. You understand the trust I place in you?"

Mongoose nodded.

"I doubt I will be able to help much while I get myself into position. Cobra is going under cover again. Now I am simply Jared Tindall, woodsman and refugee."

———— • ————

Shayla sat for a long while staring at the blank wall.

Most of her office was decked in the trappings of a ferociously busy life. A map of Eloon dominated the wall to her right, barely discernible beneath a clutter of charts and reports on a hundred construction projects in progress around the globe, schedules of arrivals, and immigrant processing statistics.

Other walls were obscured by bookshelves laden with oldworld tomes, the framed Freeworld charter of Eloon signed by the heads of the Grand Families, a set of ceremonial knives hanging in a presentation case, and a Chensing pottery urn, a gift from Emperor Julian Skamensis. A collision of functional and personal, dimly seen in the muted glow of a single standard lamp behind her chair.

This wall facing her, stark and unadorned, was an anomaly.

"The comms link is ready, My Lady."

"Thank you, Simone. Leave me now."

Without turning around, Shayla listened while her servant closed the door, then she took a deep breath and composed herself. She glanced down at her notepad and checked the tiny glowing shield in one corner of the page. Free from surveillance. Her security agents had been working for the last half an hour sniffing out and quietly silencing unwanted electronic intrusions. Neither as ingenious nor as elegant as the security arsenal concocted by her dear dead brother Brandt, but still probably the best in the known worlds. Simone had been a good find, but her cryptic skills would never be a match for Brandt's. One day Shayla would try to retrieve copies of her old software, still stashed tantalizingly out of reach on the university Freeworld of Chevinta, but this was not the time. Too much else to deal with right now.

Satisfied, or at least as satisfied as she could reasonably be, Shayla scribbled a few commands on her notepad. The wall in front of her glowed a pearly blue. It shimmered, then a complex pattern appeared in one corner. It seemed to hover in front of the wall like a hanging ornament of fine gold filigree. Shayla dredged her memory, dimmed by long years of neglect, and scratched a coded response. A patchwork of emerald appeared alongside the gold. A few moments later, cornflower pinwheels blossomed. More responses followed, alternating between Shayla and the unseen person at the end of the communications link. Each one added new colour to the wall. Each an almost-pattern hinting at hidden geometry.

Finally the patterns slid into the centre of the wall, merging to form the crest of the Firenzi Special Service.

Shayla heaved a silent sigh as the crest dissolved to reveal a round face framed by close-cropped red hair. She noted graying skin and deep lines around the eyes. *Something's been keeping him up these past few days.*

"Jai Marx, greetings," Shayla said, careful to keep her tone and expression neutral.

"Lady Carver." The Firenzi security chief's response was also a study of disinterest. "A person of your standing has little time for pleasantries. I assume you have something of importance to discuss."

He's fishing. "I have some abandoned property of yours."

Jai's expression relaxed slightly. "You are ... well?"

There was curiosity in his tone, with only a tinge of disappointment. So he must have been aware of the plot, but only distantly. Not close enough to have a strong interest, or to have heard of its failure. "I survive." She paused. "Thank you for your concern."

"You understand, of course, that this is not strictly *my* property."

"This link is secure and my office is clean of snoops, so let's quit fencing. Firenzi agents using mimetic implants to disguise themselves. Whether or not they are yours, you don't want that technology to become known. And, Jai, although Eloon sits in Firenzi space it is still an Imperial protectorate. You understand that a plot like this will draw the attention of Imperial security."

Jai grimaced at the implied promise and threat. "You have the means to ensure adequate disposal?"

"I do."

"And in return for safeguarding our technology?"

"Your help."

Jai's face set like stone, but he inclined his head slightly in acknowledgement.

"My work here is hard enough already without fighting off threats from my own doorstep."

Jai snorted. "You surround yourself with threats."

Shayla accepted the statement at face value. Yes, her aborted attempt on the Emperor's life seven years ago had upset many plans and made many enemies, some with long reaches and deep pockets. What was done, was done. She had to live with it. "All the more reason to wish for peace from some quarters."

Jai pursed his lips. "Even my intelligence has its limitations. And many here hold you responsible for the death of Pere Josef."

"You know the truth of the matter. Scipio Firenzi and Ivan Skamensis bear that burden. I am not the enemy."

"Not all here would agree."

"Then I leave their education in your capable hands."

<hr />

Jai Marx scowled at the blank desktop long and hard after breaking the connection.

I could have done with retrieving those bodies!

He dismissed the thought immediately as wishful thinking. He had no leverage for one thing. And sending a ship to Eloon, or arranging for more discreet transport, would be impossible to organize without raising unwanted questions. All the same, he didn't like leaving them out there, unaccounted for.

The implants would degrade quickly. The invasive fungus depended on its host for nourishment. Within a day or two, anything but the most careful autopsy would reveal nothing of the bio-mimetic technology.

Unless, of course, the bodies were preserved. Would she do that, to keep a bargaining chip over him? But surely Carver wanted the secret kept intact just as much as he did.

With an effort, Jai put that problem out of his mind. He had more pressing matters. This plot appeared to have been a simple assassination attempt. He'd been telling the truth about the people who wished Lady Carver dead, but that was only part of the story. Most of his attention had recently been on murkier factions with more subtle aims. With a weakling like Giovanni Firenzi heading the family since Pere Josef's death, Jai had his hands full fending off yet another bloody change of leadership. He chided himself for neglecting more simplistic threats.

He poured a glass of water from a tall pitcher standing at one end of his desk. He raised the glass, watching frost form as he turned it slowly in his fingers.

I need to rein in my loose cannons. Or at least know where they're aiming.

Jai swallowed and set the glass down, grabbing a stylus instead. With a few strokes, he pulled a chart of his organization across the surface of the desk.

He hesitated, replaying the recent interview in his mind. *She was testing me. Seeing if I had anything to do with this.* A cold chill ran down his neck as he recalled the hard expression on Carver's face. Her abilities and determination were still talked about, by foe and ally alike, in hushed tones in the corridors of the Firenzi Special Service.

I think my evident ignorance just spared me a midnight appointment with a shimmerblade.

He shook his head irritably and set to work on the chart, his movements becoming more purposeful as he reviewed notes and made annotations.

Ignorant once is forgiven. Ignorant twice is willful.

Chapter 3

Shayla set aside the never-ending flow of reports and briefings infesting her notepad. Every security breach redoubled the workload as she and her team reviewed events, identified weaknesses, plugged loopholes. This last week was no exception. An hour's blessed solitude in the confines of her personal air cruiser allowed her to keep up with neglected essentials, nothing more.

The relative tranquility was soured by roiling emotions still raw from that attack. She closed her eyes and turned her mind inward. As usual, after so many years as a warrior and assassin, the instinctive anger abated into a clinical assessment of the attack and a grudging professional admiration. But for the first time in her years as governor, she was plagued by deep foreboding that haunted the few precious moments of peace in her days, and stalked her dreams at night.

These assassins had come so close and had covered their tracks well. Too well. This had the mark of an altogether new level of sophistication. *Peritax.*

If they'd simply wanted to kill her, they had ample opportunity. There was more to it than that. Lurking on the fringes of awareness, she sensed something larger than personal revenge. Deeper plots moved in the shadows. Plots maybe with more weight behind them than her limited resources could handle.

An alarm warbled on the navigation console. Back to immediate business.

She shrugged into a snow suit, leaving it unzipped in the climate-controlled cockpit, and draped a winter hood and cloak across the vacant co-pilot's seat. She slid back behind the cruiser's controls and took over from the autopilot.

Frozen pinnacles of The Sharks Teeth reached towards her, gleaming bronze and white in the low morning sun. As she banked over the dormant caldera of The Sombrero at the northern end of the range,

Shayla set a heading on an old-fashioned gyro compass she'd had mounted on top of the more standard controls.

The arctic prison, built by Grand Duke Ivan Skamensis and the renegade Scipio Firenzi, had remained hidden for decades behind an electronic veil that misguided the navigation systems of any craft that strayed too close. After so many visits to check on her high profile prisoners, Shayla could find her way by dead reckoning.

These visits gave her a deep chill every time.

Along with rebuilding Eloon, Emperor Julian Skamensis had tasked Shayla with keeping these two aristocratic traitors in safe custody. At the time, it had seemed only fitting that they be imprisoned in their own facility, where they'd held the Emperor's family hostage. That, and the fact that there had been then no other intact structure left on the planet, let alone one built for this very purpose, had made the choice inevitable.

But as months turned to years, choice reverted to the inaction of simple inertia. There were always more pressing matters to deal with on a limited budget than to solve a problem that already seemed to be taken care of.

Shayla felt this duty more keenly than her own exile and confinement to her burned-out birthplace. The prisoners' safekeeping weighed on her more with each passing year. With so many volatile factions in both families, either escape or assassination risked dropping the civilized worlds into a bloodbath.

Way over to her left, above the dark horizon, a too-bright star betrayed the orbiting presence of an Imperial warship. *Vanquisher* was the capital ship currently on patrol, soon to be joined by Shayla's old acquaintance, *Merciless*, another *Implacable*-class heavy cruiser. Imperial security was getting twitchy as the date of inspection drew near.

So was Shayla. This place was still hard to find in the white expanse, but its very existence had ceased to be a jealously-guarded secret years ago. Back in the days when Eloon was an abandoned shell, stealth and secrecy were essential. Nowadays, stealth wasn't enough. She made a note to talk to her head of security again about perimeter security, and about moving their troublesome guests to the new site they'd been preparing.

The cruiser settled in a brief, swirling blizzard under a deep pewter sky. The last driven flakes drifted to the ground as Shayla stepped down the ramp. A short distance away, the ground sloped up to a shallow escarpment cut through with blue-green icy crevices. Ruby light glimmered deep within the nearest cleft, the only hint of human presence.

Shayla pulled her cloak close around her. Although the morning was clear and bright, the arctic cold pierced the smallest gap in her clothing. Already her nose pinched, and the trace of a tear froze on her lower eyelashes. She trudged away from the cruiser and entered a red underworld cut into the ice shelf. A few yards in, the cave opened into a dim-lit antechamber.

The room was empty, but Shayla knew her approach, her landing, and her every move was watched.

Stairs cut into the floor near the far wall led down through a series of flights and short landings. Rough matting gave footing on the ice-carved steps. Lights buried in the ceiling gave steadily brighter illumination as she descended.

Walls of ice turned to white plastic trailed with condensation. An armored door at the bottom remained firmly closed. Shayla thumbed the communications panel alongside and announced, "Lady Shayla Carver. You know me well enough. Open up."

A nervous voice on the other side said, "Please key in the passcode, Milady."

"Do you not know who I am?" The door shook at Shayla's bellow, but remained locked.

"Nevertheless ..."

Shayla smiled to herself. She'd chewed out the last poor fool who'd caved. The lesson seemed to have stuck. She keyed the code. The door swung open. "Well done ..." Shayla peered at the guard's insignia, "... Simon."

She'd seen the youngster before, a recent recruit to the guard. He seemed unusually pale. Sweat slicked his forehead above darting eyes.

"We've suffered recently at the hands of imposters clever enough to fool my own house staff." She kept the anger out of her voice, simmering still at the memory of that intrusion. This youngster was nervous enough and looked like he could do with reassurance. "Nobody gets through this door without the right code. No matter who they *claim* to be, no matter how they bluster. The Emperor himself could be outside and you will not let him in without the code. You did well."

She spied an old friend in the corner. "Jevin Colt," she drawled. The stocky guard struggled to suppress a laugh. "You still believe in throwing young cubs to the wolves, I see."

"Experience is the best teacher, My Lady." He gave the slightest of bows, enough to satisfy protocol, then he gestured to the door opposite. "Your guests are waiting."

Shayla allowed him to lead the way down stairs, past the guards' living quarters, and down again to the secure level separating them from the prisoners' accommodation.

Through a guard room at the foot of the stairs, Shayla emerged into a corridor dominated on one side by a clear partition. She stopped and squared her shoulders, muttering her ritual curse to the Emperor for imposing this duty, and stepped into the interview room. The partition turned opaque as she shut the door.

Heavily-built Scipio Firenzi glowered at her. Ginger hair and neatly-trimmed moustache held hints of white. He heaved himself to his feet with an insolent sneer and gave a mockingly theatrical bow, complete with elaborate hand flourishes. Shayla could see no hint of fat yet under his tunic.

Grand Duke Ivan Skamensis, by contrast, looked gray with defeat. Although he held his lean and angular frame straight and his hair was as black as when she'd first seen him, his face was creased by new lines and his gaze was vacant. He acknowledged her with barely a nod. The arrogance that used to define him had long since fled.

How long ago had this transformation started, inch by inch, unnoticed in her monthly visits? From her intelligence reports she knew that only Ivan's continuing influence—and the remote hope one day of the release his lawyers kept pushing for—kept many unstable factions in the Imperial navy from wreaking havoc. With a shock, Shayla realized that it needn't take an assassin's poison to rob her of one or other of these still-powerful figures.

The room was lit by a pair of free-standing glowtubes and furnished only with a clear plastic table and three transparent chairs. Scipio settled back into his seat and planted his feet on the table, leaning the chair perilously back on two legs.

Walls, floor and ceiling were coated with a smart material from the Firenzi laboratories. As long as no electrical signal intruded, the surface shimmered like a windblown meadow. Any attempt to spy remotely, or to install any kind of surveillance device within the enclosure, would disrupt the holographic effect for all to see.

Shayla had seen fit to leave the coating in place, knowing that Scipio himself had commissioned this room's construction and trusted its privacy. Conversations in here were truly in confidence, no record could exist as evidence of treason, so tongues may occasionally be loosened.

She briefly eyed the shimmering walls. She'd choked when she'd seen how ruinously expensive this smart material was. Her head of security had ordered generous stocks for the new prison and the Emperor's accountants were raising hell. Just another detail in an overcrowded life.

Disdaining the vacant chair, Shayla clasped her hands behind her back and gazed down at her high profile prisoners. "The Emperor sends his greetings."

"Oh, cut the pleasantries," Scipio hissed. "The usual bland reports. Yes, we are well fed, our health is attended to, we've received the books and entertainments we requested, all praise to the Emperor." His gaze pierced Shayla. "The important questions remain unanswered. How long will the Emperor hold us without trial in flagrant violation of the Trown Plains Accord?"

"That is not for me to answer." Shayla's voice dripped frost. This was well-worn territory. "Your legal representatives—"

"I'm sure my dear nephew is following due process," Ivan cut in smoothly. "More to the point, I'm curious what the upcoming Imperial inspection will make of our ... *unusual* ... situation."

The inspection. Shayla hesitated on the verge of a response. Even though she was confident she knew how to handle this, admittedly unusual, situation with the inspectors, unease tugged at her senses. She teased the worry out. Nothing the pair in front of her had said. There was something subtly wrong with the air. Not a poison or a drug, she was sure of that, which is why it didn't register at first.

She sniffed more carefully, and left the interview room. Out in the corridor she sniffed again and turned to the nearest guard. "Keep a close watch on those two. They stay here until I say." Striding down the corridor towards the lower level, she signaled to Jevin to unlock the doors leading down to the prisoners' quarters. He raised an eyebrow, but complied without a word.

Jevin followed Shayla down to the main living area. The odor, still faint, became more pronounced. Shayla looked sidelong at her guard sergeant for some reaction, but he gave no indication that he sensed anything amiss.

She surveyed the room from the foot of the stairs. The area had been designed to give a clear view, with no opportunities for ambush. "Do you or the guards have any cause to go further than this?"

"Not routinely, My Lady. We deliver food and other items here, to that table yonder, then leave them to it." He scratched the back of his neck. "My standing instructions are not to engage in idle chit-chat. I know the poison webs these men's tongues can weave."

Shayla strode to the open staircase leading down to the sleeping quarters. At the bottom of the stairs, even Jevin wrinkled his nose. A stale, damp odor permeated the level. Peering inside each door, the source was clearly the plumbing. "When was this last checked?"

"Routine maintenance every six months. The crew empties the cistern and gives the whole system a look-over. I'd have to check records, but my recollection is about two months ago."

Puzzled, Shayla checked the facilities, and cautiously tasted the water from the faucet. "Everything seems okay, apart from that musty smell."

Jevin shrugged. "We have system monitors everywhere. They are watched around the clock. Nothing is showing any signs of a failure, on that I'd swear."

"How long, do you think, before someone noticed?"

"You must have the nose of a bloodhound." Jevin frowned. "With all the sealed doors in between, this stench could take weeks to find its way upstairs, if ever. We rarely come down here in person. We watch on the monitors. Unless something got picked up on one of the sensors we'd have no cause to be here until the next maintenance crew arrived." He paused. "Or the inspection."

Shayla nodded, mouth set in a grimace. The inspection. Was that their game?

She returned to the interview room, struggling to keep her expression neutral. "There is a bad odor down in your quarters."

Ivan inspected his fingernails, his ramrod posture relaxed, a deliberate picture of casual innocence.

"You knew of this." Shayla fought to keep her voice level. "Why did you not report it?"

"Why? Is it dangerous?" asked Ivan.

Scipio slouched in his seat with his hands jammed in his pockets. "Why do you care? Our comfort means nothing to you. Much like our opinions or rights."

Shayla gazed long and hard at the pair lounging insolently in front of her. Something was amiss, far more than just an odor hanging in the air, but without more to go on she had no lever with which to pry. She would have to keep an exceptionally close watch on these two.

Silence weighed for long minutes after Shayla had left. Finally Scipio stirred and pushed a ten franc coin across the table. "I honestly thought we'd have to nudge her."

Ivan pocketed the coin. "Told you her nose was sharp." His gaze roved across the shimmering holograms. "She's suspicious."

Scipio grunted. "Of course she's suspicious. All the Firenzi Special Service get truthsense training. Very few have the true talent, but some awareness rubs off in many cases. *She* was never an adept, yet sharper than most." His mouth twisted in distaste. "In this case it should serve us."

Ivan allowed the smallest of smiles to intrude, a rare house guest these days. "A little knowledge is a dangerous thing."

Airborne once more, Shayla punched the cruiser through atmosphere into a suborbital loop to clear the disruptive field as quickly as possible. Cloudless sky above darkened from slate to gunmetal as the cruiser climbed. Dazzling white gleamed below from one horizon to the other. She handed control back to the navigation system and reached for the comms screen.

"Brin?" she said, when her head of security glowered from the screen. "It may be nothing, but arrange for a maintenance team to check out the habitat systems at the prison. Especially sanitation. I want a full team on this, the works. I get a sense they're up to something."

He nodded.

"I know work has been affected by preparations for the inspection, but how soon can we have the other site ready?"

Brin didn't need to consult his reports. "The site can be put to use now, but I wouldn't recommend considering a transfer until things quieten down. There are too many new faces in the guard and the work teams right now, with all the preparations going on."

"No let-up in security checks though." It was a statement, not a question.

"No amount of checks can reduce the risk to zero. Statistics alone say we are at increased risk until we can offload the extras."

Shayla chewed her lip. On the one hand, accept the risk of an increasingly vulnerable site. On the other hand, the security nightmare of moving two prisoners that half the civilized world wanted free and the other half wanted dead.

An alarm rang out across the cockpit. "More on this later, Brin," Shayla yelled as she checked the readouts. "Shit!"

A contact registered on the horizon, closing rapidly.

Shayla wrested control back from the autopilot and flung the cruiser earthward.

The contact resolved into two blips, flying in close formation.

The tactical system's tentative annotation of 'hostile' was superfluous. The more detailed readout a few seconds later confirmed Shayla's fears—a hunting pair of Wasps.

The ground rushed closer. The seemingly featureless wasteland fractured into an endless network of low bluffs and icy chasms.

While Shayla hugged the tortured landscape a detached corner of her memory dredged up details of the long range Wasp surface to air missile. Deadly alone, these tiny killers were often deployed in pairs. With a backup following just outside the blast radius, even a near miss from the lead missile would be enough to disorient the target for that instant needed for the second to close and kill.

Her only hope was to outrun them or outfox them.

And Wasps were fast.

The tactical display showed the missiles closing in.

With dismay, Shayla saw that they were staying out of the maze of canyons and managing to track her despite the ground clutter. Right now, the obstacles were only slowing Shayla and not affording any protection.

She pressed her lips into a thin and determined line. They would eventually have to close in for the kill. Plan 'B' would need precise timing.

With one eye on the tactical display, Shayla ground-hopped from one bluff to the next, always keeping a cliff of ice in her sights.

A change in course. The Wasps were closing in.

At the last moment, Shayla fired her forward beams. An icy knoll exploded ahead. Shayla punched the throttle and flung the cruiser through the sparkling debris and up into a loop. As she rolled out of the loop, she checked the display and swore. The Wasps had overshot, caught out by her maneuver and momentarily blinded by the distracting cloud, but they hadn't taken the bait. She'd bought herself only a few seconds of time while they circled and reacquired their target.

Shayla scrambled through her training for other evasive measures, and came up wanting. The cruiser had beam weapons but no effective defenses. Not that traditional countermeasures meant much to Wasps. Wasps were small and light, but highly sophisticated. And smart. They had high-end tactical and navigation systems.

Navigation.

Shayla noticed the cruiser's navigation display drifting out of true against the gyro compass. She was heading back into the prison's defensive field.

She pushed the cruiser to its limit, gaining altitude to clearer skies. Behind her, the Wasps closed in once more but were noticeably drifting to one side, confused by conflicting signals.

The missiles corrected, then drifted again, their paths growing more and more erratic. Simple dumb trackers would have killed her by now, but with onboard intelligence and navigation to identify and hunt a target from half-way across the globe, these weapons were too smart for their own good.

On an impulse, Shayla jinked to one side and drifted across their path. For an instant, she was in direct line with the two missiles and hidden from the trailing Wasp. Its confounded senses mistook the lead

Wasp for its target. The double concussion hammered the cruiser and flipped it end over end, out of control.

Shayla gasped for breath through a haze of pain, doubled up over the edge of the cockpit console. The force of the craft's suicidal spin pinned her in place, face grinding against the jury-rigged gyro compass, arms outstretched towards the canopy, legs crushed against the underside of the console.

Through a surge of adrenalin, Shayla's instinctive self-check reported in. Cracked ribs for sure, internal bleeding possible but not immediately relevant, limbs functional ... if only someone would untie the ton weights attached to each. She assessed her balance on the edge of the console, acutely aware of the ground rushing closer. If she slipped either way she would spill over or under and be unable to move against the vicious tug of the end-on spin.

Regaining control of the craft was out of the question. She could barely move, let alone manipulate the manual joysticks. Speaking of which, that stabbing pain in her gut told her the guidance stick was currently inaccessible anyway.

Gritting her teeth, Shayla inched her right arm down the instrument panel towards her. Her breathing came in sharp shallow pants. Red mist clouded her vision. She screwed her eyes shut and clung desperately to consciousness as she pictured the layout of the console. Working blind, groping fingers sought out the navigation panel.

She clicked on the autopilot.

Navigation might be screwed up. That didn't matter. Who cared what misguided direction the craft took, as long as it was not into the ground.

For a second, nothing seemed to be happening, then Shayla felt correcting pulses through her strained ribs as the craft's guidance system tried to make sense of their wayward tumbling.

The pressure on her limbs lessened. Shayla eased herself back into her seat, ignoring for now the blood smeared across the console and her clothes, and pulled crash webbing around herself.

Just as the buckles clicked into place, the seat hit her like a piledriver. Through the cockpit canopy there was a brief glimpse of sparkling ice, then another shock threw Shayla into the webbing. Her head snapped forward, and she tasted blood.

Another impact, then another, weaker this time. An angry serpent's hiss outside, and bone-jarring bumps and rattles within, told Shayla they were on the ground shedding speed.

Sound and sensation stopped, far too abruptly. Shayla tensed and clutched the webbing, counting the seconds. Three ... four ... five ... straps cut deep into her shoulders and she granted herself the luxury of a scream as tortured ribs protested. The cruiser harmonized her scream with the shriek of rending panels.

Winter breathed through the cabin.

The world whirled, and stilled.

Silence.

Groggy, Shayla eased her white-knuckle grip on the straps and lifted her head. The sight of a wall of snow through the shattered canopy confirmed they had indeed come to rest. Out the corner of her eye she regarded a shard of clear plastic piercing the headrest next to her ear. She reached gingerly and plucked it free. It fell upward. That would explain why her ribs were still giving her such hell. Shayla swallowed and checked herself over for more injuries, dusting smaller fragments of splintered canopy from her jacket. She checked overhead for obstacles before releasing the webbing and swinging herself out of her seat.

Treading carefully on the sloping cabin ceiling, Shayla inched her way aft. She felt for any signs of movement. She might have landed on level ground, or might be hanging over a crevasse. Whether buried, dusted with snow, or crazed by the impact, the few windows in the main cabin gave no clear view of the world outside.

She reached the starboard hatch and hit the release. A clunk, but no movement. The hatch on the other side gave slightly but opened no more than a few inches. Shayla put her shoulder to it, wincing with pain, and gained a few more inches. Rage colored her vision. With a warrior battle cry she grasped the armrests of the two nearest seats hanging above her head, and swung at the hatch with both feet.

The hatch surrendered. Shayla spilled onto the snow after it.

She groaned, caught her breath, and struggled to her feet. She blinked a few times to clear her vision, then turned on the spot to survey the horizon. The cruiser had ploughed a long furrow, littered with debris, before burying its nose in a steep bank. Two hundred yards behind, the morning sun winked off the green carapace of the power housing.

"Guess I'm not flying out of here, then," she murmured. She returned to the cockpit and checked the comms panel. Dead. Even the emergency backup supply must have been lost somewhere along the way. No matter, the identification beacon was self-contained and would keep transmitting even if the rest of the craft was blasted to oblivion. Plus Brin knew she'd spotted trouble and her own security forces would have tracked her descent.

The big question was, who else was tracking her?

She retrieved her cloak, an emergency medical kit, and a ration pack. She didn't know how long she might have to wait. Checking that her knife was still securely in its sheath, Shayla stumbled fifty yards back along the cruiser's track. Where the craft had ploughed through a snow bank, the sides grew steep and high enough for concealment.

Shayla pulled out her knife. Hard-packed snow offered no resistance to the shimmerblade; a few swift strokes freed a block a foot square. Shayla pulled it to one side. Another, and another. She carved a shallow cave into the overhang, piling the blocks to form a low redoubt between her and the cruiser.

A whoosh overhead reminded her that she was expecting company.

Jeez! That was quick.

Shayla wedged herself into her foxhole, and squinted at the pink snow. Funny. Last she remembered, snow was supposed to be white. She gazed down where blood pooled dark in her lap.

A muffled roar in the distance snapped her attention outward once more. A large transport settled next to the wreckage.

Were these rescuers, or a backup assassination team?

It was hard to stay focused, but she was sure assassins would travel light and in small numbers.

Wouldn't they?

Chapter 4

J ared Tindall settled the haversack on his shoulders and joined the stream of humanity straggling down the loading ramp of the battered transport. Clean air replaced the reek of hot plastic and engine oil that pervaded the transport's interior, and not before time. They'd been held two days in orbit, chafing to reach the ground and escape their confines. With communications limited, reliable news was hard to come by and rumors ran rife. Some sort of security scare was the closest Jared could come to the root of the matter. His jaw clenched. If anything *premature* had happened to Lady Carver ...

At the foot of the ramp, he kicked at the stony soil, inhaling a whiff of wood smoke as fine dust hung in the still air.

He turned on his heel and raised his eyes to the cloudless flint sky, where the fierce white disk of Eloon's sun peered over the top of the transport.

"Doesn't look much, does it?"

Jared turned to see a round-faced woman in a guard's uniform strolling towards him. She cradled a high-performance beam rifle, but its snout was angled towards the ground. Jared could detect no threat in her demeanor. The knots in his jaw and shoulders relaxed slightly. "It's not what I'm used to."

"The Empire made a pretty thorough job of burning this place up. I'm told this ridge used to be green. Popular picnic spot for folks from the city down there. But all the burning's gone and messed with the weather. No rain's fallen up here for thirty years." She grinned. "Don't worry. It's not all like this. And we've got lots of hands to help put it back together again."

Jared pursed his lips. "I hope so." Although he knew all about the planet and the vast development projects scattered across the main continent, he could imagine the impact that the desolation here would have on someone used to life on a fertile world.

"Now, if you'll just follow on with the rest of the new intake over there ..." She waved the snout of the rifle to where Jared's shipmates were lining up in ragged rows at the edge of the landing field. He gave a casual salute as he hastened to comply.

While he walked, he kept up an unobtrusive surveillance of his surroundings. Another transport a hundred yards away started to disgorge its human cargo. The guard he'd spoken to was already beckoning the first of them towards the assembly area. Further away, more transports squatted like queen termites amid a bustle of attendant machinery.

The parched soil gave way to an apron of dressed flagstones. There was no balustrade to obstruct the view across a wide bay and out to sea.

Jared glanced over the rows of his fellow immigrants. Odd, he thought, it was impossible to gauge the population in the cramped warren of corridors and bunk rooms of the transport. It had felt like a lot more than the two hundred or so he could see lining up here.

He joined the back row, nearest the far edge of the flagstones. From here, he had a clearer view over the edge of the escarpment on which the landing field stood. The sea shore he estimated lay a few miles away. Clear blue gleamed in the distance, ruffled into white horses by a breeze that failed to reach the heights. The sea looked welcoming but all sense of normality ended at the shore.

Part of the mystique of planetary cleansing lay in the scarcity of information surrounding it. Scenes like this never featured in the state-run media, and few returned in person to a planet touched by Imperial *Swords*.

Here lay a capital city, once. Only a few decades ago Torremis had been beautiful. Jared had seen pictures in the archives and was well acquainted with Eloon's capital city of old.

What lay before him was impossible to reconcile with those images. The heart of the desolation was smooth and level, like a salt flat. The glassy surface had long ago dusted over and looked almost natural. It was the periphery, starting two or three miles out from the epicenter, that gave him the creeps. Here and there low mounds broke the level plain, becoming more frequent and sharp-edged. After another mile, the true nature of the ruins revealed themselves in a jagged wilderness of slagged rubble. The ghostly lines of streets traced an obscene web through the devastation. Here and there a more recognizable structure aimed skeletal fingers at the sky.

An official flunky stood on a podium and lectured the assembled immigrants. It was all the expected officious stuff. Her Imperial High-and-Mightiness welcomes all who seek sanctuary. Great rewards and opportunities for those who gave freely of their time and their skills. Some notes on security and personal safety. Blah, blah, blah.

Although pretending to take in the official's words, Jared listened with only half an ear. His attention kept getting drawn to the sight over his shoulder.

How many lives were extinguished, down there? He knew the statistics, of course, but numbers on a page couldn't prepare you for the stark reality.

Briefly, Jared felt a tug of empathy for the former assassin, now planetary governor, he'd come to kill. This had been her home, her life. That she should seek revenge against the Empire that had wreaked such destruction was only natural. He and the Insurrection wanted much the same thing—an end to Imperial rule. But there their paths diverged. Jared sought much more: an end to unearned privilege. But in her personal quest Shayla Carver had betrayed him and the Insurrection. She had come from a life of privilege and had pursued her course for entirely selfish reasons, not caring who she used and discarded along the way. And she'd returned to her cozy privilege now, and had become part of the machinery she'd tried to destroy. That, he could not forgive.

Shayla settled in her seat at the head of the conference table, trying not to wince as she adjusted her posture to limit pressure on the dressings under her tunic.

She took a moment to catch her breath, gazing out the windows to her left where the distant buildings of the planetary Legislature glowed in the morning sun. The sight normally cheered her, but today fatigue and the fog of pain meds dulled her spirit. She glanced down at the polished tabletop, barely registering notes for the daily briefing already laid out, before meeting the eyes of each of the five others standing around the table.

Shayla saw genuine concern in each face. Some for her personally—
they had been working together on a common goal for too many years
not to have developed mutual fondness and respect—but more for what
she represented.

The Emperor had charged her with rebuilding this world, and she
was the focal point for their efforts. She had the strength to see this task
through, but that dependence was also a fundamental weakness and
they knew it. If she fell, they all fell. Maybe not immediately, a replacement Governor would be appointed, but this task was as much a punishment for her as anything, and building a world was ruinously expensive.
Who knew how long the political will would remain once she was gone?

"Forgive me if I don't follow normal protocol. I find bowing somewhat uncomfortable right now." She waved them to sit and turned first
to her head of security services, Brindis ap Silessi. "Brin, the attack in
the Residence? I hope you've made good use of the extra few days' grace
my convalescence earned you."

The attempt at levity failed to crack Brin's chiseled granite mask.
He frowned and consulted his notepad.

"One of the assassins was holding a thermal grenade. You can guess
how much useful information we got from her." His eyes sparked anger
as he read more of the report. "The other had started to decompose
badly even before the examiner got to him. We believe there was some
post-mortem agent at work. Something biological, maybe, but we could
find no trace of it."

"Not surprising," said Shayla, concealing a sigh of relief. Simone had
done her job well. "You can't blame yourself for that, Brin. The Firenzi
are masters of biological and chemical agents. I'm sure it would be easy
to engineer something to accelerate necrosis."

Not for the first time, Brin glowered at Shayla and leveled his old
complaint. "You were part of their Service. You must know more about
their methods than you're telling."

"And my past knowledge stays with me. To do otherwise would nul-
lify the strict neutrality our provisional Freeworld status demands. You
know this. It's the same reason you keep your knowledge of Imperial
security to yourself, no matter how useful it might be to us."

That wasn't strictly true. Brin kept his secrets because he was an
Imperial appointee and loyal first to the Emperor's security service, not

to Shayla. But the presence of hidden agendas was an open secret and not something either side was going to acknowledge in company.

"*Do* we know for sure this was a Firenzi plot?" Felicity Marr, Shayla's legal head, speared her with an appraising stare.

"I think we can guess," Shayla lied, suddenly aware of her slip. "Only the Firenzi have shown themselves able to infiltrate our inner defenses like that."

"And I guess you'd recognize their methods." Felicity pursed her lips. "Old friends, perchance?"

With an irritated shake of her head, Shayla said, "Peritax is a uniquely Firenzi drug."

"And it leaves no residue behind. The air was clean by the time the guards arrived on the scene, so Milady's testimony is the only hint that a drug was even used." Brin grunted and scowled. "It's so slippery that many in Imperial circles doubt such a drug even exists."

"And many in Firenzi circles would be keen it stays that way." Shayla glanced sharply at Felicity and Brin. "If anyone jeopardizes our neutrality, I will personally skin them alive."

"However," Brin continued smoothly, "there is other evidence that points to the Firenzi. There *was* one item of interest we managed to recover from the burned one."

Shalya's heart thudded. She tried to show only professional interest. Surely no evidence of the mimetic implants could have survived that roasting.

"It was badly distorted, but from the general shape and a more revealing chemical analysis we think that one was carrying a *shakra*."

Shayla twisted too sharply in her seat and gasped in pain before she could recover herself. "A ceremonial knife? How sure are you? And what would an assassin be doing with an item like that?"

"If not a *shakra*, then something else made from a rare and millennia-old alloy formulation, which would beg different but equally hard questions. And I don't think it was for her own use."

Shayla narrowed her eyes. "You have a theory."

"Impossible to prove, but with the use of a drug like peritax to disable you, I suspect the plan was to stage your ritual suicide."

Lines of weary travelers shuffled towards a row of desks. The air in the cavernous reception area was mercifully cool and fresh after the deceptive onslaught of the tiny white sun.

Many people sat on the painted concrete, heaving themselves upright from time to time as the line advanced. Men, women, the occasional child. Mostly lone travelers, though Jared did see what looked like an extended family still together. Few elderly or infirm. Wars had a way of singling out solitary survivors. The elderly didn't typically make it this far.

Jared was thankful to see many people sporting signs of injuries old and recent. His own scarred face was one factor that had kept him away from active fieldwork. Impossible to disguise and too distinctive for someone whose job it was to blend into the populace, here he fit right in and the evidence of an embattled background bolstered his cover.

In other contexts, tempers might be expected to fray at such lengthy waits, but one thing these faces held in common—the weight of defeat, of flight, of oppressive fatigue. The crowd couldn't be described as patient. They had simply had the fight knocked out of them by their experiences, nightmares they'd come here to escape. The overwhelming mood was of resignation.

Guards strolled up and down the lines, weapons lowered. Jared held himself upright throughout, but gratefully accepted a cup of water proffered by a pair of smiling guards doing the rounds.

Jared's hair-trigger senses clued him in to guards around the edge moving with more purpose than they wished to display. He seethed inwardly, caught in the rush of adrenaline, until he confirmed he was not the target. It was over in moments. Half a dozen individuals scattered through the crowd found themselves singled out and escorted towards the nearest exit before they had time to react. One struggled, turned and chanted, "Try them! Burn them!" as he was dragged through the door.

Jared shrugged and rolled his eyes to his nearest companions as they settled back to their wait. The planet's high profile guests attracted a steady stream of agitators trying to slip in amongst the genuine refugees, intent on ineffectual protests either for or against the prisoners. Well, he'd relieve them of that problem soon enough.

The shed could have hangared a medium-sized warship. The few hundred arrivals today felt lost in its echoing emptiness. The planetary authorities had planned on a massive scale. All around, hundred-foot-high moving murals showcased some of the many development projects slowly restoring a measure of sanity to Eloon's blasted surface.

As he neared the far wall, Jared studied a time-lapse scene taken over many years. Tiny pockets of green appeared in an ash-gray landscape, expanding, creeping towards the distant horizon. Narrative in a dozen languages told the story of planetary rebirth in simple words. No boasting, none of the brassy triumphalism that would have accompanied Imperial projects on such a scale. The mural next to it showed the same work to scale against the backdrop of the whole planet.

For the first time, Jared felt the true magnitude of what these people were attempting. An involuntary shiver had nothing to do with the cooled air blasting from massive vents high up on the wall. He swallowed. The audacity was breathtaking. It would take someone as bull-headed and arrogant as Shayla Carver to contemplate success.

"Name?"

With a start, Jared saw he was at the head of the line. A clerk gazed at him, expectant, no hint of impatience in his eyes. A faint smile twitched the corners of his mouth. He must have seen this awestruck expression a thousand times.

He stepped forward. "Jared Tindall."

"Any identification?"

Jared shook his head.

The clerk sighed and made a note on the scroll on his desk. "Planet of origin?"

"Recently ... Scorflac."

The clerk looked up. "Before that?"

"Teth."

"Farmer?"

"Arboreal ecologist." The clerk's eyes widened. Jared pressed his advantage. "Certified in the school of Drooe ... before it got wasted."

"So, I'm guessing no surviving records, either. No matter, this world is all about fresh starts. That's not just the official line, either. We judge people by what they can do, not what scraps of paper they hold." The clerk made more scribbles on his scroll and pointed to a row of desks behind him. "Number twelve."

Jared grunted, and slouched past him to the next row, lining up behind a gangly youth waiting at desk twelve. It looked like ecologists were in short supply. But Jared already knew that.

Shayla sank back, closing her eyes for long moments. She would surely have been unconscious when they performed the suicide ritual. They wouldn't have risked her struggling and leaving tell-tale marks from any bindings. But that was not the kind of death she envisaged for herself. Helpless. Unable to fight back. That was not a warrior's death. She shuddered, then took a deep breath to compose herself.

Looking around the table, the others also seemed shaken by Brin's revelation. It was Felicity Marr who broke the silence. "This suggests new levels of subtlety." Deep frown lines darkened her pale golden skin as she thought. "And I see a worrying logic at play."

"How so?" Brin asked.

"Compare and contrast. What would be the motive of a simple assassination?"

"Revenge?" said Shayla. "I've made enough enemies."

Felicity inclined her head. "Yet an enemy who'd content himself with merely settling a personal grudge is too shallow to pose a serious threat. So think beyond the killing. What next?"

"Heightened security," Brin mused. "Intense investigations. Martial law."

"The planet needs a new governor," Shayla said. "The Emperor would appoint one. There would doubtless be more grumbles about his right royal prisoners, and maybe some unrest."

"And, I suspect, added strength to the Emperor's efforts to reign in the more lawless forces. So far, so petty. A simple killing couldn't be dressed as anything more than that. But a *suicide*," Felicity leaned forward, eyes narrowed, "especially such a poignant ritualistic statement ..."

Cogs clicked in Shayla's mind. "People would look for a motive."

"*Look* for one? Think of the scandal! The whole Empire would be gagging for *anything* to feed their voyeuristic little minds. All the gossip vultures would happily embellish and inflate the slightest hint of a rumor."

Shayla thought back to her brief time in the Emperor's service as the Master of Circuses. That office knew the value of perception and propaganda, and how to twist the media to the Empire's ends. "Who knows what kind of a media storm they might have been ready to unleash on my death. Rumors, speculation ..."

"Clearly a disgrace to the Emperor for one of his high servants—"

"Not to mention close family ..."

"The Emperor's hold could be seriously weakened. It might even give Ivan's supporters the courage to stage a revolt." Felicity sat back with a grim smile. "When you look for motive, with the right whisperings in the right places, someone could spin such a death any number of ways."

With an irritable shake of her head, Shayla said, "That also means there could be any number of groups behind this. Let's focus on what we know. Brin, any progress uncovering how they entered the Residence?"

"Only that we've scoured the Residence and the grounds thoroughly and the real Barras and Gingallia have yet to be found. We have records of them coming and going in the course of their duties, so there could have been a switch somewhere off site."

Coldness swept up Shayla's spine. Helplessness came in many guises. "Their families will find it hard to grieve, to find closure," she muttered.

Brin sat back and steepled his fingers. "We will keep searching, for that reason amongst others. We need to establish how long the imposters were able to remain undetected. Their disguise must have been impeccable just to get in, but did they walk among us for any length of time? I suspect not, my staff heard reports of something amiss in their behavior and alerted the guards, but the very thought chills me."

The chiefs exchanged looks around the table. The thought troubled them too, and there was nothing Shayla could offer in the way of hope. The Firenzi mimetic disguise could be penetrated if you knew what to look for, but that was a secret Shayla was not prepared to divulge. Not yet. For now, her hopes lay in persuading Jai Marx to keep his factions under control.

"As I say," Brin continued, "investigations are ongoing, but we are stretched thin. There is also the matter of the Wasps."

The wound in Shayla's belly throbbed at the memory of that attack on her cruiser. She eased herself into a more comfortable position and waved Brin to continue.

"The launch site was easy to find. It seems *Vanquisher* had records of the track—"

"The navy was *tracking* the missiles?" Shirley Chavas, the financial brains on the team was half out of her seat, face flushed. "And those Imperial asswipes didn't see fit to *tell* us?"

Brin's face darkened. "They have their own protocols and priorities—"

"The Imperial guard is under strict instructions not to meddle in planetary affairs," Shayla interrupted, sensing an upwelling of pride and offended Imperial loyalties that she could well do without right now. "The neutrality of a Freeworld cuts both ways. They would only be interested if there was a direct threat to our prisoners. My safety is in Brin's capable hands, not theirs." She hesitated, following her own train of thought to its conclusion. "How *did* you persuade them to share their information?"

"It did not come freely, and the fact that they shared at all stays within this room." Brin gazed around the circle of faces, ensuring he had their compliance. "Suffice to say, *we* discovered the missiles were launched from forty miles outside of Scale."

"Well *that* narrows down the list of suspects," Frank Wu snorted. The stocky manager of Eloon's development program had been silent throughout the exchange, his normally unquenchable good cheer absent today.

Shayla gave a weak smile. The coastal town of Scale was the largest settlement on the planet, and far more the center of civilization than the seat of government here at the old capital of Torremis.

"Given the timing," Brin said, "they must have launched before you left the prison complex, before you were even in the air."

"That would point to someone tipping them off ..."

"Maybe not knowingly. The guard signaled to the operations room here that you were making ready to leave. The signal could have been intercepted."

Shayla's eyes widened. "That's not normal procedure. We never broadcast my movements ahead of time for exactly that reason, and especially not from the prison."

Brin grimaced. "There's a new guard up there. A youngster. He was, of course, briefed thoroughly on standard operating procedures but Sergeant Colt will be at pains to remind him."

"Hmm ..." Shayla let the thought slide for now. She knew Brin would chase down all lines of inquiry. Meanwhile, though, "How the heck did they manage to smuggle Wasps down to the surface?"

"They didn't," Brin said. "They were already here."

"Well, that's a relief." Shirley made an exaggerated show of mopping her brow. "Thought you were going to ask me what else I've been buying."

"It's both a relief and a worry," said Frank. There was something deeply unsettling about his serious demeanor today. "I'd be going mad figuring out how to secure our supply lines against unauthorized shipments. We are wide open to all comers."

"An irksome but necessary condition of our Freeworld charter," Shayla reminded him.

"Not arguing that, but I'm actually surprised nobody's tried this before. Anyway"—Frank squinted at Brin—"what makes you sure they were already here?"

"Back before the Cleansing, Wasps were deployed here for close planetary defense. Caches would have been hidden deep, away from centers of population. Some will have survived, we can be sure of that. Either someone unearthed these by accident, or someone has access to old planetary records. Either way, we found the discarded launch tubes in a clearing alongside a forestry track—they made little effort to conceal them—and the serial numbers correspond to batches shipped here decades ago."

Frank nodded. "That brings me to my concern, how many more are there lying around?"

"A good question, and something else for Brin's team to look into. That's a deeper question than we can afford to dwell on in this conference." Shayla headed them off from the rabbit hole. "We have to assume there are more of them ready to be used. Prevention is a fish that's already slipped the hook. We need to take suitable precautions against the worst. Meanwhile, I'm wondering if there are any leads on who set the trap?"

Brin scowled. "There were no useful forensics at the site. The road is quiet enough that there was little chance of them being observed, but used often enough that there's no knowing which tracks might belong to the traitors."

"Come on," Shirley spat. "That's barking madness. How can someone launch a missile attack from, what, two, three thousand miles away, and not leave a trace?"

As Brin was the only other military person at the table, Shayla could understand Shirley's scorn. She cocked an eyebrow at Brin.

He said, "A pair of Wasps could easily be transported in a small air or ground cruiser. It would take no more than three, though more likely four, to manhandle the tubes out of the vehicle and set them up. Someone with a knowledge of the target to give them their orders, but it wouldn't have needed a weapons tech."

That's the great thing about Wasps, Shayla thought sourly. They were designed to be easy to hide, easy to program, easy to launch. And they were intelligent. Fire—from a safe distance—and forget.

She gazed at Brin long and hard. He averted his eyes. There was more on his mind than he was prepared to bring to this table. She took a deep breath. "Okay, there's a lot still to unearth and I know it's still early days. Meanwhile, we face an approaching threat no less deadly than assassins and smart missiles."

"The inspection," Frank said.

"The inspection, indeed," Shayla answered. Growing a planet from its transitional state as an Imperial protectorate to full Freeworld status was a decades-long journey. Every five years along the way, the Emperor would send an inspection team to report on progress. Though seemingly benign in intent, the Inspectorate wielded almost limitless power, answerable only to the Emperor in person, and could easily halt them in their tracks.

"I believe our progress has been good," Frank said. "We're establishing new, stable ecosystems and centers of population." He glanced over at Yamen Kondosa, the fifth member of Shayla's council.

The tall and elegant young woman took her cue. "Our intake numbers are strong." She gave her head a tiny shake, heavy braids brushing her shoulders. "There's no shortage of people displaced by conflict. I think the purpose of our charter will be fulfilled many times over."

"We should have a viable and self-sustaining population ahead of schedule," Frank added. "What worries me is not the practicalities, it's the politics. No matter how well we're doing, if they come in with an agenda ..."

"A possibility," Shayla said. "We arm ourselves as best we can against that, but we concern ourselves first and foremost with those factors within our control." She pulled up this morning's messages on her note-pad. "The head of the Inspectorate has been appointed. Lady Josephine bin Mellion. Not a name I'm familiar with, anyone know anything about her? Any clues we can glean from her appointment?"

"A distant relative of the Emperor," said Felicity. "Other than that, not a name I've come across either."

"Anything to hint as to her alignment and loyalties?"

"The Emperor." Felicity's expression was deadpan.

"Beyond the obvious," Shayla murmured. "The Emperor would have appointed someone loyal for this job. But what about hidden associations?"

"Now we have a name, I'll get my team onto it," Brin growled.

"Thanks, Brin. Felicity, do we have answers on protocols yet?"

"Are you kidding? Those bureaucrats at the Mosaic Palace would choke on their own snot before giving a straight answer to a simple question."

"Who've you been dealing with?"

"The client relations department in the Office of the Master of Circuses, as you suggested."

"Hmm. And they were unable to advise?"

"Too much advice, more like!" Felicity's voice deepened a few tones, and her face set in mock gravitas. "Some sources say that, as the Governor of a Freeworld, you are technically on a par with the Grand Family heads," she droned. "That would imply that a public servant would defer to you. But this is an Imperial Inspectorate, a direct repre-sentative of the Emperor himself, and the Grand Families defer to the Emperor. However, that's a matter of historical convention. They offer allegiance by treaty not by rank. Then again, the Trown Plains Accord is not too clear on the standing of the Freeworlds." She snorted, face twisted in disgust. "I got the feeling that they were skirting around any kind of real help."

Shayla nodded. *Mind games.* From her brief time working in the heart of the Imperial hierarchy, she was sure that her old office would have had no trouble answering a question like this. Instead, it sounded like Frank might be right. They wanted to wrong-foot her with a proto-col gaffe. There *was* an agenda at work.

Shadows reached long across the ground by the time Jared climbed aboard one of the slug-like ground transports idling outside the immi-grant processing complex. Despite his peak of fitness, his body resigned itself to the soft embrace of the worn but clean seat. It wanted nothing more than sleep, but his mind was a whirl. Sleep would be a long way off yet.

After the welcome speeches, the interviews and sorting in the intake hall, the stream of newcomers filtered into a maze of halls and lecture rooms beyond. Utilitarian painted concrete was tempered by more murals. Information, engagingly presented, immersed him in the wonder that this world represented. The Insurrection was no stranger to propaganda, and the hand of communications experts was not lost on Jared. They'd done a marvelous job, he grudgingly admitted. To people fleeing strife-torn worlds, people who'd lost everything they'd known, this was the gateway to a new life.

Everything here had been built on the same gargantuan scale. A factory designed to take in thousands at a time, not the mere hundreds present today, and fire them with enthusiasm for the back-breaking task ahead.

The indoctrination lingered in the background, present at every turn yet not ostentatious, while they worked through the process: orien-tations, briefings, assignment to a work team. He took a quiet moment to compare his notes against a fifty-foot-wide map of Eloon set in the floor of a spacious concourse at the heart of the complex. Jared was pleased to see his local contacts had succeeded in getting him assigned to a project near his ultimate goal.

Somewhere along the way a hot meal gave much-needed suste-nance. His health was checked, meager possessions assessed, essential items of kit and clothing offered from a well-stocked warehouse. It was amazing what a welfare system the Imperial budget afforded.

Finally, a billet assignment to a sprawling immigration camp nearby. In Jared's case, this would only be for the night. The Eloon authorities were keen to put his skills to use. As keen as he was to take up his position and review the preparations his team of contacts had made.

The transport glided across cindered ground leaving the immigration complex behind.

Even though he'd read about it and expected it, the sudden appearance of the Garden of Hope left Jared breathless.

Through an opening in a stark concrete wall, grassland stretched a mile either side, dotted with stands of trees and vibrant splashes of color. Manicured lawns cut swathes through acres of less formal wild meadows. Jared had done his homework in readiness for this mission and knew the whole garden was planted with native species, resurrected from the ashes.

The Garden of Hope straddled the network of roads between the landing field and immigration processing center, the temporary housing camp, and the official planetary legislature. Anyone arriving, leaving, or simply going about everyday business on this desolate plateau would pass through this reminder of what could be.

The garden was as much a show as the propaganda lining the concrete walls. Nothing like this could yet sustain itself on this world. There was no life-giving climate, no ecosystem established. Everything, he knew, had to be tended carefully. Even so, the verdant oasis made a shocking contrast to the desiccated surroundings.

After the subliminal brainwashing of the Imperial spin doctors, simple nature spoke with dumb eloquence.

As the setting sun reflected off a still lake, a lump formed in Jared's throat. He pursed his lips angrily and brushed a reluctant tear from the corner of his eye.

———— ◆ ————

Shayla poured tea from the silver service laid out on a glass-topped table in front of her. The setting sun angled in through the windows of her study, highlighting a riot of colors from the bookshelves and glass cases lining the near wall.

She picked up her cup and regarded Brin over the rim while she blew steam from the bitter drink. No point beating around the bush. "I sensed this morning there's something on your mind. Something you're not yet ready to share."

"It's nothing, My Lady."

"Don't go all formal on me. Someone may have access to a basement full of Wasps. If you have so much as a half-baked notion to get us closer to this threat, then you've a duty to divulge it. There is no saving face if I end up creamed across the countryside."

Brin chewed his lip. "This is nothing more than the ghost of speculation."

"Understood. And, Brin, I'm always mindful of the burden you carry. This is not a challenge to your judgment, but a support. Better to over-divulge what may be nothing, than to be over-cautious."

Although Brin looked troubled, he shrugged and gave a resigned sigh. "There is a man, something of a mystery, who lives out in the mountains around Scale. Known only as Randall."

"Do we have any record of him?"

"We do not. He's not enlisted on any of the work teams, but there's always been a handful who choose to make their own way rather than join the organized programs."

"So, what specifically about this man has caught your attention?"

"He has been speaking publicly against you, against our work here." Brin hesitated. "Says it's a desecration of the memory of those who died."

"Aah." Shayla had been on the verge of asking why he'd been allowed to roam free, preaching sedition. Now she understood. "It's a sensitive topic. And from a certain perspective, he's right."

"We've found nothing whatsoever to link him with anything overt. No connections to outside bodies protesting one way or another about our treatment of our Imperial prisoners. As far as we can tell, he's a religious madman. A rabble rouser, but not otherwise dangerous."

"Nevertheless," Shayla said, tapping her teeth thoughtfully with her forefinger, "I think I will look into this, personally."

Chapter 5

Shayla joined Simone in the cockpit of the heavily-modified transport she'd requisitioned years ago for longer excursions. Battered and nondescript on the outside, the interior of the forward cargo hold had been converted into a comfortable suite. A bedroom, little larger than the bed, and a pair of bunk rooms could accommodate Shayla and a handful of staff. A small but well-equipped galley, cramped bathroom facilities, and a combined sitting, dining, and office area filled the rest of the hold. To compensate for the limited space, the bare metal of the hold was screened by wall hangings, imitation wood panels, and throw rugs over the non-slip decking. Nothing lavish by Imperial standards. Nothing, she was sure, that a bean-counting auditor could complain about, but it served as home and office when she traveled.

Green water heaved far below, the Straits of Gehenna, where tide-driven torrents boiled back and forth between the Sea of Cordoon and the northern ocean. On the horizon, spray-lashed cliffs towered, bleak and inhospitable.

"We're getting close, My Lady." Simone's voice held a barely-perceptible edge.

"We have time yet. You don't imagine I'd risk this flight, do you?" Shayla smiled, reached for the comms screen and scrawled a series of clearance codes. Nobody had asked for clearance, nor would they. A curt warning to stay away was all that any interloper would get before the ring of automated defenses took action.

There was no acknowledgment. The only clue that the codes had been accepted would be their continued existence.

Glistening cliffs passed below, guarded by fierce fangs that broke the foaming swell. Shayla's smile hardened. This wild seascape, these cliffs, held fond and painful memories from another life. She pictured young daredevils from the town launching themselves into the updraft on gaily-decorated flimsy wings. Young Shayla clapped her hands in excitement, looking up into the eyes of her father. "Pappi! I want to try!"

"Next year, maybe." His smile could light continents. His long fingers jabbed her belly, sharp yet playful. "You need to put on a few more pounds yet or you'll be blown clear to Bandallis."

There was no next year.

Beyond the cliffs, the landscape bore decades-old scars of Imperial punishment. Here near the coast the signs were subtle. Only someone familiar with the previous heavily-wooded terrain would be shocked by the thin scrub stubbling the desert like a youth's first try at a beard. This had been Shayla's home. The sight never failed to bring a tear. Further inland, unnaturally smooth plains miles wide, still shunned by vegetation, marked the locations of towns and villages. She could name each one.

At last the new prison complex stretched to the horizon, though it took a keen eye to see it. Nothing more than a low mound here and there cresting the dry scrub and an occasional scattering of buildings showed the hand of man. Those mounds hid state-of-the-art defenses, ever watchful. The buildings housed barracks and the multiple entrances to the prison itself deep underground. They slowed to a non-threatening crawl, honoring a safe approach path unmarked on any navigational chart.

Simone landed the craft under Shayla's guidance, and disembarked. Officially Shayla was still recuperating. Today, Simone would be her eyes and ears on this unannounced in-person visit.

Shayla watched her stride across the parched soil armed with a scroll full of people to question, and her own sharp instincts for the slightest hint of deception. The visit had a serious purpose. Events at the old polar prison had unnerved Shayla. She knew the risks of underestimating the influence and cunning of her dangerous captives and sensed they were plotting something. But then, when were they not? Still, she was determined that as soon as the inspection was over they would be moved and this new facility had better be in good shape to receive them.

But this visit concealed a murkier purpose. Her recent escape gave Shayla an excuse to remain out of sight for a few days and this was a window she was going to take full advantage of.

She reluctantly lifted her gaze from the door in the nearly feature-less bunker into which Simone had vanished, all calm competence and efficiency, and settled back into the depths of the co-pilot's seat. She pulled her cloak tight, closed her eyes and poured her energy into mor-phing her implants.

The dense network of fungal filaments, a skin within her skin, responded to her mental summons. Like stretching long-disused mus-cles, she willed the implants to squeeze *here*, to plump out *there*, to start their microscopic chemical factories churning out pigments. A fierce itching and crawling under her skin nearly made her gag. Even after so many years, she never grew used to the eerie sensation.

Taking on the looks of another person well enough to fool close acquaintances was an art that took days to complete, and crippling amounts of effort. The task this time didn't need such finesse. She was taking on a fictitious identity and all she needed to do was look like someone other than Shayla Carver.

Eloon's chief of security, Brindis al Silessi, scowled while Sam Kattergee, Shayla's senior medic, fussed with the nargile on his desk.

Brin had never truly got used to the Firenzi social rituals around the traditional water pipe, but Lady Carver had introduced it into Eloon culture and Sam was a fiercely traditional Firenzi at heart. He'd reached into a drawer for his tray of dried leaves and assorted spices the moment Brin entered the inner sanctum of his office. Always a bad sign. Brin stifled impatience and practiced one of the mindfulness techniques Sam had taught him. There was no hurrying the process and Sam would not interrupt his preparations to be drawn into conversation.

Heavy drapes drawn against the night, Sam's private office in the Residence offered a warm haven from the bleak desolation outside. Walls and shelves distracted Brin with a profusion of artworks and orna-ments from a hundred cultures. Normally such a clutter would have seemed untidy yet the collection gave a sense of subliminal order and unity, as if each piece was a necessary facet of an unseen whole, each in its own precise and unfathomable place.

Sam hovered like a pale ghost in the mellow glow of a single desk lamp. Skin tones light even by Firenzi standards, hair grayed as befit his age, it was his eyes—little more than white on white—that gave him an alien appearance. At last, he sucked a draught of fragrant smoke and large teeth flashed a smile of satisfaction.

"Now then, Brindis, this will take the edge off your worry." Sam offered the mouthpiece to Brin, who gave an inward sigh as he accepted.

The smooth coolness of an alpine meadow washed through him. In all his visits, he'd never quite tasted the same blend twice. Sam's tray held only a few dozen containers, but the possible combinations were endless. The Firenzi aristocracy regarded it a high and subtle art to concoct a flavor fitting to the occasion and, though Sam shunned narcotics, many of the ingredients reputedly held medicinal and subtle mood-altering qualities.

Despite the soothing effects of that one inhalation, Brin's impatience turned to concern. If the doctor had *good* news to impart, he wouldn't have needed the pipe. "Do I have something to worry about?"

"Your face is being a constant picture of worry of late."

"You know what I mean."

Sam took the pipe and drew a pensive puff. "True enough, my dear Brindis. There is little I can say to lighten the news."

With sudden insight, Brin saw the calming ritual of the nargile was as much for his friend's benefit as for his. "It's still progressing, isn't it?"

"Slowly." Sam nodded and took another puff. "But yes."

Brin declined the offer of the pipe, and sat back, fingers steepled in front of his face while he digested the news. Ever courteous, Sam allowed him the time. "And there really is no treatment for this?" His voice was little more than a whisper.

"Firenzi medicine is far beyond the reckoning of any other in the collected worlds of humanity. I retain some small openings with my former colleagues and can endeavor most secretively to procure treatments only the military have access to." Sam took another delicate puff, then handed the pipe back to Brin. "Even so, Brindis, I am not in the business of miracles."

"So, how long before I'm reduced to slack-jawed drooling?"

Sam sat erect, hands clasped on the desk in front of him. "You must understand the rarity of this disease, and the sorrowful lack of understanding in our possession."

Brin gave him an impatient wave to continue.

"Prognosis from the point of diagnosis varies from weeks to years. We do not have the data to answer those questions you want answered. However," Sam hastened on, "I will watch for early signs of cognitive impairment. From the tests I've completed, my best estimate is that point is months away yet."

"I'm used to logic guiding my judgment, but nowadays I find I'm reviewing and second-guessing the tiniest decision." Frustration ached, along with growing dread at the future in store. "I know this sickness will affect my judgment, open me up to unwarranted risk-taking. You taught me to be alert to the signs, but what if I'm now over-compensating?" Brin's mind went back to the matter of Randall. His first impulse had been to action ... arrest, maybe covert assassination. He'd been on the verge of readying a flyer and seeking Randall out himself. He shuddered. But in reining himself in, had he gone too far the other way? Lady Carver seemed to think it warranted investigation, so what had stayed Brin's hand? "Inaction can be as damaging as a risky plunge."

As if reading his turmoil, Sam said, "You must practice calm above all else. We have observed that stress hormones catalyze the spread of this prion."

"My role is inherently stressful," Brin growled. "I need you to keep me fit for duty."

"At present, Brindis, you have the necessary measure of control and the disease is not yet too far progressed. You must of course be on your guard, and seek counsel when you are troubled by indecision."

There was little comfort to be found in Sam's words, but it seemed the best he could hope for right now. "Well then." Brin sighed. "Lady Carver is aware of my ... condition. I could fob it off and say it's up to her to remove me when she see's fit."

"But you are afraid that she, being of honorable indebtedness, will hold from causing you hurt. Maybe to her detriment."

"Indebtedness? Pah! Pity is what I'm afraid of."

"Then you do Her Ladyship a grievous disservice." Sam's voice grew stern. "Do you truly believe she would hold from doing that which she knows is needed? Even at the cost of a friend?"

"Of course not. You mistake my point, though. I *could* easily lay the decision at her door, but I won't. This is my burden to bear, and I will not shirk it."

"What, then?"

"If my judgment fails me utterly, I need to know that I can count on you to bench me before I can do harm to our endeavor here."

"Brindis, never doubt that for a moment. I am at all times most earnestly attentive to Her Ladyship's best interests."

"And, Sam"—Brin took a deep drag on the pipe—"when I start drooling, shoot me."

———◆———

The transport's cockpit was lit by nothing more than the ready lights of the instrument panel by the time Simone returned with her reports. Much of the prison was still a building site crawling with excess personnel, but the essential facilities were at least functional. "You should rest." Shayla's servant regarded her with fond concern. "You've made good use of these past hours. No one, not even Brin, would recognize you."

Fatigue washed through her in waves. Shayla pursed her lips. "Need to deepen skin tone a bit more. I'm from Wala space, remember?"

"Bloody perfectionist." But the jibe was kindly. Her face grew serious. "There will be time for finishing touches on the flight up. Right now, we eat. You sleep."

Shayla couldn't argue.

In the two years of preparation between the Emperor's pronouncement and the formal establishment of the new colony on Eloon, Shayla had taken great care in assembling her staff. She'd had little say in the most important posts. Brin, Frank, and Felicity were excellent people and Shayla was profoundly grateful to Emperor Julian for his choices, but when it came to her closest personal servants she'd insisted on a free hand.

Of all of them, only Simone was entrusted with the secret of her implants. Even that had been a soul-searching decision. Only a handful of operatives in the Firenzi Special Service knew about the technology and Shayla was as keen as them to keep it hidden. It was times like this that she offered thanks for this small leap of faith.

It had been years since she last used her implants. She'd forgotten just how draining it was. The disguise was remarkable, the closest anyone had come to true shape-shifting, but it carried a cost.

She allowed herself to drift as barbecue smells wafted from the galley. Protein and carbohydrates in generous quantities. Simone knew the drill.

After a night's uneasy rest, Shayla woke with what felt like the mother of all hangovers. A large jug of cloudy liquid sat on the ledge beside her bed. With shaking hands Shayla poured herself a glass, tossed it back, and poured another. "Thanks, Simone."

"You're rounding out your face, the bulk has to come from somewhere," Simone answered from the galley. "Breakfast, while it's hot, then we're on our way."

Once more in flight, Shayla snuggled in the co-pilot's seat and willed her appearance ever closer to the image she held in her mind. It was like flexing muscles, adopting a posture and holding it.

The western coast of Bandallis unrolled below, much of it parched and seemingly lifeless. Shayla knew better. Away from the centers of destruction, seeds survived. They needed just the right encouragement to spring forth once more. Life could never be wiped away entirely. And now pockets of green appeared where the work camps nurtured fragile new ecosystems. A few miles further, and isolated patches merged into an unbroken carpet stretching up the coast and for miles inland. They were nearing the main center of activity at Scale.

They set down in a remote corner of the landing field. Simone unloaded a couple of small ground cars from the rear hold while Shayla checked her own appearance and equipment. She matched perfectly the picture on the fake ID Brin had made for her. A chemist from war-ravaged Scoon in Wala territory. Many immigrants came from those disputed border territories so she wouldn't be conspicuous, and she'd studied the Wala customs and dialects over many years as a Firenzi agent.

She threw a plain threadbare cloak over her worn and stained technician's tunic and collected her travel bag. As she threw the strap over her shoulder the bag bumped against the unaccustomed bulk of a civilian-issue beam pistol in its holster. A necessary evil, for show rather than serious use. This was a frontier nation and she'd have looked undressed without it. The knife snugged in its sheath against her waist was a more reassuring feel.

Shayla sealed the outer hatch of the transport and took a deep breath. Here, in the midst of hundreds of square miles of newly-planted forest, the air had almost lost the pervasive smoky aftertaste she'd come to take for granted. She sighed and resolved to visit here more often to remind herself why she was doing this—breathing new life into a ravaged planet. She climbed into the smaller of the two vehicles waiting alongside, little more than a fat-wheeled trike with a lid, dented and dust-caked.

She tossed her carry bag behind the single seat and turned to Simone. "I'll check in this evening when I've had a chance to look around. Maybe Brin's people will have tracked Randall down, or maybe I'll get lucky."

Simone pursed her lips and looked Shayla up and down. "Even after all these years at your side, that's still an impressive trick." Worry edged into her eyes. "Remember that even though this is technically home territory, the rule of law is thin on the ground."

"Yes, mother, I'll be careful." Shayla struggled to keep a straight face.

"Such a deep disguise is two-edged." The worry lines deepened. "Your status can't protect you if you are so demonstrably *not* who you would claim to be."

"Under the skin I am still Shayla Carver, Firenzi assassin. That should be protection enough."

The second vehicle was a more standard two-wheeled gyro-steadied roadster, clean black and green with the Imperial acacia blazoned on the side. Simone mounted the two steps up into the cab slung between the wheels. She had official business here, too, on Shayla's behalf. The sprawling forestry operation here was a vital foundation to breathing life back into the desolate continent.

Shayla touched fingertips to temple in a casual salute, and gunned the engine to life. She waited for Simone to disappear onto the road towards the center of town, then picked her way around the perimeter of the field in the opposite direction.

Miles crawled by on a rutted dirt road. The soft tires and suspension of the trike evened out the bumps, but Shayla was on constant watch for sharp dips deep enough to roll her.

Alerted by a deep booming don't-fuck-with-me horn, Shayla pulled over and waited while a monster truck thundered past with ponderous disdain for ruts and potholes. Choking and blinded in a billowing dust cloud, she realized why her outfit came with scarf and goggles. She rinsed her mouth and face and ruefully acknowledged the learning experience.

The road here clung to the side of a river valley. Miles-wide gray water glittered under the morning sun. On the horizon, the unnaturally level and featureless far bank marked the old town of Scale, another reminder of her purpose on this planet. Shayla grimaced and turned the trike back onto the road with fresh determination.

At last, unruly vegetation to one side of the road gave way to sprawling acres of neatly-tended plantations. Regimented mile-wide plots held trees at stages of growth from seedlings to head-high saplings. In the distance, a spiderlike harvester picked its way with deceptive grace through the rows, plucking trees ready for harvest, bundling the root balls in degradable wrapping, and stacking them in the back of a heavy transport idling patiently alongside.

A few miles further, a cluster of low buildings appeared. Shayla sought out the work camp office and loitered near the desk under the pretense of collecting instructions from headquarters. She chatted to the clerks behind the main desk, playing the newbie card to ask about local conditions, terrain, weather, and where to find the cheapest beer. All the while, she tuned in to the gossip around her as booted and overalled workers came and went, swapped notes, bitched and bantered.

At the next camp, Shayla repeated the performance, probing as directly as she dared for news of Randall. Again, she came away empty handed.

Another thirty miles of numbing tedium and Shayla was growing heartily sick of trees. With a sigh of relief she saw the outlines of more substantial buildings peering through the leaves.

Some classically-literate wag had scrawled a homemade sign and hung it on the side of the water tower standing guard over the road into the unnamed distribution center. 'Welcome to Mirkwood' it read.

Beyond the tower, long rows of prefabricated sheds gleamed orange against the surrounding greenery. Many were labeled as storehouses— seed, fertilizer, food, machinery. Towards the center of the complex, buildings with windows showed human habitation, bunkhouses, administration, and a canteen.

Shayla wheeled the trike into a gap at the side of the road, lined up with a dozen assorted work vehicles, and dismounted. It was still early for lunch, but her stomach growled in protest. Stretching cramped limbs, she climbed steps up to the canteen and pushed through swing doors into the darkened shed.

Suffocating mugginess engulfed her after the crisp outdoors. A heady blend of spice and charcoal washed her nostrils setting her stomach gurgling again.

Rows of mess tables stretched into the distance. The only natural light came from windows behind her overlooking the street. Elsewhere, yellow ceiling lights served only to enhance the shadows at the edge of Shayla's vision. Small huddles of early diners covertly regarded her as she made her way towards the serving counter near the far end of the room. The nape of her neck prickled.

Joining the line at one end of the servery, Shayla flashed her work badge to a sleepy attendant and took a mess tray. She glanced at the hot trays, and spooned a portion of sweet fries.

Her scalp crawled once more at the sudden silence nearby. The attendant had miraculously wakened. "Umm, you can't ..." He stammered to a stop when Shayla treated him to her best ice warrior glare.

"Hey," someone hissed behind her. "I guess you're new here." The speaker used a dialect common on the Wala home world.

With a sidelong glance, Shayla noted the dark skin and hair of a Wala native, similar to her chosen cover identity. "Trouble with the locals?" she asked in the same tongue.

The young woman behind her nodded. "The good food is reserved for Firenzi workers." She gestured further down the counter where cauldrons of greasy stew simmered. "We get to enjoy their misbegotten take on *chakchouka*."

For the first time, Shayla saw that the scattering of workers around the room was anything but random. There were no signs, no barriers, but the tables were clearly segregated with the prime seats near the windows occupied exclusively by Firenzi crews.

From the corner of her eye, the attendant made what he probably imagined were discreet hand signals, and a pair of thugs lounging near the door got to their feet. Bloody amateurs. Her cheeks flushed, and she forced herself to calm.

"Oh," she whispered, "so I guess I'm not supposed to take these either." She helped herself to two plump barbecued chicken breasts and a generous spoonful of locally-grown green beans.

The girl's eyes widened in fright.

"What happens next, I wonder?"

"The best you can hope is they just take your rations." The girl nodded towards the front of the room.

"Rations?" Shayla murmured. "There *is* no rationing on the work crews."

"Tell that to the Quartermaster," her companion muttered.

"I think I will." She finished loading her tray and sauntered towards the front, angling towards an empty table near a window.

A lanky youngster in a guard's uniform intercepted her. By his worried expression, Shayla guessed he was hoping to keep the peace. He glanced over his shoulder then jerked his head towards the back of the room. "You should find somewhere with your own people."

"Back off, soldier." Shayla kept her tone low but firm. She held his gaze, expression set like stone. "I have vermin to deal with. Be ready to fetch the clean-up crew."

He swallowed and nodded. Shayla breathed a sigh of relief that he wasn't too green to catch on to the Firenzi military slang.

She pushed past him and found her way barred by a wall of muscle. The two thugs she'd originally marked stood a respectable distance behind, clearly nothing more than lieutenants in this bully ring.

The wall of muscle was topped by a face wearing an amiable grin. "Your folks sit back there." He glanced down at Shayla's tray. "And I see you've brought me my rations." The grin widened.

Shayla gazed back at him, unfazed, expressionless.

"Stupid Woolly," one of his henchmen muttered. "Dumb bitch can't even understand you."

"I will sit by the sun as befits my complexion," Shayla announced, in carefully-accented but perfectly clear Imperial dialect, "and I will eat my lunch in peace."

"You have a lot to learn." The grin was gone.

Shayla placed her tray down on the table alongside her, just out of his reach. He leaned across, hand outstretched. Her balled fist lashed out, striking him squarely in the solar plexus. As he staggered back, she landed a couple more lightning blows to make sure damage would be visible for the next few weeks. Blood gushed from a broken nose.

He crashed into the table behind, eyes rolled up in their sockets. His henchmen leaped forward then stopped as they took in Shayla's casual contempt and her fighting stance.

When they hesitated she widened her eyes, pretending to notice her downed assailant for the first time, and brought her hand to her mouth. "Oops. I didn't realize I hit him *that* hard." A picture of innocence, she picked up her tray and stepped over the comatose figure and past the nonplussed sidekicks.

By the time the young guard returned with a sergeant and a medic in tow, the gang had already left. The two thugs had been joined by three others who'd edged out of their seats at the start of the fracas and hastily backed down when they saw how it played out. Between them they carried their unconscious leader out. Others hesitantly came forward to right the toppled table and benches. Eating voraciously all the while, Shayla scribbled on her notepad with her free hand.

The medic scratched her head and left. The sergeant, a portly woman in her sixties, sat opposite Shayla and unrolled a scroll on the tabletop. The youngster hovered behind, eyes bulging at Shayla's rapidly emptying plate. She stripped the remaining flesh from her second piece of chicken and threw the bones down with a sigh. "This country air does bring out people's appetites."

"It brings out a lot more than that, too," the sergeant growled. "It's good to be able to look after yourself."

Shayla shrugged. "I got in a lucky blow."

"You don't fool me. You knew what you were doing."

"He was lucky I was hungry and not looking to prolong things. Now"—her tone became brusque and businesslike—"this is the part where you will want to ask lots of questions. My advice is to forget them because they will not go well for you." Shayla packaged up her scrawled notes and pointed her stylus at the sergeant's scroll, transferring the package across. "These folks are probably already known to you, but here are descriptions and details of their insignia that I observed. There will be others, hangers-on, but these are the ringleaders. Keep them in check and the others will likely toe the line."

The sergeant's mouth opened, closed, and opened again. After a few moments she took a breath. "There's only me and Owen here to keep the peace in a camp of ten thousand. Budget's stretched. We're stretched. The most we can hope is that they don't hurt each other ..." She chewed her lip. "... Too badly."

"I know." Shayla wrote out a comms code. "I have a contact in the central security office in Torremis. They have covert operatives and ways to deal with troublemakers. Word will spread that crap won't be tolerated. All you need to do is keep an eye on things."

"How ..."

"I've traveled widely. I have connections. Questions are bad, remember?"

The sergeant eyed Shayla, who gazed back, arms folded across her chest. Eventually the sergeant snorted in disgust. "Getting way too old for this." She glanced down at the information Shayla had sent. "Thanks, we could use some help."

"Don't think on this as a kindness. You should have called for help before things reached this point. People coming here have been through shit already, I should know, and they don't need more of it on the ground here. This is a refuge and a place of opportunity. Lady Carver will expect this camp to be cleaned up by the time someone next visits."

The appraising stare sharpened again. "You're no mere chemist. Who are you?"

"Me? Just another technician trying to make good on a second chance." Shayla leaned back in her chair. "So, what else do you do for entertainment around here?"

An afternoon's hard ride brought Shayla to another work camp, much like the others she'd passed along the way. Her shadow stretched long in front of her when she pulled up outside the ubiquitous field office. She hauled a crate of soil samples her staff had provided as part of her cover, and lugged it into the office.

Just another soil analyst bringing home her day's catch, she busied herself sealing the crate into a padded transit container and labeling it with a destination code that would ensure it didn't end up anywhere that would raise questions. She landed it with a thump on the shipping counter.

The clerk scrutinized the code. "This going to headquarters?"

Damn him, he was observant. Shayla knew Scale had its own laboratories where most analysis work was done. She shrugged. "Don't ask me. I have my instructions. Special survey. I guess they don't trust us oiks out in the wilds."

The clerk gave a sympathetic nod. "Always keeping an eye on us, aren't they?"

They exchanged pleasantries. Shayla got directions to a billet for the night, and asked after the local watering holes. Her lunchtime conversation with the elderly sergeant had finally got her a lead. "I hear Drake's has good beer. Well"—she made a face—"good enough around here, anyway."

The clerk shrugged. "I guess it depends what you want. They get some odd folks in there, though." He gave her directions and she turned to leave.

"Hey! You forgetting something?"

Shayla gave him a blank look. For a moment she suffered that wrenching disconnect she sometimes got working under cover. Dual identities fought for expression. Like pulling on an unfamiliar overcoat, she settled her mind back into the persona of a lowly soil analyst. She cocked an eyebrow at the clerk. "Give me a hint. I'm bagged."

He nodded to the back of the office where, amongst a heap of boxes and crates, stood a pile of empty sample containers.

Smothering a sigh of relief, Shayla chose instead to roll her eyes and curse. "Forget my own fucking head next. Thanks." She grinned as she grabbed a crate and swung it onto her shoulder. "Good night."

In the bustling camp kitchen there was no sign of the overt tribalism she'd met in the larger distribution center, maybe because the crowded room held only serving counters and a limited choice of dishes. The air, thick with the reek of sweat, steam, and simmering gravy seemed as much a physical barrier as the press of bodies besieging the counters. Trays scraped and clattered, talk and laughter ebbed and flowed. Shayla elbowed her way through the crowd, filled a covered mess tin and sought refuge in her assigned bunk house.

Refueled, and on the scent of her quarry, she pulled cloak and scarf close around her and set off once more into the chill night.

Drake's pub turned out to be a prefabricated storage shed near the far end of the camp. From its location and the evident newness of the row it stood in—only a few of these sheds had so far been put into use— Shayla guessed some entrepreneur had appropriated the space and claimed squatters' rights. The possibility of backhanders to the camp authorities also crossed her mind.

That did beg interesting questions, though, harking back to her earlier conversation about entertainment. There seemed to be little to do out here other than work, eat, and sleep. Not a healthy situation. Shirley would bitch about frivolous expenses but they had to do something more for these folks. She also made a mental note to talk to Frank about encouraging some free enterprise on a more officially sanctioned basis. The planetary population was growing, and needed a more sophisticated infrastructure than the rudimentary work camps they'd started off with.

She pushed through the door and caught her breath at the warmth, bustle, and explosive level of alcohol vapor. She grabbed an outrageously expensive beer from the makeshift bar and settled near the back of the room. Her hunched posture and fixed scowl discouraged company.

Three beers later, Shayla was wondering how late the bar stayed open and how much longer she should wait.

Sam Kattergee took an experimental puff on the nargile and beamed in satisfaction before handing the spout to Brin.

The single desk lamp cast the same warm light on the same dizzying array of memorabilia as the previous evening. This evening, though, the draft Brin drew into his lungs cut through his mind like a hot knife. For an instant he glimpsed a wholeness in the room's disorder, like seeing the rows in an apple orchard appear from the confusion of trees. The moment passed, but the sharpness within his mind lingered.

"Now then, Brindis, are you ready to discuss what is on your mind?"

"Is it that obvious?"

Sam waggled his head. "You are not so lacking in expression as people think. I am seeing last night that medical matters were not the end of your worries. But I am believing in fighting just one battle at a time."

Brin hesitated, wondering how many of his misgivings he was ready to share. "I need some points of reference to baseline my judgment. Look on it as a sanity check."

"You are troubled by a course of action?"

"Not a decision I have to make, but one I made some months ago. I find I'm second-guessing my reasoning now." Any failing on his part was hard to contemplate, Brin knew. For a man in his role, the potential for harm was too severe for any margin of error. Under his friend's steady gaze Brin felt like a moth on a pin. He realized this conversation could lead to his suspension from duty if he'd misjudged.

He took another puff on the pipe. Another brief wave of clarity showed that delaying tactic for what it was. "There was a particular requisition for the new prison. It was"—Brin sucked his teeth—"*expensive*."

"The whole project is a drain on the Emperor's purse, I believe."

"Lady Carver was angry. I stood my ground, but the experience left me shaken. She so rarely questions my judgment, when she does I should take it seriously."

"What was the nature of this requisition?"

"The interview room in the old prison has a smart coating. Firenzi technology. It gives reassurance that the occupants are not being spied on."

Sam nodded encouragement.

"I used some unorthodox contacts to procure stocks of this material for the new prison."

"That seems like a prudent measure."

"If that were the end of it, I would agree. But I ordered thirty times the quantity needed for the room alone."

Sam's pale gaze revealed nothing of the medic's opinions. Brin marshaled his own thoughts. "It seemed like a good idea to set up a secondary barrier in the surrounding caverns, but when it came to it, I found it hard to justify my decision. *That* failing is what troubles me."

"Hmm. You are not one for relying on instinct, are you, Brindis?"

Brin shrugged. "I'm used to my instincts staying firm, and being backed up by logic. This one felt so strong at the time, but my certainty evaporated under pressure."

"And what do you think now?"

"I think that what is done is done."

"Aside from the cost, any harm done?"

Brin gazed long at the wisps of smoke curling in the bowl of the nargile. "At first, the technicians said what I wanted couldn't be done. I asked them to set up detectors to alert a communications office if anything triggered the holo material. But how do you spy, undetected, on a coating designed to detect attempts at electronic spying? Nevertheless, they assure me they've engineered a solution. The remaining question is—why? To what purpose did I put so many people to such effort? That, I can't answer." Brin struggled to keep the pleading out of his voice. "Am I losing my grip?"

"I am of the opinion that only time will tell. Your first instinct felt *true* to you, did it not?"

Brin nodded.

"Then that is good enough for now, but Brindis"—Sam's voice grew stern—"I think you are having another misgiving too."

Brin gave his friend a wry smile. "This whole business with Her Ladyship chasing a phantom in the wilds."

"You have forces keeping watch over her."

"At a distance. She values her freedom of movement." Brin shuddered at an imaginary draft on his neck. "If anything happens to her ..."

"That decision, at least, you cannot be laying at your own feet."

"But should I have stopped her?"

"The question is, *could* you? This is being Shayla Carver we are talking about," Sam said firmly. "One cannot babysit a hungry hoklok."

Shayla noticed the man even before talk in the room stilled.

It wasn't his size that marked him out, though he could comfortably stand toe to toe with a bear. It wasn't the startling contrast between graying, almost white hair and beard framing his florid face. It wasn't even the motley layers of many-times-patched clothing that drew her attention.

It was his eyes, his expression. Not blank, not vacant, but not *here*. He steered himself to a seat in the corner, heedless of the people scurrying out of his way. For all his immense physical appearance, the man was utterly absent from the room.

For a moment, Shayla felt herself being pulled from her world and into whatever alternate reality this man inhabited, as though her *presence* here was a substance that could be siphoned off into a vacuum.

With clear certainty, she knew she'd found her target.

He sat. A drink appeared in front of him. The server backed away, unacknowledged.

He scarcely seemed to notice the glass as he picked it up and tossed it back. His eyes flicked back and forth, following imaginary or remembered events in his own head.

Another drink appeared.

Out the corner of her eye, Shayla noticed the group at the next table flag down a server. Coins clinked. More drinks flowed with no perceptible effect on the giant in the corner, but the mood in the bar grew tense with anticipation.

"Hey, Randall," someone jeered from the back of the room. "Tell us a story."

For the first time, Randall reacted to another person. His eyes swiveled in the direction of the cry, then lost their focus again. "Hellfire," he roared.

People cheered and clapped.

"Fire from the sky!"

More cheers. This is what the crowd had come to see.

"The earth melts. It opens up before me." Tears glistened on ruddy cheeks. "Buildings gone. Trees like torches. People are matchsticks in the wind."

"Yeah, the wind," a man near the back of the room called. He made a farting sound and collapsed, laughing.

"Fear the wind," Randall bellowed. "It roars like a lion and sweeps all before it. It levels whole streets at a single breath, turns them to glass."

Shayla wondered about this man's story. Somewhere in his deranged mind there must lie a germ of truth. Military? Had he seen combat somewhere in another life?

"Glass, I say! There is an airfield, a multitude trying to flee. A star-liner proud and gaudy like a peacock. It is paper before that hot breath. That hell wind picks it up like a child's toy and flings it against the hillside. Metal burns. People turn to ash." Randall staggered to his feet, arms flailing. "I watch the skies fall. It is Judgment Day. We harbored snakes in our midst and the punishment is swift and terrible."

The rant sounded insane yet curiously convincing. It had the appearance of religious zeal, like Brin had surmised, yet Shayla puzzled. In her undercover assignments she'd studied the Book of Unity and many other holy works. She knew the Pillars of Duty inside out and could quote sermons wholesale from a dozen mainstream religions. This was nothing she recognized. Besides, the details were too precise. This man had *seen* something. And it had driven him mad.

"We are all being judged and we will be judged again for our sins."

"We're doing no harm," someone yelled.

"My home is gone," another called out. "I just want to start over."

"We shouldn't be here. This town is an abomination, a desecration." Randall eyed the crowd. This was the first time he'd acknowledged anything close to reality. It should have seemed like he was regaining his senses, but it felt instead as if they'd intruded into his madness. "What you are doing here is wrong. The Emperor should know better. The Governor should know better, she of all people. You must cease your building, your planting, your grubbing amongst the graves. Leave the dead in peace."

The room grew quiet. This was getting a bit close to home.

"We do not remember. We do not honor those who have fallen. The fire will return. It will take you all!"

"You're crazy!"

The baiting sounded half-hearted and distant. An awful suspicion formed in the back of Shayla's mind, impossible to contemplate yet too compelling to ignore.

"The flames take everything. Towns, people, trees. They took the very soil beneath my feet and the sun from the sky." This last came out as a whisper. Tears ran freely down Randall's face.

"How did you escape the fire?" Someone trying to keep the talk going, but it was obvious the sermon was running dry.

"Paul tells me. Dark ways under. Dark and cool. He leads me to safety. Away from the fires and the endless night that comes after."

"Who is Paul?"

"Paul knows everything. Keeps everything safe, all the hidden ways of this world. Paul hides me from the fire."

"What color is the fire?" Shayla called. She ignored the puzzled stares nearby, focused entirely on the answer, hardly daring to breathe.

Sightless eyes turned towards her, then lifted to the ceiling. Randall raised his arms, hands outstretched like a priest before the altar of Unity. His voice was hushed. "It is the purest, cleanest, palest lilac. Too bright. Too bright. No mortal eyes should see that light."

Despite the warmth in the room, goosebumps raced up and down Shayla's body. The table in front of her swam in and out of focus. She pushed herself upright, steadying herself against waves of vertigo, ignoring angry protests as she stumbled from table to table towards the door.

Outside, the night air restored a measure of balance. She gathered herself and, with an effort, walked around the corner to the shelter of a dark alley. There she doubled over and was violently sick.

There were no immigration records of this man because he hadn't arrived and dropped off grid as Brin supposed. No, he had always been here.

Shayla and a few hundred others had escaped the Cleansing, taking flight while the Imperial navy closed in, but this man had lived through it. He had just described perfectly the flash from an exawatt plasma cannon, the signature weapon of Imperial *Swords*.

He had been here, on the surface when the planet burned, and had survived three decades alone on this cindered land.

Shayla leaned against the wall, taking in the sounds of the night. Shouts and raucous laughter drifted through the near wall, tinny and distant. Further afield wind rustled leaves, an unaccustomed sound from a lifetime ago.

Thoughts whirled through her mind, muddy, fragmented. A survivor. From his speech he was obviously educated. What had the years alone on a global tomb done to him?

And how had he survived? She'd watched the Cleansing broadcast from remote drones—propaganda to keep the peasants in line. The fleet of *Swords* systematically slagged large towns and cities, then bathed the remaining landscape in province-wide swathes of plasma, a gentle good-bye kiss after the fierce intensity of those first thrusts.

Yes, maybe some people could have found safe refuges from those fiery caresses. A planet was just too big to smother completely, even for *Swords*, but then what? Years-long darkness followed as the earth cooled and fine ash settled from the sky. Years more before seeds buried far from the worst ravages once more took root. Food on land would have been scarce, but the oceans lay untouched. Maybe he fished?

A few revelers spilled from the bar and reeled, laughing, down the street.

Shayla came alert. Looked like the party was breaking up. The door opened again. Light spilling onto the packed dirt road framed an unmistakable silhouette. Stately and disdainful, seemingly unmoved by the humiliation he'd suffered, Randall glided up the center of the road, a one-man procession heading out of town.

Just about to follow, Shayla paused. A subliminal unease played on her nerves. She melted back into the shadows. Randall would be easy enough to trail from a distance.

Across the street, two figures detached themselves from the darkness of an alley and flitted from doorway to doorway. Their fluid movement, little more than a flicker in the night, and their utter silence marked them as professionals. They must have been watching the whole time, would likely have seen Shayla emerge. Would hopefully have drawn their own conclusions at the sound of retching and subsequent quiet.

Noting the direction they took, Shayla pictured the layout of the camp from what she'd seen of it. She withdrew deeper into the darkness between sheds and glided down the narrow alley as fast as she dared, eyes adjusting to the gloom but ever mindful of the rough terrain. As the camp spread, little effort was made to level the ground other than bulldozing the largest obstacles. The prefabricated structures were simply airlifted in and lowered onto piles. She rounded the back of the hut that housed the unofficial watering hole, and crossed the next alley paralleling the path Randall and his followers had taken.

Past the back of two more huts, she was close to the edge of the camp. Shayla judged she should have overtaken Randall by now. She eased her way back towards the main street, straining for any sounds. In the distance, Randall crossed her line of sight still making his slow but sure way up the road.

She cursed under her breath. If he left the camp altogether she'd have a hard time following without being seen. She doubled back and crossed behind the last huts in the line, then slunk alongside the minimal cover offered by the side and overhang of the roof.

As she neared the road, Randall appeared around the corner. Shayla flattened herself to the ground and rolled into the gap under the shed. She crawled forward and peered around the corner of one of the piles supporting the structure.

"Hey, Randall." A woman's voice, harsh and demanding. The larger of the two figures closed the gap. Shayla had a moment to see the trailing figure more clearly in the moonlight before she entered the darkness beside the shed. Another woman, small and thin-faced beneath a bulky cloak.

Randall appeared not to hear. He'd reached a decrepit trike and was about to climb in when the larger woman stepped out of the shadows, grabbed him by the shoulder and whirled him around to face her.

"I'm talking to you, Randall."

His eyes widened, seeming to focus from a great distance onto the here and now.

"Looks like you sold someone a stash of nasty little stingers."

"Ease up! I'll handle this." That was the small, wiry one talking. Her voice was low and soothing. "Now, Randall, we're your friends aren't we? We're going to help you move these people on, respect the dead."

Randall licked his lips and nodded.

"So I'm wondering, Randall, have you got any more help? Any new friends? Maybe we can all work together to help you, hmm?"

Randall's eyes rolled up till the whites showed. He seemed to think long and hard, then he shook his head emphatically. "The wolf and the rabbit," he chanted in a sing-song voice. "The lion and the walrus. No others."

"So," said the small one. "No new friends. Shame. But you did find the Wasps, didn't you?"

Randall nodded.

"Who did you show them to?"

"None but the king."

"Lion?"

Randall nodded.

"Good man. Thank you."

Randall's eyes glazed over once more. He hauled himself onto the trike and roared away into the night. Shayla thought hard. She had no chance of following him now, but it seemed like he was nothing more than an unwitting finder. These two were another matter.

"Lion," the smaller woman muttered. "Never was keen on that one. He has a smell of the Imperial about him."

"You've gone soft in the head. Why would an Imperial want to take a pop at 'Er 'Igh'N'Mightiness?"

"You're the one who's gone soft," the small one growled. "She's no more popular there than anywhere else."

The two watched Randall leave, then they turned back to the main street.

As soon as they were around the corner, Shayla eased herself silently from under cover and sprinted back the way she'd come, around the back of the sheds to where the bar was housed. All the while, her mind raced and chills ran up her spine. Lion? And Randall had reeled off a list of animal names. At first Shayla presumed this was his way of identifying people in whatever world his mind inhabited, but the way the smaller woman spoke it sounded like a name that meant something in the very real world. And she was all too well acquainted with people who habitually used animals as code names. The Insurrection.

As she neared the street once more, Shayla fumbled in her pockets for a pair of tiny spray dispensers.

She waited for the sounds of approaching footsteps, still soft but no longer being actively hushed, then staggered out into the street.

Keeping her head low, and keeping a safe distance, she scrutinized the pair for their reactions while she stopped and swayed, a drunk trying to get her bearings. It didn't do to startle trained killers.

Straightening unsteadily, she made a show of spotting the two for the first time and stepped closer with arms outstretched. "G'devening, my fine fellows." Shayla steadied herself with hands on the women's shoulders, and peered close into each face. "Beg pardon, leshhtry again. G'evnng, fine ladieshhh. Can you do me the honor of direct-ect-ing me to"—she screwed her eyes in concentration—"shed sixshteen."

The larger woman brushed Shayla's hand off. Unbalanced, Shayla pitched to one side and struggled to keep her footing. "Now thatshh a fine welcome, I must say!"

The two gave her a look of contempt and hurried on, oblivious to the chemical tracer they now wore. Shayla let them go before sobering miraculously. Back at her billet, she picked up her bag and slipped once more out into the night. Taking care to watch for any signs of being followed, she slunk behind the bunkhouse and into the undergrowth beyond. Senses alert, she took out her notepad and pinged Simone.

"I need a ride out of here fast. Looks like we have an Insurrection cell at work and I need to brief Brin on what to look out for." Voice low, Shayla recounted the evening's events.

"On my way. Where will I meet you?"

Shayla gave Simone directions to a clearing a few miles west of the camp. "We'll need to find Randall again, but first get Brin to send a team out here tonight with noses. I managed to tag the two, but the chemical tracer will only be good for a few hours, and if they take off in a vehicle we'll lose the scent."

Signing off, she hurried back towards the bunkhouse.

At the corner of the building, she paused. She was missing something. She ran through a quick inventory. She'd gathered her meager belongings from the bunkhouse intending to make a quick exit. Keeping a safe distance, she'd seen the two Insurrection members enter another bunkhouse. Brin's team would find them soon enough and would have the resources to track them properly without being spotted.

Still something felt wrong.

Defensive instincts kicked in, too late.

Hammering agony burned through her back. Her legs collapsed and she pitched forward. Sucker punched? Where the heck did that come from? Too paralyzed with shock and pain to defend herself properly, let alone fight back, Shayla was dimly aware of more blows around her body. She tried to wrap her arms around her head, all training forgotten and animal survival taking over.

Something wet and sour-smelling slapped over her mouth and nose. As pain-free darkness enfolded her, a hoarse voice rasped in her ear, "There's someone dying to meet you, Woolly."

Chapter 7

Ocean rolled to the horizon, oily dark shot through with silver in the setting sun. Jared glanced over his shoulder to where the rest of the survey team made camp around the beached transport. Satisfied that he and his companion wouldn't be overheard, he turned his gaze back to the horizon. "So Lion has become a liability."

"Randall fingered him. There was no deception in him." The wiry assassin perched on a rock beside him. Her tone was quiet, matter of fact.

Jared humphed. This one possessed a small measure of truthsense. She must have had a rare talent because she'd had no formal training. The Imperial service and a few of the Families had the specialized knowledge to nurture this slippery skill, but those schools were closed to the Insurrection. Elsewhere, those with the gift were mostly on their own to develop their sensitivity and the path was notoriously treacherous, yielding misinformation as often as it revealed truth. But Timber Wolf's sense was keener than most. Enough to give Jared confidence in her assessment.

Enough to be dangerous if his own purpose ever came into conflict with the Insurrection's. Even now, she scrutinized him for signs of hidden agendas. Even now, seven years on, the Leading Council regarded him with suspicion after his spectacular failure on Magentis. Damn that Carver woman!

"So," he said, "we must remove him from play."

Timber Wolf nodded.

"Send Rabbit to deal with him. I need you here to escort me."

When the assassin didn't respond, Jared glanced at her. Something in the set of her shoulders troubled him. "There's more?"

At first, Jared wondered if she'd heard, then she heaved a deep breath. "Carver has vanished."

Jared's stomach clenched. "How?"

"Rumors are rife but not openly spoken, and officially she's holed up in her Residence still recuperating."

"But you don't believe that?"

"She was last seen inspecting the new prison site. In fact, even that's not certain. She sent her lackey to do the actual inspecting while she waited in her transport. All I know for sure is that the security team is riled up like a nest of fire ants, all the while pretending nothing's amiss." Wolf tilted her head as she regarded him. "How important is Carver to the plan?" She paused. "As distinct from important to you?"

Jared knew where this conversation was heading. Personal revenge was understandable given her role in his fall from favor, but it would not be allowed to endanger the greater mission. "We need her to order the prisoners' movement." That much was true. "She has to be irretrievably implicated in what happens next. With all the rumors and propaganda our media techs are ready to unleash, fingers will point to the Emperor."

"And the Families, particularly the Firenzi, won't sit still for that kind of betrayal." Wolf nodded. "The deeper the connection, the more the instability. You realize this will end in all-out war. Are you prepared for that?"

"Regimes like this never go quietly. There will always be a blood price to pay."

"Just checking." The tone was light, but the hard look in her eyes chilled Jared.

Dim light caught Shayla's eye. An ill-judged turn of the head earned her thumping pain across her temples. She closed her eyes and breathed through it. Memory surfaced like flotsam from a shipwreck. She'd been drugged. Caught by surprise. The admission shook her. The beers she'd consumed in the line of duty probably hadn't helped, but all the same it was a rare measure of stealth that could take her so completely off guard.

She cracked open her eyes once again and risked a cautious movement. Her first concern was the use of a control drug like trylex. Any voluntary movement under its influence brought paralyzing agony, but she knew how that felt. The texture of this pain was different. Not trylex, then. That would have been serious, it was a sophisticated drug only available to the most ruthless of secret services.

This was a more primitive effort. *Woolly!* That was the last word she remembered from her captors. A common enough insult to Wala people, but it was the same slur used by one of the thugs at the canteen.

The pain was still there, but manageable. Shayla worked up a droplet of saliva to moisten her parched lips. The sour taste persisted.

Trying to ignore the pounding in her head, she eased herself around in her seat. She found her wrists, ankles, and waist were bound by some kind of industrial tape.

Light spilled from the crack under a door in the far wall, illuminating little more than the planked floor. Windows would have revealed moonlight or pinpricks of stars. Nothing was visible around her. Not surprising, most of the storage sheds she'd seen were windowless.

She hadn't been gagged, either. They had no fears of her making herself heard.

Throbbing aches across her back and gut reminded her of the beating she'd taken. A sensation of stickiness around her waist suggested the stomach wound had opened up again.

An earthy smell hung in the air. Shayla tried to place it. Farmyards came to mind. Fertilizer? They must be holding her in one of the work camps, but which one?

She tested her bindings. Too tight to wriggle free, and too strong to break.

Raw fury made her head spin. These jerks would have a shock when they found out who they were dealing with. Simone's words taunted her. They couldn't have known her true identity. That thought enraged her even more. Shayla Carver, planetary governor, was a legitimate target but they'd attacked a defenseless worker who'd done nothing more than stand up to bullies.

Footsteps outside roused Shayla. She didn't recall the lure of sleep, and she had no sense of the passage of time. Anger boiled again, at herself this time. She would never have allowed herself this kind of lapse in her long years of working under cover. Too much of her former training was little more than a dim memory. Not the physical side, she still worked out daily and practiced combat skills, but her fieldcraft, the habits of survival, had dulled. Sure, they were regularly exercised by the attempts on her life, but the environment she inhabited was hers, home turf, controlled and familiar. She'd lost the edge of alertness that came from living and breathing in enemy territory.

The door opened. Overhead lights outside were blinding. Screwing her eyes against the glare—though in reality it could only be one of those dim ceiling lights she'd seen everywhere in the work camp sheds—she made out a group of silhouettes. Couldn't figure out how many.

A flashlight stabbed her night vision, brought a strangled gasp at the sudden intensity.

"Are you sure this is the right one?" A woman's voice.

"I was there. Tracked her to Spitball." A man, voice laden with contempt. "Same clothes. Look at them. Nearly new. This one's had it too easy."

"She looks pale." Another man. Closer. The urge to struggle, to lash out, died stillborn as Shayla processed the words, numb. How long had she been out of action? She'd paid no attention to her disguise. For her looks to have reverted that noticeably, she must have been out for at least a day, maybe two.

"Eric will throw a screaming fit if you've dragged in the wrong fucking Woolly."

"I drugged her." The admission was cold, devoid of remorse. "Of course she's going to look like shit. Feel like it, too, I shouldn't wonder."

"Sitting in it, you mean."

For the first time, Shayla took better note of the smell in the air. Realized it was her.

"Feed her. Give her water." There was no compassion there, just business. "Eric will want her well enough to know the real meaning of suffering."

———————

Jared planted his feet and folded his arms across his chest, letting the two engineers and the surveyor in front of him bluster. Timber Wolf lounged on the steps of the transport behind them. Jared tried to ignore the faint smile playing on her lips. She was enjoying this confrontation far too much.

He let the tirade run its course, until the three realized he wasn't responding. Like a swordsman over-extending himself, their attack petered out finding no mark to strike.

When they paused, mild embarrassment on their faces, he said, "I agree, this site is ideal for a desalination plant and that's your area of expertise, not mine. However we're expected to seed Veshi oaks along this coast. They won't take on their own. We'll need to start with yellow cherries and indigenous ground cover. I'm going to suggest aromatic fireweed."

"Fireweed?" one of the engineers snorted. "Naught but a pest. Why of all plants bring that one back?"

"It's aggressive, true, but it will bind the soil fast, and in a few years the cherries will outgrow it and keep it in check. But that requires steep south-facing slopes to give them the edge they'll need." The advice was sound, he knew, even though it differed from what the previous—and sadly late, courtesy of Wolf's professional skills—ecologist had recommended. It threw a spanner in plans already in gestation, but nobody at headquarters would be able to fault it for an ingenious, if unorthodox, approach. Not that Jared really knew an acorn from an artichoke. That's what the resources of the Insurrection were there for. Their expertise might not match the Imperium's, but they had surprising pockets to draw on and their researchers could efficiently plunder the libraries of civilizations when they had the need. Field support, they called it. Literally true in this case.

Wolf stretched and stood. She put on a serious face for the benefit of the others as she lined up with them. Her body language said she was their ally, not an adversary. "So, Jared, this is a big departure from the original plan. Why such a difference?"

"Nothing wrong with the original plan. It will get you there ... eventually. And it will need intensive mothering for decades to come."

"This is a long term venture." Wolf gave a deprecating smile. "You're a new arrival. You haven't got used to the kind of scale we're working on here."

Jared inclined his head. "Nevertheless, I sense we're under pressure to show solid results. Feel free to deny the rumors, but I hear we're on shaky ground. The Emperor could pull funding at any moment."

"And you think your approach would do better?" Just the right blend of skepticism and curiosity.

"That plateau we flew over fifteen miles down the coast looked promising. If I'm right, we could have a robust and self-sustaining ecosystem established within twenty years."

Gasps of surprise said he'd hit a nerve.

Wolf made a show of pondering the problem. As the survey team leader, this was ultimately her call. "Okay, this is what we'll do. It'll extend our field trip by a few days but we have plentiful provisions and I think this is worth exploring." She turned to the other three. "You'll take the transport and complete a more detailed survey four hundred miles north and south from here along the coast. Just look from an engineering perspective. Desalination, obviously, and sites for other infrastructure. I want a list of options. I want our asses covered if we do go back with a change of plans."

The grunts and eye rolls signaled reluctant assent.

"But first," Wolf said, "you'll drop us off at that site that caught the noob's eye and we'll check it out. We'll take tents, provisions, and two of the ATVs with us so we can cover some ground, but I want to take back some thorough seed and soil analyses to show if this idea has a chance of holding water."

"And then?"

"Then it's up to the development planners back at HQ. Remember how Milady Carver is always twatting on about initiative? Let's take her at her word."

━━━━◆◆━━━━

Time passed, uncounted. Her captors' words circled like vultures.

Spitball? Really? She'd have to talk with Frank about naming these places properly. A coded designation served, but who could feel a sense of *belonging* to a string of letters and numbers?

It hadn't been a priority. Nothing important had been a priority, it seemed. All the focus on numbers—immigration statistics, buildings constructed, acres planted, crops harvested. Where were the people in all this? Where was the sense of awe at breathing life into a world? Where was the hope of a fresh start? A better life than the ruins left behind?

Nobody got inspired by a production target. You got drawn by the light on the horizon, but Shayla saw no signs of that light here, only the rot filled by human greed and opportunism.

There were things that needed fixing. Urgently. Before the inspectors lifted the lid on her incompetence.

All very well, but where was 'here' and how was she getting away from 'here' that didn't involve reincarnation as fertilizer?

'Tracked her to Spitball.' The man's tone and choice of words suggested that Spitball, where she was attacked, was somewhere else, somewhere distant from where they now held her. She'd been moved. Her heart sank. Simone knew where she'd reported from. Spitball would have been turned inside out by Brin's team by now. They hadn't already found and freed her because she'd been moved.

Not sure whether she'd drifted off again, Shayla came alert at the sound of footsteps approaching. Once again, she tested her bonds. No use. And yet, was that a slight slackening around the wrists? Not enough to wriggle free but definitely there. How long did it take for starvation to have that sort of effect?

Still, no use to her and she couldn't even move her feet enough to rock the chair. It was wooden, creaked slightly when she moved. Might smash given enough persuasion, but even that faint hope seemed beyond reach.

They were being cautious. Her own fault. In downing their leader she'd taught them the need for caution. Despite her half-hearted protestations to the sergeant back there, they wouldn't believe it was a lucky blow. By her manner in the canteen, her fighting stance and casual insolence, she'd been at pains to make it clear she was in charge of the situation. That bravado had served its purpose at the time, ending a messy fight before it began, but she was paying the price now.

She took stock, reviewing her surroundings as the opening door spilled light into the room, alert for anything that might be of use.

The room was bare.

She wouldn't waste energy in a futile struggle, but she would need to be alert to any slip that she could take advantage of.

Three figures took up positions to one side, features impossible to discern in the half light, but there was no mistaking the glint off drawn weapons. Even bound, she merited an armed guard. A fourth approached. Despite the futility, Shayla tensed, but he held nothing more threatening than a water bottle and a bowl of stew.

Alone again, Shayla screwed her eyes shut and concentrated. The bio-implants that permeated her skin could work wonders with her appearance, not just color and texture, but within limits they could also bulk out her physique.

For this disguise, she'd chosen to plump her appearance, face, neck, and thankfully arms and legs. Now she was attempting something she'd never before managed—a reverse transformation against the clock. Something that should take at least a day she wanted to achieve in a few hours.

On the bright side, she wasn't trying a whole-body change. She focused just on her arms and wrists. The rest would follow in its own time.

After half an hour she relaxed, panting, drenched in sweat. She tested her bindings again. There was definitely some play in them now. A few minutes rest, breathless gulps of fetid air, then she gritted her teeth and focused inwards once more.

Another few stints of similar effort and she could slide her wrists back and forth under the loops of tape. The adhesive seemed to have surrendered the battle to keep its grip on her sweat-slicked skin, but the edges of the tape balled and restrained her when she tried to work it past her thumbs.

Her shoulders sagged. There just wasn't enough slack to pull loose.

———————

"Speaking of Carver," Jared said, once the transport dwindled to a speck on the horizon, "what news?"

Wolf grimaced. "There's a large but very discreet search going on around Scale. We've got an extensive network here but mostly in low-level admin positions. Nobody close to the heart of the hierarchy. All we've got are a few rumors leaking out."

From the top of the plateau, Jared gazed out to sea. Beyond the horizon lay the island, inaccessible from sea or air, where the new prison complex was nearly finished. "What makes you sure she's even missing?"

"I'm *not* sure. It's just the exceptional secrecy around this activity. There's *something* Magister ap Silessi is desperate to keep quiet, and he doesn't scare easily. Draw your own conclusions."

Jared had no answer to that.

Wolf laughed, brief and bitter. "Wouldn't it be ironic if someone's managed to do our jobs for us."

Jared gave her a puzzled look. He'd been so determined that Carver would die at his own hands, he felt nothing but keen disappointment at her disappearance. Where was the upside to this?

"There's a political powder keg ready to blow. I don't care which match lights the fuse." She gave him a sidelong look.

Aah. Now he could see Wolf's line of thinking. "Ivan and Scipio were meant to be the trigger, and Carver is key to bringing them out where we can reach them." He gestured towards the distant horizon. "It was a genius insight on someone's part to use her alive rather than dead. Do you really think her loss *alone* will be enough to achieve our ends?"

"Hard to say. We've made our attempts on her life, along with many others, but more out of habit than anything. She's got such an irritating knack of not dying that nobody's really analyzed what would happen if anyone actually did succeed."

"So, analyze then." In the Insurrection's ranks, Jared had always been a foot soldier, a doer. Competent, reliable, but he was no motivational analyst.

Wolf shrugged. "There's so much sensitivity in Imperial and Firenzi camps surrounding those prisoners, factions on both sides wanting one free and the other dead, only someone so visibly neutral can hope to hold them in custody. With or without Carver, Eloon is a Freeworld—"

"An Imperial protectorate still," Jared reminded her. "Real Freeworld status is decades off yet, and hangs on this inspection and many others to come."

"True." Wolf gave a slow and pensive nod. "And if she's gone, who's to say how long that will last? Whether this world remains in Imperial hands or reverts to the Firenzi doesn't matter. Just a whiff of allegiance in place of neutrality and one side or the other will bring things to a head with force."

"The Emperor should have executed them when he had the chance."

"More fool him, and good for us. He's left himself a cancer that's ripe to kill its host."

———◦•◦———

A deep breath. Another. This was something Shayla had never tried. Had never even heard of being tried. Homing in on her left hand, she felt inwards for the conscious control of her *alter*-body—the mesh of microscopic fungal fibers that permeated every part of her skin.

After years of practice she knew how it felt to flesh out, to change color, and alter the contours of her body. Now, she wrapped her mind around her left hand, snuggling her awareness into the network of filaments, and *squeezed*.

Tendons and joints popped in protest. Her hand was gripped in a crushing pressure. Elation flooded her and gave her renewed energy.

She squeezed again and pulled against her binding.

A sharp stab of agony as something dislocated. She stifled the urge to vomit and focused on the subcutaneous web, ignoring the protests of her native flesh. A desperate squeeze and pull.

Her hand popped free.

Shayla gazed blankly at it in the gloom, unable to believe it.

Wincing at the acid sting of returning circulation she felt around the right-hand binding for an edge of tape to worry loose. Found it. Worked at it. Unraveled it.

Repeated the process at her waist. That took longer, they'd cut off the end of the tape behind her back.

Leaning forward to reach for her ankles, she came up short. Stabbing pain in her gut stopped her. Shayla sat back and forced herself to relax, muscle by muscle, before easing herself forward inch by inch. At each stage she allowed her innards to settle into position and quit bellyaching before easing down another inch.

She had the tape started on one ankle. Footsteps down the corridor lent urgency to her movements. She threw off the last clinging strips from that leg and tore savagely at the bindings around the other.

The footsteps stopped outside. No time to free her other ankle, the chair would have to come with her. It would severely hamper her movements, but on the other hand it might be pressed into service as a shield or a weapon if she played this right.

She staggered, dizzy, to one side of the door, lifting the chair as she went and setting it silently alongside. A few deep breaths restored her balance, just as the door opened.

Without knowing how many opponents she'd have to deal with, Shayla had to make the first blows count. Mentally, she was already forming an image of the figure still invisible beyond the door, anticipating their posture from the position of the handle and the sound map of their steps. She lined up a disabling, possibly fatal, blow. She didn't care. No messing around.

As the intruder crossed the threshold, Shayla was gratified to see the silhouette closely match her mental image. Her fist was already flying.

Chapter 8

Only the slightest whitening of a fist betrayed Jared's reaction as the small air cruiser hugged precipitous cliffs and hopped from canyon to crumbling canyon. He was used to hurtling small craft down twists and turns in narrow confines, but used also to being at the controls at the time. Buttock-clenching helplessness was for others to endure.

Walrus threw their craft through clefts and ravines with reckless abandon, and while his competence as a pilot was amply demonstrated, his cavalier manner did nothing to instill confidence. "Should'a packed yer brown trousers, mate," he said with impossible cheerfulness, one arm resting along the cockpit ledge. "We gotta stay low. Not a lot of surveillance out here and it's all low tech, but we don't want to attract the Carver cavalry, do we now?"

Jared gritted his teeth. It didn't help that in order to cram his lanky frame into the cockpit, Walrus slouched almost sideways on in his seat and seemed to be more interested in studying his passenger than their flight path.

"So, you're the legendary Cobra," he drawled. "Right royal fuck-up, that Magentis lark."

"Carver played *everyone*, from the Executim down." Jared kept his voice level and tried to keep his attention on the wider landscape beyond the tan-gray rock rushing past.

Freed from inquisitive companions, Walrus had met him and Wolf at their landing place. Wolf stayed behind to keep up the pretense of serious fieldwork, while Walrus ferried Jared to a rendezvous with Randall. They'd headed straight inland, hugging the skirts of a craggy mountain range to the north.

Jared's preparation for this mission included an extensive briefing on Eloon, its geography, its history. Before the Cleansing, the land they now traversed with ground-hugging bravado had once been a sprawling wine-producing region. An arid landscape even in its heyday, the vintages from here graced cellars across the worlds of humanity, jealously hoarded and occasionally traded for fabulous sums not only for their quality but for the fact that there would be no more. Jared's interest here was more than professional. Local wineries used to distil a fierce and sweet liquor from the lesser vintages. The taste, the name, was etched in his memory. Not even into his teens, a young thug with a score of gang kills to his credit in the harsh underworld of Derrin's industrial slums, he'd once ransacked a store frequented by rich factory owners and made off with a bottle. Dragon's Breath. His tongue pricked at the memory. How could such extravagance live side by side with the desperate poverty he'd grown up in?

That realization sparked a burning curiosity, fanned into incandescent outrage, leading him ultimately away from the slums and into the ranks of the Insurrection.

Now what providence brought him back here, to the place that produced the luxury that had started him on his rebellious path? To the place where he meant to bring the whole rotten edifice crashing down around those well-to-do ears?

He closed his eyes, picturing these slopes thick with vines, villas gracing the hillsides. There had been towns here, too. How many ghosts had the rush of their flight disturbed?

The bare rock outside gave few hints of that prosperous past. Only the occasional outlines on the ground, profiles on the brows of hills, that were just a bit too square and regular to be natural.

"Ye'd still bang 'er though, wouldn't you? Before slitting her pretty little throat?"

The bizarre tangent caught Jared off guard. Not knowing how to respond, suspecting that the infuriating Walrus was just playing with him, he contented himself with a stony gaze.

"Imagine them thighs twined around yer, knowing what they could do to you if she'd a mind." He chuckled and licked his lips. "Adds a spice of danger, don't ya think?"

"I didn't realize a death wish was still a job requirement."

Walrus pursed his lips. "So there *is* a touch of humor in there after all. Was wondering. Gotta find laughs somewhere or ye go mad out here." His expression sobered so suddenly Jared glanced out the cockpit to see what had caught his eye, but there was nothing to be seen but more shattered rock. "Nearly there," Walrus breathed. "You got what I asked for?"

Jared silently handed him a dull white ball the size of a marble.

Walrus set it on the console alongside the navigation screen and, piloting with one hand, deftly manipulated a trio of tiny bumps around the equator of the ball. He tapped a few instructions on the navigation screen and nodded. "Baseline set."

The craft touched down, and Walrus pocketed the ball. "This 'un's a touchy bugger. Blindfolds, and always scans for trackers."

Dust settled around the cruiser. Jared craned his neck to take in their surroundings, but nothing much was visible. Rock walls hemmed them in. A strip of blue-gray above marked the course of the canyon. Jared wondered if a river flowed here only a few decades ago. It looked like nothing had ever lived or grown here. Walrus slouched even further back in his seat, winked, and pulled his cap over his eyes.

Jared settled back to wait and keep a wary watch.

Shayla pulled the blow short at the last moment, took a few more moments to process what her subconscious had registered. She helped the guard to his feet, winded but thankfully unharmed by her mostly-aborted attack. She recognized him, and the two others pressing close behind him.

Relief hit like a plasma bolt. Thoughts of the last few days raged through her mind, bringing with them a storm of suppressed emotions. Anger at what had happened to her, the lonely hopelessness of her dark cell, and fear of what might have been. Cold determination to right the wrongs she'd discovered bled away on the overwhelming tide of giddy relief. She'd been found. Essence of Unity, but that was a close call.

Her abused body, too, clamored for attention. For once, her automatic self-check floundered, not knowing where to start. Wounds lay untended. Hunger and thirst gnawed. Her legs spoke for the rest of her, lowering her far from gracefully onto the chair still attached to one ankle.

The first guard caught his breath and gave a rueful grin. "Well met, My Lady. They did warn me you'd likely be unarmed and dangerous. Guess I should have paid more attention."

"Space alive," growled the one behind him. "What's that smell?"

A few minutes later, a faint rumble in the distance alerted Jared.

Walrus pushed back his hat and sat up with a smirk. "Punctual as ever," he drawled. "Probably watched us land and made sure we weren't followed."

"Commendable," Jared said drily. "Do we know anything of his background? Why would a civilian be so cautious?"

Walrus shrugged. "No one knows where he came from. Never found any official records."

It was hard to judge distance with the noise echoing off the canyon walls. Each time Jared expected to see a vehicle round the corner, the grumble quieted before resurging once more. At last a large-wheeled quad bike roared into view and pulled to a stop a few yards away.

Walrus waved a greeting. "Randall, this is a very dear friend, Cobra."

"A snake in the nest, hmm?"

The open-topped vehicle sat high on suspension designed to clear rough terrain. Jared eyed the giant of a man peering down at them. Sunlight glinted off a darkened visor. Between visor and straggly gray hair and beard, little of his face was visible. Layers of dust-caked clothing had seen better days, but the military-issue beam pistol at his waist had a used and cared-for look.

"A friend, all the same." Walrus gave a broad grin, wrinkles creased the dark skin at the corners of his eyes. "And I can promise he'll be quick to strike those you want gone from here."

Randall grunted and climbed down from his perch under arching roll bars. He sidled over, looking ready to run at the first sign of danger. In one hand he clutched a palm-sized silver-blue box that Jared guessed was a wide-band detector. The other hand held a pair of soft black hoods that he silently handed to each of them.

"Get strapped in first," Walrus said to Jared. He nodded to the quad, where a pair of bucket seats hung at the front of the spindly vehicle.

They strolled over to the quad and settled themselves in. Meanwhile Randall passed the detector up and down over their bodies, glancing now and then at a tiny screen on its front. He appeared satisfied, but waited, scowling, until they'd secured the blackout hoods over their heads.

The quad creaked and lurched under Jared. "No cheating now," Randall growled from behind.

Any further words were lost as the engine roared to life and they lumbered off. The quad weaved back and forth over rough ground before picking up speed. It occurred to Jared that after a few turns he had no idea which direction down the canyon Randall had taken. They'd met in the shade of steep cliffs, without even the warmth of sunlight to hint at the compass. It wouldn't do to assume he'd arrived from the direction of his hideout. Then again, he could be double-bluffing.

He soon gave up trying to guess their movements and concentrated on stopping himself being thrown around in his seat as the bike sped up, slowed, took sharp corners and banked in lazy turns. Some movements were likely dictated by the terrain but Randall seemed cautious enough to put in a few extra moves of his own. With a chill, Jared realized that without Randall they'd have trouble finding the flyer again in this broken landscape. By now it was impossible to guess even how far they'd come, let alone in which direction.

At last, bruised and sore, their drive ended. The sudden hush was a blessing.

"No peeking," Randall breathed in Jared's ear. Halitosis overwhelmed the desert tang of sun-baked flint.

Jared sensed movement alongside. Still blindfolded, he unbuckled and eased himself from his seat, feet feeling for the ground.

A rough hand took his and placed it on Walrus's shoulder. Walrus moved. Jared shuffled after. He stumbled briefly before catching himself as the ground fell away at his feet. Without sight, other senses came to the fore. The sound of feet rasping on pebbly soil gained timbre and a faint echo. They were entering an enclosed space. Coolness washed over him, the sun no longer beat on his shoulders. Wherever this was, it opened to the south-east.

They stopped. A hand whisked his blindfold off, along with the sting of a few trapped hairs.

Jared squinted at dazzling sunlight streaming through an opening behind him. The ground underfoot sloped downward into a dark corridor cut into the rock. The entrance tunnel had been partially blocked by rockfalls and drifting soil from further back, and he had to duck under a laser-cut lintel.

Jared's eyes adjusted to the gloom as Randall led them along the corridor. Rooms opened out to either side, gray steel doors standing ajar, nothing but inky black beyond. A dim glow ahead, startling after the darkness, came from a cluster of free standing glowtubes in a large room. Two tables, littered with empty ration cartons and water bottles, stood surrounded by an assortment of chairs, some broken, and crates.

Bare walls were painted a military gray. The floor, free of drifting soil this far in, was covered in dark green flooring tiles. This looked like some kind of shelter. Maybe a guard outpost, judging by the underground location. Only such places could have survived the Cleansing.

Jared turned to Randall, who stood in the middle of the room, huge hands twisting in front of him. "My friends tell me you know of a way under the sea."

Randall's head bobbed. Somewhere along the way he'd ditched the sun visor. "Found it long ago. Paul showed me."

Jared glanced at Walrus, who shrugged. "Haven't been able to get much out of him. Just this mysterious Paul who seems to know everything."

"Have you been along this path under the sea?" Jared asked.

Randall shook his head.

"So how do you know it leads to the island nobody can reach?"

"Paul says it does. So it does."

"This is all we can get," said Walrus. "Wolf thinks he's sincere. At least, he believes what he's saying."

Jared pondered. Too much rode on this man's knowledge. "Can we meet this Paul?"

Randall's eyes flicked from Jared to Walrus and back. A wild gleam lit their depths.

Sensing Randall's hesitation, Jared said, "Wolf told you, we need to see how good your information is. That's why we're here."

Randall chewed his lip.

"It's all right, Randall." Walrus's tone was surprisingly serious and earnest. "I know this is asking a lot, but we are risking a lot, too."

Jared recalled something Wolf had told him about her interactions with Randall, and added, "We want to make sure the dead are properly honored."

The vacant gaze regained focus. Randall regarded Jared for a long while, as if seeking the truth in his words, then he nodded. He slipped behind a curtain to a darkened corridor leading deeper into the shelter, emerging a minute later with a rectangular burden covered in dusty sacking. He placed the bundle carefully on the table and, suspicious eyes on Jared, pulled the sacking away.

With a start, Jared recognized something like an oldworld book—physically printed, rather than an image on a screen. Not quite, though. The handful he'd seen had been neatly trimmed and bound, objects of great age and beauty. This was something along the same lines, but clipped together with crude staples punched through one edge of the yellowing pages.

On the plastic cover, large letters offered little insight: PALL. Jared peered closer and read finer lettering underneath: Planetary Asset Lists and Locations. "Space alive," he muttered, realization dawning. "The planetary systems would all have got fried in their bunkers, but you've got a printed copy of the old administration's database."

Randall smirked, then eyes widened in alarm as Walrus reached for the heavy binder.

"Easy," said Jared, as much warning to Walrus as reassurance to Randall. "I'm satisfied with what I've seen."

Randall clutched the binder tight to his chest and scurried back through the curtain with it.

Walrus nodded to Jared to show he understood. The binder was priceless. As a source of reliable information it was beyond compare and it certainly explained how Randall unearthed a stash of Wasps. But that could wait. Right now, they still needed Randall's co-operation.

And once they had access to a navigation computer they wouldn't need a remote tracker to find this location again. The miniature inertial compass he'd procured for Walrus, with the known starting point from where their air cruiser touched down, would replay their tortuous route for them later.

Curled up in the corner of her transport's dining nook, Lady Carver nursed a steaming mug of broth, barely able to hold it in trembling hands. Her whole body convulsed from time to time but she refused offers of help.

Head of security, Brindis ap Silessi, cursed himself thrice and thrice again for a fool. The alternating feelings of rage and helplessness that had beset him these past three days now ebbed away, replaced by guilt. After all the attempts on her life over the years, all the high tech and sophistication, she'd nearly succumbed to a bunch of petty thugs who would never even know who they'd captured.

He should have had his agents trailing her more closely, but she'd been under an assumed identify and could look after herself more readily than his people could. And she'd spot and evade a tail a mile off. That, she'd proved time and again.

Regardless, her vehicle, like all works vehicles, housed a tracker. They'd known where she was. He'd had teams standing by to act on whatever information she gleaned. Had he let it become too much of a game? Too confident in her infallibility?

Brin took a deep breath of nicodyne, the stimulant that had kept him and his team going through the days-long search, and studied her more carefully. She'd already suffered the indignity of having her soiled and blood-caked clothing cut off her, and the worst of the filth sponged off by the side of the road before she deemed herself fit to enter the transport. There, a more thorough bathing restored some sense of humanity. Only Simone had been allowed to attend to her. She'd refused medical aid, insisting on dressing her injuries herself. There'll be time for that back at the Residence, she'd said. Brin knew from her tone there was no arguing the point, and wondered how long this intransigence would last. The wounds to her pride cut deeper than the physical variety, and would take longer to heal.

She even disdained the lift of nicodyne, though Brin could see she was hanging by a thread. With the adrenalin from her ordeal and rescue dispersed, she was now too weak to stand unaided. The cleaning and scrubbing had yet to remove all trace of her disguise. Dark shadows still tainted her skin.

Her eyes remained sharp, though. Brin shook himself from introspection and resumed his report. "We were on the scene even before Simone reported you missing. The nose picked up your tracers. Three distinct trails, though, not two like we expected."

Simone held out her hand. Cupped in her palm lay a trio of twisted capsules—chemical spray dispensers. "These were in your pocket. They must have been crushed in the fight."

A shadow crossed Lady Carver's face. "Not much of a fight, I'm sorry to say."

Remorse twisted Brin's stomach.

"The two agents?" she prompted.

"Lost them." Brin's pain sharpened.

"It was a long shot," she murmured. Her eyes drifted half closed and her head flopped against the back of the dinette's bench. "I'm guessing they got in a vehicle. Not much of the tracer would escape."

Brin nodded. "That's what it looked like."

"But they moved me, too. How did you track me down?"

"We lost your trail, too. Realized what must have happened when Simone sounded the alarm." Brin's mouth dried out and throat constricted at the memory of those tense hours. He took a swallow of unsweetened tea. "The camp sergeant at Mirkwood gave us the name of your friend, Eric Voortrek. He has a works vehicle registered to him. We ran the history from its transponder and backtracked every mile it had been, looking for a whiff of your tracer."

"Was it him?"

Brin huffed. "He was miles away at the time. I had other teams chasing down all his known associates and tracing *their* vehicles. The details you gave the sergeant helped us there. We knew we were running out of time. We can usually only follow a trail for a few hours, maybe half a day, but you gave yourself an extra dose."

Lady Carver managed a weak smile.

"The dry climate helped, too," Simone added. "Humidity breaks down the chemical faster."

"All the same, that was too close. The trail to your shed was nigh on invisible. Another few hours, and you'd have been lost to us."

"Any time I go under cover there is risk involved. Simone reminded me of that." She sipped her broth again; a touch of more natural color returned to her cheeks. "And even as Lady Carver my life is one long risk."

"All the same, next time I *will* insist on you wearing a tracker."

"That would light me up like a beacon to enemies as much as to friends." One corner of her mouth twisted in disdain. "So, this Eric Voortrek was behind all this and yet we have nothing to nail him with."

The disappointment in her tone was almost comical. At last, here was something Brin could feel some satisfaction over. "Your friend Eric was up to his neck in nastiness. A long way beyond terrorizing a small camp. That shed they held you in was stuffed with supplies. He's set up a tidy black market business for himself."

"Which you are in the process of disbanding?"

Brin nodded.

"Would you consider it ... unwise ... for me to meet Mister Voortrek?"

Brin shuddered at the chill in her voice. "He'll bother us no longer." He pressed his lips thin and met Lady Carver's piercing gaze without flinching. Justice on the frontier was rough and uncompromising. This was a loose end he'd not burden her with.

She nodded. She understood.

———◆———

Timber Wolf had sent the rest of the survey crew on another day-long mission on a pretext, supposedly to give her and Jared time to complete the last of their analyses. Randall met them as arranged, a hundred and fifty miles nearer the coast than their previous meeting point. He seemed more at ease in Wolf's presence than Walrus's; she had a soothing way of talking to him.

This time there were no blindfolds. This was a secret Randall had agreed to share. Their bumpy journey took them to the outskirts of a level plain stretching to the horizon, the kind of feature that Jared had learned marked the demise of a city. A river meandering around its edge looked like it once ran through the heart of the metropolis, but the stellar heat of the plasma beam had altered the contours, forcing the water to find new paths. Randall followed where it resumed its course downstream. A mile further, and he angled up the bank.

Ash lay on the ground, fused to mortar in the last rains of a dying world then baked hard under decades of unrelieved sun. The quad left a barely-perceptible track in the surface. Where the bank climbed steep, on its brow the broken edge of the ash layer lay exposed, inches thick.

Randall stopped the quad and sat for a long while, gazing at the bleak landscape. "Forests here once," he said. "Wild and thick. This place passed from living memory under the green."

Jared wondered what place he was talking about, then he noticed the barest hint of a line in the slope ahead, a beveled edge maybe twenty feet along.

Randall dismounted and walked past the edge, disappearing down a dip behind. Jared and Wolf hurried after him. Randall moved aside a few lumps of rock, carefully placing each to one side, then lifted the edge of an ash-caked tarpaulin.

Somebody had been excavating here, carefully exposing a few feet of buried wall and a sliver of an opening just wide enough to squeeze through.

Without hesitation, Randall eased himself into the scrape and slid into the darkness. Jared and Wolf exchanged glances then followed.

They wriggled down the slope to where it was possible to stand, and wound their way past a thicket of dead tree roots, iron hard in the parched air.

Bright light, unannounced, made Jared squint. Randall held a glow-tube in front of him. Jared and Wolf fished out their own. Jared also understood now the advice to bring coils of lightweight line and the collapsible shovel tucked into a holder at his waist. This place had lain abandoned to the elements for an age. Soil and rock washed into the passageway over countless centuries brought the floor to within a few feet of the ceiling. The lintel of an almost-buried doorway showed the depth of the neglect.

A little farther, the corridor opened out on either side into a circular cavern thirty feet across.

"Have a care here," Randall whispered.

The ground sloped away ever steeper towards the center, disappearing into a sheer drop tens of yards deep.

Randall hugged the left hand wall and edged down the treacherous slope to what must have been the floor level of the corridor. A narrow ledge ran around the inside of the circle. A few rusty stubs along the edge showed where a railing had long ago corroded to nothing. Peering over, Jared could just make out the bottom of the pit. Above him, a circular grating a few yards across may once have opened out to the air above. It had long since been grown over, silted up, and finally sealed by the burning above.

With a start, he realized Randall had vanished. He edged along the ledge and felt his way into an opening. Footsteps clanging on iron echoed up from the depths.

Mindful of the decay around him, Jared knelt and inspected the steps. Randall's light flashed through open grille-work from several flights down the shaft. The metal appeared sound, more protected here from the elements.

"They seem safe enough for the big man," Wolf whispered in his ear. "I think they can take our weight."

"He does seem the cautious type," Jared agreed.

They followed, flight after flight, in no great haste. Jared felt confident Randall would wait for them assuming his intentions were true. If he had treachery on his mind, well, Jared had no plans to blunder unwary into a trap.

Just short of twenty flights down, the access shaft opened out into a room filled with machinery. Rusting carcasses of pipes and pumps cast jumping shadows in the light of their glowtubes. Jared caught himself on the uneven floor, unexpected after the clean steps above, and found it littered with debris. A mound of soil spilled from a blocked doorway leading back to the filled-in main shaft.

Randall beckoned from another doorway across the room. "More careful now."

Another shaft, more flights of steps, but these were in a poor state of repair. The handrail had all but disappeared, and many steps looked too fragile to hold the weight of a person.

Randall flattened his back against the wall, testing each step as he went. The occasional creak of brittle metal punctuated the sound of their breathing in the stale air. They used their lines to rappel down the last forty feet, the last flights seeming more rust than metal.

A short corridor led into a broad arched tunnel easily wide enough for four of Randall's quads to ride side by side. Past spillage from the choked ventilation shaft, the tunnel ran into the distance in either direction. Jared checked his mental bearings and pointed. "This heads towards the sea. You say it leads out to the island of Sherrin?"

"Nothing else of importance between here and the sea so where else can it be headed? Besides, I seen it on old maps."

"Why build a tunnel all that distance?" Wolf asked.

"The seas around the island are nigh impassable," said Jared. "We know that, and the tidal motion won't have changed with the Cleansing. I'd guess some founding fathers with more money than sense tried to open those islands up to regular traffic as alternative to air."

Wolf frowned. "There were no records of Eloon having such a transit system."

"No *recent* records. But regardless, I'll go with empirical evidence."

Randall turned to face them, his ruddy face demonic in the ghostly uplight of the glowtube. "Do none of you young'uns study history any longer?"

Jared glanced at Wolf. Formal education of any kind was unknown to him. She shrugged.

"These tunnels go all the way back to the founding of this world. Before the surface was livable they lived and worked underground." Randall cleared his throat and spat. "Back then, hole boring was a well-practiced art, as easy as flying. All forgotten now, but to those folks then, this"—he gestured around him—"was nothing."

"Are you saying these tunnels have survived, what, five thousand years?"

"Seven," growled Randall. "And why not? They were used and maintained for an age. And this world has no plate tectonics to disturb the earth this deep."

"Okay," Jared muttered, "by my reckoning it's about four hundred miles to Sherrin. I don't see an easy way to get a vehicle down here."

Wolf chewed her lip. "Maybe a small two-wheeler?" She glanced at Randall. "You told me you'd been there."

He shook his head. "Not all the way. Gets wet under the sea. Randall doesn't like wet. And the air gets bad."

"Under the sea," Jared echoed. "That's still further than you'd walk. How did you travel?"

"Two miles back"—Randall pointed in the opposite direction—"there's a siding. Garages, workshops, some vehicles. Some still working. I brought power packs."

Jared's hopes lifted. "That sounds promising." He made a mental note to bring breathing equipment. "How about getting out at the other end?"

"More shafts like this one when you reach land. Shown on the old maps." He gave Jared a sly smile. "One comes up inside the prison fence. I reckon they never knew it was there."

"But you've never been there, so no knowing what state they're in."

He shrugged. "The top was built over, not left open to the elements, but who knows? I show you a tunnel to the island. Getting out's your problem."

As they neared the sunlit entrance once more, the distant slit of light dazzling after the underground gloom, Jared said, "I've seen enough. Randall, you've fulfilled your work admirably. May the dead rest forever in peace."

He nodded to Wolf. In one swift, fluid motion, she swept up a fist-sized jagged lump of rock and slammed it into Randall's temple. The giant's face held a momentary glimmer of surprise, then he folded quietly to the ground.

Wolf regarded him for a few moments, then she sighed. "I've always said you should never explore the wilderness alone. One slip in this terrain, and ..."

Chapter 9

The barren landing field stretched into the distance, to where the Heights of Scithea plunged down to the vitrified wasteland that marked Torremis, the old Eloon capital city.

Normally busy, the landing field was now cleared of all traffic. The precautions irked Shayla, but the disruption to the usually bustling activity was the least of her concerns.

Fury rose once more, a visceral upwelling, as Shayla replayed this morning's events. The fresh, clear dawn had seemed to presage a busy and productive day, but she could still feel the knot of dread in her stomach from when Simone handed her the message capsule during the morning's operations briefing.

Simone's grim expression had warned her to brace herself.

Shayla had taken a few minutes to digest the implications of the capsule's contents, the silence lengthening amidst increasingly concerned looks between her chiefs of staff.

Eventually, Shayla had calmed herself enough to speak. "It seems the Imperial inspection team will arrive ahead of schedule." She held up a hand to silence the ominous muttering that swept around the table. "We must clear the landing field and prepare to welcome our guests this afternoon."

This time she could not quieten the uproar.

"But we're not ready!"

"What are they playing at?"

"A full week early?"

Shayla's mind raced while the sounds of outrage spent their course. Then she'd fought to keep her tone matter-of-fact. "This is a perfectly typical tactic. They want to see us as we really are. No opportunity to hide our dirty laundry."

Dirty laundry!

But they'll still expect an impeccable showing, of course.

A metallic glint high overhead caught Shayla's eye. She squinted to see if it was a descending transport, but it was too far off. A sharp quality of light told Shayla that it circled way above atmosphere. *Hammer of War.* The vast battleship which carried the Imperial inspection team here.

Early.

Somewhere up there, her tormentor was still playing mind games. This afternoon, the message said, but it had been curiously light on specifics. She and a select welcoming committee had now been standing out here in the dry afternoon glare for over an hour.

So, what parts of our operation were they going to pick on? Shayla had directed her staff chiefs to the profusion of status reports vying for prominence. "We pay attention to the most pressing matters. The rest we can deal with as we go."

She'd skimmed through the mess of detail. "Let's see. Are the accounts ready for audit?"

Shirley Chavas, in charge of the planetary purse strings, sat straight. Teeth flashed white against russet skin. "All up to date, but we haven't packaged them up for presentation yet."

"They can either wait or take the raw data." Something nagged at Shayla. "Nothing in there we'd be worried about?"

"They can dig all they want. They won't find anything."

Shayla met Shirley's level gaze for a few moments then turned to Frank Wu, the head of planetary development. "What's the state of the accommodation?"

"Their compound will be ready for use in two days."

"No sooner?"

Frank looked up from his scroll, on which he'd been scrawling furiously throughout the exchange. "That was after stripping out all the frills and dispensable touches, and ... paying attention to only the most pressing matters." He'd met Shayla's gimlet glare without flinching. "No sooner."

A tiny flickering lightbulb had sparked at that moment. Despite the unwelcome wait, Shayla smiled to herself as she recalled Frank's horror at her proposed solution. With her eyes still on Frank, she'd instructed Marconi Collsen, the head of her domestic staff, "Find a suite for Milady bin Mellion in the Residence. At this short notice, it will have to be one currently vacant. See what we have available."

"But the only vacant suites are those being refurbished after that attack."

"I know. I will be responsible for explaining arrangements to the Governor of the Inspectorate."

After a few more seconds of open-mouthed silence, Frank had sat back, nodding, his characteristic cheerfulness slowly returning. "And we'll have to billet her staff in the Residence reception hall. It's either that or the immigration processing halls, and I'm sure that wouldn't do."

"You have the right idea."

Marconi had been looking back and forth between Frank and Shayla, clearly at a loss. "And the welcome banquet ...?"

"Will proceed on the planned day. The inspectors will want to get down to business so we'll respond in kind. Besides, I think we've got enough to deal with without trying to bring that forward."

You'll see us as we are, dirty laundry included.

For the twentieth time since that morning briefing, Shayla faced down her anger and channeled it into constructive energy.

You can't achieve anything by games like this. We're ready for you.

But she knew that her rage masked a deeper fear. This inspection was vital to the future of this world. Every five years, an Imperial team would arrive and audit her whole operation. They would report back to the Emperor in person. And the Emperor could cut off essential funding, or even close them down altogether, just as quickly as he'd granted them their coveted status.

The fact that the Inspectorate would pull a trick like this was disturbing. But it was all part of a pattern. They wanted her to fail.

A warning chime sounded from the depths of the field offices behind Shayla. She scanned the sky for signs of her Imperial guests.

A troop transport, belly swollen like a pregnant goat's, swooped overhead and settled to one side of Shayla's entourage. Loading ramps on either side thudded onto dry soil.

A platoon of guards in ceremonial livery tramped down the ramps, their boots kicking puffs of dust as they took up positions in front of Shayla.

Another transport landed opposite the first.

As the inspection team disembarked and lined up to one side of the guards, Shayla studied their robes and insignia with interest. Lots of auditors. *Hope Shirley's done her work well.*

That was to be expected, but ... *she's brought her own chef?* Shayla was incredulous. *Marconi will not be pleased.* More to the point, this was a calculated insult to a planetary governor.

As she scanned the faces, one in particular stood out. A diminutive figure near the center of the line, almost insignificant, other than her unusually pale face amongst the largely swarthy Imperial citizens. Beth Silvani.

Beth the Knife.

Shayla knew the face well from her research notes. Her intelligence team had spent months speculating on who would be chosen to lead the audit, and Shayla had familiarized herself with the most likely candidates. The choice spoke volumes, confirming Shayla's suspicions. They were out to find fault.

Finally, a small air cruiser plunged into the gap between the transports, pulling up hard at the last moment. The subtlety of the display was not lost on Shayla. Small air cruisers did not typically mount the grav fields needed to shield their occupants from such harsh maneuvers. This was an exceptional luxury, and a deliberate show of extravagance.

The cruiser's door opened.

Shayla's heartbeat quickened. Now more than ever, she felt exposed and unprepared. She couldn't explain why this unknown woman should hold such power over her, but she struggled to contain her anxiety over this first meeting.

Damn this Imperial obsession with protocol!

She knew all too well that this greeting would set the tone for the inspection. Get this wrong, and she risked either delivering a grave insult to the Emperor, or handing the Inspectorate a psychological advantage.

Lady Josephine bin Mellion appeared at the top of the steps and cast a disdainful gaze across the bare field and the few dozen people ranged in front of her, like she owned the planet. Unhurried, head held high, she swept down the steps and stopped a few feet in front of Shayla, clearly waiting for some sign of obeisance.

Outwardly cool, Shayla's mind seethed with anxiety. She kept her gaze fixed on a point on Josephine's forehead, almost but not fully meeting her eyes, not quite acknowledging her.

After a prolonged pause, Josephine's eyes wavered. She inclined her head.

At the first hint of movement, Shayla also inclined her head, to exactly the same degree.

To the expectant onlookers it was effectively simultaneous.

"Lady bin Mellion, I bid you welcome to the Freeworld and Imperial Protectorate of Eloon."

We greet as equals.

"The Emperor commends your gracious hospitality."

Amongst all the mind games, Shayla was thankful to salvage this small victory.

Whitewashed walls of Scale's medical center passed by in a blur. Two sleepless nights since the inspectors landed and one full day in between, Shayla felt like she'd been hit by a whirlwind.

While a posse of crew members from the orbiting battleship invaded the Residence with bedding and baggage for her Imperial guests, the guests themselves went straight to work. They seemed to have planned their assault like a military campaign, and knew exactly where to sniff out weakness. But even their onslaught of demands and veiled criticism had to take a back seat today.

Ignoring the protests of angry bruises and newly-patched skin, Shayla's pace hardly slackened. She strode corridors and down stairs to the coastal district's only mortuary, as she dealt with one last priority call on her notepad.

The faces of Shirley Chavas and Frank Wu gazed back at her from the surface of the notepad. "Damn barefaced *cheek* of the woman," Shirley raged.

"This meeting was with Beth Silvani in person?" Conflicting pressures clouded Shayla's mind. The uncharacteristic urgency of Brin's earlier call this morning dragged her away from a meeting with the Inspectorate. She'd requisitioned a single-seat *Lance* fighter, the fastest craft available, and piloted it herself. She'd ignored protocols and landed in a square in front of the medical facility, burning with curiosity, but before that curiosity could be satisfied here was another unrelated emergency.

"It wasn't a meeting. It was a *summons*." Shirley paused. "Can she even *do* that?"

"Don't let her rattle you." Of all Shayla's senior management team, Shirley was the least accustomed to the machinations of the Imperial court. "She has the right to *request* a meeting. You have the right to refuse, but *my* instructions are to extend full co-operation. Remind them of that at every opportunity. When you accept invitations, it is because you *choose* to do so, not because they insist."

Without breaking stride as she took another flight of stairs, Shayla added, "Feel free to make them wait once in a while if it's not immediately convenient. Just enough to remind them you don't *have* to jump when they snap their fingers."

Shirley nodded. "But what in Space made her home straight in on expenses for maintaining the Garden of Hope?"

"More to the point," Shayla said, "what was her gripe?"

"Wasteful extravagance," Shirley spat. "She even tried telling me we had to shut it down."

Aah, that's what was really getting her steamed up.

Shirley caught Shayla's eye and must have noted her concerned expression. "Oh, I'm not dumping my problems on you. I know they can't give us operational direction. I can handle that poison dwarf but I thought I should share what's going on back here so you're not blindsided. Those asswipes are playing mind-fuck games and I wouldn't put it past them to hit us on more than one front at a time."

A pair of guards ahead came to attention and her guide pushed open a door for her. Shayla paused on the threshold with a twinge of guilt. She'd not told anyone else in her inner circle of Brin's urgent message. She'd just upped and left. Not that there was anything to tell, yet, but what if this was the second prong of the same attack? "It's right to keep me informed. In fact, we all need to keep each other abreast of what the Inspectorate are up to. We need to support each other through this." A thought struck her. "Frank, have they visited the immigration center yet?"

"Tomorrow morning, as I understand it."

"Do we have incoming tomorrow?"

Frank nodded. "They want to see the center in operation. Sit in on interviews and briefings. That kind of thing."

"Good. Make sure at least one of the inspectors rides a bus to the camp, and make sure they interview a few of the drivers."

Frank pursed his lips then grinned. "Consider it done." Shayla could see he understood her intent. On the many occasions she'd visited the center herself, the drivers often talked of the effect the Garden of Hope had on their charges. It was one of the unwritten perks of the job, to see the looks on people's faces. All the propaganda in the processing center could do only so much. It set the scene, but the reality outside had the power to move grown men to tears.

And, damn it all, the concept and the psychology behind the Garden had come from Imperial advisors in the first place. She was sure this upstart auditor would have known this already.

Shayla's own words to Shirley came back to her. Don't let them rattle you.

She clipped her notepad back into its holder at her side and turned her attention finally to head of security, Brindis ap Silessi, and the two naked bodies on slabs in front of him.

One corpse Shayla recognized immediately. Even without his motley patchwork of dusty, faded, multi-colored clothing, Randall's build was unmistakable.

Unlooked-for grief tore at her. She stood silent for long minutes, probing inwards for the source of the darkness that had gripped her so unexpectedly. "Oh, Randall," she whispered at last. "You came through so much. Lived beyond all odds, and now this." A fellow survivor, one who'd been here, on the surface, when her world was torn apart and who had nevertheless lived. In all of recorded history, nobody on the ground had ever walked away from a Cleansing.

"I should have looked after you." A hot angry tear pushed past her lashes. She brushed it away with a flick of trembling fingers. "What happened?" The words rasped out.

Brin's face was set in its usual granite mask, but his eyes betrayed his pain. "We found him at the bottom of a hidden shaft."

"Big guy took a tumble out in the badlands near Arnie's Vineyard." The pathologist's cheery voice contrasted the grim scene. He turned from a worktop to one side where he had been scrawling notes on a scroll. He caught himself as he recognized his visitor, and bowed deep. "Pardon, My Lady, I hadn't expected you to arrive so quickly."

Shayla gave him a distracted wave, signaling him to stand easy, and frowned. "What the heck was he doing out there? That's two thousand miles from his known stomping ground." The frown deepened as she looked Brin in the eye. "And how did you find him?"

"A few days ago we picked up his trail again near Scale, like you asked, and put a passive tracer on him."

"Passive?" Shayla's mind seemed to be crawling at a snail's pace. She should know this jargon but the meaning slipped tantalizing at the edge of her awareness.

"We've tried tracking him before since we first heard of him. Always managed to shake us off. I assume he's got access to military band detectors."

Brin's eyes were red-rimmed and new lines had creased his wiry face. More worrying, his normally sour manner had slipped behind pure exhaustion. No, worse, he had a look of defeat about him. This string of setbacks was taking its toll, and he would take this personally. That was a failing in herself she knew all too well, but she couldn't bear to see it tearing apart someone in front of her.

"Aah." Shayla nodded, remembering. A passive tracker would listen for a command signal and respond only with a nanosecond pulse. It was effectively invisible to detectors unless they caught it in the act. "Good work, Brin." She put as much warmth into her voice as she could. Was gratified to see his back straighten slightly.

"We pinged him every three hours, just keeping an arm's-length watch. You'd be surprised how widely he traveled."

"So," she breathed, "what were you doing down there, I wonder?" She peered closer. One wound in particular caught her professional eye.

The pathologist saw the line of her gaze. "Yes, that's the blow that did it. His other injuries were serious, but not directly life-threatening and look post-mortem."

Shayla brushed her finger around the indentation in his skull. It could have been accidental, but the positioning was too precise, and the angle of entry made it unlikely this could have been caused by falling.

His shoulder would have got in the way. "Brin," she murmured, "this was an execution."

Brin's sour face almost managed a smirk. "We already knew that. We found him in a blocked-off ventilation shaft. Some old piece of infrastructure. His tracer was pinging from under the search team's feet. They took soundings and saw they were sitting on top of the shaft, so they broke through the cap to get at him. They realized he must have had a way in, but it took some finding."

"It was hidden? That seems to fit with his lifestyle."

"It was hidden," Brin said with grim satisfaction, "from the *outside*."

"Oh!"

"And there were faint tracks but no sign of his vehicle."

"So he was dumped. Someone killed him to take his vehicle?"

Brin shrugged. "You can rest assured we're retracing his movements as best we can. We'll try to correlate his track with any traceable vehicles. See who he might have crossed paths with."

"You know your job, Brin. Just give me any conclusions."

"He had a hideout a ways from the coast. Some old militia installation. With supplies."

"A structure left standing?"

"Underground. Far enough away from settlements not to be a direct target, and deep enough to survive the aftermath."

"So, that's how he survived then." Shayla gazed down at the body. Despite the bruises he looked at peace. No more nightmares.

"I think he must have been someone in the old Eloon public service," Brin said. "Someone with access to the old planetary infrastructure."

"Wonder what else he knew. Weapon stashes, maybe?"

"The thought had crossed my mind. The trouble is ..." Brin trailed off into thoughtful silence.

"The Randall we've seen didn't seem the murderous sort," Shayla finished for him. "I agree. And I'm not sure he had the faculties or information sources to co-ordinate that Wasp attack. That took sophistication."

"And as if we didn't have enough mysteries in this one," Brin said, "we have stiff number two."

"No mystery about cause of death there," the pathologist called from across the room. "He was knifed. From behind. Not likely an accident."

Shayla arched an eyebrow at Brin. His seemingly casual tone rang with discordant harmonics. "Something about this one you'd care to explain?"

Brin pursed his lips and jerked his head towards the second body. A clear 'be my guest' signal.

Puzzled, Shayla moved closer. The man was well-muscled, Magentis native by his features and skin tone, though his face was distorted in the rigor of a silent scream. Yet there was something familiar about him. A memory tugged from years ago.

Shayla gasped and her legs weakened. She clutched at the table edge to hold herself upright. "Brin, what in Space was Corporal Kurt Weiler of the Imperial Palace Guard doing on Eloon?"

Chapter 10

From the air, the sheer scale of what had befallen Eloon decades ago became clear. The unnatural plain that marked the demise of a city lay like a raw blister across once-fertile ground. The edge of the destruction swept away on either side describing a perfect circle.

Jared shrugged off a sudden chill and focused on the meandering river below. As agreed, Wolf had secured him an assignment to carry out a solo survey further down the coastal stretch. He'd swapped the heavy transport for a single-seat air cruiser loaded with survey and sample equipment, amongst other things. He needed time away from prying eyes to put Randall's information to the test.

Jared followed the river at high altitude to scan the land around the tunnel entrance for unwelcome company.

A glint down below caught his eye. The craft wavered momentarily in its course before Jared recovered from his shock and brought it steady again. He could normally identify every make of craft from the merest glimpse, no matter how distant or how camouflaged. Right now his mind had gone blank. It didn't matter *who* they were, they were sat right on top of the fucking ventilation shaft.

That could not be coincidence.

He was screwed.

Faculties came back online in a rush. Jared shed height and circled in a lazy arc. No attempt at hiding, he willed the air cruiser to fly with nonchalant innocence. Whether these were innocuous passers-by or official didn't matter. Out here so far from habitation travelers who chanced on each other *always* stopped. In this emptiness, people looked out for each other. His fly past couldn't have been missed, and to continue would arouse suspicion.

He circled the landing site at a respectful distance.

"Air cruiser, please identify yourself." The comms screen showed a military call sign. *Fuck.*

"Jared Tindall, ecology survey. You boys okay down there?" Without waiting for an answer, he settled the craft down fifty yards away and popped the hatch.

Putting on his best game face, Jared climbed down and gave a cheery wave to the soldier striding across the face of the slope towards him. "Long way from home, mate."

"What's your business here, sir?" The soldier's beam rifle wasn't exactly aimed at Jared, but it wasn't exactly not.

Jared masked a prickle of unease. A second soldier loitered in the distance. Their craft looked like a two-man job. Jared calculated the odds of disposing of the two of them, then balked at the odds of evading the combined might of Eloon's forces descending on these two's last known location when they failed to report in. "Scouting land and soil conditions for a new stretch of planting. What brings you guys all the way down here?"

Just the hint of evasion in the man's eyes before he said, "Following a line of inquiry. Nothing I can talk about. You understand." He sounded almost apologetic.

"Police work, huh?" Jared grinned and glanced at the sun high in the sky. "From what I hear about military field rations I guess a plate of pulled pork wouldn't go amiss?"

The soldier's mouth twitched. "Spiced?" The rifle dangled all but forgotten in his hands.

"Like Momma used to make." Jared smacked his lips. "Out here I look after my feet and my stomach. All else follows." He mounted the ladder and rummaged in the back of the cruiser, thankful that he genuinely did believe in looking after basic comforts wherever practical. He emerged with an insulated pot and a plastiwrapped loaf of bread, noting that the second soldier had joined them, curious.

Jared resisted the temptation to gaze over at the military cruiser. From here the top of the shaft was hidden and there was nothing visible to arouse the interest of an innocent visitor. So Jared stifled his burning curiosity and kept the conversation turned to innocuous subjects. Just passers-by breaking bread together.

"Got to ask," the more senior one said eventually, wiping his bowl clean with a last hunk of bread. "Survey work, you said? Where you been working?"

"Started sampling a hundred miles or so north of here, working my way down for the past few days."

"Seen anything odd out here?"

"Strange. I was told this place was empty for a thousand miles around, but seems it's got real crowded."

The soldiers exchanged looks.

"Well, there's you guys, obviously, but ..." He shook his head. "Nah. Just the sun in my eyes." *You fucking tease, Jared.* He could see the carefully masked interest in their eyes.

The younger one took the bait. "Even if it's nothing, better to spit it out and let us judge its importance."

"Well ..." Jared hesitated. "I thought I saw something moving in the distance, maybe three days ago?"

"And?"

Jared shrugged. "I headed over, but couldn't see anything. Figured I was mistaken. All this emptiness." The shudder needed no faking. "You think this place will ever be green again?"

Face hooded, a shabby anonymous figure near the back of the field canteen, Shayla sipped a large mug of steaming tea and pondered ... if the churning chaos of her thoughts could be said to constitute pondering.

Kurt Weiler. The guard she'd promoted to look after her security when she infiltrated the Mosaic Palace seven years ago on her abortive mission of revenge. She'd never found out what happened to him afterwards.

He'd unwittingly revealed himself a close supporter of Grand Duke Ivan in the hours before she closed her trap. She knew that, but who else might? And would it matter? They could hardly bench everyone who'd shown loyalty to Ivan, that would leave the Imperial service perilously thin. That was part of the problem the Emperor wrestled with. Support for him was too finely balanced against support for many other factions, Ivan included.

So what *had* Kurt been doing here?

She smiled thanks, brought out of her introspection as Simone dropped a tray of food in front of her. Simone, equally hooded although less likely to be recognized, sat beside her. "Gem's doing a good job."

Shayla had been paying little more than subliminal attention to the presentation one of her senior overseers was delivering. It had been Felicity Marr's idea to bring the inspection team out here, flying low over the hundreds of square miles of greenery around Scale. An hour-long truck ride, a sore trial for soft city-dwellers accustomed to Imperial luxury, ended at one of the distribution centers. Yes, they could easily have landed the transports closer but Felicity, her sharp legal mind now relishing the mental swordplay of political one-upmanship, wanted to impress on them the breadth and sheer audacity of their operation and the brutal conditions this world endured.

So they roughed it, and mixed with callused and grimy fugitives from a hundred planets. No air-conditioned boardroom today. Cooking smells, heavy with spice, did nothing to dispel the unwashed stench as curious workers fresh from the field crowded long benches. Standing room only. Frank Wu had hardly needed Felicity's prompting to declare time off for anyone who wanted to greet the inspection team. The impish grin as he'd listened to Felicity's proposals had lifted years off his face.

They even ate the same food, although Shayla wryly noted a marked uptick in the quality of today's fare. Someone had tipped off the canteen boss.

Yes, she agreed, Gem Brigga *was* doing an excellent job. The elderly Wala woman, midnight-skinned and muscular, cut a striking figure at the front of the room. Her rough and scarred face, one eye a blank wall of white, roved the front rows of their esteemed guests as she delivered her lecture. Her gravelly voice, as rough as her face, nevertheless mesmerized with its soft accent and rhythmic, poetic cadence. Passion for her work shone like a beacon.

She talked of the water cycle, the nurtured acres of artificial forests slowly re-invigorating the air above with moisture to be carried ever further inland, and the fields of crops now interspersed amongst the woodlands.

Some sharp mind from the ranks of the inspectors drawled into a momentary pause, "If you got no precipitation, how come there's snow on them mountains up there?"

Gem Brigga turned her one good eye towards the interruption. She bared her teeth and inclined her head. "Glad t'see always one sharp tool in't ranks. You're right. Snow falls on mountains ... sometimes ...

but it takes them mountains to squeeze out what precious little mist as in t'air. Falls only on highest ground. Ne'er where'ts needed." This year, she went on to explain, they had celebrated the first genuine rainfall recorded on this coast since work began, an inspiring sign that they were starting to make a difference and that a self-sustaining ecosystem was within reach.

As Shayla picked at her food, her thoughts turned again to Kurt Weiler. Space! That had been a close call back then. She'd let her guard down, came close to letting him in. Had come close to having to kill him when he'd shown his true allegiance. How had she misjudged him so badly? Now here he was, dead.

He was the real reason Brin had hauled her out from headquarters in such a hurry. She'd been saddened to see Randall on the slab, but Kurt had shaken her to the core.

Brin had had his suspicions about Kurt's identity, but needed her confirmation. Had needed to see her close up, in person, and see her reaction as recognition hit.

Kurt Weiler, Brin's investigations revealed, had transferred to the security service after Shayla's exile, and eventually been sent to infiltrate the Insurrection. There, Brin's information dried up, but it was hardly a leap of the imagination to see Kurt winding up here in bad company.

The shock and puzzlement in Shayla's face had been genuine. That was what Brin needed to see. She'd known nothing about Kurt's presence here.

So what had happened to him? Had his cover been broken? She recalled the two Insurrection agents who'd met Randall. It was even more vital to find them. Brin was already ahead of her. Another to-do on his list.

A cold chill swept over her. Those two had talked about the Wasps. Sounded angry, but why would they disapprove of an assassination that came so close to succeeding? One of their own had launched that attack against Shayla. Had that been Kurt?

———————

Once more in the air Jared cursed his luck. It took little imagination to deduce they'd found Randall. How? The man had been paranoid about trackers, but that seemed the only explanation. If Jared himself had been spotted visiting this site previously, he'd be dead or captured by now. He'd detected no trace of suspicion in those soldiers. Nothing beyond the ordinary, anyway.

All very well, but how long did they plan to camp out there, and what were they looking for?

He flicked the comms screen and called Wolf. "Hail, Wanderer," she greeted him. A pre-arranged signal that they may be overheard.

"Run into a problem. The deep sampling operation hit a rock on the surface. Any chance you can manage a flypast and help me shift the blockage?" Jared hoped to hell Wolf would decode his improvised code. She'd fend off casual eavesdroppers at her end but there was no knowing who might tap into even a direct link like this.

"Sure thing," she responded. "By the way, some friends of yours were asking after you. I told them you were out in the field for a few days." Okay, so the soldiers *had* called in to check out his story, and Wolf had backed him up.

Jared set down a few miles away from the annoyingly guarded shaft and deployed sampling equipment for show. Next, he unpacked some less standard equipment from hiding places in the back of the craft.

He checked the time and calculated how long it would take to retrace his path on foot. It was time to get moving.

The sun hung low on the horizon by the time Jared, hidden below the rise of the sluggish river's bank, neared the shaft entrance. When his pocket inertial navigator showed he was half a mile out, he unrolled a tissue-thin sheet of thermal fabric and draped it over himself. He wormed on his belly to the crest of the slope until the cruiser came into view. He flipped a visor over his eyes and magnified the view, overlaying heat signals onto the visible wavelengths. The cruiser radiated a blazing light show in infrared. They were keeping it fired up and ready to launch. The two soldiers worked nearby in the fading light.

Jared settled down to wait.

At the prearranged hour, a low rumble from the north grew steadily louder. Minutes later, Wolf's transport made a low-level pass not quite overhead but too close to ignore. The soldiers scrambled and took off.

The moment they were out of sight, Jared sprinted the remaining few hundred yards. He slowed and moved more cautiously as he drew near, ears straining for the sounds of the craft returning.

An adjustment of his visor, and the image enhanced to a high contrast view. Randall's quad bike track, practically invisible to the naked eye, showed clearly. He advanced slowly, scanning the ground ahead. There. Trails of footprints traced a spider web a hundred feet across centered on the shaft cap.

Jared froze. The trails converged on several points around the circumference. He backed off and circled to the nearest point of convergence then crawled forward once more.

Oh, you sneaky buggers. Camouflaged so well he wouldn't have noticed it even up close, a pebble the size of a coin was just a bit too round to be natural. The soldiers were here to guard the exposed shaft and question anyone who strayed close, but they had no plans to stay here indefinitely. They'd surrounded the site with an automated perimeter alarm.

Was it active yet? Doubtful. They'd still been working until Wolf's diversion. All the same, Jared tuned his visor up and down the wavelengths scanning for any traces of a signal. Nothing.

Aware of the passing time, Jared took a deep breath and stepped past the perimeter. Nothing flared on his visor. The alarms remained quiet. He hurried to the shaft and examined the hidden entrance.

Randall's crude tarpaulin was still there, pushed to one side. So they'd found the entrance. Wary of traps and alarms, Jared slid into the tunnel. He worked his way forward by feel and by infrared, not daring to shine a light even down here.

At the main shaft, something felt wrong. Jared froze where he stood, barely breathing, while he probed his senses for whatever had raised the hairs on his neck. At last he let out a relieved sigh. Above his head, the grating that had capped the shaft was gone. It was open to the sky once more, allowing an unexpected draft.

A distant drone of engines spurred Jared to action. He eased himself down the slope and into the stairwell. He rattled down as many flights of steps as he could under cover of the aircraft's noise, before slowing and slinking silently the rest of the way. As he reached the transit tunnel, Jared wondered if the authorities had been this way. They'd broken into the top of the shaft to recover Randall's body—dammit, that shaft had seemed like one place on the planet that would lay undisturbed for many more years, who'd have thought of a tracker?—so they probably only found the excavated entrance afterwards. They would have had no obvious cause to explore further. They likely assumed the shaft held no significance other than as a hiding place, and the soldiers' actions up above showed they were more intent on trapping the killer should he return to the scene of the crime.

Even that was surely a long shot. Who the heck returned to a body dump?

Jared's lips curled in self-recrimination. Who the heck dumped a body right on the doorstep of their operations? Water under the bridge. Moving on. He switched back to visible wavelengths and lit a glowtube, then set off inland at an easy lope.

After a quarter hour, the tunnel widened and branched. Just as Randall had said, here were workshops eerie in their millennia of solitude. Garages held a few decaying hulks, ghosts of machines. Nothing looked fit for service. A few wheeled cars looked promising at first but were missing parts. Otherwise, nothing appeared to have been disturbed.

Jared sat back on his heels and pondered. He switched his visor back to enhanced contrast and scanned the floor for tracks. The floor was criss-crossed. He mentally retraced his own steps and subtracted his movements from the traces visible. Randall had been here and had explored thoroughly, probably over a period of time.

Bingo. Here was the track of a vehicle leaving the garage. A one-way trip.

Jared smacked his forehead with sudden insight. Randall had plundered parts from almost-working vehicles to patch one up to a useable state. He'd mentioned bringing a power pack but omitted the labor in between. Jared sighed and retraced his steps, edging past the bottom of the ventilation shaft with senses on a hair trigger before picking up the pace once more.

An hour passed. Jared paused and used the high contrast view again. The trace of a vehicle showed faint, almost indiscernible this far along the tunnel. The floor was too clean. There was little for a vehicle to disturb.

Another hour, and Jared wondered how much further he'd have to go. Near the end of the third hour his persistence was rewarded. A gleam in the distance resolved to an open-topped work vehicle lying abandoned in the middle of the tunnel.

Grinning, Jared stripped out the spent power pack and replaced it with one of a pair of spares he'd toted with him. With a brief prayer to whatever deities ruled the world of machinery, he thumbed the vehicle to life. The grin broadened and Jared let out a whoop that echoed up and down the tunnel as he whirled the car around in the confines and sped towards the sea.

—— • —

The security field office in the heart of Scale was cramped, noisy, and crowded. And hot. Brindis ap Silessi shook a drip of sweat from the end of his nose as he addressed the two dozen security agents crammed into the briefing room.

Professionals all, some were identified by insignia and dark olive uniforms of the security services. Many others wore work clothes, pulled in on various pretexts from their undercover posts in forestry crews, supply depots, haulage teams and kitchens. Men and women, young and old, the one feature they all shared was the hard set of their eyes.

"Your lieutenant has given you a good run-down of the task in hand," Brin said. "We have two bodies in the mortuary. There is a connection between them. You will track down contacts and associates, sightings and movements. They used vehicles. Those vehicles have transponders leaving traces in our logs. See who they intersected with."

Brin planted his balled fists on the desk in front of him and locked eyes with each of the men and women around the room.

"This is all standard procedure, you know it in your sleep, but I want to be clear about one thing. The Insurrection is now active on Eloon. Not just the occasional sleeper cells biding their time that we like to sniff out and keep tabs on. These agents are on a mission. They have an interest here, an intent that we cannot let them achieve."

—— • —

A few monotonous hours later exhilaration had given way to weariness. Weariness in turn surrendered to sullen frustration. When Randall had talked about getting wet, he wasn't joking.

At first, the only sign was a hint of moisture in the chill and stale air. After the bone dryness everywhere he'd been, the softness was a blessed relief. A few miles further on, Jared realized the truck was leaving a distinct track. Soon he splashed through a miles-long shallow puddle.

Jared slowed the pace as the water gradually deepened. When the lapping water crept over the truck's axles, he stopped and checked his position on the navigation unit. By his reckoning he must be well under the hundred-mile stretch of treacherous water that separated the island of Sherrin from the mainland. In fact, he must be nearer the island's shore than the coast he'd left behind.

He checked over the vehicle carefully, estimating how deep it could go before either losing traction or shorting a critical circuit. With a wary eye on the depth, he pushed on at a snail's pace.

Just one game of fucking chicken. Water inched higher up the wheels. At any moment the almost-but-not-quite-level ground might start to rise again and he'd be through. At some point the vehicle would give up, probably with no warning. At that point he'd be walking and would very likely not see the light of day again.

Another check on the vehicle's critical systems and Jared judged the latter point was close. He stopped the truck and marked the water level on the side, then backed up a hundred yards. The level had dropped by a fraction of an inch. He marked that and backed up again. Repeating the exercise a few more times it was clear the tunnel here was still on a very gradual but steady slope. He returned to his original point, checking the level against the side periodically.

When he'd gone as far as he dared he took a deep breath and slipped over the side. Needles of ice shot through him. If the truck quit here, he'd die of hypothermia before clearing this flooded section. Carefully noting the depth against his waist he waded slowly and deliberately until the headlights were a gleam in the distance. He confirmed his fears. The tunnel continued its downward slope. He needed a better vehicle for this stretch.

Shivering violently, Jared clambered back into the truck. His legs had lost all sensation and barely had the strength to lift him past the running board. He turned around and set off slowly for home.

Brindis ap Silessi sat ramrod straight on the unforgiving metal bench in the main cabin of the transport. Icy stratospheric air whistled past the machine's skin behind him. Through the window opposite, sunlight flashed off the cockpit of an escort fighter. His breath steamed in front of his face. These vehicles were pressurized but that was the only sop to human comfort. Structural girders and exposed wiring decorated the walls and ceiling. Harsh glowtubes lit the utilitarian white of the interior. Slate gray non-slip metal floor panels sucked all warmth through the soles of his work boots.

Normally, these transports flew loaded with workers. The press of bodies kept the chill at bay, and the passengers had suffered enough hardships in their past to put this slight discomfort into perspective. But Lady bin Mellion had insisted on sending most of her entourage on ahead so she could make use of her precious time to hold a private debriefing, and she was visibly suffering for her choice. She huddled in her cloak, more showy than practical, and deep lines around her mouth accentuated her grimace at each jolt through the airframe.

There was only her, the venomous audit chief Silvani, Lady Carver and him occupying a passenger bay built for a hundred. And the auditor had the cheek to lecture *us* on waste.

The physical environment didn't trouble Brin. It was the human irritants that got under his skin.

"In short, my team reports widespread dissatisfaction out in the planting projects. Ethnic segregation and maltreatment of workers." Beth Silvani concluded a long catalogue of woes. Not a single mention of the remarkable achievements of the last seven backbreaking years.

The words were directed at Lady Carver but each new accusation cut Brin deep. Never mind that his overstretched team's combined efforts were barely enough to handle life-and-limb security, the general policing of the whole planet was still his responsibility. Damn the Freeworld charter that, by its nature, required them to give sanctuary to people with unknown backgrounds. They were wide open to all comers.

He recognized the welling of blind rage that threatened to overwhelm his normal composure. At least, he reflected, he was still able to recognize it. How long before those defenses rotted away leaving him helpless to dreaded irrationality?

He took a small measure of satisfaction in the discomfort of Lady bin Mellion and her pampered entourage. The harshness of their quarters and transport over the last two days clearly pained them, although it probably contributed to the severity of this impromptu grilling.

At least Lady Carver seemed to be taking it in her stride. She lounged across from Brin, braced casually against the bumps and dips as they punched through air pockets. Even wearing her blazoned robes of office, hanging open despite the chill, she looked perfectly at home in this spartan environment. "I am aware of all that," she said. "We're dealing with it."

Brin clung to her calm in the face of such ill-informed criticism.

"Is that so?" the audit chief sneered. "I hear stories of one of the oppressed factions making a stand ... and disappearing."

"When you have something more than stories, let me know."

"She was last seen being taken by your security team." Lady bin Mellion gave Brin a pointed glance. "Nobody has seen her since. That smacks of a cover-up at best, and complicity at worst."

That was too much. "Planetary security is none of your business," Brin barked. "And if your meddling compromises it, you will answer to the Emperor." He had the satisfaction of seeing the governor's eyes widen in surprise. "I will say this much, but only to show you how close to the line you tread. The woman you speak of was one of my own agents. She came across the issue of maltreatment while investigating matters of greater concern. The Insurrection is present and making trouble. There is no record of her because the identity she assumed never existed."

"Why would The Insurrection be interested in this barely habitable world? They have no argument with Freeworlds."

"They *do* have an argument with this world's governor," Lady Carver whispered.

"And," Brin added, "with the unwelcome guests the Emperor has lodged with us."

———•••———

A ping on his navigator alerted Jared that he was nearing the ventilation shaft once more. He had almost drifted off, keeping the truck straight for the hours of the return journey through little more than reflex, and the alarm jarred him awake. He'd drawn a beam pistol before he realized what had disturbed him.

Space, but he was cold.

He killed the lights and coasted forward until the shaft entrance, just a faintly glowing patch in infrared, drew near. He decided to continue and stash the vehicle back in the garage. There was no sign the soldiers had explored this deep, but there was no point leaving evidence of recent use lying around.

The walk back to the entrance, nothing more than a shamble on legs afire with pinched circulation, felt like an eternity. The climb to the nearest stretch of solid stairs almost defeated him. He sat a while and munched on a ration bar before continuing.

The shaft top was closed once more. The heavy grating that had survived the passage of time was replaced by a smooth sheet of rigid polymer. He puzzled over this before answers suggested themselves to his fuddled mind, then he remembered the perimeter alarm. If the soldiers hoped to trap whoever had dumped Randall here, they would leave the place looking undisturbed from the outside. Of course they needed to block the hole again, and they'd probably replaced Randall's tarpaulin too.

The question was, were they still camped up top or had they finished setting their trap? Either answer posed a problem.

They'd kept their cruiser powered up and ready for flight. Jared switched his visor to infrared and scanned the ceiling for any signs of its heat signature. On its most sensitive setting, the rock walls of the shaft gave off a sullen glow. The ceiling above was an inky pool, all warmth sucked into the chill of the desert night. The cruiser had blazed in thermal glory, surely something would trickle through if it was still stationed above?

Jared wormed his way up the entrance tunnel to the flimsy tarpaulin. Here he stopped and listened. Nothing but the occasional rustle where one edge of the tarpaulin flapped loose, and a patter of wind-blown grains.

He retreated a few feet, then sent Wolf a prearranged signal. He settled back to wait.

Jared drifted into a wakeful doze, brought instantly alert by the sound of distant engines. The rush of adrenalin faded as he recognized the heavy growl of a slow transport, none of the turbocharged overtones of a military cruiser.

The sound settled some distance away. He waited, patient, his beam pistol drawn as a matter of habit.

Faint sounds reached him, someone making a slow circuit. Eventually Wolf's familiar voice murmured their prearranged recognition. All was clear. Jared slid on his belly out of the entrance tunnel. "I assume the alarms were no bother?"

Wolf grinned and waved a tiny box in his face. "That's the trouble with portable distributed systems. They have to talk to each other and that makes them open to attack."

Jared replaced the tarpaulin and joined Wolf outside the perimeter of the alarm system. Wolf circled the site, pausing now and again to adjust settings on the palm-sized device. "All closed up again. No sign we were ever here."

Chapter 11

A t this altitude, the white blanket rolling to the horizon around them seemed featureless. Still haunted by memories of her last flight over this frozen land, Shayla knew different. Somewhere down there, the wreckage of her old cruiser seeded a new drift of windblown flakes.

She checked the heading on the gyro compass she'd scavenged from her shattered craft, and glanced out the window at the accompanying flight of *Lance* fighters holding formation around her. They were taking no chances on this trip.

A murmur of conversation sounded louder behind her, then muted as the cockpit door closed again. Caleb ap Scoth, one of the inspection team leads, settled in the co-pilot's seat. He gazed for long minutes at the endless winterscape.

"Are the inspectors ready?" Shayla jerked her head towards the cabin behind her.

"Passing time. We received our briefing notes and instructions before we set out." He sniffed. "I was hoping the view from here might be an improvement."

"Don't worry. We're nearly there."

"How can you tell?" He gestured at the navigation screen that currently showed them roughly fifty miles west of their true position.

Shayla simply gave him a cool sidelong glance. Caleb seemed decent enough. From the few direct interactions she'd had with him, he appeared honest and at least had investigated impartially and delivered balanced reports. Her staff liked him, although he might still be a stooge, the good cop to Beth Silvani's bad.

"Well, I had to ask, didn't I?" He made a show of checking off a box on an imaginary scroll. "I understand security's pretty tight up here. Even so, there's nowhere for them to go if they did manage to get out."

"They brought it on themselves." Shayla's voice was cold. Her gut felt colder still. "They held the Emperor's family hostage here for twenty-five years. Whatever you see when we land, remember that you owe them no pity."

The last few minutes of the flight passed in silence. Finally, Shayla keyed the comms screen and told the fighters to take up covering positions while she landed a hundred yards from the prison entrance. Today the sky above was obscured by hard-driven flurries.

Caleb gazed around at the hostile landscape. "You're kidding, right?"

Shayla was already out of her seat, zipping her suit and reaching for a thermal gilet and fur-lined cloak. "Hope you all heeded my instructions to dress for winter."

Caleb sighed and followed her into the main cabin where the rest of the team was making ready for the outdoors. At the far end, three of Shayla's own guards faced off against three from the Inspectorate. Lady bin Mellion in person had come to see the high-ranking prisoners, along with two of Caleb's team and a legal overseer.

Shayla gave a curt bow and gestured to the hatch. "After you." She threw a mask and goggles across her face and pulled her cloak around her.

One of her guards hit the hatch release, not waiting for the tardier members of the inspection team to finish fastening their outdoor wear. He flashed Shayla the hint of a wink as he marched down the ramp into the teeth of an arctic gale.

Shayla loitered, allowing everyone to assemble at the foot of the ramp before she exited. Her own guards stood smartly at parade-ground attention. She'd picked old hands who'd done many tours of duty up here and knew what to expect. The rest huddled in the scant shelter afforded by the cruiser's landing struts.

Without a backward glance, Shayla strode confidently through the blizzard leaving it up to her guards to shepherd any stragglers. She paused in the cleft in the ice that marked the entrance, sheltering in the lee of the crevice, and counted bodies as they shuffled past into the depths of the prison. Everyone accounted for, including her own guards, she brought up the rear again as the team filed down the flights of steps cut through the ice.

Nearing the bottom, a one-sided argument shrilled up the stairs. Shayla took her time squeezing past the line of people in the corridor.

"Do you have the faintest idea who I *am*?" A fleck of spittle flew from Lady bin Mellion's quivering lips as she raged into the intercom.

Shayla recognized the voice of Jevin Colt as he calmly acknowledged that he was well aware that he was addressing Lady Josephine bin Mellion, Governor of the Imperial Inspectorate, and no, she was not entering without the correct pass code. Shayla's own guards struggled to hide smiles as she pushed past.

"Your career is *over*, you impudent little rat, and I will decorate my living room with your upstart *hide!*"

Shayla interrupted the tirade. "No harm will befall a member of my staff simply for executing his duty."

The Governor rounded on Shayla. "By Imperial decree, I am to be given free access *everywhere* on this benighted rock!"

"The arrangements and operational procedures here were laid down by Magister ap Gwynodd's team, and we follow them stringently."

"This is absurd. The man admitted he knew who I was."

"We've had our share of imposters, disguises good enough to fool close colleagues at anything more than a close inspection. The door would not open to the Emperor himself without the necessary codes. And"—she gave the Governor a pitying smile—"I have utmost confidence the Emperor would not feel so slighted by the measures keeping his esteemed guests safely in custody."

Shayla folded her arms and waited until the Governor, her round face hard as brass, yielded her position at the comms screen. She entered the series of code words issued for this visit.

The door swung open and Lady bin Mellion swept through, salvaging a few shreds of regal dignity. Shayla signaled Jevin Colt and the other guards to stay back, deciding to dispense with the usual niceties of introductions, and ushered the inspection team down the stairs.

Confirming that Ivan and Scipio were secured in the interview room as instructed, she paired off members of the inspection team with members of her own guard and ordered that they be given free access throughout the facility. She nodded to one of the remaining guards then turned to the Governor. "After you, My Lady."

"Lady bin Mellion," Ivan drawled as he stood to greet her.

"My Lord." The Governor of the Inspectorate gave a deep bow.

Shayla hid a start of surprise at the warmth in the Governor's voice. Her face settled into a neutral mask as she processed the implications. Why would Julian keep one of Ivan's supporters in such a prominent position of power?

In exile on a remote planet, Shayla was hopelessly out of touch with the court politics of Magentis, but even after these years she recalled something from her brief contact with that world. She smiled inwardly at the memory. Imperial Chief of Security, Chalwen ap Gwynodd, had taught her a hard lesson. The Empire was still fractured. Even now, Ivan's supporters were strong. Peace hung on a knife edge and Emperor Julian's hold on power was precarious. And in between those camps there were many other factions with their own agendas that had grown fat on the old repressive rule. Julian was still following the slow and gentle path to better days.

Another teaching from her Special Service days surfaced. "Keep your friends close," her old instructor once said, "but keep your enemies closer." It was a proverb from pre-history recorded in the Book of Enemies, and it had never seemed more apt. She wondered if a copy of the Firenzi assassin's handbook had ever found its way into Imperial hands.

"What brings you to this sorry part of the universe, Josephine?" Ivan's voice oozed innocence, but the harmonics were off-key. He knew perfectly well about the inspection and could deduce the Governor's role. Even amongst old friends, Ivan was never one for idle small talk, and his innocuous words hid deceit.

Shayla couldn't shake off the nagging feeling from her last visit, but nor could she substantiate it. On her orders, a maintenance team had checked every inch of the prison's pipework and processing machinery and found nothing amiss. The rank odor had disappeared as mysteriously as it had arisen, with no hint as to its source.

"I am here to make sure they are treating you well."

"We have a list of grievances as long as my arm," Scipio growled.

"I'm sure." The warmth Lady bin Mellion held for the Emperor's disgraced uncle clearly didn't extend to his sidekick. Interesting.

"Lord Scipio's many and repeated grievances are all on record for your inspection," Shayla said dryly.

The Governor gave Shayla a quizzical look. The lines of her mouth softened just a fraction.

"You will find that they mostly relate to the legality, or otherwise, of their incarceration."

"Indeed." Where Shayla's tone was merely dry, Lady bin Mellion's could desiccate oceans.

"They have all been forwarded to the Imperial offices for consideration. I remind my guests on each visit that my role as our Emperor's servant is to hold them safe and to ensure their continuing health and comfort, within reasonable constraints."

"Of course."

"I think you'll find that any legitimate grievances within my realm to address have been dealt with appropriately."

A loud gurgle from behind the wall interrupted Shayla's train of thought. Wide-eyed, she motioned to the nearest guard to check out the disturbance.

Before the guard could report back, though, one of Caleb's assistants appeared in the corridor, panting. Through hurried breaths he gasped out, "Come quickly! Down ... prisoners' quarters ..."

Ever mindful of diversions that might cover an escape attempt, Shayla checked that her own guards maintained discipline. She snapped her fingers at two of them waiting outside. "Prisoners stay here. Everyone else out." To a third, she said, "Report to the control level and lock down this base. Signal the main base and the air cover. Albatross protocol."

The guard gulped, "Albatross, aye!" and disappeared.

Shayla pounded down the corridor in the opposite direction and leaped the stairs three at a time. 'Albatross protocol' was code for threat of imminent attack, size and direction unknown. Was she overreacting? Maybe, but better that than fail to act when needed. The full-scale military response she'd just invoked could be stood down when the threat proved to be nothing. And she could easily pass this off as a drill designed to show the Inspectorate their state of readiness.

But half-way down the stairs, Shayla's earlier misgivings resurfaced. Another gurgle and a low, drawn-out rumble echoed through the confines. Someone in the Governor's retinue trailing behind her gagged. The sewer smell was back with a vengeance. She paused at the entrance to the living quarters and called over her shoulders, "Stay there. I want this level cleared and we'll send a team in to check properly."

A thought seeped into her awareness. The timing was precise. She didn't believe in co-incidence.

The main living area was empty. She crossed to the stairs, senses on high alert. Down in the sleeping level she found a guard standing outside the main washroom area. He glanced around as Shayla appeared. "Seems to be a problem in here, somewhere in the maintenance shaft."

A member of the inspection team backed out through the door, holding a cloth over his face.

Another thought hit Shayla like a trip hammer. Neither Ivan nor Scipio had shown any surprise at the disturbance. "Out," she roared. She grabbed the guard and the inspector by their collars and threw them towards the stairs. "Get out!"

Another boiling rumble sounded, but instead of trailing off, the volume grew to be joined by a metallic shriek. Without looking back, Shayla hurdled the stairs, only to be brought up short by a small crowd of ashen-faced onlookers milling around the upper level. With the sound of liquid rushing behind her, she pushed them towards the far stairs. It was like herding cats. Those who could, staggered towards the exit, but others doubled over, retching. The stench was overwhelming. She had to seal the level before the whole base became uninhabitable.

"Milady bin Mellion." Shayla grabbed the Governor by the shoulders and steered her ahead of her. One look in her eyes told Shayla what she needed to know. The Inspection team had played no part in these events. The Governor was as surprised as she was.

After checking that nobody was left behind, Shayla pulled the heavy door closed. Up the stairs. More doors. Her breathing became easier as she shepherded everyone past the interview room. She was thankful to see Ivan and Scipio still there, and her guards still on duty in the corridor.

She caught up with the Governor. "I should ask exactly what you understood by my instructions to clear the level."

"I am not under your orders," Lady bin Mellion gasped. A tinge of color returned to her cheeks. "My inspection team needs to see everything."

"This is a security breach and falls under my jurisdiction."

The Governor opened her mouth, then caught the determined look in Shayla's eye and chose not to press the matter.

"Report back to the control room on the upper level and make sure your team is all accounted for." She signaled to one of the guards to accompany the team.

Shayla beckoned to the guard she'd found on the lower level and spoke in a low murmur. "You were with that inspector the whole time?"

"Yes, My Lady."

"And?"

The guard caught on quickly. "Nobody down there had any opportunity to carry out sabotage. I'd swear to it."

Shayla nodded. "Keep watch here while I consult with the base commander. These two go nowhere until I collect them in person."

Like truthsense, the ability to divine useful meaning from barroom gossip was, at best, a slippery skill. But it was a skill that Jared Tindall had practiced and honed over the years. Truthsense relied on a deep analysis of one person's words, their tone and the stress harmonics that only revealed themselves to the most sensitive ear. Jared had no such sensitivity, indeed was pretty much tone deaf, not helped by overly-close proximity to too many loud explosions. He relied on accumulating snippets of gossip from many sources, mentally filing and correlating to build a balance of probabilities. And the balance of probabilities said that the accounts, growing more elaborate with each passing beer, were at their heart reliable.

"As I understand it, the prison is underground." The vehicle mechanic, who Jared mentally labeled 'Beetroot', expounded well-oiled engineering wisdom. "Prisoners held on the lowest level. Trouble is, all the bleedin' cisterns are set up above."

"Naw!" That was the 'No Man', another of the bar's inner circle, fulfilling his conversational duty that appeared to consist of wearing an incredulous expression and interjecting suitable negatives.

Beetroot nodded sagely. "Designed so they can be more easily pumped out from the surface."

"Never!"

"I say in truth, must be the work of an ivory stylus jockey, 'cos any batbrain can see the risk in *that* thinking. Any failing in the plumbing and ... well, you can guess the rest."

"I hear Her Ladyship was in a right tizzy." That was the political-ly-savvy storesmaster, a short, dumpy woman that Jared labeled 'Slime'. "Move them? Keep them put? Problem is, this whole thing looks like it was rigged to force a move, and she don't know what might happen along the way. Was there an ambush planned? And if so, assassination, or kidnap?"

"Sounds like they got moved, all right."

"Fucking great *Sword* hovering above, no one's going to try nab-bing them, and I guess they figured they'd handle anything else that got chucked at them."

"Must have been worried about someone taking a pop at them, though. Someone nearly got 'Er 'Ighness just couple weeks ago. Could have been a dry run, with benefits."

"She moved quick, though, give her that. No messing around. Maybe fooled 'em by not dicking about setting up security protocols and planning the ass end off the logistics. Just brought in a dozen armored cruisers with enough air cover from that battleship to sink a continent, and whipped them all off on different courses."

"Smart, that. By the time anyone could'a figured out which ship the prisoners were actually on, they were back below ground."

Jared allowed himself a small glow of satisfaction as he sat on the edge of the conversation. Something, at last, had gone right. The Insurrection planners had concocted a high-tech plot to force the evac-uation of the prisoners. He'd had his doubts, but that Firenzi substance his pet engineer had introduced into the plumbing had worked better than he'd dared to imagine. All it needed was a few drops of catalyst to set off the chain reaction, corroding the pipes in a matter of minutes.

That catalyst, and the harmless substance to produce the earlier suspicious smell, had been easy to smuggle in, and that oaf Scipio had played his part well. Imagine him thinking his own supporters were trying to help him. Jared smiled at the thought.

Even that missile attack on Carver, which had so nearly robbed him of his personal victory, had worked out to the best in the end. Moving the prisoners was always going to be risky but the heightened state of security helped. They were now where he wanted them. All he needed now was to get himself and Her Ladyship into place.

Chapter 12

Midday sunlight streamed through high windows of one of the smaller conference rooms in the Governor's Residence. Like most rooms in the formal reception wing, unadorned walls and simple furnishings bespoke modesty. Stained polymer between the upper mullions showed pastoral scenes and tinted the sunlight splashing across the inner wall, the only hint of color in the room.

Alone on one side of the plain wooden table, Shayla faced a small contingent from the Inspectorate led by Lady bin Mellion herself.

"You say that the facility has been regularly inspected and well-maintained," the governor said.

"You have the maintenance records in front of you. There is nothing more for me to say on that point."

"Agreed. The records appear to be thorough and all in order."

Shayla raised an eyebrow.

"Here's the thing, though. We brought down engineers from *Hammer* to carry out an independent inspection."

"I'm sure they will get to the bottom of the matter." Shayla inclined her head. "Of course they will have the full co-operation of my team."

"I've no doubt. But you needn't trouble yourself. They've already made their report."

Shayla's stomach lurched. "How? Who guided them to the prison? It can't be detected from the air, and only a select few of my staff have the directions and navigation markers to find it."

"Your security chief handed over the co-ordinates and switched off the navigational disruption."

"What? I gave no such authorization."

"On *my* instruction. I am the Emperor's personal representative." Lady bin Mellion's voice dripped liquid helium. "Anything less than full and immediate co-operation anywhere on this planet carries a summary charge of treason. I need nothing from you."

Something seemed to have gone wrong with the environmentals in the room. Hot and cold chills chased each other up and down Shayla's back.

Lady bin Mellion leaned back with a serene smile. "Furthermore, I was curious why you would keep such secretive measures in place after they served no further purpose. What were you keen to keep hidden? Caleb, perhaps you would care to summarize the engineer's report."

The smug face in front of Shayla swam in and out of focus. There was nothing to hide, other than the facility itself which could still have a future use. Was there?

Caleb had been avoiding Shayla's eyes throughout the interview. He consulted his notepad, looking like he wished he could crawl into the digital underworld. "The pipework throughout the sanitation system was heavily corroded. Over half the pipes and joints were on the verge of failure. It must have been degrading over the course of years."

"Most likely from the start of your Governorship," Lady bin Mellion added calmly.

"That can't be so! The maintenance team has been in there every six months. There's no way they could have missed something that extensive."

"Given that the maintenance records show an unblemished history, quite in conflict with the indisputable physical evidence, my conclusion is that the records have been systematically falsified over a period of many years."

"That's absurd! I am certain nothing like that could have happened without ..."

"Without your full and express knowledge." Lady bin Mellion smirked. "I couldn't agree more."

For once, Shayla would have welcomed the scrutiny of a truthsenser. She had wondered why an inspection team, intent on uncovering truth, wouldn't include an adept in their ranks. It occurred to her now that they might not welcome truth getting in the way of their conclusions.

She gathered her composure. The timing could not have been co-incidental. She had been trapped somehow but there was nothing she could do about it right here and now. "If you have charges of corruption or other wrongdoing," Shayla said, astonished at the calmness in her own voice, "then I suggest you bring them with requisite evidence to the appropriate jurisdiction."

"This is not a court of law," Lady bin Mellion chided. "Nor are we an inquisition. We collect and report facts. Nothing more."

Shayla stared blankly at her. Where the heck was this leading? "So, what happens now?"

"We continue as planned. Our role is to inspect, and report findings to the Emperor. It is up to him to judge the fitness, or otherwise, of this colony and its leadership."

Brindiss ap Silessi glowered at his desk as he cut the connection to his spycam hidden in the frame of the conference room windows. The faces of the Imperial inspection team faded from the desk's surface, but their words lingered long in his mind.

Although appointed to this post on Eloon, he was first and always the Emperor's servant. So when another Imperial appointee—no, far more than that, the Emperor's *personal* representative—ordered access to the polar base, was he in any position to refuse? He'd agonized over that capitulation long and hard since yesterday, yet even now he could see no reasonable alternative. But he had also assumed his action would be harmless, the findings would surely point to an external act of sabotage.

A deep chill settled on his mind like damp fog when he thought of the trap so neatly sprung on Lady Carver, and he had been an unwitting instrument in arming that trap.

With a shudder, Brin pushed himself away from the desk. He stood and gazed out the windows, reaching inside for the mental armory of calming techniques Sam Kattergee had taught him.

We collect and report facts. The governor's words mocked him. He knew how slippery *facts* could be. Could the inspection team have some-how fabricated evidence and their report?

Deep down, Brin couldn't credit that line of thought. The physical damage was real enough. The inspectors hadn't been here long enough to wreak such serious harm, and he'd ensured Eloon's own engineers accompanied the party from *Hammer of War* summoned by Lady bin Mellion. The evidence was hard to deny.

Yet how could the prison plumbing have fallen into such a state of disrepair? Nagging doubts resurfaced. There was one conclusion that fit all the visible facts. It was a conclusion he sought to avoid, but cold logic forced him to face it. Could Lady Carver really have been complicit in such negligence?

Brin mouthed a silent howl of anguish and ground the heels of his hands into his eyes. The thought violated everything he had come to know about Her Ladyship. And it made no more sense than sabotage on the part of the Inspectorate. What could she have gained by letting prison maintenance lapse? In the overall planetary budget the savings would have been negligible.

Or had his own judgment been so badly compromised already?

The problem seemed beyond his analysis, and that fact alone terrified him more than anything else about this situation.

With a leaden feeling in his gut, Brin turned back to his desk and the reports he'd been reading before eavesdropping on that interview.

His field agents had made progress. They'd identified a suspected Insurrection agent linked to both Corporal Weiler and to Randall. Someone long known to his security forces, along with many other potential or confirmed agents. Someone they'd been content to keep watch over.

Brin glanced once more at the images from her dossier. A small, hatchet-faced woman, her eyes appeared soulless. A killer if ever he saw one. More to the point, she matched the description Lady Carver had given him of one of the Insurrection agents she'd seen questioning Randall.

His agents' reports showed her going about her normal duties on one of the survey teams. She didn't seem to be making any special preparations. Brin suspected she was nothing more than a contact, a link in the chain.

Was this important enough to bring to Her Ladyship's attention? Feeling unusually at a loss, Brin agonized over this question. Even when he had his answer, he found himself questioning his motives. No, he convinced himself, it was not a matter of trust. This piece of intelligence would wait until he had something more substantial to report.

With her back to the room, Shayla gazed out across the grounds towards the Legislature half a mile away. Off to her right, a huddle of low buildings marked the temporary encampment where the Inspectorate was housed. Security fencing and patrolling guards surrounded the camp. Tips of green peeped above the fence, an extravagant gesture of homeliness that Shayla had denied herself all these years. She could so easily have built her Residence inside the walls of the Garden of Hope, but she instinctively shied away from such a gesture. That oasis was held in trust for *everyone* on the planet. Besides the Garden, the Inspector's camp held the only greenery on this stark plateau. *And they had the nerve to accuse us time and again of waste.*

Anger and despair collided. Around the table her inner circle of chiefs made their morning reports, but their words rolled over Shayla like the tide over unmoving rocks. She turned to a sideboard next to the window and began preparing her nargile, a family heirloom salvaged from her late and unlamented mother's ancestral home on Ploorbellin. With only half a mind on the reports, she drew on ancient folklore to prepare a blend of aromatic flavorings reputed to bring calm and perspective.

The inspection continued apace. That the last two days had turned up no new disasters did nothing to dispel Shayla's dark mood or the emptiness that ate at her. She tried to recall the fierce determination that had driven her for so many years through her teens and twenties, the thirst for revenge against the Emperor since the burning of Eloon.

That feeling was a distant memory, eclipsed by the burning passion she'd found since. With the Emperor's decree, she'd found a new lease of life as a builder rather than a destroyer. Now, that future hung in the balance.

She tried once more to find that iron resolve, but there was as yet no focus for her wrath. Nothing to conquer.

She took a few moments to compose her expression before turning back and placing the nargile in the center of the table. Marconi Collsen, head of domestic staff, was reporting on final preparations for the welcome feast that evening. He looked up as she turned, and she caught the slight widening of his eyes before he resumed his report. Maybe she wasn't masking her feelings as well as she imagined.

"Everything is on course." His voice took on a forced gentleness and reassurance. She detected undertones of worry, but nothing in his harmonics betrayed any falsehood. Things really were going to plan. At last.

Shayla squeezed her eyes shut. "I'm sorry, folks. I know I need to be the strong one here. Protocol demands it. But if I can't let myself go just a little bit in this room, then ..." She let the thought dangle. "I don't need to remind you how much this world means to me. To us."

She opened her eyes, fearful of what she might see in their faces. Brin's flint expression had softened. He nodded thoughtfully. Even the waspish Felicity touched a discreet finger to the corner of her eye.

It was left to the effusive Frank to break the silence. "Your openness commends you." The uncharacteristic simplicity spoke volumes.

A commotion outside the door broke the moment.

"Dammit, Max, I must see her."

A muttered response.

"No, it can't fucking wait!"

Shayla's heart sank. Whatever it was, she'd probably better hear it sooner than later. She opened the door and recognized an engineer, one of Frank's chiefs, a gifted woman and someone Shayla trusted completely. "It's okay, Max," she said to the guard outside. "Come in, Cally."

Chief engineer Cally Cordero peered around the door and took in the circle of questioning faces. She grimaced then shrugged, and crossed the threshold cradling a foot long cylinder sealed in clear plastic. She laid the package on the table, careful not to scratch the polished surface.

Shayla peered close. The metal cylinder bulged in the middle, pale blue powder coating glowed in the morning light. At one end, though, the coating became dull and patchy, and the metal looked paper thin. Even as Cally set it down, a few fingernail-sized flakes fell from the fragile rim.

"This valve is brand new," she announced.

Shayla looked up, startled. Cally stepped back and folded her arms. Smug satisfaction battled for face time with baffled fury.

After a closer examination, Shayla shook her head. "The inside here has been corroded through." She turned the piece of machinery towards her and squinted down its bore. More pieces flaked off under her touch. "This can't be."

"The old valve was on our 'when you get a chance' list, nothing urgent, but slated for replacement next time anyone happened to be working on that section of the plant."

"So I'm guessing the records say it was replaced. How can you be certain this really is new?"

Cally pointed to a serial number embossed on the casing. "This shows it was manufactured only last year. There's no disputing that evidence. Plus"—she looked Shayla squarely in the eye—"it just happened that I replaced this part myself."

The implications caught up with Shayla's reeling mind. With startling clarity the pieces of the puzzle fell into place. She felt behind her for the arm of the nearest chair, and sat heavily. How could she have missed this?

Frank Wu gasped. "How the heck can anything corrode that quickly?"

With a dismissive wave of her hand, Shayla muttered, "Sabotage."

"What?"

"How?"

"Someone introduced a hyper-corrosive agent into the system. Most likely during the overhaul I ordered." She barked a short, bitter laugh.

Cally frowned. "Something like that would be dangerous. How did it get smuggled in? And how the heck did the timing work out so perfectly? Or was that just luck?"

"I've used something like this myself, out in the field." Shayla planted her elbows on the table and cradled her face in her hands. "It's a two-stage process, something the materials scientists are brilliant at. The primary agent is inert and perfectly safe until it's triggered by a catalyst. You can plant bucketloads of it days ahead, give it time to work its way right through the system, then when you want fireworks you just add a small trace of catalyst and, poof!" She threw her arms up wide.

"The inspectors?"

"No. This kind of thing is Firenzi science, not Imperial." She thought hard, and eyed Felicity carefully. If anyone was going to have problems with her next instructions it would be honest Felicity.

"Although I don't believe the Inspectorate would stoop to outright sabotage, do not make the mistake of thinking them to be our friends." She turned to Cally. "Image this, date it, take samples from the inside for analysis—I can maybe dig up some clues on what chemical signals to test for that would nail it. Then lodge it in a vault for future reference. Brin and Felicity will sign and witness the records. Let's keep this item of evidence safe. I wouldn't want it to ... vanish."

"And the inspection team's own investigation into this matter?" As expected, Felicity had questions. "Won't this be considered withholding evidence?"

Shayla allowed herself a smug moment. "Their inspectors already had access to this evidence, and missed it. Remember, their engineers had already submitted their completed *independent* report before I was even notified they were on the ground." Her tone turned harsh. "We owe them *nothing*."

When Felicity tightened her lips to hide an unaccustomed smile, Shayla knew she was on-side. She would fight this argument to the end and mop the floor with the scalps of whatever lawyers Lady bin Mellion brought to the fray.

"Friends, let's enjoy this evening. At this stage of the game we have the Inspectorate right where we want them."

———————•◆•———————

"Does the fish not agree with you, My Lady?"

Lady Josephine bin Mellion had only eaten a few mouthfuls, and toyed with the remains in their rich golden sauce while surveying the room with a deep scowl.

Shayla followed her gaze, trying to second-guess what had earned the Imperial Governor's displeasure this time. The reception hall in the Governor's Residence had been cleared of its temporary occupants and returned to its proper use. Like the rest of the Residence and other buildings in the complex that served as Eloon's capital, it was sparse to the point of asceticism. As befitted a fledgling colony on a no-frills budget, no hint of unseemly luxury adorned its walls. The only perma-nent decoration was a portrait of the Emperor, frowning down at the assembled guests from high over her shoulder.

Shayla and Lady bin Mellion sat at the center of the long high table, flanked by their respective chiefs of staff. In front of them, a less formal arrangement of round tables seated the rest of the inspection team, their guards, and an equal number of civilian and military staff from Shayla's entourage. At Shayla's insistence the seating plan mingled people from both sides and all ranks.

While the cavernous hall itself was bare—stone walls, open rafters above, and plain glass in the windows—the austere setting accentuated the splendor of the diners themselves and the tables they sat at. Dress uniforms vied with civilian evening attire, and both challenged spotless linen, crystal, silverware, and sumptuous bouquets of cut flowers.

It seemed unlikely that this temporary display of extravagance could be a point of contention. Everything had been dressed according to strictest protocol for such an occasion. The Governor could surely expect no less.

This banquet was meant to be a welcome and a chance to meet, but after a week of business, the meeting had already happened and the welcome was already thin.

Maybe the Imperial Governor's scowl was aimed at the rising buzz of conversation that had finally dispelled the somber mood. Anticipating the mutual hostility, Shayla had instructed Marconi Collsen to freely plunder her own cellar to oil reluctant tongues, and hand-picked especially congenial staffers to ease the mood at each table. Her plans were starting to bear fruit, which was unlikely to please Milady.

But Lady bin Mellion made no comment on the growing conviviality, and returned her attention to her plate. "Yellow Snapper Margerite." She sniffed.

"Is it not to your liking? I was led to believe you'd requested this dish specifically." Shayla set aside her fork, her own appetite suddenly gone.

"It is a rare delicacy. My chef recommended it. I was curious to see what this planet could offer that was superior to home-produced fare."

There it was again. The blatant slight so clearly implied but not quite uttered. This woman was a master at delivering diplomatic offence. "We only recently discovered surviving stands of the local Eloon sumac. It was suggested fitting that we prepare as much of this meal as possible with local ingredients."

"I understand that the local spice has some unique qualities that used to make it highly prized."

"That is so." Shayla struggled to keep her tone conversational. "A combination of minerals in the soil and water I believe. There are many similar varieties of spice on other worlds, but nothing else quite matches ours for its richness."

"I'm surprised to find the Emperor's funds spent on such extravagance."

Shayla's right hand itched to show this haughty intruder the edge of her shimmerblade. All this political maneuvering made her sick. She was damned if she failed to honor her Imperial guests with sumptuous hospitality, yet, it appeared, equally damned if she did. She longed for the certainty of a straight fight.

"Think on it as an exploration of a possible source of revenue." Frank Wu's cheerful voice carried from his station further along the table. "If this rediscovered variety meets the approval of the educated palates we are graced with tonight, I'm sure we can establish an export market to our civilized brethren. As you say, it is indeed a luxury commodity."

"I must say, this *is* an excellent dish," Caleb ap Scoth added from his side of the table. He caught Lady bin Mellion's glare and returned his attention single-mindedly to demolishing the last of his fish.

———————

Shayla threw off her ceremonial robe, leaving it where it fell, and loosened the fastenings of her stifling dress tunic. She flopped back on her bed, arms outstretched. "Is there nothing we can do to please these damnable inspectors?"

"Granting Freeworld status is an uncommon event, and not to be taken lightly." Simone scooped up the discarded robe in a graceful movement and draped it on a hanger. "I've been searching the histories for accounts of past inspections. It seems to me they are always intentionally harsh, especially those early on the road."

"Harsh I can live with, but I was expecting the process at least to be fair."

"How do we judge fairness? They have their own protocols to follow, intended to ferret out weaknesses. Who can guess how they process what they find to arrive at a conclusion?"

"Appointing auditor Silvani was no random act, I'm sure of that. They mean us to fail. Why would Julian set us up like that?"

"Who ever asked a sword how it feels to be tempered?"

Shayla raised her head and squinted at her assistant. Simone gazed calmly back. Shayla growled, "Hit me with the philosophy lesson when it's less likely to end in bloodshed."

The corners of Simone's lips quirked upwards. "All I'm saying is that maybe there's nothing ominous to be read into their actions."

———————

Shayla lay awake. The first tinge of dawn edged the window frame by her bed. She would usually be rising soon anyway, but not quite yet. She had been awakened early by a barely audible disturbance in the passageway outside.

Words beyond the closed door hovered on the edge of meaning.

She slowed her breathing and closed her eyes, forsaking other senses and pouring all her awareness into the world of sound.

"Let me speak to her first." That was Simone's voice. Low but urgent.

The reply was too faint to make out.

"Brin, you know full well she either comes with you willingly, or not at all." Clearer this time, no attempt at concealment.

Something's happened. Why would I be reluctant to accompany my own head of security?

Possibilities raced through Shayla's mind while she reached for her knife and needle gun. Was there some treachery afoot? Brin was an Imperial appointee, chosen by Chalwen ap Gwynodd in person and loyal to the Emperor. But he was also in the early stages of a mind-rotting sickness. Sam Kattergee had warned them both to be alert to signs of lapses of judgment. She dismissed the thought. Sam was monitoring Brin closely and wouldn't let him continue his duties if there was any question of his abilities.

"I don't care how many guards you have with you, or how many snipers surround the building with every window in their sights, you cannot hope to take her by force without bloodshed."

Loyal to the Emperor, of course, not to me. Shayla realized that Simone was speaking as much for Shayla's benefit as to the guards outside. *She knew I would be roused and listening. She knows me too well.*

Shayla rose and pulled a gown from the closet. She was not one for running. If there was trouble, best to meet it head on.

She threw open the doors. Brin met her gaze, unflinching. The posse of guards behind him, hardened soldiers all and each one known to Shayla, shrank back visibly despite being at the safe end of leveled weapons. That reaction, the fear in their eyes, distressed her more than anything, but she sensed this was not the time for weakness.

"Well?" she demanded. "What brings you mob-handed to my door at this hour? Is this treachery?"

It was left to Simone to answer. "My Lady, we are in serious trouble."

We?

"The Inspectorate ..."

Shayla's heart faltered. "What?"

"They have all fallen gravely ill."

"All of them? How can that be?"

Worry lines creased Simone's pale forehead. "It sounds unlikely, impossible in fact, but the medic from *Hammer of War* has examined them and declared poisoning."

Shayla's mind failed her for a few seconds, weighed down by a galaxy of burning questions. "Wait. *Hammer's* medic has seen them already? When did this happen? And why was I not informed immediately?"

"The alarm was raised over four hours ago," said Brin.

"Brin has spent the time trying to decide how to deal with you."

"What do you mean?"

Simone hesitated, chewing her lip. Without meeting Shayla's eyes she said, "It seems that you are the chief suspect."

Chapter 13

The detention block behind the planetary Legislature had seen little use in the last few years. Its construction, not a high priority in the early days of the settlement, had been felt a grudging but necessary display of civilization and the rule of law. In reality, justice out on the working frontier was still rough and quick. Minor offences were dealt with by fines, loss of privileges, or a few nights in the local slammer overseen by camp guards. Serious infractions tended to be dealt with before the authorities had a chance to intervene. The resulting informal justice was probably as equitable as anywhere in human space.

This sub-basement contained a handful of solitary cells and a secure entrance, intended for any dangerous miscreants who survived to face the official judicial system, which mostly consisted of an up close and personal interview with Shayla.

A whiff of new paint still permeated this level. The universal prison smell of sweat and urine and, for reasons Shayla had never fathomed, boiled cabbage had not had a chance to establish itself.

Beige painted walls stared back at Shayla as the door banged shut behind her. She had at least been allowed to retain her own clothing, after a thorough search for her inevitable armory of silent weapons.

Not that she had any thoughts of fighting. Brin had surrounded her with men and women from her own guard. People she knew. People she trusted with her life. If any one of them had raised a weapon to her in an act of treachery she would have killed them on reflex. She would have mourned a friendship lost, but that would have come later. In the moment she would have not hesitated. But they surrounded her in the course of their duty. She couldn't have harmed them even if doing so allowed her to escape. She could sense the reluctance with which they escorted her from her suite. There was no treachery there, just fear, incomprehension, and deep sadness.

Once the moment to act had slipped by, her spirit left her. Her whole life since the burning of Eloon had been one long battle, but most especially the last seven years when she not only had something to fight for, but more importantly something to lose. The moment she abandoned the fight, the enormity of her situation overwhelmed her and, like the spent shell of a firework, the fire that had driven her through those decades now fled.

It took all her remaining strength to walk the halls and stairs of her Residence with her head high, without betraying the emptiness inside.

She hugged her cloak tight around her, but the chill in her core had nothing to do with the air. Her mind stayed as blank as the wall opposite. What had happened couldn't possibly have happened. All the inspection team fallen ill.

No, not all. One of them had missed the banquet, taken ill with a mundane infection—a not unusual occurrence when exposed to a new planet's biosphere—and was otherwise unharmed. Little details like that made the truth all the more difficult to deny. The banquet. Something must have happened at the banquet. And yet her mind balked at the sheer impossibility of it. *None* of her own staff had been affected. How could poisoning, where every dish, every drink, had been served from common platters and carafes be targeted so precisely? Nothing like that could have been planned without massive collusion amongst her staff, and that could never have happened without her knowledge.

Despair gripped her, cold and raw. Was that it? However it had really been engineered, it would be obvious to all outside observers that she *had to have known*, had to have approved.

It was the same ploy as the prison sabotage. Set her up with an act that, to all appearances, could not have happened without her knowledge. Except this time she was in no position to fight back.

———•◆•———

Brindis ap Silessi paced the halls of the temporary residence where the Inspectorate lay. Literally.

During the month prior to their arrival, Frank Wu had diverted precious resources to building a compound within sight of the Governor's residence. Brin knew they trod an impossible balance between insulting the Imperial representatives with less than stellar hospitality, and objectionable excess. In Brin's opinion, Frank and Shirley had done a fine job. Any complaints of erring on the frugal side were easily met by the observation that this was nevertheless the most luxurious place on the planet.

The standard prefabricated sheds used everywhere on the planet were recognizable here only by their outline and dimensions. Exteriors were decorated and lines softened by stands of nearly-mature trees borrowed from the planting projects. Windowless interiors were made homely by soft furnishings, carpeting, rugs and drapes. The air was soft and scented.

Now, the filtered air reeked of sickness.

In each room he passed a person lay dying, but the place was hardly a chapel of rest. The entire medical team from *Hammer of War* had landed, bringing with them mountains of equipment. Even now, a muted roar vibrated through the walls signaling the arrival of yet another transport. In addition to the naval medics, Brin had issued a planetwide summons to anyone with medical expertise.

He'd also recalled as many of his own agents and regular guards as he could spare from the field. The place was crawling with marines and spooks from the Imperial navy, accepted grudgingly in the name of cooperation, but none of them went anywhere without an escort from his own ranks. There was practical sense in the Imperial presence too. It had taken all his stoic reserve to mask his pain at placing Her Ladyship under arrest, but in a murky business like this perception was everything, and the last thing he needed was any pretext for the darker Imperial factions to cry 'cover up!' Whatever his team unearthed, they saw too, visibly and on record.

If he'd had the slightest reason to suspect Her Ladyship's involvement he'd have been the first to lock her up and throw away the key, but logic had sneered at that suggestion. He'd spent too long observing her at work. She wanted to *pass* the inspection, not derail it, and they were now plunging off a cliff edge, everything they'd achieved under threat. She had no reason to wish the Inspectorate harm, no matter how scathing they'd been.

Yet the Imperials insisted in pursuing their one and only suspect, and for all the granite obduracy he displayed to the world he knew when to bend with the wind. Besides, their single-minded insistence reeked.

There was more at play here and the best way to unearth it was to appear to go along with this madness. For now.

Raised voices echoed down the hall, cutting through the bustle. Brin hastened his steps, signaling two of the Residence guards to follow.

In the largest suite at the far end, where Lady Josephine bin Mellion resided, the normally placid Sam Kattergee looked fit to bust. Sam, Lady Carver's senior medic, faced off against the chief medical officer from *Hammer of War*, a tall, russet-skinned woman with waist-length hair severely tied back into a ponytail.

In between them, the Governor of the Inspectorate sat upright in bed. By all reports she'd been least affected by the illness. Her eyes peered out from folds of waxy skin, but they followed the heated exchange with bird-like alertness.

"They cannot be moved," Sam insisted. His gray hair and abnormally pale eyes and complexion gave him an ethereal appearance, as if death had already made its presence felt.

The Imperial medic blurted, "You expect me to leave them here, among their would-be killers?"

"None of them are fit for any kind of transport, and the facilities down here now surpass anything you have on board."

"My orders are to take them back to *Hammer*."

"That would kill some of them at least. Do you want that on your conscience?"

"Our fate lies on the Governor's conscience," Lady Josephine croaked. She coughed and sipped a glass of water. "Whatever happens to us lies at her door."

That was too much for Brin to ignore. "If you insist on laying that burden on her, then you must remain within the Governor's purview."

Lady bin Mellion looked shocked. "I'm in agreement with the good doctor here. Why should we remain here after what's happened?"

"And exactly what do you suppose *has* happened?"

"A blatant assassination attempt."

"Maybe, maybe not. There are other explanations, and others who could be to blame. She willingly allowed herself to be taken into custody. Believe me, despite all the weapons pointed at her that was *never* a foregone conclusion." Against all protocols, Brin overrode the Governor's enfeebled attempts to interrupt. For an instant his rational

mind questioned his motivation, but was quickly swamped by the imme-
diacy of the moment. "Your egocentric view of the universe has blinded
you. What makes you assume *you* are the ultimate target? Have you
considered that your deaths laid at Lady Carver's door might be someone else's intent? That moving you from here could be exactly what was
planned, and that it might only hasten your end?"

"Magister ap Silessi—"

Brin silenced the doctor with an upraised finger and a ferocious
glare. "Magister," he hissed, "is an Imperial mode of address. This is a
Freeworld and neither you nor your Inspectorate have jurisdiction here.
You may address me as 'Sir' or as 'Acting Governor.' "

"But—"

"Lady Carver is currently indisposed and in no position to discharge
her duties." Brin's gut twisted as he spoke. This was the final step he'd
been trying to avoid, but he felt he had no choice. Once spoken in a
moment of precipitous haste, the words could not be recalled. "It is clear
we are dealing with a security emergency, and planetside operations
therefore fall to me. That being the case, and according to standing
orders of succession in the Trown Plains Accord, I am assuming the role
of Acting Governor in Governor Carver's *temporary* absence, or until I
am instructed otherwise by the Emperor himself."

Governor Josephine bin Mellion's protests spluttered into silence.
With a shaking hand she brought the glass to her lips once more. At last
she grimaced and whispered, "So be it."

Once more out in the hall, Brin summoned the two doctors close.
First, he addressed the Imperial medic. "What is your assessment of
these people's condition?" A warning glance at Sam calmed his evident
frustration.

"Slow but steady tissue degradation," she said. "Nothing we've
tried seems able to stop it. At this rate the first will die of organ failure
within days."

"And what progress towards identifying the cause?"

"Screening for known toxins and biological agents. Nothing so far."

"And meantime, what treatment have you offered?"

"Against an unknown agent?" The medical officer's tone dripped
contempt at the question. "We've managed to slow the spread in three

control patients by slowing their metabolism. The spread does appear to be mediated through the bloodstream."

"So, in summary, you've reached the extent of your ability to help." Brin turned. "Well, Doctor Kattergee?"

"All the aforementioned are reasonable lines of inquiry," Sam said, "but pointless if the patients don't survive long enough for a cure."

"We're doing everything we can," the medic protested. "Their fate is outside our control."

Sam shook his head. "Your medical science is somewhat less than current. You know that perfectly well."

"We're working with what we have available."

"I may be long retired, Acting Governor"—Brin raised his estimation of Sam a notch or two for catching on to the shift in power that had occurred back in the Inspector's room—"but I still have contacts in the military. I'm sure I can obtain assistance."

"But—"

Brin silenced the medic again with an upraised hand. He knew Sam's background and battled a deep unease himself at the thought of inviting any kind of intervention from the Firenzi. He sympathized with the Imperial medical officer's instinctive rejection of the very notion, but, as he'd reminded her only minutes ago, this was a Freeworld. Yes, still under Imperial protection, but technically neutral. They had as much right to ask for assistance from other quarters as they had accepting the current Imperial aid.

"What do you recommend?" The question was pointedly addressed to Sam.

"At the very least, we must obtain stocks of a proper metabolic retardant, *Firenzi* military grade." He glared at the Imperial doctor. "We can put these people into a near stasis and stop the spread of damage while we isolate the active agent."

"Do what you can. I expect the Imperial medical staff to continue to assist you in every possible way." Without waiting for a response, Brin turned on his heel and stepped smartly down the hall.

———◆◆———

As soon as they were airborne, Jared leaped from his seat and attacked the bindings on the crates Wolf had loaded. 'Machine parts' and 'sample boxes' the labels read. The larger crate broke open to reveal a compact single-seat airbike.

Most airbikes provided some sort of protection to the rider—a forward-facing canopy for example, overhead roll bars, maybe even a surrounding crash cage. This machine was little more than a hard saddle mounted on the power and grav unit. No sops to creature comforts and, more to the point, no extraneous bulk. Bare utility and able to be handled in tight spaces.

To Jared, it was a thing of beauty. He felt like hugging Wolf. A rare impulse, and one likely to prove fatal. He contented himself with a flicker of a smile and a curt nod. She responded in kind.

He turned his attention to the smaller crate, unpacking and inspecting the catalogue of supplies he'd ordered long ago in preparation for this mission. Each item he checked over carefully and laid out on the deck. From the pilot's seat Wolf watched him out of the corner of her eye. There was no question of mistrust here. As an experienced operative herself, Wolf would know perfectly well that no one went out into the field without checking their equipment personally. And mistakes and misunderstandings did happen, even to the best.

Where Jared was going, mistakes and misunderstandings came with unwelcome consequences, and this was a hurried departure following the news from the planet's capital. Their sources of intelligence on the ground informed Wolf that all non-essential troops had been recalled to Torremis. Keeping a remote watch on a disused ventilation shaft did not count amongst the essentials. It was too good an opportunity to miss.

He quashed a pang of regret that Her Ladyship might be out of the picture for good. His trap had been designed to eliminate her as well as the two noble prisoners. He drew little comfort from Wolf's observation that pinning the blame on the Emperor became more credible if Carver wasn't targeted at the same time. She was nothing more than the most obvious catalyst that would bring all the right ingredients together, but killing her would have been the icing on the cake. The mission, the bigger picture, came first. He almost convinced himself of that.

Satisfied, he packed everything away into panniers straddling the airbike fore and aft of the saddle.

As they approached the ventilation shaft, too many thousands of feet up to cause alarm or arouse suspicions, Jared manhandled the laden bike to the transport's cargo hatch. Wolf left the piloting in the hands of the navigation system and came aft to help him.

Jared mounted the bike. Wolf clipped on a safety line and slapped the hatch open, overriding the altitude alarm. She turned to Jared, expressionless. "Luck."

"Shouldn't need it."

With a shake of her head, Wolf grunted and heaved the bike out the hatch.

Chapter 14

The slipstream slammed into Jared, a living howling demon. He'd braced for it and hung on with both hands, knees gripping the power unit casing beneath him, but still he feared he'd be swept off.

He plunged a mile and a half groundwards on a craft with the aerodynamics of a housebrick. This was a maneuver well outside the recommendations of the owner's manual. He ignored the vertiginous gyrations of the dusk-lit horizon and focused on the makeshift altimeter strapped to the handlebars. Airbikes were not aircraft. They usually had an operating height of a foot to a few tens of feet. Drops like this were not part of their normal repertoire.

At the last moment, Jared eased the grav unit on a fraction to steady his wayward motion and orientation, then more fully to cushion his descent. The ground rushed towards him in the gloom then steadied a few feet beneath him.

Jared released his pent-up breath and checked his bearings. He was close. Little chance of being tracked by routine ground surveillance.

He stopped a little way outside the guarded perimeter, checking as he went that there were no signs of human occupation. Highly unlikely—they'd set an automated alarm and left the site undisturbed hoping to catch whoever had dumped Randall's body should they return to the scene—but paranoia ruled in this game.

Donning his enhanced visor, Jared scanned the wavelengths and found the milky veil of radiation that bathed the circle. The alarm was active. He worked his way around the perimeter with Wolf's scrambler unit. She'd explained the principles behind it. Nothing subtle, just a brute force temporary freezing of the alarm's sensor circuitry. Not useful against the more intelligent security systems, but adequate for non-military building alarms or simple quick-and-easy mobile systems like this.

With the alarm system blinded, Jared hurried to the center and inspected the covering the troops had placed over the top of the shaft.

He worked his fingers under an edge and lifted. As he thought, they'd used a rigid but lightweight polymer sheet, something the two of them could maneuver easily into place, weighted down with a few rocks. Jared slid it to one side, then collected the bike. He flew down the shaft and into the top of the stairwell.

Returning to the surface on foot, he replaced the sheet and wormed his way into the slipway of the original entrance. He pulled the tarpaulin back as best he could. It wouldn't be perfect. If anyone visited in person the disturbance could, perhaps, be dismissed as the result of a gust of wind. But the moment they checked the perimeter alarm, which Jared had no means of safely arming from within its circle of influence, the game would be up. Leaving the alarm disabled was a risk, and one which he and Wolf had debated long and hard.

With all the upset over the Imperial inspectors and Her Ladyship's arrest, the planet's forces had their hands full. No one was likely to return to this site in person—the only way they'd discover the tampering—so that risk was outweighed by the intense scrutiny of all air traffic. Upsides and downsides.

Even though the airbike was compact, riding it down the stairwell was a tight squeeze. The flights zig-zagged down with too small a gap to allow a straight drop down the middle. At first Jared followed the path of each flight, but soon smoothed that out into a carefully-judged spiral. Where the stairs had collapsed near the bottom, the going was easier.

Out in the transit tunnel, Jared felt the same rush of excitement as when he'd brought the ancient works truck to life. Once again, he gave a whoop and opened the throttle.

Miles sped by. This time, when he came to water there was no need to slow down. In minutes he covered the miles that had taken so long in the car. More miles followed. The only way to gauge the depth was by the headroom above as he skimmed the water's surface. He would never have made it in the truck, that much was obvious, but he'd been right to judge that he was close to the far side. Inch by inch the depth lessened again until he was once more in dry tunnel.

Eventually Jared slowed and check his navigator. He'd already passed a shaft off to one side, blocked like the one he'd descended, and openings to another network of workshops and garages, but that was near the coast. His target, if the old charts could be trusted, lay hidden within the new prison's perimeter fence.

Whether or not it was useable was another matter.

His pace slowed to a crawl. At last the shaft came into view. Jared gaped and tried to stem the elation that washed through him. The mouth was clear.

He dismounted and took a powerful glowtube with him. Resisting the urge to rush into the shaft mouth, Jared went a step at a time, inspecting floor, walls, and especially the ceiling for signs of decay. Everything looked as solid as the rest of the tunnel network. Like Randall had said, those old folks had certainly known about tunneling. The floor lay under a thick layer of dust. That suggested that there was, or had for a long time been, an opening to the air outside. He stepped into the foot of the shaft proper and shone the glowtube up. The shaft vanished into the distance as far as the light could show.

This was going to be easier than he'd dared hope. Jared mounted the airbike and steered it through the opening. He drifted upwards. Smooth walls, almost featureless, gave little sense of movement.

A shadow above startled Jared. He halted the bike's upward progress and shone the glowtube up. A bitter laugh escaped through clenched teeth. It was never going to be quite *that* easy. If this shaft followed the same pattern as the one across the water he must be about half-way up. His path was blocked by a steel grating and the still blades of a massive fan.

Thank Space for standardized designs. Back down at the transit tunnel there was a stairwell just like the shaft he'd descended. The difference was that the ancient stairs were intact all the way down. Conditions here hadn't led to the same centuries-long decay. The machinery space alongside the ventilation fan was free of debris, and a passageway, barely wide enough for the bike, led back into the main shaft above the fan. From there, the ascent was easy.

Jared parked the bike in the top passage that must once have led to a maintenance entrance on the surface.

Randall's charts, from the binder that Walrus had retrieved, showed the top of the shaft had long ago been sealed. A small settlement once lay above, with generations of buildings built, leveled, and rebuilt on top. Only ruins remained by the time the Imperial navy came to burn the planet. If this region had felt the full force of Imperial wrath, then emerging at the top would have meant tunneling through a dense layer of vitrified rock, but there had been nothing here to warrant more than a light toasting.

Beyond that, Jared had no idea what to expect.

He was not surprised to find the far end of the entrance passage closed off. A steel door barred his way. The question was, what lay beyond? Was there any point trying to breach the door?

Jared rummaged in one of his panniers and returned with a scanning device the size of a small glowtube. He donned his visor and activated the multi-frequency probe. Patiently he swept the device back and forth, adjusting frequency and depth of focus to probe the volume behind the door. The picture built up gradually. The thickness of the door showed clearly, the boundary between metal and whatever lay beyond sent back a bright echo. Past that, a murky gray shot through with sharper boundaries as far as he could see. No dark cavities. The way beyond was filled in solid.

The road between the Residence and the planetary Legislature had never seemed to stretch so long. Brin's footsteps dragged through treacle, his subconscious delaying the coming interview even though he knew she must hear this from his own lips.

For someone accustomed to working in the shadows, assuming control of the planet was an outrageously risky step. Not one he could undo if he'd miscalculated, and one that would be seen from all quarters as an outright show of no confidence in Lady Carver, maybe even an affirmation of her guilt. How would she react to this betrayal on top of all his recent failings? Even unarmed she was deadly. Maybe a swift snap of the neck would put him out of his misery.

He berated himself for this self-indulgent weakness as he rounded the corner of the legislative building and approached the detention block behind. He squared his shoulders and forced a spring into his step. What was done was water under the bridge and he'd have to make the best of the course he'd chosen.

A nod to the guards in the entrance lobby, he passed through pairs of sliding steel grilles, each one slamming shut behind him before the next would open. Along a brightly-lit hall and down stairs to the main detention area. Empty holding cells radiated off from the main guardhouse.

Brin paused to look around. Were jails a sign of civilization, he wondered. Historians talked about semi-mythical primitive cultures, people who lived close to the land gathering just enough to sustain themselves. There was never any mention of police, of security, of prisons in those societies. It seemed the closest those primitive peoples ever came to incarceration was to tie prisoners up while they decided what to do with them. His gaze roved across bare cages, almost unused since the building's construction, and wondered just how far civilization had come. If prison institutions were a hallmark of a civil society then Eloon still had a long way to go, but he would be happy to see this building crumble unused.

As he rounded a corner and started down a steep flight of stairs a servant from the Governor's household passed him. A twinge of sadness washed over him at the sight of a barely-touched tray of food in the servant's hands.

"How is she?" Brin whispered.

The servant paused on the stairs, started to say something banal then thought better of it. Most members of staff had worked here for years, many from the days the first transports had landed. This proud and elderly Firenzi was one such. "The helplessness weighs on her," he said, before bowing his head and continuing on his way.

And I'm about to add to it, Brin thought. Down the last flight of stairs to the sub-basement that passed for the planet's maximum security prison, excepting the accommodation for the Emperor's two special guests of course, Brin passed through the last ring of security. Shayla Carver was immaterial, he reminded himself. Even the success of this planet's mission, however laudable, was not his primary goal. His role as security chief was little more than a cover. He had to remember that.

The sight of her tested his new-found resolve. Sunken eyes turned towards him as he entered the cell. She'd aged a decade in the past day. She stood, but that simple act clearly took its toll.

He hoped his shock didn't reflect in his eyes and he steeled himself once more. He had a duty to perform. He'd been placed here to ensure the safekeeping of the Emperor's prisoners. That was all that mattered.

Not Eloon, not the displaced population rebuilding it into a habitable world. They paled beside the billions of lives in the balance if anything happened to either of those dangerous noblemen. Not for the first time Brin wondered just how long the Emperor could play his balancing act. He had the tiger by the tail, and sooner or later the tiger would turn. In the bloodbath that would undoubtedly follow, who would notice if this place returned to ashes? And, when all was said and done, what allegiance did he owe this haggard woman standing in front of him, looking at once frail and yet cored with tungsten carbide?

"How are the inspectors, and how goes the search for a cure?"

The firmness in her voice, so at odds with her appearance, startled him, and right there, that was his answer. No thought for herself. No questions about moves to free her. Her first concern was for the stricken, for the health of those who'd tormented her.

"All the measures I last spoke of are in place." Brin tried to match Lady Carver's resolve. "The entire Residence has been locked down. The kitchens, everything used in the preparation of the feast, all scraps left over, are being examined for any hint of how a poison could be dealt. All members of staff and all recent visitors are being interviewed, thoroughly."

"Have you summoned a truthsenser?" The question was straightforward, but Brin caught the edge in her tone. He sympathized. He had his own misgivings about the truthsense adepts. Some truths should never see the light of day.

"I have made a request. Whether or not it's granted will itself reveal some clues about who's behind this."

"You mean someone might not be too keen for your investigations to succeed."

"The Imperial party is trying to get the Inspectorate moved to *Hammer of War*. I've so far blocked those attempts. I feel they can be cared for as well here as anywhere, and I want to ensure no further harm befalls them."

Lady Carver nodded, her expression grim. "I wish you luck in that aim."

"There's more." He hesitated, then the words tumbled out in a rush. "My Lady, I've declared myself Acting Governor for the duration of this emergency."

"Thank you, Brin," she whispered.

Brin searched her face for any hint of sarcasm. All he saw was a clear brow, and a face at peace such as he'd not seen in years. "You *approve* of this?"

"What use am I here? My visitors are numbered in single figures. My communications with the outside world are even more restricted. I cannot govern from here, and now more than ever this planet needs a strong Governor."

Red rage blinded him. "I agonized over this act and spent the last two days seeking ways to avoid it. I felt it a betrayal. If this is what you wanted all along, then why put me through that when you could have simply decreed it so?"

A small shake of the head. "No, Brin, that is one thing I couldn't do."

"Did you think me not up to the task?" The rage intensified. "Did you think I might refuse the burden?"

"That's not it. It *is* a heavy burden, I understand that, and the fact that you talk of it in those terms shows that you're the right person. Yes, I would be reluctant to lay this on you with everything else you have to deal with, but"—her tone hardened to tempered steel—"I would have had no hesitation in doing the right thing for Eloon."

That was a relief. "But, if not that ..."

"I *cannot* appoint a Governor, nor can I relinquish the duty. Only the Emperor has that power."

Light dawned. "You needed me to *assume* control. You needed me to declare you unfit, and to invoke security protocols."

"And you had to be seen to be your own man in doing so. Not my puppet." A sad smile. "What took you so long?"

<hr />

Once Brin had left her cell, Shayla sat back on the bench that served as a bed. The thin mattress barely softened the steel underneath. She closed her eyes and felt all life drain from her.

Even now, she'd not noticed the tension in her muscles until it finally washed away. With the last dregs of strength she lay down in little more than a controlled fall.

Brin had taken over the mantle of governorship, a burden she'd not wish on anyone right now, but he'd taken it of his own free will.

He'd realized what she couldn't voice—that she was a spent force. There was nothing she could do for her planet, her people, from here. He talked about it as a temporary measure—*for the duration of this emergency*—but he must know as well as she did that there would be no returning from this.

Someone back on Magentis, someone with a very long reach, had engineered an impossible crime and laid it at her door. Who knew what other damning evidence had been stacked against her?

As she settled herself more comfortably on the hard bed, she tried to imagine what would become of Eloon. The Emperor surely had more in mind for this planet than simply a punishment, an exile, for her. Resources for the rebuilding were stretched, everything needed to be prioritized and hard choices made, but those resources still amounted to a Duke's ransom. He wouldn't have poured all those billions of Imperial francs into this project if he intended to let it wither. No. He would appoint a new governor to continue the work.

That, and the problematic question of her two prisoners, who still held the power to ignite a powder keg with little more than a word, was no longer her problem. Long-sought release enveloped her. Surrounded as she was by cold stone walls, Shayla felt more free than she could remember.

As long as they had their sacrifice, things would proceed as before. Shayla may not be around to see it, but Eloon would grow green again. For that, she walked willingly into the trap prepared for her.

Jared returned to the main ventilation shaft and shone the glow-tube up at the ceiling. He worked his way around the ledge that circled the shaft, testing his footing with each step. The railing separating him from a drop into the depths appeared intact, but he had no plans to put it to the test. Every few feet he gazed up, inspecting the ceiling from all angles. He also checked the walls behind him. The cut stone was still smooth and firm even after all these centuries.

He returned to the bike and hauled out a compact pack of climbing equipment. The largest item resembled a shortened rifle. Jared slipped a wickedly-barbed piton into the barrel and paid out a length of lightweight line, double-checking for snags or tangles. Bracing himself against the wall, he took aim at the far angle between wall and ceiling and fired.

Before long, a cat's cradle of lines spanned the ceiling a few inches beneath the grating. Jared tested each anchor, and pulled the lines taut. He stepped into a harness, clipped himself to the nearest line and hauled himself up and over the void.

Up close, peering through the circular grating, it was clear this shaft had indeed been closed deliberately at some point. Instead of the accumulated dirt of neglect, a metal cover lay overhead. Working his way across the ceiling, Jared probed with his scanner. It was too much to hope that the way above would be clear, but the jumble of reflected planes and shadows hinted that the filling was looser. It was still many feet in thickness, though, before larger gaps and voids started to show.

Once more on solid ground, Jared paused to replenish his energy from a small stock of rations, then swapped the scanner for a much deadlier piece of kit. One of the panniers held little more than a bulky package which he lay gently on the ground beside him. He unrolled a softly quilted covering to reveal several loose coils of what looked like inch-thick rope. He selected four ten-foot lengths and clipped them to carabiners at his belt. They were joined by a can of solvent spray and a pack of detonators. The remaining coils he carefully re-wrapped and stowed back in the pannier.

A chalky odor hanging in the air caught at the back of his throat. He drank and gargled to soothe the irritation, then stretched to loosen his limbs for the next task.

Back in his spider's web, Jared unhooked one of the coils and sprayed a bead of solvent along the first foot of its length. He waited a few seconds for the solvent to soften the outer coat of the rope, a combination insulator and adhesive putty, then pressed the end of the rope up against the ceiling. He worked his way, foot by foot. Spray, wait, then massage the softened side into place, pressing the thermal core of the rope into close contact with the grating.

Dangling upside down over a dark drop, he eventually formed a circle in the ceiling. A final inspection, and Jared reached into the pack at his waist and pulled out a handful of tiny thumb-tack detonators. He pressed one into the rope every few feet, twisting the top of each one to arm the electronics. Last of all, he pulled out a bulkier master detonator and set a timer before pressing it into place.

Unhurried, Jared descended, untied the lines and systematically hauled in his supporting web. Pitons he had to spare; high tensile lightweight rope was more bulky and a precious commodity.

He stowed everything back in his bike and descended the shaft. Out in the transit tunnel he backed a hundred yards and checked the time. As the last seconds ticked by, the result was anticlimactic. There was no explosion, nothing so obvious to alert anyone up on the surface, just a faint rush of falling debris at first. A few seconds later a loud clang reverberated up and down the tunnel as the cut-away grating hit the ventilation fan. Jared wondered whether the fan housing would hold in place or come tumbling down to the bottom. Nothing but a brief patter of stones.

Patiently, Jared waited another ten minutes before venturing near the foot of the shaft. Once more up the winding staircase, faster now with practice, he paused in the machinery space. He left the bike there and went on foot to inspect. The fan assembly had indeed stopped the fall. Debris filled the shaft, some of it spilling into the passage where he stood. He waited and listened. Silence. He leaned out and peered up into the gloom. Shining his glowtube up, the air was thick with dust. Relieved, he saw no glimmer of light from above. It would have been bad news if he'd broken right through to the surface.

Equipped with face mask and breathing filter, Jared rode the bike on up to the top, twisting all the way up the stairwell this time rather than chancing the main shaft. Once again, he inspected cautiously on foot. In the light of the glowtube thick wreaths of smoke and dust all but obscured the neat ten-foot hole in the ceiling. With the light off, the lip of the grating glowed a dull cherry red circle in the dark. With his visor set to infrared the glow became a searing ring. The heat signature extended upward outlining a ragged chute. It was impossible to tell how far up it extended, or how stable it might be.

Chapter 15

B rin took a deep breath of nicodyne and slipped the spray back into his pocket. He dismissed the mess of documents obscuring the conference room table before acknowledging the knock on the door that had startled him from the ambush of sleep. His own Captain of Guards, Bard Jovin, marched in and bowed stiffly followed by Commander Annelise ap Terlion, *Hammer's* security officer.

Brin straightened his tunic and belatedly glanced around the room tucked away in one corner of the immigration processing center. With landings and normal operations suspended, and with the Governor's Residence still off limits, he'd appropriated this room as temporary quarters and an office. A camp bed lay unused in the corner. He was thankful to see that someone had cleared the remains of last night's meal, though equally miffed that he'd failed to awaken at the intrusion.

"Report." He pointedly addressed Bard, aware of a slight stiffening in Commander ap Terlion's posture and a hastily-disguised hint of a pout. Fuck her. This was not her jurisdiction. He'd hear the report from his own man and he was too fucking tired for niceties. "Keep it brief."

"As you wish, Acting Governor. The brief version is that there is no trace of poison, common or exotic, anywhere in the Residence. All traces from the feast have been put to the most stringent tests. We've looked for air- or water-borne contaminants. Nothing. And cross-examination of all staff has satisfied me that nothing of this precision could have been orchestrated without someone noticing something, or some inconsistency in people's accounts."

Brin absorbed this. He eyed the Imperial Commander. "And your people have worked alongside my team? Been given full access to all materials? Are your conclusions in accord with Captain Jovin's?"

A hesitation. A grimace. "Everything the good Captain reports is in accordance with my own views." The words seemed torn with utmost reluctance from the Commander's lips. She still managed to hold herself with dignity, despite her evident distaste at the admission.

"So, there is no evidence that the inspectors could have been poisoned here."

"And yet we are faced with the empirical truth of a sick and dying Imperial inspection team."

"Yes," said Brin heavily. "There is still that." He peered close. "And do you still insist that Governor Carver has a crime to answer for?"

"Despite the lack of an obvious mechanism, the Governor is ultimately responsible for what happens in her jurisdiction."

Brin's fists curled at the smug expression on her face. He reminded himself that he'd expected nothing else.

———— ◆ ————

Jared eased the airbike through the passage and up the shaft created by his incendiary rope. As he'd hoped, with a circle of grating and a few feet of hard-packed spoil cut away, the looser debris on top had fallen through the resulting hole. The flash heat of the pyrotechnic had fused the lower section of the shaft, stabilizing it. Further up, it fanned out in a steep cone. As he ascended, vibrations from the airbike dislodged small runnels of grit and debris that clattered down and into the depths.

The light of the glowtube reflected back from lingering clouds. Despite his mask, fine dust coated his mouth and nose. Sharp metallic tangs cut through a gagging reek of sulfides. Jared wondered what kind of space lay beyond the swirling luminous tendrils obscuring his view. How stable was the structure above?

Hazily at first, then with increasing clarity as he rose, the light picked out the outline of ancient brickwork overhead, a barrel vault still intact. He brought himself as close to the ceiling as he could. This must have been a cellar once, now choked almost to the top with soil and stones. A treacherous slope spilled down to the hole he'd made.

There was nowhere to land the bike.

No matter. That's what climbing gear was for. Jared surveyed the far recesses of the cellar, where a brick wall was just visible, and fired more pitons to anchor a line leading down into the ventilation shaft.

———— ◆ ————

"Shayla! No time for lazing around. We have work to do."

Brandt's voice.

We?

Shayla looked around. She was lounging on a swing seat her father had built in the walled orchard at the back of their family home. Fruit trees grew in profusion and in no particular pattern, not the straight lines typical of an orchard. "Nature isn't to be regimented," Pappi often said.

The seat lay in the dappled shade of an ancient spreading cherry. High walls around kept stray breezes at bay. Within their confines the air was still and heady with the scent of spring blossoms.

"Snap out of it, Shayla!" There was urgency in Brandt's voice now, but he was nowhere to be seen. Why was he hiding?

Shayla stood and almost collapsed, knees weak and trembling. She'd been curled up on the bench too long, dozing in the afternoon warmth, comfortable. She must have sat awkwardly; her legs had gone to sleep.

Brandt appeared in front of her, arms outstretched to support her.

"Brandt! Space alive, I've missed you, brother." Shayla hugged him tight, then held him at arm's length. Something wasn't quite right. Her fingers traced the deep burn mark on his chest. "I did this to you, didn't I?"

He nodded.

"You're dead."

He nodded again.

She looked around the garden, tears welling. "This is all gone, too, isn't it?" Memories drifted near, or was it the memory of a dream? "I've failed, haven't I? I'm in prison, waiting to be taken to the Emperor for killing his inspection team."

A slap stung her to silence. There was no anger in Brandt's face, just sadness. "They're not dead yet. You cannot give up. There's still work to be done."

"What work can I do from inside an isolation cell?"

Brandt spat. "When did four walls ever make a prison? Opportunities will present themselves. Remember your training. Ready yourself to make opportunities, and to take them when they arise."

"It would help if I had some idea who was behind this."

"So, think! Someone set you up."

"Someone in the Palace."

"Maybe, but I think Ivan *and* Scipio are behind this. Everything keeps coming back to those two, together. That means they have Firenzi as well as Imperial resources to draw on."

"Meaning ... ?"

Brandt shrugged. "Spaced if I know."

"But you're a genius. You should be able to think your way through this!"

"I'm not here, am I, dummy? This isn't me talking. We just have your two disconnected brain cells to work with."

"Oh." Yeah, good point. Something sparked between the two brain cells. "Where does Kurt Weiler fit into this?"

"He doesn't. A loose cannon. You know he was assigned to infiltrate the Insurrection, which he succeeded in doing. They have a cell operating on Eloon. Something they were doing here gave him an opportunity to pursue a personal agenda against you, that's all."

"The Wasps." She paused in thought. "I guess his Insurrection handlers weren't happy with his display of initiative." She thought some more. Something about that reasoning was off. "Which means they didn't want me dead. Yet."

Brandt grunted. "Odd, isn't it? Lucky for you, though. If it weren't for that Wasp attack you'd never have investigated Randall. He is the more important figure here. The Insurrection had an unhealthy interest in him."

"They killed him."

"Which means whatever it was they were after, they've found it."

Shayla shivered.

———•+•———

Brindis ap Silessi ran a finger along one edge of his polished desk, glad to see the cleaners had been allowed in, and glad to be back in his own quarters at last now the painstaking examination of the Residence was over. In principle one setting was as good as another for him, and the stark lines of the immigration center's conference room suited him, but here was cold familiarity.

The cool tones of the walls, the minimal furniture, and the space black surface of the desk all worked to clear his mind of unwanted distractions. Focus on the matter at hand came with no wasted effort. He glanced at the only adornments hanging on the wall across from him. Two plaques. One, the Imperial Order of Merit, signed in real ink by the Emperor's hand, was a rare tribute to his lifetime of service. The other was even rarer. Plain black, no writing, no image, no hint as to its purpose, it puzzled visitors. They either knew its meaning already, or Brin was not prepared to enlighten them.

He took a deep breath. He had a feeling clear focus would be needed for this next meeting.

A guard ushered in Commander Annelise ap Terlion, *Hammer of War's* security officer, and her oily sidekick, Lieutenant Haalv Lekk.

Brin had seen little of Commander ap Terlion in the whirlwind nightmare of the past five days. She'd stayed mostly out of the way on *Hammer*, her primary responsibility, but he realized with a shock that his normal acute observation of personal details had mostly failed him. He felt he was looking at a stranger. Yes, he'd previously taken in her dark— almost midnight—skin and close-cropped gray hair, but only now did he notice the fine lines and slight stoop that placed her age somewhere in her seventies. She moved with a careful poise that gave her a look of fragility, as if a sudden move would snap brittle bones.

Lieutenant Lekk was another matter altogether. He had been underfoot the whole time, quiet, observant. Predatory. For all the apparent softness of his fleshy face he moved with the fluid grace of a trained killer. Yes, Brin knew Lady Carver's background and she'd certainly ended enough lives in the time he'd known her, but you'd never know it to look at her. She kept her skills hidden, to be brought out only when needed. In contrast, Lekk oozed menace like a malevolent cane toad. His very presence brought a winter chill to the brightest day.

"Commander. Lieutenant." Brin's greeting was curt to the point of rudeness. Lieutenant Lekk prowled the edge of his office, silent but, like a bad smell, impossible to ignore. "I understand you have news to report."

Brin stayed standing, forcing his guests to stand also and hopefully speeding up the process.

Commander ap Terlion stopped a few feet away, ill at ease, with her hands clasped behind her back. "Our investigations here have concluded, as far as we can conduct them."

"Then am I free to release Lady Carver?"

"Oh, no," Lekk breathed from somewhere behind him. "Milady stays where we can find her."

Commander ap Terlion said, "Henri Chargon has commandeered a fast frigate from Cendithor and diverted several of his own agents to Eloon. They will take Lady Carver into their custody and bring her back to Magentis."

Henri Chargon. The Emperor's most senior inquisitor. Brin shivered.

"They'll be here in a matter of days." Lekk's voice oozed from somewhere near the windows behind Brin's desk.

"Days? From Cendithor?" The math momentarily escaped Brin.

"Oh, they were dispatched immediately." Lekk tutted. "Serious business."

A red mist clouded Brin's vision, enraged as much by the tone as by the words. He swallowed hard. "So you prejudged her guilt!"

Commander ap Terlion's eyes glazed slightly. Her expression clouded as if in pain, and Brin recognized the depths of an extreme nicodyne debt, along with a hint of distaste and resignation. "An Imperial inspection team is gravely ill under her care. Unless you can suggest an innocuous cause, we are assuming malicious intent."

"That is not in dispute—"

"Then she will account for her actions to the Emperor in person."

Brin bowed his head. "If that is the Emperor's wish."

Once alone again, he sat and took a few moments to restore his calm. Hot rage slowly subsided and reason prevailed. When he replayed the meeting in his mind, he saw how close he'd come to drawing the beam pistol at his side.

Commander ap Terlion he could understand. She was under orders and doing her job, and Brin held grudging respect for a fellow professional. But Lekk! Shooting was too good for him.

Brin held his hands out in front of him, willing the trembling in his fingers to subside.

He turned once more to his work. A flick of his stylus brought the desk's surface to life, restoring the orderly stacks of documents vying for attention.

A new dossier caught his eye flagged "urgent". Brin leafed through the pages with mounting disbelief.

It looked like that sharp-faced Insurrection agent was only a local facilitator after all. Someone had pulled strings to add a newcomer to her team. A newcomer with no record of a past life, although that was nothing unusual on Eloon. But a newcomer who just happened to have the skills to replace the previous specialist who'd died in suspicious circumstances. And a newcomer who himself had now dropped out of sight without a trace.

Coincidences were piling up. Brin was not surprised that his security staff had chosen to follow up more closely.

But then there were the tentative identity hits his analysts had dug up from what little biometric and facial data they'd been given to work from. This was the reason for the "urgent" tag. One entry in the list had rung alarm bells all the way to Magentis.

Without hesitation, Brin issued orders to the security forces to find and detain both these agents and all known associates. His faced twisted. Despite all his misgivings, this was one piece of news he had to bring to Lady Carver, before it was too late.

———•—•———

It took Jared another two days of painstaking, backbreaking toil to excavate up through layers of collapsed sub-basements into the remains of a more recently inhabited building. With the last of his thermal ropes, he finally broke into an almost-intact parking garage beneath the melted shell of a dwelling.

While the dust from the collapsed wall settled, Jared squatted in one corner and listened. Sweat trickled down his collar, and slicked the grime caking his forearms. He ignored the chalk taste on his tongue and poured all his awareness into his surroundings.

He knew he was close, by the scorched outlines of a well-baked ground car in one corner. He couldn't identify the model but the lines of the fragile skeleton were of a recent design, this century for sure. Soot-blackened walls around it looked fresh still after a mere thirty years, compared with the decaying brick and timbers crumbling to dust further back.

All was quiet.

A glimmer of light peeped through the top of a choked entrance ramp. Jared squinted against the unaccustomed brightness, and gave his eyes time to adjust before he ventured closer.

He crept up the slope, pausing often to examine his surroundings and to listen for signs of activity. Someone had cleared a rough path down into the garage since the building's destruction. Here and there, scuff marks and yellowish soil showed clean through the baked ash gray surface. A few boot prints marred the blackened floor by the burned-out car, but the overlay of dust suggested this place had not been revisited in the last year or more. He guessed the early survey and security crews had examined the terrain and buildings when they started work on the prison. Their survey would have shown nothing more than layers of long-abandoned history beneath the ground.

Stopping short of the evening daylight spilling into the entrance, Jared extended a fine telescopic wand and tuned his visor to the miniature camera feed on its tip.

From his hiding place inside the perimeter of one of the most secure locations in habitable space, Jared surveyed his hunting ground and smiled.

<hr />

"Shayla, wake up!"

Simone's voice.

Shayla opened a bleary eye, squinting against the bright lights of the cell. Simone stood over her, freckles showing stark against her pale skin. Her brow was pinched in a frown, though her voice was light and matter-of-fact. "We need to get you showered and cleaned up. I have fresh clothes for you."

Shayla sat upright, panting at the effort. The room swam then settled into sharp focus. She looked down at her hands, little more than wrinkled claws lying in her lap. The hands of an old woman.

She puzzled. These were not her hands. The answer came in a flash—her mimetic implants. While she'd been wallowing in self-pity these past days her subconscious mind had mutated her external appearance into a mirror of her own self-image. An old woman. Spent. Useless.

She stood and gave vent to a howl of outrage. Simone backed up a step, eyes widening, but Shayla didn't care. She let the anger burn through her. How had she allowed herself to grow so weak? This was *not* who she was.

The last echoes of her cry rebounded off tiled and painted walls and ceilings, fading through the security gates and startling guards from their posts. A pair of worried faces peered around the door and retreated again on seeing Shayla's ferocious glare and the absence of any blood to mop up.

Shayla took a few deep breaths and composed herself. Finally she said, "Thank you, Simone. A shower would be most welcome. To what do I owe the privilege?"

Unfazed by the outburst, Simone laid a neatly-wrapped package on the bed. "You have visitors."

For the first time, Shayla noticed head of security—no, Acting Governor—Brindis ap Silessi, hovering just outside her cell door. He seemed reluctant to enter. He clutched his notepad, one index finger drumming the surface in a nervous tic. His normally stern features sagged.

Profound misery threatened to overwhelm Shayla, seeing the pain she brought down on the heads of everyone around her. Her own selfish relief while she languished here reminded her what a terrible responsibility Brin had taken on.

As if sensing her dismay, Brin abruptly straightened himself and marched into the cell. "The planet and its security are mine to manage, have no fear on that score. I'm not here to burden you, you have problems enough of your own, but I have one question to pose that I believe you can answer."

"Better make the most of the opportunity then." Even as she spoke, Shayla felt the attempt at humor fall flat.

Brin scowled. "My team has been following various leads relating to the Insurrection."

"You've found something?"

"There is a person of interest." He hesitated. "I think we have an identification, but you would be best placed to confirm it."

Without further ceremony he opened his notepad and turned it towards Shayla. She puzzled over the image. From scraps of detail intruding around the edge of the scene, she saw it was taken from one of the monitors in the immigration processing shed. She focused on the figure slouching in the center of the frame. A man, young but careworn with a vicious scar down one side of his face. Nothing remarkable, given the kinds of troubles that drove people to seek refuge on Eloon.

Shayla squinted in concentration. There was definitely *something* about him, some tug of recognition. Then it hit her. In her mind's eye she took away the scar, and imagined tightly woven braids of hair in place of the military buzz cut.

Another ghost from times past.

"Cobra!"

Brin hissed a sharp intake of breath.

Shayla looked up. "Not what you wanted me to say?"

"What I feared to hear."

Her heart sank once more. This, on top of everything else. "He survived Magentis."

"So it would seem."

"He was high in the Insurrection's ranks back then."

"No word of him since."

"Regardless, Brin, if Cobra is active on Eloon there is something bigger happening than sabotaging an inspection. Don't underestimate him."

Helplessness weighed Shayla down like quicksand. Of all the people she'd fought in her past life, Cobra had come closest to matching her for ferocity and skill. If he'd been sent to Eloon, the situation here was dire. Brin was good and his team was more than competent, but they were only equipped for backwoods planet policing. This level of threat was beyond them. She had to free herself, somehow.

Shayla turned to Simone. "You mentioned 'visitors', plural."

"There is an ambassador from the Emperor's service wishing to begin fact finding."

Senses alive at long last, Shayla considered this. "I take it they are waiting for me?"

Simone acknowledged.

"I will shower and eat first. I'm sure they have nowhere else to be at this time. Let them wait."

She was Shayla Carver, assassin, governor, and a blood cousin of the Emperor. Whoever was doing this to her would have to come out of the shadows sooner or later, and they would find her ready and spoiling for a fight. She was *not* going down quietly.

Only once she'd refreshed and fed did Shayla realize just how weakened she'd let herself become. She cursed herself soundly for that foolishness. Who knew what opportunities might already have passed her by unnoticed, or how many more might she yet be too enfeebled to grasp?

Like a spent firework, that was history. She had to look to her future. While waiting for a servant to clear away the tray of dishes she practiced calming meditations and focus exercises, the kind that used to keep her mind sharp and whole through long assignments behind enemy lines. She'd grown far too lazy for her liking.

She was escorted from the high security basement and through the lower guard house by a squad of guards. Imperial guards, she noticed. That was disquieting because it signaled a shift somewhere in the balance of power above ground. On the plus side, she would have no qualms dispatching any or all of them if the opportunity or necessity arose.

They led her through a tunnel into the basement of the Legislature itself. This was how prisoners were brought into the courtroom on those rare occasions when the full weight of a formal court hearing was needed. Alert to her surroundings, seeing them afresh no matter how familiar, she looked for subtle clues as to her standing here.

The courtroom was empty. This wasn't a full trial then. Not yet. Relief turned to puzzlement, then to anger as the guards marched her out into the lobby and then into the anteroom to her own judicial office.

Was she really being made to wait, in her own waiting room, while some interloper lorded it behind her desk? She swallowed the hard knot of rage that threatened to break her focus. This was the Governor's office, she reminded herself. Maybe Brin was behind those doors. Somehow she doubted it. That was not Brin's style.

Her misgivings proved well founded a few minutes later when a guard, listening on a lapel communicator, nodded and threw open the door.

Shayla stepped through, bracing herself, and delivered an icy glare to the stranger sitting in *her* high-backed chair, behind *her* desk.

There was no chair on Shayla's side of the desk. Without waiting for an invitation she strode purposefully forward, stopping just short of the desk so the seated woman would have to look up at her.

The thin-faced woman gazed back, brown eyes regarding Shayla solemnly. Black hair, swept severely back, framed a high forehead. Why do truthsensers always look like carrion crows?

"Who are you?"

"Senior Inquisitor Tyree, at your service, Governor Carver." The bob of her head as she spoke barely paid lip service to protocol. From someone so high up the hierarchy the slight was finely calculated.

"Where is Henri Chargon?"

"*Commander* Chargon is unavailable. He delegated preliminary interviews to me."

Delegated? "So, he sent a lackey to do his job. Does the cousin of the Emperor merit so little respect?"

The woman's eyes betrayed her shock. She was too used to subjects cowed by the fear her profession evoked. Defiance she'd probably faced often enough, but righteous outrage seemed like a new response.

The moment she'd entered the room, Shayla had discerned the true purpose here. This interview was not about fact-finding. This was straightforward intimidation. Softening up. Show her how little she counted in the grand scheme of things. Her spirits soared. *They were still afraid of her.*

Shayla had no intention of allowing this truthsenser to lead the way. "You are a truthsenser," she hissed. "If you have *any* skill in your craft then this will be a very quick process. Know this, that I had nothing to do with the state of the Emperor's Inspectorate, nor would I have wished such a fate on them."

She leaned her hands on the desk, towering over the startled woman. "Do your job, you old crow. Discern the truth and report accordingly."

Chapter 16

Now that he'd established a way into the prison grounds, Jared camouflaged the hole in the corner of the burned-out garage. There was no hiding the hole itself, but a few well-placed blows with a pry bar and some work with dust and soot disguised the nature of the opening from casual inspection.

It then took Jared two more round trips under the sea to ferry the remainder of his supplies into his hideaway. He'd only carried with him the climbing and demolition gear needed to break through to the surface. There followed more specialized equipment for the next stage of the operation, clothing, and supplies for the possible wait. With her fuckin' Governorship banged up in prison, some element of predictability had fled the scene. When news came of the chess pieces moving in the right direction he might have to move fast. He needed to be waiting on site, for Space knew how long.

Safe on the mainland, he arranged with Wolf to drop supplies and equipment in a cluster of small grav-braked containers. She made just the one supply run. Any more was too risky. The containers were too small to register on any surveillance but of course they landed across a wider area than Jared was comfortable with. He scurried back and forth on the airbike, keeping low to the ground, until each one was accounted for and stashed in the tunnel entrance. Only then did he begin the painstaking task of hauling them under the sea and up through the ruined basements.

Fast torpedo frigate *Vixen* squatted in the landing field, resting on her outlying drive pods. Three hundred feet of oily blue ugliness towered over the bustling transports, ground and air cars, and crowds of field staff, guards, and new arrivals.

Traffic parted in front of Shayla's car as it crossed the field and entered the shadow of the starboard pod. The car stopped under the fuselage, where a boarding ramp stretched like a silver tongue up into the forward bulge.

Shayla stepped out and looked up. She could feel the weight of the ship pressing into the dry soil of the landing field on either side of her. That weight mirrored the oppressive gloom in her own mind. She was needed *here*, on Eloon, but she was being shipped off to Magentis and she could see no escape. The best she could hope for was to plead her case to the Emperor in person and be returned before it was too late.

Another car pulled up alongside. Senior Inquisitor Tyree stepped out and favored Shayla with a poisonous glare. She'd made two more attempts yesterday to interview Shayla after that first disastrous encounter. She'd changed her approach on the last occasion and visited Shayla in her cell. Abandoning the failed tactic of intimidation, these interviews were more genuine. She probed savagely with barbed and double-edged questions, and listened intently not just to the words of the answers, but the stress harmonics in their delivery. A detached part of Shayla admired her skill. Given other circumstances, one such as Tyree might have made a useful addition to her own staff. But she left just as frustrated. She couldn't trap Shayla in a lie, because there was no lie in her account.

Another figure emerged. Shayla gasped. "Simone! What are you doing here?"

"I thought you could use a friendly face in the days to come."

"I can handle the Emperor." *I think!* "You understand that you risk sharing my fate?"

"Acting Governor ap Silessi felt you could use my services rather more than he." Simone's eyes twinkled. "He also sent me with gifts to ease the passage of time."

Shayla's heart lifted at the message hidden in Simone's words. She herself had been thoroughly searched, every stitch of clothing scrutinized, but with Brin's clearance Simone wouldn't have been subject to quite the same inspection. And—Shayla only now noticed the incongruity—she wore a many-layered winter outfit far too heavy for the season. Who knew what Brin had secreted in those folds?

Simone pressed a worn scroll into Shayla's hands. "Of course they wouldn't let you have your own notepad, who knows what dangerous secrets it might carry? So I drew a scroll from the stores for your comfort and entertainment."

The Imperials here had no idea what skills Simone possessed. They saw a simple elderly personal servant. Shayla saw a cunning technology expert giving her a knowing wink.

This part of Scale was laughingly called "The Old Quarter". The warren of prefabs along with some real poured-polycrete structures behind the medical and administration centers was all of five years old. The Old Quarter sat at the heart of the town, amidst a sprawl of the ubiquitous multipurpose steel boxes that had been imported in their thousands to serve as everything from housing to workshops to stores to warehouses for this fast-growing population.

Wall screens in Scale's oldest and most popular bar normally showed off-planet sports channels, with the oft-fatal ground races and jetski tournaments perennial favorites, or even rougher local pastimes such as forest-rules wrestling and bush racing. This afternoon they showed local news, an unheard-of departure, but the heaving throng had eyes for nothing else today.

Overpowering even the reek of sweat and stale beer, Jared realized that raw anger had an odor of its own and the town today was rife with it. The din in the bar, an endless thunder of outrage vented at the newsfeed, drowned out the commentary but the images on screen needed no interpretation.

A small convoy of ground cars settled in the shadow of a hulking warship in Imperial livery. The sight sent a tingle of fear up Jared's spine. He pushed it to the background and focused on the scene that drew the crowd's ire.

Soldiers scurried, keeping onlookers at bay. The image danced and juddered, a long range view at extreme magnification from outside the security cordon. Nevertheless the figure of Lady Carver was unmistakable, standing maddeningly serene in the midst of the surrounding activity.

Jared's own anger at today's events was genuine enough, although rooted in a different motivation. The population of Eloon had united in fury at Her Ladyship's arrest ten days ago. The move by Imperial forces to ship her off-planet was the last straw, a slap in the face to a million refugees who'd arrived here spent and broken, and in whom she'd rekindled a fierce pride.

For Jared, her extradition dashed his last hope of achieving a deeply personal revenge. His anger at the Imperials momentarily aligned with the locals. He allowed himself the rare luxury of venting his feelings along with the hundreds of other hoarse voices.

A subliminal impression, sensed rather than seen. Jared turned in time to see Wolf forging a path towards him through the press of bodies. The diminutive figure should have been swamped in the crush of burly construction and forestry workers, but she projected such an intensity of purpose that the way before her cleared effortlessly.

Jared heaved an inward sigh of relief. He'd taken a huge risk to make this rendezvous, emerging from the mainland shaft and hugging the river valley to evade surveillance before finally meeting with Walrus, who'd then brought him up the coast to Scale.

He handed Wolf a beer he'd been clutching. "You've talked to the planners?"

She took a deep swallow from her mug.

Jared nodded to the screen. "How does this affect things?"

"She's served her purpose. The targets are where we want them. Ap Silessi is holding the planet now, but apart from that nothing's changed." Wolf's voice was soft, for his ears only. "Now you've got physical access to the site, here are the papers and data you need for the next stage."

As Jared accepted the palm-sized package, his spine tingled. Something about the flow of people around the pub's entrance suggested more purpose than was normal. "You were followed?" he hissed.

"Of course." Wolf took another swallow from her glass. "My days here are numbered. Just you make this happen! Pull this off and nothing will matter any more."

At least three men eased their way through the crowd from the main entrance. Two more from the rear. They wore working clothes and their appearance was perfectly in keeping with the rest of the clientele, but their manner and movements screamed law enforcement.

"On my mark, make for the bar. The server over there"—Wolf jerked her chin towards a mousy-looking woman of indeterminate age lounging at one end—"will let you out the staff entrance."

"Which will be watched, no doubt."

"Already taken care of." Wolf winked and slid, wraith-like, into the crowd.

Sudden commotions broke out on either side. The security goons found themselves at the wrong end of some imagined insult, maybe too hard a jostle sloshed someone's drink. It was like a match to tinder in the crowd's current mood.

Jared grinned and slipped, unnoticed, towards the bar.

Chapter 17

S hayla sat bolt upright, ducking just in time to avoid cracking her head on the bunk above.

Why am I not breathing?

Her barely conscious mind took a moment to catch up with the instincts that had so often saved her life. Then she was fully alert, senses sharpened by a sudden dump of adrenaline. Shit! Not peritax again.

Apart from Simone's shallow breathing above, a quick scan in the dim red night light reassured her that the cramped officer's cabin—her prison since leaving Eloon—was empty. For how long? She slipped out of the bunk, working saliva around her mouth and spitting to expel what she could of the drug.

Whoever did this was expecting her to be unconscious by now. Still holding her breath, Shayla listened for a moment. No sounds outside.

She opened the closet and felt around the hem of Simone's robe. There! Well concealed in the heavy folds of the fabric was a tiny cylinder. Thank Space they hadn't searched Simone too thoroughly. They'd paid more attention to Shayla. Even that had been cursory, looking for obvious weapons. Most members of the Imperial forces knew her reputation only too well. The crew of *Vixen* knew she'd have needed no hardware to kill them given the inclination and the opportunity.

Her probing fingers found the hidden pocket and worked the cylinder loose. She slipped the breathing unit into her mouth and took a deep breath.

Another quick listen while she checked Simone. Out cold, in the grip of the drug. Peritax was remarkably consistent in its effect. It would be at least an hour before she woke.

Shayla unrolled her scroll and cautiously tapped into *Vixen's* network. Working through the camera feeds that monitored every passageway and compartment, she scanned the nearby corridors for signs of movement. Here and there, crew members lay sprawled wherever the drug had hit them. No signs of life, and no immediate danger.

With an inward curse, Shayla realized that she was taking a huge risk simply sitting here in her cabin. Someone had incapacitated the crew and could be scanning the ship just as she was doing.

Peritax. It had to be someone on board. Somewhere, someone had a task to complete.

Her stylus flew across the face of the scroll as she opened an electronic toolkit. Simone had done an effective job of building up Shayla's security arsenal, and the camera hidden in the cabin quickly succumbed to her commands. Shayla skimmed back in *Vixen's* archives for the moments before she woke up. She locked the camera feed onto a static image. That should fool anyone making at least a cursory check on her.

Now Shayla began a more systematic search of the ship, her stylus flicking the view from one camera to the next.

In order to flood the whole ship, the peritax must have been introduced through the main habitat systems. A couple of engineers had collapsed on the deck of the machinery space, but the compartment that housed the ventilation control and distribution system was empty. In the recreation room and mess hall, crew members slumped across tables or sprawled at awkward angles half on and half off benches. Toppled drinks and scattered trays of food bore witness to the speed of the drug's action.

While she searched for movement, Shayla wondered at the purpose of such a brazen attack. Was she the target? Or was this coincidental? Could they just be after the ship? Somehow, that seemed unlikely. There were easier opportunities to disable a small warship than when it carried an important passenger under heavy guard.

A clatter of feet outside startled Shayla. She flipped the scroll over and whirled to face the door, glancing around the cabin for somewhere to surprise whoever might try to enter. She'd barely started when she realized that the footsteps had passed the cabin and were heading towards the ship's forward sections.

She suppressed a curse and returned to the scroll, hunting for a useful camera feed.

There! A flicker of movement in the main corridor caught her eye, heading down to the command deck. She switched views and recognized Trovor Scarth, one of *Vixen's* communications technicians. He vaulted into a seat in front of the communications console and wrote briefly on the desktop.

Shayla scanned *Vixen's* communications channels, hoping to trace any transmissions. All she could find was a simple low power beacon. There must be another ship nearby. Shayla turned her attention to the external scanners.

While she instructed *Vixen's* command system to alert her to any incoming vessel, she kept an eye on Trovor's activities.

Huh?

Shocked, Shayla realized that she was looking at her own sleeping body on the screen over Trovor's hunched shoulder. Checking up! So she was the target. Another thought occurred to her. He's a comms tech. Would he notice her deception? But he seemed more preoccupied with the outside view. He looked nervous as he quartered nearby space.

Worry tugged at the back of Shayla's mind. She finally teased out the thought nagging at her. Trovor must have been somewhere up in the engineering compartment in order to drug the ship's crew, but there'd been no sign of him when she'd started her search of the ship. So, what was he doing for those minutes in between?

Shayla quizzed *Vixen's* archives once more, searching for the moment when she'd heard running feet. There he was. But he hadn't come from the direction of the habitat control room and machinery space. He'd emerged instead from a companionway that led up to the weapons pod.

Shayla searched for a different view, and watched in horror while Trovor tinkered with three squat cylinders on the loading rack of the torpedo ready room.

Fifty feet above her head.

Fingers trembling slightly, Shayla set to work once more on the locks imprisoning her in the cabin.

Damn! I wish Simone was awake to help me! But Simone had already spent the last two days trying to crack the door codes that Henri's agents had set. They let me keep my scroll, she thought bitterly. They had complete faith in their security codes.

An alarm pinged on the scroll. Shayla snapped back to the here-and-now and saw Trovor sit up, visibly agitated.

A Firenzi scout ship had appeared on the communications console, and was closing in on *Vixen*.

Trovor took a breathing unit out of his mouth and dropped it onto the desk. Then he fished a slim cylinder from his pocket and spoke briefly on the short range communicator.

Shayla checked the time and removed her own breathing unit. The drug would have broken down long ago in the presence of oxygen.

Trovor slid across to the helmsman's console and tapped out a few commands. A docking tunnel extended from *Vixen's* prow and snuggled into the scout's flank. So their rat had his escape route. How long did she have? Now becoming frantic, Shayla checked the cabin once more for any hope of escape. But Henri's agents had made good use of the time on their voyage to Eloon.

She glanced back to her view of the command deck. Her stomach turned to ice. Trovor had moved to another console. The weapons console. She swore, and reviewed her situation once more, casting around desperately for options.

It'll take him a while to override the safety codes and arm the warheads. Let's see ... locked cabin ... armored walls ...

Vixen was built to traditional standards for close combat warships. Lots of sealed compartments. Lots of inbuilt structural strength.

Only one door ... ventilation and facilities inlets just about wide enough for an escaping ferret ...

She returned to the scroll. It seemed to be her only connection with the outside world.

Can't unlock the door. Access to communications may be a possibility, but how would that help? Can I get at any of the ship's systems? Cameras and archives are one thing, but ... Could I seal him into the command deck?

Shayla's fingers flew as she thought through possibilities.

Movement in the corner of the screen caught her eye.

There was someone else on board.

Trovor spoke briefly to the newcomer, pointing first to Shayla's slumbering image, and then to the schematics of *Vixen* displayed on the wall of the command deck. The newcomer, a muscular woman in Firenzi uniform, nodded and strode out of Shayla's view. Heart pounding, Shayla found a view down the forward corridor of the main deck.

The Firenzi strode towards Shayla's cabin, with a collapsible stretcher over her shoulder.

This wasn't an assassination, it was a kidnap.

Shayla rolled up the scroll and slid back into her bunk, trying to still her breathing.

She counted heartbeats ... ten ... fifteen ...

Footsteps outside.

A pause.

The door opened.

Through slitted eyes, Shayla watched a shadow appear at her side. An arm reached for her. She was expecting the Firenzi to simply pick her up, but the movement of the arm approaching her exposed neck was wrong. In the dim light, Shayla discerned the tip of a medical applicator.

Crap!

Shayla's hand whipped out to grasp the woman's wrist. With the advantage of surprise, Shayla twisted the hand around to meet a uniformed thigh. She heard a faint hiss and a choked gasp as she slid out of bed. Shayla squirmed behind her attacker, thumbs probing for pressure points. But the woman was already slumping to the floor.

Shayla took the Firenzi's head in both hands and gave it a business-like twist just to make sure.

She switched on the overhead light, picked up the medipen from where it had dropped to the floor, and checked the color coding. You have to be kidding! They wanted to make sure she stayed helpless, and it seemed they weren't too concerned with her long term health. Trembling slightly, Shayla placed the medipen on the tiny desk in the corner and peered out of the door.

The stretcher was leaning up against the wall. Shayla noted magnetic clamps and manacles. They weren't planning on taking any chances. She hesitated. How much time did she have? She turned back and hurried to the captain's cabin. A quick rummage through locker and desk. Relief. Her personal effects were here in a neat bundle. She retrieved her shimmerblade and tucked it into her belt.

She hurried down the corridor, stepping over sleeping bodies.

At the head of the ramp leading down to the command deck, she stopped, listening intently.

A faint murmur of voices told her that Trovor was still down there.

She glided ghost-like down to the door of the command center.

"Crawford has gone to fetch our passenger," Trovor said. "Three warheads armed and control turned over to you."

"Encryption signature confirmed. We have control."

"Confirmed. And in the name of Unity keep your paws off those triggers until we're well clear. Just remember you'll go up too if you fuck up."

Shayla waited until Trovor had ended the transmission before closing in. He never knew what hit him. As his body slumped to the floor, Shayla hooked his beam pistol from its holster.

She grimaced in distaste as she pocketed the pistol. She despised such inelegant weapons, but right now it was better than nothing.

"Scarth! Report! I can't get word from Crawford."

The voice sounded tense.

Shayla ignored the communicator and studied the weapons console.

I can't disarm this in time.

Simone would probably know how to, and it would have been a cinch for genius Brandt.

Simone!

"Scarth, check in please. Bring the passenger and let's get the fuck out of here."

This time, there was real panic in the voice.

Crap! How long before they give up and blow the charges anyway?

I need to disable those torpedoes.

But she had little chance of achieving that without raising the alarm. She'd have to board the other ship and stop them from triggering the warheads.

Shayla closed her eyes and concentrated on her memory of Trovor Scarth's voice.

She breathed deeply, forced the choking tension out of her throat, then thumbed the communicator. "All wrapped up. We're on our way."

Even before completing the response, Shayla was out of the command deck and sprinting for her cabin. Her ploy might have calmed the crew on the other ship for now, but it could only be a matter of minutes before they realized something was up.

She'd do what she could. *Vixen's* crew would have to take their chances, but she was damned if she was going to lose someone like Simone.

In the confines of her cabin, Shayla dragged the lifeless Crawford out of the way and hauled Simone out of the bunk and onto her shoulders. *Shit! She's heavier than she looks.* Staggering back out into the corridor, Shayla realized that she had to cope with the Imperial navy standard gravity, somewhat greater than that on Eloon.

Mental note: include high gravity workouts in training regime!

Cursing the narrow corridors on the cramped warship, Shayla tried to keep Simone's head away from bulkheads and projecting machinery as she hastened to the nearest escape pod.

That was the best chance of surviving a blast. It would have to do. Shayla dumped Simone unceremoniously inside the pod then stepped back and sealed the hatch.

She gazed at the launch button, indecision for once gnawing at her. Send her off? But she'd be a sitting target for that scout. So how much protection would the pod give her here? It was designed to take quite a battering.

It's not going to come to that. Shayla gritted her teeth and sprinted back through the bowels of the ship, drawing the beam pistol as she went. She slowed as she approached the corner of the mess hall. She pressed her back to the wall and edged around the corner, senses straining.

All clear.

The corridor skirted the secondary power housing, which shielded her from the docking tunnel and also barred her view. She peered around the curving armor of the power housing. The near end of the docking tunnel was empty. Silently she crossed the few feet of open space and entered the airlock. The tunnel stretched ahead of her. Thirty feet of narrow emptiness. Brightly lit.

And guarded.

Another woman in Firenzi uniform gazed at Shayla from the open hatch at the far end.

She raised a weapon.

Her eyes widened in horror, quickly obliterated as Shayla's beam charred her face.

Shayla raced along the tunnel.

Too late!

The far hatch slammed shut.

A ripping sound was quickly overwhelmed by the rising shriek of escaping air.

Shayla's feet left the floor and she bounced off the roof of the tunnel. Grav field cut! She hastily pocketed the pistol as she was propelled towards the growing ring of blackness edging the end of the tunnel and the receding hatch.

She allowed the last dregs of air to vent from her lungs, resisting the impulse to hold her breath. She held her arms out and steadied herself against the rushing walls, using the last few feet to aim her flight before the blast of air ejected her into the interstellar void.

The hatch drew closer again, then started to drift to one side. *Shit!* The ship was turning away.

Shayla reached for the hatch. An outstretched finger caught the edge of a vent housing. She hooked it and pulled herself towards the hatch, grasping for the nearest handhold.

Got it. She hauled herself closer. *Where's the access panel?* Shayla looked in confusion for a few moments.

Her mind drifted.

Holding on with one hand, Shayla's weightless body pirouetted slowly.

The black of space beckoned.

Beautiful.

Silent fire blinded her. She tried to gasp. *Simone!* Vacuum seared her throat.

Get a grip!

Ignoring the glowing wreckage of *Vixen*, Shayla turned back towards the hatch. With the sharpness of cold fury welling inside her, Shayla realized that she'd become disorientated. She was hanging upside down. She righted herself and found the access control panel, searching her memory for Firenzi navy emergency codes. It's been a long time. Hope this still works.

But she'd already noted the scuffed and pitted surface of the hull. This ship was long overdue for an overhaul. Its access codes had probably last been reset before Shayla was born.

She'd only get one chance at this before the crew realized and locked her out.

Furiously blinking away lights dancing in front of her vision, she punched in the code.

Nothing happened.

Blackness bled from the vista outside and seeped deep into Shayla's eyes.

What now?

The hatch opened.

Of course! The airlock needed to cycle first!

Shayla pulled herself inside and slammed the hatch shut.

Her skin tingled.

She gulped deep breaths.

Sound returned.

She realized that she was screaming.

The far door opened. A hand appeared, aiming a beam pistol.

Shayla's own weapon was already out, firing through the widening gap.

Still screaming, heedless of danger, Shayla strode across the airlock pumping charge after charge into the blackened body outside.

———•◦•———

Shayla sat, huddled in the angle between floor and walls.

If she made a sound, she couldn't hear it.

If she cried, she didn't feel it.

Some corner of sanity wondered whether there were any more people on board. It reassured itself that Shayla's reflexes would deal with them. Probably.

The little corner of sanity retreated to where it was safe from the roiling madness.

It would just have to ride out the storm.

———•◦•———

Unknown time passed.

———•◦•———

Blackness ebbed.

Pain returned. Pain she hadn't realized she'd earned.

Shit. That bastard nailed her after all.

Shayla ached all over from her brush with the depths of space. Her chest and throat hurt from the anguish she'd voiced. But it was pain from her arm which had finally penetrated the shell that her mind had built around itself. A long, cauterized gash across her left upper arm demanded attention.

She wiped at wetness around her mouth. Her hand came away red. She staggered to her feet, still clutching the pistol.

Two bodies here, and one on Vixen. That made sense. This class of ship would typically have a crew of three.

All the same, Shayla cautiously inspected the tiny craft from end to end.

The bunk room held kits for three, confirming her assessment. Wonder if they'd have taken Trovor Scarth with them? Probably not, he'd have served his purpose.

A storeroom next door was empty save for a low table with clamps welded down each side. Shayla puzzled over that for a moment, then remembered the modified stretcher that Crawford had been carrying. Cold fingers kneaded her stomach. This was going to be her room.

Hands slightly unsteady, Shayla closed the door before continuing.

A few minutes later, search complete, her legs weakened under her. Shock setting in.

She returned to the galley, fumbling for the medical cabinet next to the door.

She could barely control her trembling fingers.

Shit! Shit! Shit!

She tipped a drawer out onto the floor. A kaleidoscope of blurred colors skittered across the blue tiles. *There! Green stripes on white.* She groped for the medipen, her heart fluttering like a trapped bird inside her chest.

Not caring where it hit, Shayla pressed the tip of the pen against her neck. The drug worked quickly, calming her palpitations and soothing her breathing.

The chemical calm brought a symphony of pain into sharp focus. Shayla closed her eyes for a few moments, reaching inwards to search out the sources. *Arm, and lungs. Probably ruptured capillaries.*

She coughed and spat blood. Nothing that couldn't wait. She had more urgent things on her mind. Clutching at bulkheads for support in the narrow corridor, Shayla stumbled to the cramped control room and sat at the navigation console.

She hesitated, not wanting to see what was left of *Vixen*. Memory of twisted wreckage haunted her, indistinct through the afterimage of the glowing fireball. But she had to know.

Shayla checked the outside visuals.

Vixen was nowhere to be seen.

Chapter 18

"It was honestly that straightforward, was it?" Brin felt utterly deflated. "They had the encryption codes to our comms network, and simply ordered the squad around to the front of the pub leaving the staff entrance unguarded?"

Brin slumped one side of a cluttered desk in a windowless office, deep in the warren of rooms and corridors that was Scale's security field office. The air reeked of cheap food, stale beer, and unwashed bodies. The lieutenant in charge of security operations along this coast squirmed in his seat opposite Brin.

"Not entirely." If Brin felt disheartened, the lieutenant looked like the world had collapsed on his shoulders. "They left one agent at her post ..."

Brin grunted. They had at least kept some wits about them in the heat of the moment.

"But on her own she was an easy target for a paralyzing dart. The Insurrection had people stationed on the roof opposite. Our targets slipped out the door and escaped over the roof. The street was unguarded for only a matter of seconds, but that's all it took."

"And the agents would have wasted precious seconds working out what had happened to their colleague before starting a pursuit."

The lieutenant nodded, then straightened in his seat. "We're quartering Scale, building by building. Their mugshots are posted up in every guard post, works office, bar and canteen—"

Brin waved him to silence. "All commendable and proper actions. Keep up the search, but I believe our targets are long gone to ground, somewhere beyond the reach of our sources of intelligence."

"Surely they can't stay hidden forever?" the lieutenant protested.

"It looks like the Insurrection is more deeply entrenched than I gave them credit for." Brin gave his head an irritable shake. "This wasn't a random meeting place. The whole rendezvous was carefully timed and staged. Their escape was equally carefully planned. They knew we were watching them." And I failed to prepare you for what you were up against, thought Brin. *And Lady Carver really thought I was the right man to look after Eloon in her absence?*

Guilt and anguish cut through his mind and blinded him to the room with its clutter of files, equipment and crumpled food cartons, but with the pain came a more profound realization. His people meant well, but they were outmatched. He could have spent all night briefing them on the wiles and trickery to watch out for, but it was now clear that the Insurrection had a high caliber team in place.

Brin shuddered inwardly as he saw what had to be done. "You have a new priority." The sudden edge to his voice startled the lieutenant to fresh alertness. "Work with your counterpart on Sherrin to redouble vigilance on traffic to and from the prison site. There is nothing else on this planet that the Insurrection could possibly be interested in. This agent may have slipped from sight here, but he must not be allowed to set foot on Sherrin."

"Are we just giving up hope of finding him, then?"

Brin tried to keep the distaste out of his voice. "This has gone beyond police work. You will keep up the visible efforts you already mentioned, but understand that this is only for the sake of appearances. Meanwhile, I'll need a small team of your best-connected undercover operatives. People who can be trusted to keep eyes and ears open, *and mouths shut*. The less you know about this side of the operation, the better."

Brin dismissed the lieutenant, then opened his notepad and reviewed a list of contacts. Finally, he wrote a series of codes on the screen. "Get me a secure and private connection to Commander Annelise ap Terlion on board *Hammer of War*."

———◆———

There was nothing out there, not even wreckage. Shaking uncontrollably, Shayla did a three-sixty scan of her surroundings in case she'd got her orientation wrong.

Numbed, it took her a few moments to fathom what was happening. She struggled to beat her mind into action.

Then she checked the helm. She bit back a curse, and forced herself to stay calm. Panic and sloppy thinking would not help. While she'd been in the airlock, the remaining crewman must have launched the ship on a preset course. The helm was locked out. She was heading for somewhere, no idea of the destination, no clue how long the flight might last, and no way to interfere or take back control.

She switched back to the navigation screen. At least tracking was still accessible. She could see where she was and where she'd been. There was the rendezvous with *Vixen*, two light years away already. How long was she out of action?

Regardless, it was clear that the scout was burning through space at the limits of its ability.

Moving over to the comms screen, Shayla composed a coded message to Henri Chargon summarizing the kidnap attempt—she scowled at that, the kidnap had actually worked, up to a point—and giving *Vixen's* position.

Who knows, there might be survivors.

A survivor.

She spat more blood on the floor, and gazed at it. There must be something she could do, should be doing right now, but her mind rebelled.

Her pain-wracked body demanded attention, and was that *hunger* gnawing at her? In times gone by she'd have shrugged off the discomfort while her mind outlined courses of action with laser clarity. She'd been out of the field far too long for this shit. She was growing soft.

Reeling from one wall to the other, she returned to the galley and began a careful self-examination. Working more purposefully at last, Shayla collected the spilled applicators from the floor. Most she returned to the drawer. A few she laid out on the galley worktop. She plundered the cabinet for more drugs and tools, then set about repairing herself.

While she worked, she checked the storage lockers for food. Pre-packed military rations. Her mouth twisted in a wry smile. *Oh! Memories!* Hardly what she'd been used to in her years as a planetary governor. She took a few packages at random and put them into the compact oven, leaving it to process the contents according to the instructions coded into the packaging.

While she finished dressing the deep burn on her arm, the oven decanted her selections onto a mess tray.

A heady aroma filled the galley, awakening a ravenous appetite.

———•—•———

Fifty miles east of Scale, across a sluggish river, an ashen scar on the landscape marked the location of the original city. Piloting a *Lance* fighter, Brin circled his chosen landing site a few miles beyond the devastation, where the green of new planting met the barren wastes.

He set the craft down as close to the maturing forest as he could without causing damage. The chances of onlookers out here were remote, and the Scale security office was under orders to keep the skies free from traffic without being obvious about it, but Brin believed in tilting the odds in his favor by any means he could. The contours of the land screened him from sight, and the trees provided some cover. It would take someone flying directly overhead to spot him.

An hour passed by. Brin hunched in the cockpit, keeping one eye on his surroundings and the other on the stream of reports clamoring for attention on the screen of his notepad. The demands of governorship, it seemed, never slept.

One by one, a rag-tag group assembled, arriving on an assortment of battered and dusty ground cars, bikes and transports. They emerged from among the rows of trees, or skirting the edges of the greenery.

Brin watched patiently from the cockpit, glad to see the vehicles remained under cover, awaiting orders. He kept the *Lance* warmed and ready to leap into the air at the first threat. His plea to Commander ap Terlion was a desperate gamble and he had no way of knowing how she might respond.

Minutes ticked by, until the prearranged hour arrived. A roar overhead, and an unmarked shuttle settled opposite Brin.

He breathed a deep sigh when the shuttle's passenger door opened and a robed and hooded figure stood at the top of the ramp. The figure's face was hidden, but even through clouds of swirling dust the posture and careful movements identified Commander ap Terlion.

Brin raised the cockpit canopy and climbed down. Chalky dryness coated his mouth and nose. He strode to the edge of the tree cover, where his hastily-assembled crew gathered, and turned to face the shuttle.

Commander ap Terlion stalked towards him, stiff-legged as if a misplaced footfall could result in injury. A half dozen men and women emerged from the shuttle and accompanied her across the few yards of open ground. Their movements appeared casual, but a spot in the middle of Brin's forehead prickled. Between them, they had formed a perfect perimeter around their leader, each of them maintaining a clear field of view. He knew he and each of his own team were pinned in the cross hairs of unseen weapons.

"Commander." Brin nodded as ap Terlion reached him and threw her hood back from her face.

"Acting Governor." She inclined her head fractionally deeper than Brin's greeting.

Brin jerked his chin towards the shuttle. "Can we dispense with the hidden threats?"

Commander ap Terlion tilted her head a fraction, one eyebrow raised.

"This is a joint operation. If we can't show trust now, we should return to our homes and pretend this meeting never happened."

The commander's lips quirked a fraction and she threw a glance over her shoulder.

Nothing visible changed, but the atmosphere lost its electric charge. Brin's shoulders relaxed, and he thumbed a remote control in his palm to the 'off' position. The *Lance's* weapons, trained on the shuttle, powered down to a warm standby.

Brin motioned his team to approach. They stood in a solemn circle on the edge of wilderness and completed introductions.

On Brin's side stood plain clothes guards who knew every inch of Eloon's towns and work camps, every bar and canteen, every bunkhouse, flophouse, fight ring and gambling den. Brin had greatly expanded his covert network on the ground in the weeks since Lady Carver's kidnapping. These guards had some training in undercover work but were outclassed by this new opponent.

Commander ap Terlion had brought hand-picked counterintelligence agents, wise to the techniques of tracking and evasion. They were as familiar with the mental labyrinth of human deceit as were Brin's guards with the Eloon underworld.

Brin briefed them on their targets, and what was known about the Insurrection's activities on the planet. Eventually the discussions concluded and the questions tailed off. Local guards paired off with visiting spooks. Everyone had their instructions. Brin grew somber and faced the group. "You are all accustomed to clandestine work, but I must remind you that you are entirely off the grid here."

"I understand the need of secrecy," a short and balding man said. "We must catch the Insurrection unawares, but why is this off the record from our own line of command? The Imperial navy has already landed teams of medics, engineers, and forensic investigators."

Commander ap Terlion nodded an acknowledgment of the question but remained silent.

"Those missions were all under the auspices of the Inspectorate," Brin said, "so they were legitimately within Imperial remit. This is different. I am inviting direct Imperial intervention in a matter of planetary security. This act jeopardizes our neutrality."

"Are you asking for help as Acting Governor of Eloon, or as head of security tasked with safeguarding the Emperor's house guests?"

Brin looked askance at Commander ap Terlion. That was a penetrating question. How much did she know about his real purpose here? "That line of thinking might salvage Eloon's Freeworld status in a court of law, but that would be cold comfort. Freeworld neutrality is one thing, but far more important is the perceived neutrality of our role as jailors. If Lord Scipio's supporters in the Firenzi hierarchy got so much as a sniff of Imperial military intelligence on active service down here all hell would break loose."

He caught each person's gaze in turn, seeing the implications of his words sink in. "That is something neither I nor the Emperor will risk. If anyone is caught, you will be on your own. Both I and Commander ap Terlion will have no choice but to deny all knowledge of your actions here."

———◆———

A dim red glow suffused the cabin. Shayla lay immobile, heart thudding, automatically starting a subliminal scan of her surroundings with all her senses. She could detect nothing wrong, no sounds betrayed an intruder or systems malfunction, no taste in the air beyond the flat machine-washed tang of close confines recycling. She turned her attention inwards. Her body gave no signs of distress beyond what it had already been subjected to.

Her mind, however was another matter. With a laugh of relief, Shayla calmed her breathing and teased out the subconscious bombshell that dropped her so suddenly out of sleep.

Two stages. Source and trigger. The bloody Firenzi had been at it again. She'd been driving herself mad trying to figure out how a poison could be administered to the inspection team without also harming anyone on Shayla's staff.

The clue was in the sabotage at the prison—a dormant primary agent and a catalytic trigger. And the irony was, this was another technique she'd used herself as an assassin. The inspectors *hadn't* been poisoned on Eloon. That would have happened days, maybe weeks before, with a latent precursor. All that remained was for some non-toxic but highly specific trigger compound to be administered to *everyone* at the feast.

Her smile faded. All very well, but the consequences would still be deadly and how could she help when her actions and motives were under suspicion, and she was trapped on a ship locked onto a pre-programmed course to an unknown destination?

After eating, she'd risked snatching some sleep. Who knew how long this journey would last? She gambled on it being hours at least. She badly needed to recharge after her ordeal, and sooner seemed the least risky.

She prepared more food, not caring what she chose from the utilitarian larder, and began to lay plans.

The navigation console bore more meticulous scrutiny. Even if she could, she hadn't yet decided whether she'd take control or let the scout make its pre-planned rendezvous. That kind of thinking would come later, but meanwhile she preferred to at least have the choice. And it would be good to know where they were heading if only to know how much time she had. As things stood, she needed to be ready for action round the clock for an unknown length of time. Not a good situation.

For the last seven years Shayla had nursed a raw wound deep inside, where the memory of Brandt still lived. Her dear brother, who'd shared with her the loss of their home, their world. They'd kept each other sane through the nightmares that followed, and together they'd plotted revenge against the empire. That plan had not gone well. It had ended with Shayla helping the Emperor, the man she thought was her enemy. Her true enemies ended up either dead or imprisoned.

Brandt, had died at her own hand. A mercy killing to spare him the agony of an irreversible poison. She'd had to do it. She knew all too well the torment he'd have suffered. He knew, at the last, what she was doing and why. There had been forgiveness and understanding in his eyes, hadn't there? She'd never know for sure. He'd been unable to speak by that point, paralyzed by the poison. His death was inevitable, but she'd taken it on herself to end his life.

Every day since, she missed the man, her brother, his quiet competence, his dry humor. But it was at times like this she most missed his twisted mind. Breaking past these locks would have been little more than a warm-up for him.

Instead, even with the illicit tools on her scroll, Shayla relied on her memory. She still had a dwindling stock of access codes and hidden identities from years gone by. Many were now useless, loopholes plugged one by one by Firenzi security, plastered over by routine upgrades, or simply eroded by the passage of time. A few might still bear fruit. But after a fruitless hour Shayla conceded defeat. For now. The lock was thorough. She was no security expert but this was no last minute arrangement, and not a standard part of any ship's console that she knew of. She took grudging pride in the thought that this may have been a precaution against her escape while on board the scout. Even if she'd killed the crew, she would still be delivered to the planned rendezvous.

That suggested this might be a longer trip than just a few hours.

Wherever she was headed, her best chance lay in not being on board. If that could not be physically arranged, then misleading appearances were her next best bet.

Jai Marx rubbed his eyes and worked a bead of moisture around his suddenly parched mouth. Only the pearly light from his scroll, and the navigation charts hastily summoned to his desktop, dispelled the darkness of his apartment. Only a thin robe distanced him from the small-hours chill. Only the thud of his own heart broke the silence.

He glanced down at his desktop, and wrote a series of instructions out of Shayla Carver's line of sight. He ran a hand through sleep-mussed hair and scowled. It was bad enough being woken in the dead of night by a call direct to his own quarters, but now *this*? "According to the fleet status chart, *Blazer* is in a long primary orbit at Misa-Mesai, awaiting orders."

"Then your status is wrong. *Blazer* is here, and flying silent." Carver gazed at him from the surface of his scroll while Jai wrestled with his own dark musings, then she smiled. "If you were to visit Misa-Mesai all you'll find is a relay probe putting out *Blazer's* signature."

Dammit, much as he wanted to he couldn't argue with empirical evidence. Carver's unwelcome call had come from one of his own ships. He'd verified *Blazer's* identification encrypted into the comms link, and she'd shown him the navigation plots, far too smugly for his liking. The rot in the Firenzi military ran deeper than he'd even begun to suspect. How many more fleet units were compromised and running around the galaxy on their own private missions?

"Jai, I have a big favor to ask. An Imperial inspection team was poisoned and lies gravely ill on Eloon."

"I do have sources of intelligence, you know." He didn't quite manage to keep the sarcasm out of his voice.

"What you may not know is that it was a slow-acting combination poison."

"They're just ill. Nobody's died ..."

He caught Carver's expression. Her eyebrow quirked in a giant, unspoken, 'And?'

He could see all too clearly the analysis she'd already made.

Firstly, the targeting was too precise. According to his sources, every member of the inspection team present at the feast had fallen ill. More tellingly, no one else had been affected and nor had the one member of the Inspectorate who'd already been nursing an infection and had not been present. But to distribute an active agent so precisely at such an event would demand a level of collusion among the serving staff too great to hide. That's what she would argue, anyway. Jai had his reservations. The woman commanded fanatical loyalty in some quarters. Who knew what her staff might be able to hide?

Then there was the slow spread. With the primary agent, consisting of an anchoring molecule, a release mechanism and the toxin itself, lodged in the victim's tissues, all it needed was a minute trace of the precise—and otherwise harmless—trigger molecule to start the process. That catalyst worked its way through the body, unlocking molecules of toxin one at a time before moving on to the next. Some more sophisticated poisons released additional molecules of the catalyst to create a faster cascading reaction, but they were rare and costly. Slow and certain death was the usual hallmark of a combination poison.

"Okay, it has the look," he said, grudgingly. "But that's hardly conclusive—"

"Conclusive enough for me, given that I *know* my staff had nothing to do with it. I need you to offer assistance to the Imperial team. You know what you're looking for. Even if I'm wrong, Firenzi medics have the best chance of saving them. The Imperials are out of their depth."

Jai quelled the outrage rising as she spoke. "Slow down. If the source is Firenzi as you claim, you're asking me to turn on members of my own Service. First, please explain why I should help you." That was the polite version. It was tantamount to holding up his hand to the Emperor and saying 'I did it.' Out of the question.

"I'm doing you the honor of believing you yourself had nothing to do with this." Lady Carver's tone dripped honey. "Otherwise we would be having a very different conversation."

Dammit, even trapped on a craft fleeing to Space-knows-where, the bitch was still threatening him. And the threat felt too damned credible to shrug off.

"Someone in your hierarchy has destroyed an Imperial warship and plotted to kidnap a planetary governor." She leaned closer to the screen. "There were four of Henri Chargon's agents on board, hand-picked from his elite corps. How do you think he'll react?"

Jai's gut turned to ice as she spoke. Here was a very real and damning observation.

"And how long do you think it'll be before he links the trail back to you?"

"But this plot must have been a renegade faction." A desperate claim, and one which he knew wouldn't wash with the Emperor, no matter how true it might be.

"So, are you defending them or distancing yourself?"

Bloody stupid question! Jai's expression hardened once more. "They are doing me no favors. I need to neutralize them."

"And I think you could do with my help to convince the Emperor of that."

He shook his head slowly in resignation.

"I have already spoken with your Imperial counterpart, Chalwen ap Gwynodd."

"Why would *she* believe you?" His words emerged as a strangled squawk. Essence of Unity! How busy had she been?

"Of course she's not going to simply take my word for anything. The finger of suspicion points squarely at me, after all. Rather too squarely, in fact. Chalwen's not stupid. She was already questioning the convenience, and she at least gives me credit that if I'd wished harm to the inspectors I'd have done it without being so blindingly obvious."

"Unless you were double-bluffing." The riposte now was half-hearted. There had to be a point to all this. She wasn't just hanging him out to dry; there had to be something she needed.

"There is that." Carver smiled, feline and predatory. "But that's irrelevant. All I did was plant a seed of suspicion. It was clear from my comms call sign that a Firenzi ship is implicated in the destruction of *Vixen*. And drugs and poisons are a Firenzi specialty."

The blood drained from Jai's face. How many Firenzi secrets were at risk as long as she lived? But he caught the twinkle in her eyes. The damned woman was toying with him.

"Naturally I didn't discuss the nature of the drug technology," she said, "only that it was a specialized Firenzi technique, and that Firenzi laboratories would have the resources to isolate and neutralize it."

Jai's mouth twisted. "Seems I've been effectively herded."

"As have I," Carver reminded him. "I have little hope of escaping this, but I do want to salvage what I can. Look after the inspectors for me and you may yet come out of this ahead of the game."

"How so?"

"This scout is on a preset course. The plan must be to rendezvous somewhere with me nicely sedated. I'm inclined to allow the first part of that plan to unfold as intended."

"And then?"

"Still working on that. Let's just say I may be able to unmask your renegades for you."

As he broke the connection, Jai felt a curious lightness. He was being shamelessly maneuvered, but he had a sense that here was a powerful ally. No, maybe that was too strong. Their mutual interests aligned for now, and as long as that remained true he stood to benefit.

Chapter 19

With an effort, Shayla set aside any further thoughts of Eloon. She'd done what she could for the inspection team. She prayed that would lighten Brin's load enough for him to deal with Cobra. At least that was more familiar territory for Brin, but the idea of Cobra active on her planet chilled her. What was his game? He'd have a score to settle with her, but was he acting alone or was there a bigger goal?

Regardless, she had her own situation to deal with. Brin was now on his own.

A brief rummage through the crew's lockers yielded sets of naval-issue working overalls. None of the spare uniforms hanging there were a good enough fit to pass even a casual inspection, but overalls needed less precise measurement. She sifted through the locker and found a set with a petty officer's shoulder flash. Not the lowest in society, but low enough to not stand out in the crowd.

Next, Shayla procured an EVA suit, helmet, life support pack and—thank Space—a hand-held thruster for zero gravity maneuvers. As an added bonus there was even a coil of polymer line with a clip at one end and a palm-sized magnetic grapple at the other. She double-checked the grapple's charge.

The galley yielded a week's worth of dry rations and flasks of water. It took moments longer to find a pack of sealable bags, and a couple of spare beam pistols in the storage compartment.

Shayla donned the overalls and EVA suit, and stashed the rations in the engineering compartment at the rear of the ship. She'd noticed the secondary airlock back there, on the opposite side of the craft from the main lock, that had given her the germ of her plan.

Now it was time to set the scene. The bodies of the two crew still lay where she'd left them. She meticulously cleaned every trace of her presence and checked and re-checked the ship from stem to stern before moving on to the next stage.

She closed and checked the airtight hatch separating the engineering space from the living quarters, then propped open the inner airlock hatch. A few carefully-aimed blasts from a beam pistol welded it in position. With a savage battle cry, Shayla peppered the inside of the airlock with more blasts. Nobody examining the scene could mistake the ferocity of the gunfight that had taken place here.

The outer lock obviously wouldn't open unless the inner hatch was closed, but that was easily rectified. From the control room Shayla instructed the ship to evacuate the forward living compartments. With no pressure differential, the outer hatch meekly swung open to the black of space.

This was the point of no return. Shayla ran through a mental checklist and reviewed her movements and equipment. Satisfied, she blasted the airlock controls and sent a few glancing bolts off the outer hatch for good measure. That would explain why the airlock had failed to prevent catastrophic decompression.

She paused on the threshold of the lock, checking and re-checking the grapple and the thruster pack clipped at her waist. Nobody ventured outside a craft hopping at light speed. Logic told her that this part of the journey was safe enough, but it just wasn't a done thing.

The primary drive's field enclosed the ship in a bubble. Anything inside the bubble was carried with it. Anything outside would get left behind. That thought was bad enough, but anything making the transition from inside to outside would get left behind in hair-thickness wafers as the cycling field acted like a high-speed bacon slicer.

A shudder wracked her and she stepped back into the airlock to catch her breath. Shayla swallowed the gorge rising in her throat and snarled a curse. The memory of *Vixen's* death throes galvanized her. Those bastards would pay, but not if they caught her here.

She reached outside the hatch for a handhold on the hull and eased herself out of the grav field. Now weightless, Shayla surveyed the hull in the tiny circle of light from her helmet lamp, and plotted her movements over the top. Not knowing how much room she had to maneuver in, she glided cautiously from one vantage point to the next, pausing at each to take stock and plan her next move.

Absolute black surrounded her. No perceptible starlight penetrated the bubble's boundary as it made nanosecond appearances in real space a thousand miles apart. Where the lamp shone, the hull plating curving away in front of her seemed endless. This boat was a lot bigger on the outside than it seemed from within.

Breathing hard and wishing she could wipe away the salt sweat stinging her eyes, Shayla stopped to orientate herself. Navigating with extreme tunnel vision in the utter dark of the non-space between normal dimensions, she wondered if she might have gone around in a circle. Her eyes tried to make sense of the stark planes reflecting back at her in the lamplight.

Nothing but an unguessable horizon lay ahead and to either side. Ignoring the pain in her wrists from the death grip on her current hand-hold, she scanned in a wider arc down on both sides.

Back there. That looked like an upper wing straddling the hull, with a drive pod hanging off the visible end. She had overshot her mark. She realigned herself and took a few more moments to restore calm and focus.

Another glide, and another, and there was the engineering airlock hatch.

Minutes later, Shayla was inside. She threw off her helmet and gulped the flat, stale, oily, unspeakably wonderful air of the engineering station.

Featherlight fingertips brushed the forward hatch already slick with condensation. The dead crew compartment lay beyond, now open to space. Alongside, a ladder climbed the bulkhead to a maintenance crawl space overhead. Between the ladder and the inner door of the secondary airlock, a small repeater console echoed navigation and communications from the main control room.

She checked the scout's heading, running fast for the outskirts of Imperial space. At a guess, and given that she was on a Firenzi scout a hundred light years out of position and the wrong side of the border, she was heading back into Firenzi territory. She probably had a few days yet.

Time, at least, for food.

After her meal, Shayla cleared up and bagged the small amount of waste she'd accumulated. She left the spare rations in an untidy heap in a locker, hoping their presence would be ascribed to sloppiness, but domestic garbage back here would arouse suspicion. There should be nothing to suggest recent human habitation when the time came.

Donning her helmet, she cycled the airlock and tossed the bag gently into space. Curious, she shone her lamp on it as it drifted away. Twenty feet from the hull, it vanished like a pebble dropped into industrial sludge. No ripple marred the invisible barrier, but the bag slipped out of existence, smeared across millions of miles of space.

She wondered how many inquisitive space mariners had tried similar experiments over the years.

A day passed, and another, in monotonous absence of routine. Eat, sleep, defecate, repeat. Shayla thanked providence that even in such a tiny craft the naval architects had stuck to tradition and tucked a head in one corner of the engineering space, sparing her the task of dealing with *all* forms of waste.

Most of the compartment was taken up by the main power plant, a ten-foot-wide cylinder running up through floor and ceiling. Shot-dulled metal, a fetching shade of industrial teal, was warm to the touch and vibrated just on the edge of feeling. The plant gave out a low hum, barely noticeable at first but in the otherwise silent craft it soon set teeth on edge. There was just enough room on the strip of maroon non-slip decking around the power plant for a midget to swing a very small feline, if you didn't care too much about the feline. Lumpy machinery in the same teal finish intruded all around. Dim yellow lights peered down through thick sheaves of cables.

Shayla whiled the hours meticulously charting in her mind all the possible reception committees she might have to deal with at the other end. Ship—small or large—base, moon, planet, wary, careless, military, civilian, pirate.

Soldier, sailor, candlestick maker.

Focus!

To keep herself alert, Shayla risked her elbows jogging a few circuits around the power plant.

Ruefully rubbing a livid bruise from unplanned contact with a surge regulator, she returned to introspection.

Who could have engineered this kind of kidnap? People on the inside in both Firenzi and Imperial camps. It reeked of the Gruesome Twosome, or their followers at least. Something like this would surely be hard to plan from their remote prison.

Shayla's heart missed a beat. Is that why they went to such lengths to get themselves moved out of the polar prison? The new facility, still incomplete and overrun with new personnel, might offer more opportunities for unsanctioned contact.

No, the timing didn't make sense. She was losing her grip in the cold confines of this machinery space. The poisoning of the inspectors had to factor into this plot. That's what brought her into harm's way in the first place and *that* plot must have been in the planning long before the team even landed.

So where did the prison transfer figure into all this? It didn't make sense. The poisoning linked to the kidnapping: trigger and trap. The rest didn't fit.

And none of this was helping her guess how long to wait, or what to do when the waiting was over.

Brindis ap Silessi felt the world drop away from beneath him. Bard Jovin gazed at him from the screen across his office, one-eyed, face scarred, expressionless. Brin brought his attention back to the news his Captain of Guards had relayed.

"Gone?"

"The frigate was ambushed, maybe sabotaged by someone aboard. Our sparrow is flown."

A cold shock drenched Brin's mind. Something was off in Bard's manner. Too stiff. Too formal. Speaking from down in the basement operations room he was watching his words. More to the point, 'sparrow' was a code word slipped into the conversation to signal imminent danger and the need to flee.

"Thank you, Captain Jovin. That will be all."

In a trance Brin stood, thanking Space that he was back in his own office in the wing at the back of the Governor's Residence. As he rose, his fingers sought a microscopic indent under the edge of the desk. Footsteps already drew near in the hallway outside, a large body of people marching in quick time. Why hadn't his own guards in the entrance hall alerted him? The wash of cold numbness settled into his gut. Those guards had either been overpowered, without a shot, by an

overwhelming force or they'd bowed to a higher authority. Neither prospect gave him comfort.

He paused for a fraction of a second to consider his options. These
had to be Imperial forces from *Hammer*. As Acting Governor, he could
stay and brazen it out. Surely his authority commanded some respect?
Bard Jovin's words weighed on him. He'd obviously had time to assess
the situation and judged it dangerous. Brin's position would not protect
him, indeed might now be the source of the danger. In Lady Carver's
absence, responsibility for events on the ground now lay at his door.

This analysis needed no more than the time it took him to turn
and cover the few paces to the window behind his desk. He pushed the
window open. His first duty lay with the Imperial prisoners in their new
and woefully incomplete prison. He couldn't fulfill that duty from inside
a jail cell. Her Ladyship's gaunt face, eroded by that same frustration,
haunted him.

A final thought struck him like an ice dagger. *Commander ap Terlion.*
Had she betrayed his trust?

Without a backward glance he stepped onto the sill and dropped
over the ledge.

An alarm pinged on the repeater screen. *Blazer* had stopped running.

Cautiously, Shayla started a passive scan of surrounding space, visuals only. Nothing to betray her presence. She soon saw it was a waste
of time. The scout hung motionless deep in interstellar space. Velvety
black enfolded her, dusted with distant stars. There was nothing to illu-
minate an approaching ship. Her only hope was to spot a wink in one
of those hard, remote, pinpricks as a ship passed in front. A chance in a
million, until it was too close.

"Mother Hen to Courier, please respond."

The squawk from the comms screen made Shayla jump.

The hail was repeated twice more, each time sounding more tense.

Now the moment was here, the biggest gamble—the unwanted
thought she'd been avoiding—hit her full on. How would they react
when the crew failed to answer? Would they simply destroy the craft
and run? She expected that they'd at least board *Blazer* to confirm it

was empty first. The question was, how nervous were they, and how important was she?

Minutes ticked by. At Shayla's instruction the comms unit kept up a passive scan, seeking any active channel nearby. At last, it hit on a conversation from the unseen ship. They'd launched a shuttle to investigate. It was already on its way over.

Shayla carefully reset the repeater screens to erase any hint that they'd been used recently. After a final check of her surroundings, she scurried up the ladder to the crawl space above, thankful that she'd kept the engineering compartment tidy ready for a hasty exit.

Tucked blind inside her hideaway, she followed events as best she could from the chatter through her helmet comms. The shuttle circled *Blazer*, soon spotting the gaping airlock. They closed in, shining lights through the doorway. There was consternation when the far door was discovered also open and the main corridor exposed to vacuum.

Long minutes of anxious waiting. Silence on the airwaves. At last, the shuttle pilot reported that a small squad was crossing the gap to board and inspect.

Muffled clangs echoed through the hull. Magnetic clamps holding fast. A more solid bump told her that the shuttle had reeled in the lines to hold them steady, locked together.

Now the back-and-forth chat was almost continuous. The boarding party quickly discovered the vacuum-frozen bodies and the signs of a fierce firefight. They also noticed they were a body short.

The sealed hatch to the engineering space delayed them a while.

"Of course there's still pressure there," the shuttle pilot scolded. "If the hatch wasn't already shut, it would have closed as soon as the pressure dropped. You need to get in there and check the rear spaces, just to be sure."

"The hatch won't open. You expect us to blast it?"

The pilot sighed. Shayla could picture his sorry shake of the head. "You have access to the control room, don't you? Evacuate the compartment."

"What if there's someone on the other side still?"

"Those birds have a repeater console in the engineering space. They'd have answered our hail by now, otherwise serves 'em right."

A rushing roar announced the boarding party's response. The roar died to a whistle and dwindled to unnatural silence. Shayla's suit stiffened, accommodating the transition to vacuum. She pulled out her knife, lay the borrowed beam pistol alongside her, and settled down to wait.

A subtle vibration through the deck grating. They were in.

Eyes focused on the closed access down to the engineering compartment, Shayla ran through scenarios should she be discovered. There was nowhere to hide in this narrow maintenance corridor. Whoever stuck his head up first would be one less to deal with. The question was, how many more could she surprise? Dealing with the boarding party would be the least of her worries. Could she get to the shuttle before the pilot broke away? Alternatively, would the scout's navigation panel accept commands now they'd reached their destination?

And beyond those questions, there was an another ship somewhere out there to deal with.

Her deliberations became moot. The party was looking out for missing bodies, not stowaways, and was clearly anxious to be off this ghost ship as quickly as possible.

"Gee-Ell, shuttle boarding party—"

"Mind your comms protocol, dammit!"

"Sorry, Mother Hen." The pilot suppressed a snicker. "We're a long way from the hen house. There's no one but us chickens here to hear us."

"Nevertheless ..." The response was terse.

Shayla pressed her lips thin. If this pilot had been under her command, he'd be in for a month of kitchen fatigues for that slip. If you value your secrecy you stick to your protocols even when they seem pointless. Assume even the vacuum has ears.

Gee-Ell ... crews usually adopted pet names or abbreviations for their ships. It had been years since she'd been in the Firenzi navy, but there could only be one 'Gee-Ell' by virtue of millennia of seniority: the antiquated battleship *Admiral George Leonard*. Shayla's pulse quickened. This would be a nostalgic trip. She'd served on another *Enforcer*-class sister ship when she'd first enlisted. The whole class shared the same plan. Already her mind was cataloguing knowledge, entry points, hiding places, while her attention returned to the chat outside.

"The capture went sour." The pilot resumed his report. "Two bodies here, one unaccounted for. Pilot must have set course then got fried defending the airlock. Awaiting instructions, Mother Hen. Are we bringing Courier in or abandoning?"

"Stand by, shuttle."

Shayla knew exactly what she would do under these circumstances. This was a good time to be gone. She wormed her way back down to the engineering compartment, hampered by the stiff EVA suit and thruster pack. Thankful that the compartment was already open to vacuum, it took only moments to ease herself out of the secondary airlock, taking care to close the hatches behind her on the off-chance they'd bring the scout in for a closer inspection. She hung a few moments getting her bearings and checking surrounding space. A blocky outline of occluded stars below her feet marked the battleship's presence. Must be a few miles distant. Not a gap she intended to leap without help.

The upper gull wing spread of the scout's drive and communications pods hid her from the shuttle's viewports as she maneuvered herself, handhold to handhold, towards the shuttle's rear.

The shuttle's exterior lights bathed the scout. Reflected light illuminated the shuttle itself. From the corner of her eye, she saw the magnetic clamps let loose. The lines reeled in. Her movements quickened.

She wasn't about to make the rookie mistake of jumping high, instinctively expecting non-existent gravity to bring her down, but she needed a launching point at the right angle. The use of her EVA thruster was a last resort. The emission would certainly be detected.

The shuttle drifted away from the scout's flank. A lightning mental calculation, and Shayla hauled herself forward and up into the angle where the gull wing merged with the main hull. She tucked into a roll as she flew, and kicked out against the scout's side.

Once again, she found herself reaching for handholds as her target wheeled away in front of her eyes. This time her fingers missed.

Her gloved hand scrabbled ineffectually against the smooth armor, and she bounced.

Frantic, Shayla reached to her belt and released the coil of line dangling at her waist. She activated the magnetic clamp on the end of the line and flung it across the widening gap.

The clamp made contact and held. Shayla hauled herself in and stretched for a better handhold, knowing that the clamp would only take so much weight. She wedged herself into the angle between the hull and an antenna housing, and threw a few loops of line around her-self and the antenna for good measure.

She hoped to Space and beyond that the shuttle pilot made no high speed maneuvers.

The shuttle took a wide arc away from the scout. Shayla puzzled for a moment, scanning the night sky beneath her for signs of the darkened warship. She cursed her stupidity and screwed her eyes shut instead. Seconds ticked, the sense of anticlimax and foolishness growing, until her precaution was vindicated. Even through her closed eyelids and the reactive darkening of her visor, the flash was blinding.

When she opened her eyes and dispelled the dancing afterimage of the flash, there was nothing of the scout to be seen.

A few feet from the ground, an upward-angled grav field braked Brin's fall and snatched him into a narrow recess that appeared in the wall. The opening snapped shut again, the whole maneuver over in an eyeblink.

The grav field cut off, dropping him onto a cushioned floor. He rolled with the impact and staggered to his feet. Dim red light washed the cramped space. A polished pole threaded the center of a narrow shaft ahead of him. He grasped the pole and slid, legs wrapped around it for stability.

It had been a few years since he'd practiced this maneuver. The Residence was riddled with undocumented bolt holes, but their very secrecy made regular drills difficult. Another grav field here would have been more comfortable but it didn't do to rely on technology or a ready power supply any more than necessary. Not in the kinds of emergencies that warranted this desperate escape route.

All the while, a tumult of fragmented thoughts raged through Brin's mind. Imperial forces parading through the Governor's Residence, coming for *him*. What had triggered this madness? Had Commander ap Terlion revealed his plea for help? But to what end? She would be as deeply implicated as him. Or had someone betrayed them both? Nothing made sense.

Far below ground, a glimmer of daylight illuminated the recesses of a deep and narrow cave, one of hundreds that honeycombed the

Heights of Scithea looming over the old capital city. The drop shaft deposited Brin on a ledge ten feet above the cave floor. Hidden from below behind a natural outcrop, a single-seat *Lance* fighter squatted, fueled and ready.

As he lowered himself into the cockpit the instrument panel came to life. Brin checked that the electromagnetic shielding built into the cave wall was still working before firing up the *Lance's* drive. He counted back the seconds since he'd left his office. There was probably a search going on up there, but still too early for them to have hit the panic button. The Residence was a warren of offices and accommodation, so unless someone had stayed to watch the back of the building it would take them a while to conclude he had somehow fled from under their noses.

A non-standard panel built into the console gave him a window into the operations room systems a hundred feet above his head. He scowled as he saw that *Hammer of War* had recently passed high overhead in orbit, presumably after dropping off an unscheduled transport with extra troops to arrest him, and was now heading away to the southeast. That picture would change the moment he made his move, or when the ground team reported him missing.

He decided to forego the possible advantage of extra distance between him and that battleship, and instead use the element of surprise while it lasted. The *Lance* lifted clear of the rock floor and drifted lazily towards the cave mouth. Pumped with adrenaline from his unorthodox exit, Brin's mouth twisted in a savage grin. Through the operations room shadow console he engaged broad spectrum jamming signals, part of the planet's ring of defenses, and opened the throttle.

The stubby fighter spat from the cave and arrowed along the ravine that cut through the plateau behind the Residence. Piloting with reckless abandon, he hugged the river valley through a few turns until the Residence, Legislature, and landing field complex were out of sight behind rough uplands, then he lifted clear of the ground clutter and took the craft hypersonic.

The shuttle wheeled and sped towards the battleship, hidden now beyond the craft's flank. Shayla pictured their approach against her brief glimpse of the battleship's silhouette.

Boarding would be tricky. She could hardly expect to enter the hangar strapped to the back of the shuttle and escape notice. Even if, by some miracle, the docking controller was asleep at his screens, her EVA suit would be out of place inside the hangar bay. On the other hand, any of the ship's external airlocks would sound an alarm the moment she tried to open it from the outside. She wanted to be a stealthy passenger, not a fugitive from the search that kind of alert would trigger.

Once aboard, the going should be easier. *Enforcer*-class ships were huge, second only to Imperial *Swords*, and the mainstay of the Firenzi navy for the last five millennia. A bulky hull contained machinery and accommodation, but farsighted architects had designed them with pairs of vast docking points to mount weapons or more specialized payloads. This flexibility, and the ability to upgrade weapon systems over the years without a massive overhaul, was the secret of the ancient ships' longevity.

If *Admiral George Leonard* was typical of her class, she'd be packing six batteries of beam weapons at those docking points. Shayla hoped to identify the source of the blinding shot that had vaporized the scout. From her stint aboard a similar ship, she had the glimmer of a plan to avoid arousing suspicion.

But first, she had to transfer from the speeding shuttle. Now they were close, the battleship registered as nothing more than a void in the speckle of stars. Not good. Unlike the floodlit leap from scout to shuttle, here there was nothing visible, no reference points to judge speed or distance.

Jumping blind like this was too risky. She might have to chance the hangar bay after all. On the other hand … sudden pressure against the hull plating told Shayla they were slowing. Any second now the pilot would turn to line up with the hangar doors at the stern. Shayla clung tight ready for the turn.

Yellow striplights framed the gaping door, widening as they approached. At last she had a frame of reference to orient herself, and she knew where she was heading. To reach the forward port battery, which she judged had just been fired, she'd have to traverse most of the ship's two-thousand-foot length. It was her best chance.

Shayla untied the safety line and coiled it ready for action. Using the expanding rectangle of lights to judge their approach, she picked her moment and nudged herself away from the shuttle.

Weightless, she wafted upwards. The lip of the hangar loomed into view.

Too fast.

She threw the magnetic grapple, felt it latch. A jarring wrench at her waist as she reached the end of the line. Suddenly free again. Not good.

She hastily reeled in the line for another try, aware of the invisible mass sliding past below at unguessable speed. The battleship blotted out half her sphere of vision, a darkened landscape stretching ahead and on either side under a starry sky.

She launched the grapple down and forward, feeling the line paying out through gloved fingers. Near its limit, it went slack for a moment as the magnet caught once more. Shayla pulled herself downward, trying to bring her trajectory closer to the ship rather than away, before she sped past the clinging grapple and the line jerked once more.

Once again she wrenched free, her forward momentum too much for the palm-sized magnet. She prayed that the clip at her waist would hold up to the punishment. If the line broke free she was dead. She would never be able to hold onto it under that tension.

She was tumbling now, unable to control her movements and not daring to use the thruster this close to the ship's vigilant sensors. She brought the line in again and aimed a shot, the spinning starscape her only guide.

Shayla slammed hard into something structural.

Winded, blinking away redness from her vision, Shayla re-oriented herself and threw the grapple again.

The line paid out.

Ended.

There was no tug this time. She was out of reach.

She had no alternative. Shayla pulled the thruster from her belt. She aimed and squeezed the release.

Nothing happened.

Numb, she gazed at its dented casing, becoming aware with grow-ing dread of the pounding pain at her hip where she'd crashed into the battleship. The hip where the thruster had sat.

Chapter 20

With a sneer, Brin pictured the Imperial reaction to the planetwide enveloping static that cloaked his movements. Some thick-necked Lieutenant would doubtless be bawling orders to shut it down. Brin's staff would genuinely try to comply, but the commands issued from this cockpit console, and from a very select handful of others secreted here and there, couldn't easily be overridden. The back doors built into the system were known to only a few.

Imperial technicians would quickly step in to do the job themselves. They would have even less luck and would—he hoped—realize that his staff had not been deliberately stalling.

At some point they would turn to more senior officers to override the system. The question was, how long could Bard Jovin stall while keeping up the appearance of earnest intent? They'd built in layers of entirely credible obfuscation, elaborate re-verification procedures—triggered by the Imperials' own interference—to reassure the system that an apparently hostile breach had been contained. When needed, Bard could play that passive-aggressive finger-pointing game as well as any, but there was a limit even to his talents and he needed to remain in place as a compliant asset, not removed as a threat.

Of course it couldn't last. This could only ever be a short-term evasive measure. The cloud-wreathed pinnacles of the Blue Ridge were climbing high above the horizon when the blanket of interference lifted. Twenty minutes. Not bad. He'd hoped for longer but it could have been worse.

With the airwaves clear again, Brin tuned in to the comms chatter, receive only. Other than his engine's signature emissions he was transmitting nothing to give his presence away.

All crisp efficiency, Bard Jovin himself gave orders to scramble all available fighters from Torremis and from Scale as a precaution, on the lookout for any unregistered craft, numbers and positions unknown.

The instructions sounded sensible and earnest, but Bard's careful choice of words in issuing orders told Brin that his disappearance was still a mystery and there was no firm evidence yet of his flight. Not for the first time, Brin thanked Lady Carver's foresight in devising a thorough system of code words and phrases that allowed some covert hints to be mingled into plain speech. He allowed himself a small and rare smile. Far from helping, Bard was deliberately muddying the waters, criss-crossing the region with a profusion of tracks.

Minutes later, Brin plunged into the maze of peaks that formed the mountain range inland from Scale. He'd headed this way in the hopes of confusing his true destination. He slowed to a manageable pace and hugged cliffs and valleys as he angled south towards the distant island of Sherrin, and the new—heavily fortified—prison site.

Despair gripped Shayla. She could try raising the ship on her helmet comm. That would deliver her right back to the people who wanted her and she'd already witnessed their level of concern for her well-being. Would death between the stars be a kinder choice?

Regardless, the tumbling was making her dizzy and she was not about to either die or surrender with a helmet full of puke. She took a few rotations to plan her timing and launched the useless thruster away with all her strength. The sickening movement slowed to a more manageable cartwheel. In the light of her helmet lamp she watched the thruster dwindle, a speck against the night.

Moments later, Shayla was startled to see the thruster spinning back *towards* her. She craned her neck to follow it, then directed the flashlight downward, towards the inky silhouette of the giant battleship. A diffuse circle of light greeted her, rapidly shrinking and brightening. She readied the grapple and did her best to gauge her approach, calculating as she rolled which limbs would end up beneath her to cushion the impact.

Despite the acrobatic training of her many martial arts, it was hardly a clean landing, but nor was it a blind bounce. With the grapple holding, Shayla paid out the line, regulating the tension and slowing her movement. Before she reached full stretch she finally stopped, and hauled herself back to the expanse of armor.

With a laugh bordering on the manic she processed what had happened. While she was tumbling away into space the ship had turned towards her. Shuttle safely stowed—it felt like a lifetime since she'd parted company but it could only have been a minute—*Admiral George Leonard* was maneuvering ready to engage her primary drive. The trouble was clinging to the outside—and outside the protective envelope of the ship's artificial grav field—she would be subject to the full force of any maneuvers under secondary drive, and these ships could easily pull forty gravities when they put their minds to it.

She wouldn't survive anything that extreme, but she did want a better hold than the feeble grapple.

Nothing useable presented itself in the range of the flashlight.

The push of the armor beneath her, which had given the illusion of weight for those few seconds, faded back to weightlessness.

The stars above vanished, catching Shayla by surprise. They were under way.

She breathed a deep sigh of relief and coiled the line in her hands ready to move.

With no handholds visible, movement was tricky. Using the clamped grapple for leverage, Shayla lined herself in the direction she wanted to go. She released the magnet and skimmed it gently across the armored surface ahead of her. On the limit of visibility she activated the magnet once more, watched it snap to the hull, and tested the line gingerly. Sure it was properly clamped, she pulled herself along.

Every movement was slow and measured. Once, a too-hasty tug pulled the clamp free. For heart-stopping moments Shayla drifted away from the hull, wondering how far she could travel before hitting the boundary of the primary drive's field, while she reeled in the line and cast the grapple down. Once more snug against the armor she took precious minutes to compose herself before resuming her fly-on-the-ceiling crawl.

Damn, but these ships were *big*.

At last an edge came into view. Shayla studied the contours revealed beyond. A shallow valley with a maze of pipes and ducts criss-crossed by partitions and beams lay between her and another featureless plateau. She matched the tunnel view revealed by her tiny helmet lamp against her recollection of the *Enforcer*-class. When she left the shuttle she'd traversed the upper hull, and she was sure she'd retained her sense of orientation through all the acrobatics. She was atop one of the storage modules that ran most of the length of the ship, but she had no sense of distance.

She cast her grapple forward and hauled herself down into the valley, thankful at last for useable handholds. With the line stowed by her side ready for use—she coiled it carefully to avoid snags or tangles at an awkward moment—she pulled herself along the valley.

An airlock hatch came into view. Tempting ... if she wanted to sound the alarm. But acting on long-buried memory she studied the coded notation alongside the control panel. Thank heavens for standards. The string of letters matched her recollection from a sister ship. She was getting close.

The valley came to an abrupt end. The flank of the ship sloped down and away. Shayla resumed her crawl forwards and was rewarded at last by the protruding bulk of a particle beam emplacement.

Down there, in the gap where the weapon battery docked with the ship's hull proper, was her target. A simple access hatch, not an airlock.

The hatch popped open and Shayla slipped inside the weapon bay. How to board a ship without boarding the *ship*, that was the trick. Although she was now technically on board, safely enclosed at last within the ship's armored walls and shielding and subject once more to gravity, this cavernous hold was unpressurized and still technically open to space.

Shayla examined her surroundings with a pang of nostalgia. Life had been so much simpler back then in her days as a lowly marine. A wash of red light barely dispelled the darkness. Suspended overhead, the barrels of two particle beams—warehouse-sized siblings of the handheld weapons she heartily despised—each dwarfed the scout she'd recently abandoned.

Pale green striplights marked a maze of companionways and catwalks that weaved between the inert bulk of machinery clinging to the bay walls. She craned her neck, eyes tracing the lines of cables and conduits high above.

She had been a marine, not an engineer, but she'd heard enough shipboard grumbling back then. These weapon emplacements looked similar to the ones arming the *General Martha Sandover*, Shayla's old ship. She was banking on them being just as cranky to maintain.

Towards the rear of the compartment, Shayla started climbing.

Thirty feet up, a cradle of massive girders held the nearer of the two weapons in the battery. Another catwalk, and Shayla slowed, still picking her way up through a maze of machinery.

At last, this was what she was looking for. The Achilles heel that the maintenance engineers constantly bitched about. A forest of coolant hoses, each thicker than her body, snaked from a containment vessel and spread like veins across the adjacent beam generator. Many of them looked worn, insulation frayed and flaking.

Shayla chose a section that betrayed the most signs of age. Once-white cladding yellowed and crazed. A chunk looked loose. With her knife, she levered the cladding away from the hose beneath. The edge of the knife glowed blue as she activated the shimmerblade and stabbed it into the hose. She withdrew hastily. Coolant jetted into the vacuum, crystallizing and fluttering to the floor sixty feet below.

As an afterthought, her heart thudding as she belatedly saw her near oversight, she thrust a gloved hand into the stream of coolant and smeared it over the tell-tale insignia on her EVA suit. Details mattered. To a civilian one uniform looked much like another, but wearing a badge from the wrong ship she might as well be wearing neon pink.

Knowing the pressure loss in the hose would now be triggering alarms, Shayla scooted down ladders, careful not to disturb rivulets and pools of coolant spattering the machinery.

A pressurized workshop occupied most of the floor of the beam emplacement. Shayla stopped on the workshop roof and found a hiding place across the bay from her act of sabotage.

She checked her suit's oxygen levels, mentally backtracking from the first moments the boarding crew had depressurized the scout. Assuming her sketchy geometry held true and she'd picked the right beam battery, there should still be an engineering crew nearby. Even after a single firing, there was a long list of cool-down and safety checks to run through.

Double-checking that her suit's comms unit was still locked in 'silent' mode, receiving but not transmitting even a locator signal, Shayla scanned the channels for signs of life.

A brief vibration through the soles of her feet, barely on the threshold of feeling. Light spilled across the floor below her vantage point. A team of engineers emerged from the airlock and scurried like ants up into the machinery. Relieved to see their EVA suits matched the standard issue suits she'd found on *Blazer*, Shayla tuned in to the chatter.

"What's the damage this time?"

"Cooling hose blown."

"This the shooter they let loose with?"

A grunted reply.

"Figures. Firing practice is all well and good but they never give these babies a work out at full power."

"Heaven help us if we ever go into battle. We'll fall apart at the first shot!"

The litany was timeworn and familiar. Even though the weapon systems were new compared to the ship itself, it might have been decades since this particular weapon last felt the strain of a full blast. Meanwhile, pipes aged and grew brittle.

She worked her way back across the bay and descended the gangway the maintenance team had used. A sergeant and an orderly with a notepad lounged beside the near airlock.

"Where do you think you're going, sailor?"

Shayla ignored the question.

The glare of a flashlight gleamed off her visor. As if seeing the sergeant for the first time, Shayla turned and saluted. She tapped the side of her helmet and held a clenched fist to her ear.

"That's all we need," the sergeant muttered over the open link. "More equipment failure." Shayla pretended not to hear and hand-signaled her intent to replace the faulty unit. The sergeant signaled back. Make it snappy. With a crisp salute, Shayla scurried into the airlock.

She was in.

———————

A proximity alarm pinged on Brin's console. He suppressed a surge of irrational joy that threatened to dull his survival instincts. Crossing the lowlands between Blue Ridge to the north, and the relative safety of the Tumbledowns to the south, he scanned his surroundings for landmarks that might offer cover. Precious little looked of use. He felt exposed.

Well, if any attacker thought they were taking on a standard *Lance* they were in for a shock. This one had been upgraded to outrun other craft of its class, and some offensive weaponry had been sacrificed for a few highly non-standard countermeasures. This craft was designed for flight, not fight.

Two more *Lances* took up formation on either side. Brin recognized the insignia and gave a quiet cheer. These were part of the distraction crew sent out by Bard.

"Yellow leader to yellow seven." His comms unit chirped a fictitious call sign for his renegade craft. "See anything on that last pass?"

Brin thumbed his comms to transmit. "Negative, yellow leader. Nobody here but us chickens."

In the far cockpit, the squad leader waved and gave a thumbs-up.

Over the next half an hour, a bizarre cat-and-mouse game played out as the Imperial commander struggled to gain control of the crowded airspace. The forty or more pilots Bard had scrambled swapped invented call signs in a studied lack of military discipline, making it impossible to get an accurate count of craft in the air. When the commander tried to issue direct orders, the Eloon squad leaders, mostly of Firenzi origin, responded in an obscure Firenzi dialect and pretended not to understand. Brin's lips curled in a savage grin while the furious commander spat impotent vitriol at the insubordinate aircrews.

All the while the weathered maze of peaks and bluffs of the Tumbledowns rolled by, close enough to touch in the sharp, clear air.

It looked like Brin might make it all the way to Sherrin before the mayhem calmed, but the Imperial commander finally swallowed his frustration at 'yokel incompetence' and saw the diversionary game for what it was. Frustration gave way to anger and a no-nonsense stance. With *Hammer of War* back overhead from her ponderous loop out over the Sea of Trayn, Brin's tactical plot showed a swarm of contacts flooding the stratosphere like angry hornets. Under dispassionate direction from the commander on the ground, they targeted one fighter after another and escorted them back to Torremis.

The first pilot to be intercepted tried to give the incoming fighters the slip and was shot down without a moment's hesitation. The others got the message. They continued to play hide-and-seek as long as possible, but as each was cornered they surrendered and allowed themselves to be directed back to base.

Slowly, systematically, the skies above the continent cleared of wayward traffic.

Sunlight glinted off sea in the distance. Brin checked his tactical plot. The net was tightening as the occupying forces realized that Scale was never his destination and turned their sights south.

So close.

Brin waved to the squad leader and signaled him to pull up. His escort peeled away and headed back to the mountains. Allowing a few minutes to put distance between them, he knew they'd fly higher and show themselves to distract the hunters. He pushed the throttle to its limit and hurtled over the coast.

The challenge came while the island of Sherrin was still nothing more than a smudge on the horizon. On his plot, two tracks closed slowly from behind while another three converged from the north. The order was perfunctory: turn back or die. The pursuers hardly waited for a reaction before opening fire. Brin's finger was already on the button to engage the first of his craft's countermeasures—electronic ghosting to confuse targeting equipment.

The first shots went ridiculously wide. The next rounds came closer as the pilots behind overrode their automated targeting and went old school.

Brin jinked, hugging the wave tops. Silver bolts of liquid lightning flashed past the cockpit. The *Lance* juddered again and again as near-misses glanced off his strengthened rear shields. Each jolt felt like an electric shock through Brin's seat. Sweat blurred his vision as he scanned readouts from his battered defenses, and checked the locations of his assailants. He poured every ounce of concentration into anticipating their lines of fire ... and being elsewhere.

Fingers twitching on his controls, he waited until the flanking craft joined the line behind him—with targeting electronics confounded, the only feasible shot was along line of flight. Along with a gasp of pent-up breath he released his final non-standard surprise. A ghostly cloud of butterfly mines, each no bigger than a coin, spread into the air behind him.

The pursuing craft had no chance to spot, let alone evade the deadly trap. The leader erupted in a sparkle of pinpoint flashes, then tumbled, disintegrating, into the sea. Another one caught a few of the mines and peeled away trailing smoke. The others swerved out of harm's way.

It slowed them a bit, at least, and in this chase seconds counted. With luck, the surviving pilots would be more cautious about lining up too closely behind.

As they sped towards the unforgiving cliffs rising sheer from gray seas, the island's automated defenses issued their warning. Brin keyed in the codes to give him safe passage to the prison landing site.

His pursuers, of course, did not.

Brin counted long agonizing seconds while they traversed the buffer zone, still throwing his craft one way and another to put off the hunters' aim.

Then lightning flashed from the cliff tops. The closest pursuer vanished in a scintillating cloud of technological overkill. The next one started pulling up, but too late to appease the clifftop sensors. The final fighter screamed around in a high-gee bank, loosing off a few last futile bolts as it did.

The airlock cycled. Movement in Shayla's joints freed up as rising pressure took the stiffness out of the EVA suit. The far door opened into a maintenance bay built into the emplacement. Benches and machine tools made a maze of the shop floor. Shayla weaved between them to the far door, thirty feet away.

From the corner of her eyes she clocked three engineers huddled over a bench nearby. Two paid her no heed. One gave her a puzzled look. As she passed, Shayla made a show of unfastening her helmet. Her busy hands hid her face from scrutiny. She made sure the fastenings only came free after she'd passed.

She resisted the urge to heave a deep sigh as the air of the ship replaced the recycled staleness in her lungs.

Once through the door, she sprinted past a storeroom and around the corner to a kit locker room. She wiped her helmet clean and stowed it and her depleted life pack alongside a row of identical units.

The EVA suit itself would be a problem if anyone spotted the *Blazer* insignia. She rolled it into a tight bundle and tucked it under her arm.

Back out in the corridor, she listened for signs of movement, then continued to the armored door leading from the docked beam battery into the battleship proper.

Up a steep flight of steps, Shayla found herself in a stark and brightly lit passageway stretching into the distance. The deck beneath her feet vibrated just on the edge of feeling. A whine of machinery clamored at a closed blast door at one end of the corridor.

She wracked her memory. It had been so many years since she'd served on a ship of this class. The interior was a vast and bewildering maze, and she couldn't afford to look lost. With a determined stride she put distance between herself and the beam emplacement.

She was somewhere under the main crew quarters. Clad in anonymous—and unidentifiable—overalls, she needed to lose herself in a crowd. First things first, though. A tug of recognition. She pushed open a door and peered in. She gave herself a brief cheer on seeing both that the narrow room beyond was empty, and that her memory held true. There was a garbage chute in the corner, into which she tossed the telltale EVA suit.

Relieved of her incriminating burden, Shayla hurried back along the corridor towards another steep companionway. A wash of deeply-buried memories threatened to overwhelm her. A flood of reawakened knowledge settled into her mind.

Her next destination, according to Shayla's as yet half-formed plan, lay near the upper level a hundred feet above. Ahead of her the overhead hatch offered a dizzying view up through the height of the hull. An arrow, white on black, showed this was the 'up' route. Another set of steps a few feet further along was reserved for down traffic. You mixed the two at your peril.

She ignored a row of inviting elevator doors she'd just passed around the corner. It was an unwritten rule in the navy: elevators were the province of officers and pussies. Some authorities in the marines held that the two were synonymous.

Taking a deep breath, Shayla sprinted up. Another unwritten rule said that stairs were taken at speed.

Chapter 21

A larms wailed across the square miles of the prison surface.

From the cab of the dump truck he'd acquired with the help of his fake ID, Jared glanced skywards and cursed. The air was clear from horizon to horizon but the siren moan was emphatic.

The excavator alongside Jared's truck ground to a halt and the operator scrambled from his cab.

Dominating newly-leveled acres beyond the prison perimeter, one of a ring of automated ground defense bunkers took shape. The low structure was a hive of activity, with navvies, carpenters, welders, electricians, and weapons techs readying the emplacement for service. Activity paused. Men and women gazed upwards in disbelief, mirroring Jared's own reaction, but only for a moment. Then chaos erupted as workers emerged from the depths of the half-built structure.

The supervisor, a pale-skinned Firenzi woman, bellowed across the building site, "Hustle! You're standing in a kill zone!"

Jared had spent the last week on driving duties, added unnoticed into the works roster by a clerk on the Insurrection's payroll before ap Silessi's recent crackdown. Jared gleaned patchy information from periodic forays to the mainland end of the tunnel, rather than risk direct communications from within the prison boundary with all its electronic surveillance. That information painted a bleak picture. Until recently, the Insurrection had run rings around the bumbling local forces, but they'd suddenly gotten a lot smarter. Cells and safe houses were broken, informants and moles uncovered. Acting Governor ap Silessi was taking an unprecedented interest in the Insurrection's activities, and the net was tightening.

Even the imperturbable Wolf had come close to capture, and had employed all her assassin's wiles to escape. The Insurrection's stance on this planet had always been one of utmost stealth, low key, passive. Now Wolf was resorting to booby traps and aggressive operational procedures to deter investigating forces with lethal countermeasures. A sure sign of desperation.

For the time being, Jared had what he needed. In his truck, he ranged far and wide, observing and charting work and guard schedules.

He should have known it was going too well.

The gang supervisor signaled to him. "Emergency evacuation. Gotta clear the surface."

Jared faked momentary confusion to give himself a few seconds to think. He couldn't afford to get caught up in the crush that would by now be forming at the head of the bunker entrances. He still had scant knowledge of how carefully they tracked IDs and headcounts of people entering the underground sections of the base, and he had no intention of testing their inner security. That had never been part of the plan.

But how to get away? The supervisors would be under orders to safeguard everyone on the work gangs. This one was busy shepherding workers into the few vehicles nearby that could manage more than a stately trundle, and she now turned an irritated gaze back to Jared.

The faster vehicles had disappeared across the undulating ground within the perimeter towards safety.

Jared gestured to the remaining lines of workers setting off at a jog. "What about them lot? Where's the bleedin' bus gone?"

"They'll have to leg it. This is a level one emergency. They'll be bringing the sensor net online any minute now. We need to get off this no-go zone."

Jared gunned the truck out from under the excavator's dangling bucket. With swift jerks on the controls he span the vehicle and dumped its load unceremoniously on the ground then pulled up alongside the last stragglers. "Climb up," he yelled. "Should be room for about fifty back there, but mind you hold onto something."

The supervisor gaped, then gave him a thumbs-up as men and women scrambled up into the bed of the truck. With only minimal regard for his human cargo, Jared lurched across the three miles of wasteland to the nearest bunker entrance.

While the workers climbed out Jared looked for an opening to slip away, but the supervisor was still eying him expectantly. This one knew him too well by sight and was unhealthily watchful over her charges. Damn her!

From his perch in the cab, Jared checked everyone was down safely then gave the supervisor a cheery wave. "Work crew twenty-seven will be in the same pickle, mate. Can't leave them out there. Catch up later."

Without waiting for an answer, Jared wheeled the truck around and set off for the next zone along the perimeter.

Jared considered, then dismissed, the idea of simply driving back to his hideout. It was miles away to the north, and he was sure the control room somewhere below ground would be monitoring movements on the surface. A truck heading the wrong way would warrant investigation.

At least the next work crew was in the right direction. Jared pushed the truck to its limits, bouncing across the rough ground, while he made mental calculations. He was now equidistant between the entrance he'd left and the next one around. He could easily justify making for that one, a few miles closer to his hideout.

He spotted the straggling lines of people and slid to a halt alongside.

With a fresh load of humanity, the truck ground into motion once more. At least Jared was an unknown face to this group, but he still had to slip away unseen. He needed a diversion.

Nearing the entrance, with the strident alarms urging haste, Jared let the truck's wheel hit a deep rut. The vehicle bounced hard and swerved violently before he brought it back under control.

He winced at screams of pain from behind.

He pulled up with a skid near the bunker but out of direct line of sight of the entrance, and hauled himself out of the cab away from the bunker. He rounded the back of the truck and joined the crush of people gathering alongside. Guards and workers from other crews mingled with dazed and bruised passengers climbing down from the truck bed.

"Need a hand here," a voice called from above. "Got some injuries."

Jared climbed up and peered in. "Jeez, mates, what's happened here?"

"Got bounced around," yelled one.

"Rough ride," grumbled another.

"Guess the driver was in a bit of an 'urry, eh?" Just another anonymous pair of hands, Jared helped them lift an injured man out and lower him to waiting colleagues.

In the melee of screams and curses, Jared dropped to the ground, swung himself under the near wheel arch and clung to the truck's chassis out of sight.

The last of the guards disappeared around the corner of the bunker, and the door clanged shut.

Alarms still sounded, surreal in the otherwise peaceful morning air. Alone at last, Jared lowered himself to the ground and kept watch from his hiding place underneath the truck. He puzzled over the alarms. Something must have triggered the alert, but the scene for miles around remained calm.

Was an attack imminent? Jared eyed his surroundings, noting the scant cover afforded by the barren landscape. Three of the scattered prison entrances were surrounded by barracks, landing fields, and administrative buildings, but this entrance lay isolated. From memory, Jared figured the nearest structures were at least two miles away. Defensive emplacements. Not a good place to be with the sensor net active.

———•—•———

In the last few minutes before the prison complex came into view, the rush of his desperate flight came into sharp focus. As the euphoric high and feelings of invulnerability evaporated, the aftershock hit Brin like an ice shower. Looking back rationally, he had been out of control, flying by reflex and utterly careless that each moment might be his last. He had always ruled his life through iron logic and impeccable, cold judgment. Maybe his reckless flying had saved his life, who knew? But the rational Brin felt like his body had been hijacked by a joyrider who didn't care if the ride ended in a wreck.

It was all Brin could do to keep his fingers steady on the controls. The island's defenses had come to his rescue but might still spell his doom. If he strayed outside the approved corridor he'd be vaporized in an instant, but staying inside this narrow path carried its own dangers. If anyone aloft was tracking him with longer range weapons, he presented a tempting target right now.

By the time he cleared the prison's perimeter, he was white and sweating. He ignored the main visitors' field and continued a few miles to a secondary entrance flanked by barracks and an almost-deserted landing field.

He flung the craft groundwards and leaped from the cockpit while the engines whined down to slumber. He flashed his credentials at the armored door that led into a low bunker. Stairs and underground corridors took him to the safety of the entrance proper, a bright-lit lobby deep enough to withstand a direct hit from most airborne ordnance. Other halls off the lobby gave access to emergency exits, invisible from above but ready to be cleared by controlled blasts in the event that the main bunker was destroyed.

Brin stepped into an elevator that whisked him a thousand feet down in a matter of seconds. He met no one, but knew his every move was being watched from the operations room at the heart of the prison complex.

His normal composure restored, he finally had time to reflect on the act of betrayal by the Imperial commander. Bard's warning had been timely and accurate. They had come to take him into custody, and had tried to kill him rather than let him go free.

He'd escaped the trap, barely, and was now secure in a formidable fortress. At least here he could still fend off attempts to either kill or free the Emperor's prisoners. That was where his first duty lay. And yet why had there been a need to flee in the first place? What was their game?

By the time he stepped from a high-speed transit car and through more secured doors to the operations room, his mood boiled like a controlled quark plasma.

"Make contact with *Hammer of War*," he snarled at the nearest comms tech as he entered the cramped command center. He paced the floor, face like thunder, while the tech complied. "Get me Commander Annelise ap Terlion!"

A few moments' pause, and Lieutenant Haalv Lekk appeared on the screen. "I'm afraid the Commander is late and unable to comply."

"Late ...?"

"She met with an accident on the surface. Under *your* watch, Acting Governor."

The blood drained from Brin's face. For an instant, a rasping tightness in Lekk's tone betrayed a flash of rage before he regained his composure. His oily voice brought on instinctive nausea but the words hit home. Brin found it hard to focus on the screen in front of him.

"Under the circumstances, given your regime's apparent inability to maintain any kind of order and to safeguard the lives of Imperial servants, Captain Scorf had no choice but to declare martial law and issue a warrant for your apprehension."

"Those fighters back there were not trying to arrest me!"

"Ah, yes, you see I choose my words with the word. The word 'arrest' has entirely inappropriate connotations of preservation of life, even if only in the short term."

Brin's face flushed with anger.

"I will be happy to accept your surrender," Lekk continued, voice soft and venomous, "and take you in alive, but under the standing provisions of Imperial martial law a posthumous conviction is equally acceptable."

Up one ladder after another Shayla charged. She must have boarded during the ship's day watch. Lights shone, people bustled, but only once did she have to yell "Way!" as she emerged at the top of a companionway and bounded the two paces to start on the next flight. Regardless of rank, personnel on the ladders always had priority over those trying to join the flow.

Four flights up, Shayla almost missed her footing as the aroma of coffee and baking bread engulfed her. At 'D' deck, she hauled herself around into the corridor at the top of the steps and tried to steady her breathing. Nobody paid her any attention as she joined the human traffic on this level. Assuming this ship followed the layout she was familiar with, the gymnasium lay somewhere behind her. She hoped any breathlessness would be attributed to a recent workout.

She headed aft, to where she knew another near-vertical highway connected the ship's decks. Shiny gray walls reflected yellow-white light. Battleship gray. In her time in the navy nobody had ever been able to explain why this particular shade of gray should be associated with battleships. Tradition, they said, as if that explained everything.

She ducked through an open blast door into another corridor. Pale green decking gave way to dark blue. Refreshed by her brief rest, she bolted up the last three flights to 'A' deck.

The upper levels were given over to storage, and this deck, the only one with a clear run the length of the ship, was the main freight highway.

Here she knew she'd find a quiet corner to work in, and her general-purpose overalls would stand out less than anywhere else on the ship.

Bright striplights gleamed off aseptic white. The floor here was an engineering green, with fluorescent lines and markings showing pedestrian and vehicle zones. A klaxon brayed in the distance, rhythmic, approaching. Shayla peered down the cross corridor. An electric wagon rumbled past the far end, towing a train of carts. That main thoroughfare would be busy. She headed the other way into a warren of bulk provisions storage rooms. At last, she found an empty stores office and settled at a comms screen.

She revisited her depleted stock of phantom identities. Why in Space her long-dead brother Brandt had set up the identity of a lowly payroll clerk she never knew. Along with super users, fake admirals, and special agents he'd created a plethora of more mundane personas. Many of these lesser, more innocuous records had escaped the Firenzi authorities' notice. She thanked whatever foresight, happy accident, or simple pedantic thoroughness had led him to do so, but right now a payroll clerk was just the ticket.

A few moments silent prayer to Brandt's memory, then she joined the endless hubbub of comms traffic flowing at translight speeds to and from the ancient leviathan. Minutes of careful probing located a personnel database at one of the outlying Firenzi supply camps.

The door opened. Military self-preservation quickly taught new recruits to recognize rank insignia from a hundred paces. In the dark. Blindfolded. Shayla leaped to her feet and snapped out a salute before the senior chief petty officer had crossed the threshold.

He gave the otherwise empty office a quick glance before acknowledging Shayla. "As you were, sailor."

She stood at ease, hands clasped behind her back.

"What is your business here, Petty Officer ..."

"Petty Officer Isobel Mullin, sir." Hasty improvisation. Heat prickling the nape of her neck, Shayla wondered where the name had popped into her head from, and whether it held any inadvertent significance she'd come to regret. "Locating a cooling hose replacement for battery alpha. Sir."

"Then what are you doing in the dry provisions section? You'll find machine spares stowed midships." He leaned closer. "You're new on board, aren't you?"

"Sir!"

"And those oiks sent you all the way up here for that, *in person?*"

Shayla allowed a look of realization to cross her face. Then she narrowed her eyes and snapped out, "Figured I could use the exercise, sir." She wouldn't have needed to visit the stores section in person to place a requisition. The senior chief assumed the old hands were playing games with the newcomer, and her matter-of-fact response should tell him she'd deal with it.

The lines of his mouth softened slightly. "Work smarter, not harder, sailor. Carry on."

He about turned. Shayla saluted his retreating back and settled back into her seat. Even while she hacked into the personnel system, a part of her started the long and wearying process of morphing her implants. Just a facial remodel this time, it didn't have to fool anyone into thinking she was anyone in particular, but she needed to look like someone other than Shayla Carver and she didn't want this senior chief to recognize her if she should meet him again. The name she'd given would not yet stand scrutiny if he thought to pursue it. And she should look younger. A petty officer visibly in her forties might raise eyebrows.

On the other hand ... a slow grin spread across Shayla's face as she worked. The persona of Petty Officer Isobel Mullin took form, newly transferred to the *Admiral George Leonard* while she was in orbit last week. Still a lowly PO second class as a result of a series of minor misdemeanors and unfortunate accidents. Nothing serious, nothing sinister, but enough to keep her from advancing.

Shayla needed information. She needed to be hanging around the ship's officers in their unguarded moments. She couldn't plausibly appear out of thin air as a more senior officer, but some people aboard ship were nigh on invisible.

With murderous emotions finally held in check, Brindis ap Silessi sat in a small conference room off the prison operations center. The fury he'd directed at Commander ap Terlion melted in a rush of guilt. She was dead. She hadn't betrayed him. But what *had* happened? Had they both been betrayed by a third party? And what had prompted Captain Scorf to declare martial law? Despite Lekk's claims, Commander ap Terlion's death alone couldn't have triggered such a drastic move. There had to be more to it.

Brin's eyes widened in shock as the implications caught up with him. Regardless of motivation, Scorf's actions would soon precipitate exactly the mayhem Brin had been at pains to warn against when he'd briefed the security team only days ago. What was his game?

He looked up a series of communications codes from his private archive. Although he was officially attached to Lady Carver's staff, behind the scenes he was still on the payroll of Imperial security and privy to sensitive sources of information and direct lines of communication with many important people.

He spent an hour making inquiries, then finally made a call on a secure and supposedly secret channel.

The red and rather displeased face of Captain Arrand Scorf, captain of *Hammer of War*, appeared on the wall screen across the desk from him. "Brindis ap Silessi!"

"Acting Governor ap Silessi if you please." Brin's tone was deceptively mild.

"You've got a ruddy cheek. You're a fugitive from a lawful authority, and yet you have the damned nerve to reach out to me as a peer."

"I meet you as a lawfully-ruling governor and I challenge the legitimacy of your declared state."

"You no longer have any authority on this planet—"

"Yet here I am, and I suggest you tread a little more carefully than your goons. I think you'll find the premeditated attempt to assassinate a head of state outranks an accidental death or even a murder of a mere officer."

Captain Scorf sat back. His eyes blazed. "We seem to be at a stalemate," he hissed.

Brin also sat back and laced his fingers behind his head. "So, while we're at a standoff maybe you can satisfy my curiosity. What *did* happen to Commander ap Terlion?"

Brin's hammering heartbeat belied his casual pose.

The face on the screen darkened. "She was killed while reviewing allegations of corruption in your forestry operation. We'd had reports back from the Inspectorate before—"

"On *your* orders?" Brin interrupted, brows raised.

"Well ..."

A flicker of relief touched Brin's mind. The captain's reaction confirmed Brin's pact with Commander ap Terlion remained a secret. So, the captain had another agenda here.

Brin struggled to keep control of his features and tone. "Regardless, there we seem to have a small problem. She wasn't attached to the Inspectorate, and as I understand it she was on the planet without clearance from my staff, unless of course you have documentation to the contrary. I wouldn't condone any deliberate harm to an Imperial servant, but her covert actions rather placed her out of bounds."

"All the same," Captain Scorf blustered, "the camps down there are clearly lawless."

"And I assume Lieutenant Lekk was conveniently on hand to conduct investigations and report back to you, removing evidence from my jurisdiction in the process."

"I don't like what you're implying."

"You dispute the facts, then?"

Captain Scorf slammed his fists on the desk in front of him. "Enough! I know what you're trying to do. Martial law remains in place."

"And yet I sit here, governor still. Until a higher power rules on this it's just your assertion against mine."

"I see. Well, until then, I must insist at least that you turn over the Emperor's prisoners to my custody."

"Not happening, Scorf." Brin deliberately used a dismissive mode of address as to someone of inferior station. He yawned and stretched, a calculated movement. From the corner of his eye he observed the outraged captain splutter in fury. "You can challenge my station as governor all you like, but regarding the prisoners my orders came from the Emperor in person. Until such a time as he hands me different orders in the same manner, I remain here and so do the prisoners."

He cut the connection.

Shayla assigned herself a billet in the sprawling crew's mess on 'G' deck, reviewed her preparations, and signed off. Back down through the depths of the ship—down was less effort than up, though demanded more skill to slide the handrails, disdaining the steps, in the unofficially-approved style.

The bustling canteen was always the heart of a capital ship. Open at all hours to cater for crew on different watches, Shayla was thankful to find it busy enough to be lost in the crowd, but not too crowded to find herself a table alone in one corner. Her tray looked loaded enough to feed a platoon but her appetite was a fair match.

Down a couple more decks, the cramped warren of the crew's mess was a marked contrast to the hubbub upstairs. In between ranks of kit lockers, mess tables lay mostly vacant. A few off-duty crew members lounged, read, played cards. Shayla avoided these oases of light, tuned to the artificial day/night cycle, and scurried through the permanent twilight of the dormitory areas. Past rows of curtained sleeping racks, she counted until she found the rack she'd assigned herself, the lowest of three. Low level racks, inches off the deck, were least favored but also least likely to attract notice. She crawled silently in and drew the curtain.

No sleep, not yet. First she had to put in some hours on her implants. That gluttonous meal left her feeling stuffed to the point of illness, but she knew she'd need those reserves in the hours to come. There was a limit to how long she could stay in the same pair of overalls. One more visit to the canteen was about all she could bank on before someone hauled her up for the state of her dress.

A whispered conversation nearby.

"What was that kerfuffle about earlier?"

"Live firing exercise, that's all I know."

"Heard they found a derelict out there."

Snort of laughter. "You grease monkeys soft in the head or something? You don't *find* a derelict in the middle of The Empty. In orbit in a system, maybe, but something out here? Once lost, stays lost."

Shayla decided the whispering, that barely carried above the pervasive hum of machinery, was out of respect for sleeping comrades rather than any secrecy. This kind of gossip always did the rounds quite openly.

"Angela said they toasted a ship, not just some lump of rock like normal. And," the voice lowered, more conspiratorial, "they boarded it first."

"Had to be a drill, though. No call to quarters."

"So where'd the ship come from?"

"What makes you sure there *was* a ship?"

"Angela said—"

"Exactly."

"Look, I heard it was a ghost ship. Haunted. Shuttle crew came back freaked. Thought you might have heard more."

"I run messages, and if this was Angela saying it ..."

The voices drifted out of earshot. Shayla resumed the concentration on her disguise. She needed access to quality gossip, not the half-truths below decks.

———◆———

Long after the image on the wall had vanished, Brin sat in near darkness. He pushed aside pangs of guilt at disavowing Commander ap Terlion's role on the planet. The warning he'd issued to the undercover team applied equally to himself and to the commander. They all knew the risks.

His earlier inquiries had led him to conclude that orbiting overhead was one of many Imperial vessels steeped in old traditions and values. They wouldn't declare open rebellion against the Emperor, not on their own, but all they needed was a credible challenger to rally behind.

Brin himself was of no consequence, that much was clear. He'd goaded Captain Scorf into revealing something of his intent. He'd scrutinized the captain's reactions as the argument progressed, and saw at the end where his real interest lay. He also realized that the captain wouldn't be open to pleas or reasoning. In declaring martial law, Scorf had played his hand and there was no going back.

Whether this coup was premeditated or simply an act of opportunity, the captain's goal was to acquire the prisoners. Ivan, at least. Was his aim to bring about a change in power only within the Skamensis family, or did his alignment extend to supporting the unholy alliance with Scipio? Brin couldn't say. It didn't matter. Either path led to bloodshed across a hundred planets.

Hours passed with no sign of danger.

Jared mentally charted his position and a route back to his base. With cameras dotted around the site he had no hope of making it unobserved. The guards below ground would be on high alert.

More hours dragged by. His tongue stuck to the roof of his mouth. There was a water bottle up in the cab, so close, but he couldn't risk being seen. He settled back down to wait.

Some time during the afternoon, the alarms fell silent. The sudden hush roused Jared from an uneasy doze.

He took stock. The immediate threat must have receded, but nobody emerged to the surface.

At last, dusk fell. Jared reached into a pocket for his tiny roll of thermal fabric, thankful he always kept it with him. He draped it like a cape over himself, leaving nothing more than a narrow opening to see through, and wormed his way out from under cover.

He might be an obvious target to normal vision during daylight hours, but normal vision was no longer a danger and he'd now made himself invisible to thermal imaging.

Stiff and sore, Jared began his slow and careful trek to safety.

The first blush of a new day pinked the eastern horizon when he trudged up the last slope to his burned out shelter.

Before he ducked under cover, Jared turned for one last scan of the horizon.

What the heck *was* that all about?

Chapter 22

Another visit to the canteen at the midnight change of watch. Shayla hoped her now disheveled look would be accepted as just coming off duty after a hard shift. Refueled, she retreated to the nearest washroom to check her appearance against her mental image of the fictional PO Isobel Mullin. Normally she was finicky about details, but right now time pressed. She was no longer recognizable as Governor Shayla Carver and that was all that mattered.

Down ladders once more to the lowest level, Shayla found the laundry and clothing store. Each deck on a ship like this had its own distinctive look, smell, and sound. The similarities to her old *Martha Sandover* were uncanny, and brought back sharp pangs of nostalgia. Down here, in a space nestling between the massive frames of the lower longitudinal keels, it felt subterranean. Yellow light glistened off cream walls. Pipes twisted thick overhead. Steam and chemicals tainted the air.

A bored Chief Petty Officer, a petite woman in her early twenties, manned the counter in the issue room. Shouts and the clatter and crash of wheeled laundry bins drifted in from along the corridor.

An exchange of salutes, and Shayla said, "PO Mullin, here for my uniform."

The CPO barely glanced up from the stream of information cluttering the screen at one end of the counter. "What the fuck are you doing down here? Clean stuff gets shipped back to the pick-up point on your mess deck."

"That's what I thought, but there's nothing there so I figured I'd better ask the experts."

The CPO gave Shayla a skeptical look. "Well then, *someone* fucked up on the orientation."

Shayla shrugged. "Is there anything at all made out to me?"

"Mullin ... Mullin ..." She frowned. "Nothing here. When did you last drop laundry off?"

"This morning, 'G' deck."

"Nope. Nothing here for you."

Shayla gasped. "Are you kidding? This is all I have left." She gestured to her creased overalls.

"What in Space have you been playing at, sailor?"

"I only came aboard a few days ago, still finding may way around. I've been dropping laundry off like I was told, but only just found out where to pick it up again."

With a sigh, the CPO turned back to her screen. "I see your staff record." She tapped her teeth. "Strange. No sign of *any* requisitions made out to you. Ever."

Shayla leaned against the counter and cradled her face in her hands. As if bringing herself back to the here-and-now she stood bolt upright, guilt and trepidation flashing across her face. "Beg pardon, sir. It's just that this isn't the first time this has happened. My kit goes missing. I turn up at the landing field with transfer papers but *they* have no sight of my seat on the shuttle. I can't find my work assignments on the system. Right now I'm probably listed as AWOL except there probably isn't even a record of *that*." Her shoulders slumped. "The friggin' system *hates* me."

The stores master huffed. "Shit happens, sailor." She glanced up and down Shayla's overalls. "Can't have you wandering around the ship like that, though. What kit are you missing?"

Shayla reeled off enough to get herself started. She could have forged a clothing requisition herself, and she would do so later if needed, but right now she wanted to establish a presence in the system under identities that could be verified, from people who would remember her. "Oh yeah, Petty Officer Mullin ..." Within a day or two it would seem like she'd always been here.

The woman looked Shayla up and down once more with narrowed eyes. "Stand to attention, sailor, chin up. Hmm." She scribbled a series of codes and measurements on the screen. "Shouldn't take long. You look like an average enough size and build, there'll be spare uniforms in the ready-use lockers. No need to haul ass out to the main store."

While they waited, Shayla said, "What do you make of that haunted ship they blasted yesterday?"

The woman's eyes widened. She leaned her elbows on the counter. "We were told it was just a piece of rock they took a practice shot at."

Shayla leaned in and lowered her voice. "None of the officers will admit it, but it *was* a ship. Crew dead, open to vacuum."

"I *knew* it. The Master Chief was *too* friggin' quick to stomp on those rumors."

Shayla glanced around the room, heightening the conspiratorial air. "Heard someone from navigation say it was a rendezvous. I reckon something hush-hush went bad."

Prime gossip was hard currency at the lower levels of the food chain. From the look on the woman's face Shayla could tell she'd just bought a friend for life.

Eventually a sailor emerged from a door behind the counter and dropped a neatly-bound package in front of the CPO. She glanced at the label and pushed it towards Shayla. "Any trouble with the fit, you come right back and see me. We'll get you sorted out yet."

"One more quick favor. I know this is pushing my luck, but would you mind checking if you can see my work assignments? I think I've got locked out of the admin system. Again."

The woman whistled. "You trying to set a record or something, sailor?"

"Like I said, me and technology just don't mix."

"Well, try to stay away from anything to do with life support." The tone was light, but her expression said she wasn't really joking. "Get yourself up to the admin office to get that sorted out ASAP." She rattled off the name of an admin clerk. "Tell him I sent you."

"Thanks. I owe you a gallon of beer next shore leave."

"Better snap it up. You're supposed to be on duty in engineering in two hours."

"Engineering?"

"That's what it says here. No record of absence, so I guess your luck's still in."

Shayla shook her head. "Naw. The system still hates me. Don't know what I'm doing in engineering. Thought I was assigned to stores."

As Shayla left, a voice called out behind her, "Remember, don't touch anything important." Shayla grinned to herself.

A shower and a clean uniform felt like the height of luxury after the past week. Shayla surreptitiously consigned her grubby overalls to the garbage chute rather than laundry. They'd escaped notice so far, but a close inspection might show they weren't from this ship and that would start an unwelcome chain of events.

She stowed her meager stash of spare clothing in her bunk. She would need to sort out a kit locker if she was here that long, but that was not a priority right now.

How long might she need to stow away? How long before she could track down any useful information? The scout was meant to rendezvous with this ship, which meant someone on board, someone very high up, had plans for her. If Shayla had anything to do with it, that someone had an outstanding appointment with the wrong end of a shimmerblade.

As she climbed decks and navigated the long passageways aft to the administrative heart of the ship, she wondered what was happening back in the world she'd left light years behind. This hike was her first brief opportunity to think of anything but immediate survival.

Some Imperial units must surely have found whatever was left of *Vixen* by now. Maybe ... she cut off that line of thought with a mental snarl. Heart thudding, she wiped the expression that had crept onto her face and scared two crewmen jogging in the opposite direction.

More immediately relevant, what was happening back on Eloon? The thought of Cobra so close chilled her to the core. Was Brin up to the task? Even in full health and fully focused she judged it a close match. In his present state and with the unwelcome distractions of governorship ... her fists clenched in helpless frustration.

According to normal protocols, with Shayla supposedly dead the Emperor would appoint an interim Governor to take over, but Chalwen, his closest advisor, knew Shayla still lived. Would he stall instead, and how would he keep Ivan's supporters in check? Even trickier, who else *could* he appoint that would satisfy the Firenzi? Shayla had lost count of the number of diplomatic and legal missions trying to pry Scipio from her custody she'd fended off by virtue of her 'bad girl' status in Imperial eyes. Any one of those missions could have devolved into covert military action. The first hint of Imperial sympathy at the helm and Scipio's supporters would be up in arms.

Shayla shuddered.

She reached the ship's administration office and paused a moment to bring her mind back to the task in hand, and to the persona she'd adopted. She asked for the admin clerk the CPO recommended.

Petty Officer Isobel Mullin spun her tale of woe.

The clerk looked up her record, asked questions. Shayla had answers to match the records. Those records also confirmed that tales of woe followed Petty Officer Isobel Mullin everywhere.

He shook his head and helped Shayla access her account. Rolled his eyes when she promptly managed to lock herself out of the system again, though buggered if he knew how she'd managed *that* under his watchful eye. The system really *did* hate her. They started again, this time with idiot-proof instructions to keep her account safe.

Petty Officer Isobel Mullin blessed him with a smile to light the darkest night, and Shayla left with a spring in her step that needed no feigning. She'd just completed a paper trail of authenticity that she couldn't achieve with any of her fictitious identities. She'd created personnel records, training records, disciplinary records, transfer papers, all the administrative details within reach of a payroll clerk, but it took someone with specialized security clearance to activate her system account. She was now officially legit.

———————

"There's no interference blanket," Brin said, "and yet you can't make contact with Magentis."

His voice was flat. The sickness stalking unseen and unfelt through his mind horrified him on a visceral level. Creeping chemistry attacking his precious logic and finely-calculated judgment was the deepest violation imaginable. Ever since Doctor Sam Kattergee's devastating diagnosis, he'd gone through the expected cycles of anger and denial. Sam had given him many coping tools, but right now he needed to function under extreme pressure. Duty came first, so he ruthlessly walled off all recognition of the problem, cauterized all feeling. By now he'd gone miles beyond any emotional response to yet another setback.

"It's not interference. Our signals are being blocked somewhere along the way. They must have taken control of the relay nodes." The communications tech confirmed the conclusion Brin had already, reluctantly, reached.

The fresh-faced operations commander turned from her scrutiny of the tactical screens nearby. "How? The comms network is supposed to have too much redundancy to allow any part of it to be isolated like that."

"Apart from some of the more distant outworlds, no single points of failure," the comms tech agreed. He pulled up a schematic of the Firenzi border with Imperial space. "But we're on the outskirts of Firenzi space with not much beyond the border other than the Cutler Drift. Take out these four nodes"—he highlighted points on the screen—"and you'd have control of traffic in and out of this region."

Brin rubbed his eyes, hardly aware of the slim spray tube of nicodyne that had appeared in his hand without him consciously reaching for it. Hacking comms relays was not for the faint-hearted, but if they could co-opt a *Sword* who knew what resources they had at their disposal? "Hold on." This didn't add up. Brin massaged his temples with the heels of his hands. "Those nodes are all in Firenzi space. Surely that can't be *Hammer's* doing."

The comms tech broadened the network schematic and gestured with an expansive wave. "Those are the only attack points that make sense. Anywhere beyond those choke points and there are too many connections to set up a practical blockade."

"So, not *Hammer* then," Opscom said. "That means both us *and* the Imperials are being blockaded by the *Firenzi.*"

Sudden vertigo blurred the kaleidoscope of displays surrounding Brin. He steadied himself with a discreet hand on the back of the comms tech's seat. "Which means Magentis has no idea of the current situation." He squinted, bringing the tactical plot back into focus with a supreme effort. "Is *Merciless* still upstairs?"

"Yes," Opscom said, "but—"

"*Merciless* is loyal to the Emperor. Comms, get me a secure channel to her captain, and Opscom, keep a fresh rotation of crews on Eyes and Weapons. When the attack comes, we'll need sharp minds on duty."

"Attack ... ?"

"The Firenzi have cut us off. Do you think *Hammer* will have missed that? We *and they* can deduce that time is not on their side."

The maintenance shift engineer lounged in a bucket seat, looking askance at Shayla with his head propped in one hand, elbow resting on the desktop. "Can't wind a flux coil?"

Shayla shook her head.

"Calibrate a plasma field?"

Another shake.

"Replace a fuel injector?"

Shayla's eyes lit up. "I did that on my ATV trike once."

He narrowed his eyes at Shayla. "I'm thinking of something a bit bigger." He casually pointed out the door to where a team was wheeling an eight-foot-long cylinder on a dolly.

Shayla swallowed, and shook her head.

"Then what in all of Space are you doing assigned to my engineering crew?"

"Beats me, sir. I thought I was slated for supplies."

Alarms jarred Brin out of a restless sleep. Mind shocked and drenched with adrenalin, he sprinted from his ready room and into the operations center. With the door closed, the strident alarms outside muted to a background hum and his attention turned to the displays plastered across the front wall. This was a call to action, but there was precious little they could do from here. This was a prison, not a fortress, and most of the defenses were fully automatic.

"What's happening?" Brin tried to make sense of the crowded tactical display. There was *Hammer of War* vanishing over the eastern horizon. Hundreds of specks of light swarmed down from orbit, converging on the island.

The nearest weapons tech, a young Wala woman maybe in her twenties, sat back in her chair, arms folded. "Remote drones, sir. Maybe looking to observe, but from their numbers I think they're probing for weakness."

As she spoke, the first drones broke through the buffer zone and the outer defenses flashed to life. Status lights on the weapons boards danced a jig. She glanced casually from one screen to another as wave after wave of drones crossed the invisible line in the sky and were vaporized.

The weapons tech leaned forward. "Opscom," she called, "I now have manned fighters inbound. Low level. Long range weapons locks detected."

Opscom turned to Brin. "Acting Governor, I'd like permission to assume hostile intent. Do we have a state of emergency on the planet?"

Brin had no hesitation. Normally the defense systems assumed neutral intent until incoming craft had ignored warnings as they crossed the buffer zone. Switching to hostile intent allowed them to strike at anything not showing a recognized call sign. Pre-emptively, with extreme prejudice. Hell, yeah! He simply nodded and said, "Assume hostile intent."

"Hostile intent, aye," the tech acknowledged. She keyed a code on her console.

Up to now, the drones had been picked off as they crossed the demarcation line. On the tactical plot it looked like rain falling on a clear dome. Now the automatic weapons boards erupted in a frenzy. The bubble expanded outwards as the coastal defenses burned everything within range. The last of the drones vanished in less than a second, and the wall of fury licked towards the manned fighters.

This was no longer a passive target. The fighters were armed and shielded. The long range beams had to track them, twisting and turning in the sky, and hammer them repeatedly before they succumbed. And they returned fire. Light flared around the coastal perimeter as bolts of charged particles hit the installations' shields and ran to ground.

The exchange of fire seethed back and forth, fighters attacking, probing, loosing massive bolts from their beam weapons to splash against the island's shields.

"What are they playing at?" From her seat in the center of the room, Opscom was clearly at a loss. "Those birds don't have the firepower to harm our outer ring."

Brin was equally puzzled. "If I were them, I'd concentrate fire in one sector to open up a window. They're too dispersed to do any real harm." Their tactical director must surely know this. Maybe they were still probing for strength and weakness, but it seemed a costly way to do it. The thought nagged at him.

A bank of monitors to one side relayed live images from the battle. The seas around the island boiled from the energy discharges. Vast banks of steam roiled a mile into the air and rising. Back at the tactical display their defenses were hard-pressed but holding, and the Imperials were losing fighters at an alarming rate. But more massed behind to join the fray as their comrades fell.

Why are you holding back? "They're up to something!" Brin called. "Keep a sharp lookout."

"Oh! You sneaky bastards!" Another weapons tech next to the young Wala sat bolt upright. He was a gray-haired man, plump to the point of obesity, who'd kept quiet throughout the exchange so far. Brin had hardly noticed him, and might have assumed he was napping on the job, but his heavy-lidded eyes had remained sharp and picked up something no one else had spotted. "High altitude ballistic ordnance." He transferred co-ordinates from his screen to the tactical plot.

"Where did that come from?" the operations commander asked. "More to the point, where is it aimed?"

"Trajectory ..." the elderly tech scanned his screens. "Not entirely passive. I'm seeing small course corrections. Must be targeting something, but no active scanning which is why tactical sensors haven't picked them up."

"Target?" Opscom prompted.

"Aiming for the coastal batteries."

"They're homing in on weapons strikes," Brin said. "Those fighters are lighting up the targets for the bombs."

Opscom huffed. "Nothing we can do about that, until they run out of fighters."

The remote battle still raged, with waves of fighters making suicidal dashes and loosing off furious energy bolts before retreating again.

"Coming into range ... now." Once the falling projectiles had been identified and captured on the plot, the coastal batteries took them out without further instruction. Each one vanished in a thunderous detonation that Brin imagined he could feel through a thousand feet of rock. "And there's the bomber. A suborbital transport hoofing it north. Way out of range." The older man gave a petulant pout to the youngster at his side.

At once, the assault melted away.

"That confirms it," Opscom said. "Those fighters never had a chance to get through our shields, they were both a distraction and a targeting mechanism." She glanced at the old man, who'd slumped back in his seat, lidded eyes flicking back and forth in the shadows. "Good eyes upstairs. Those bombs could have had us."

The tricky stuff was left to qualified engineers, but nursing a piece of machinery that dwarfed the Governor's Residence on Eloon there was plenty of scope for brute strength. And there were always decks to mop once the grease monkeys had finished making a mess.

Petty Officer Isobel Mullin should fit right in.

Fitting in was not on Shayla's agenda.

Kitted out once more in overalls, and after a terse safety briefing, she found herself part of a crew manhandling that fuel injector back into place.

Industrial ear muffs barely deadened the noise echoing back and forth in the cathedral space that rose through most of the height of the hull. She'd grown used to near silence in *Blazer's* machinery space, but here the quintuplet of hulking, pot-bellied power units was anything but quiet. The curving shells that filled most of the compartment hummed an almost subsonic note that tingled her bones. Accustomed as she was to technology from the microscopic to the gargantuan, she had never been this up close and personal with the living heart of a capital ship. Despite herself, her skin crawled in awe at the unimaginable power contained a few feet away. Behind layers of armor and magnetic containment fields, humans dared subvert the power of suns.

She shivered, and returned her attention to the job at hand and the instructions in her earpiece fighting to be heard. From her vantage point high above the deck, the shrieking din of ancillary equipment that clustered at floor level was lessened, but only just.

A narrow slice of unencumbered air ran the length of the power plant on either side, giving minimally-adequate working room. Canary yellow gantries spanned the engineering space and hoisted the two ton dead weight of the fuel injector high into the air, but it took sweat and muscle, and a constant stream of commands mingled with colorful invective to line the cylinder up with its housing forty feet above the deck.

Clipped into a safety harness, legs braced on a high catwalk, Shayla hauled on her guide line when told. Sweat tickled her spine in the oily heat. All the while she observed and catalogued the members of the squad.

It took her a while to spot the person she was looking for. Every squad of grunts had one, the unspoken leader outside of any military hierarchy of rank. While she worked, she studied the more obvious candidates, the physically domineering ones, the assertive complainers, the sly and furtive ones. She dismissed them one by one on closer inspection. None of them showed the casual malice she was searching for. None were shown the deference she'd expect.

After a while, she realized that she herself was under scrutiny. Feet back on solid deck, a wiry woman stood wiping greasy hands on a rag but her eyes never wavered from Shayla. One corner of her mouth lifted in a perpetual sneer. She had a knack for blending in, going unnoticed, but on closer inspection she seemed about to explode with fiercely-controlled venom.

Shayla met her gaze. "Can I help you?"

The face hardened. "Listen, bitch, you may have a coupla stripes on your shoulder but nobody gives a crap down here. Just pull your weight and don't fuck up."

"So who are you then, the fucking queen bee?" Shayla stripped her safety harness off with a sensual wriggle, slung it over her shoulder, and sauntered away.

Push buttons, leave to simmer.

The pot she'd stirred came to the boil quicker than expected. Returning from the washroom, Shayla's hair-trigger situational awareness kicked in. Someone lurked behind a pump housing up ahead. Although she wasn't expecting anything that would result in bloodshed—these kinds of wannabe big shots had to work under the radar of officialdom—she readied herself just in case. As she drew level with the machinery, a gallon can clattered across her path, lid loosened. Viscous grease spilled across the deck.

It took all of Shayla's self-control to stop herself leaping into action. Instead, she yelped and let her feet drag into the mess. She caught a fleeting glimpse of a figure retreating into the tangle of machinery and structural supports underneath the hulking power unit. That one knew her way around the machinery space and would be the other side of the compartment in seconds, ready with an alibi from her cronies and an innocent "Who, me sir?"

"Mullin!" The chief's voice thundered from the catwalk behind her. She turned and saluted. "Have you fucking shit-for-brains got any clue how dangerous that crap is on our deck?"

Shayla stood at attention and let him rant.

"We move fuck-off big pieces of machinery around here, in close confines. One slip and you could be enjoying a lap dance from a one-ton impellor or something."

"Sorry, sir. I'll get this cleaned up on the double."

He pursed his lips and regarded her long and hard. "This is a dangerous work environment, Mullin. Watch your step."

Somehow, she guessed he wasn't talking just about the machinery.

Up in the catwalks once again, sweating engineers leaned into an open access hatch reconnecting the rehoused fuel injector and completing their overhaul of this power unit. Shayla was acting as scrub nurse to this complex operation, handing tools to the engineers from an array laid out on the catwalk at her side.

"Socket wrench, size six," one of the engineers barked.

Shayla looked down. No socket wrench. She looked up. The wiry woman leaned against the catwalk railing, anonymous in welding overalls, socket wrench dangling from her gloved hand. She'd probably helped out on this job many times herself and knew exactly which tools would be called for. She grinned.

"Snap it up, Mullin!"

Shayla gave her a pleading look, hands out.

She rolled her eyes, tossed the wrench to Shayla and disappeared around the corner. She was out of sight before Shayla even registered the welding torch in the woman's other hand and the reflex that made her drop the wrench the instant she caught it.

A metallic clatter echoed from far below. Shayla looked dumfounded at the red welts rising on her fingertips. Her heart pounded, sharp pain just starting to make itself felt. Damn, she hadn't seen *that* one coming.

"Mullin!"

Strike two.

With the gargantuan power unit back online, Shayla was on solo cleanup duty, punishment for her slip with the wrench. Even with the help of the system of hoists and gantries, collecting the assortment of heavy-duty tools from the catwalks and lowering them to ground level was backbreaking work. She finished cleaning the last spot of dirt and grease from the catwalks and ladders and inspected once more for anything out of place.

Before cleaning and returning the tools to their storage lockers, Shayla cornered the woman—Petty Officer Christy van Belling, she'd learned—in the navvy's ready room. They were not alone. "Hey, Big Shot," Shayla called.

PO van Belling ignored her. Other heads turned, curious.

"Van Belling, I'm talking to you."

She turned and gazed down her nose at Shayla. "Oh, it's the newbie. Don't you have a deck to swab somewhere?"

"Yeah, about that, I know that was you from the whiff of dog's breath you left behind you, and that stunt with the wrench was out of order."

She sneered. "I don't know what you're talking about." A few snickers behind her were quickly muffled.

"That figures. If you had a second brain cell they wouldn't know what to say to each other so let me make it perfectly fucking simple for you. One more stunt like that and I'll wear your skin for a headscarf."

Shayla stormed out and returned to her work. Each tool had its assigned place in the lockers. Each, she cleaned and shined to perfection.

She reported the completion of her work to the chief engineer. He grunted, gave her a skeptical look, and climbed to his feet. She followed him down to the tool storage room.

"Mullin! Here, on the double!" He gestured to the locker. "This your work?"

"Yes, sir! I mean ..." She trailed off then straightened her back, turned her eyes front, mouth set in a grim line. Petty Officer Christy van Belling, or more likely one of her cronies, had worked fast. The tools she'd left neatly arrayed were now anything but. True, they were all in the locker, but many were in the wrong place, not properly secured in their rack, and some lay on the locker floor.

The chief reached in and picked up a combination wrench and scrutinized it. He sniffed at it, eyes widening. "Have you been eating your fucking lunch with this, Mullin?" Without waiting for an answer, he picked up a bar clamp and ran his finger around the jaws. Rubbing his fingers together he asked, "Do you think I want caked grease and grit in my engines, Mullin? Have you any idea what a speck of grit inside a coolant nozzle can do?"

"I believe it would not be good, sir."

He glowered at her. "Clean these up, properly, then report to my office."

An hour later, and well past the end of her shift, Shayla finished and had her work checked by a CPO from the incoming watch. Then she sought out the chief once more.

"Disaster seems to dog your footsteps, Mullin. Anything to say for yourself?"

"Sir, no sir!"

The chief chewed his cheek, pensive. "Petty Officer Mullin," he said softly at last. "Is there anything you think I should know?"

Damn. He likely knew the sorts of things that went on down below, but with no evidence, no witnesses, his hands were tied. Shayla was not about to enlighten him. She stood to attention, eyes front, mouth shut.

He grunted, with a brief shake of his head. "That's it then, Mullin. Report for kitchen duty."

Chapter 23

More decades ago than he liked to admit, a young Brindis ap Silessi had visited one of the Family di Brugui estates. It had been an occasion for the newly-acclaimed matriarch, a passionate hunter and collector, to show off her menagerie.

Not much of that distant day remained, but Brin still clearly recalled a guard's protective hand on his arm as he leaned over a waist-high stone wall. Far below, a family of brown bears paced the damp concrete floor of the narrow pit.

Some other youngsters pointed and jeered, trying in vain to get a reaction from the caged animals. Brin's eyes instead locked on a shaggy giant rocking slowly by the wall, gaze downcast. The sense of confinement, of hopeless despair, rose from the pit like a sickness.

That fragment of memory burned in his mind now, mirroring the helpless frustration they all felt.

A dozen men and women sat at their stations—weapons, comms, surveillance, tactical—postures a conflict of attentiveness, fatigue and crushing boredom.

The first hour after the assault everyone remained on high alert. As more hours ticked by, the rush of adrenalin wore off leaving a hollow feeling of defeat. Eyes turned again and again to the tactical plot, to the encircling warships menacing but ominously quiescent. Nerves stretched taut, waiting around the clock for the next blow to fall.

Brin realized he was pacing the narrow walkways between stations. He *never* paced. He stopped beside the tactical plot, hands clasped in the small of his back, and caught Opscom's eye.

"What next, do you think?" Opscom stirred a cup of heavily-sweetened black coffee, and sipped.

"They lost a great many pilots back there," said Brin. "They mean business."

"Why doesn't *Hammer* just cream us then? She has the firepower."

"Don't know about Scipio, but they want Ivan alive. That is an old guard ship if ever I saw one."

"So they have to crack our shell without breaking the yolk." Opscom took an appreciative slurp. "That makes me feel better. Still begs the question, what next?"

"Time is pressing. Even without *Merciless* sounding the alert from outside the communications block, our silence must surely have aroused suspicions on Magentis. They only have until the Emperor can get other more loyal forces here. This can't be a long siege. I expect a full-out assault."

Opscom pursed her lips. "At best, any response from Magentis will take days. Do we have that long?"

————————

Before her next watch started, Shayla visited the infirmary. A senior nurse scowled at her from behind a counter. "Nothing serious, sir," Shayla said. "I guess you're about to go off watch and I don't want to hold you up. I just need to dress a minor burn before starting my next shift."

He grunted and beckoned her through to an examination room. Rats. She didn't really expect to get unsupervised access to the infirmary but it never hurt to try. She showed him her blistered hand. "Touched something I shouldn't have, down in engineering."

He turned her hand over and peered close at the track of blisters, which Shayla had already done a careful job of cleaning.

"It's nothing, sir. Just need a low-grade analgesic, an antiseptic spray, and skin sealant."

The scowl deepened. "Everyone's an expert now, eh?"

"Not trying to be funny, sir. My mother was a doctor, my brother a paramedic. I thought about med school myself"—Shayla gave a wry smile—"before I found I couldn't stand the sight of blood. I just didn't want to waste your time on nonsense like this."

His expression relaxed a fraction. "And you reckoned the navy would be a good place to avoid blood, hmm?"

"Civilian life dirtside is no health spa either, sir."

He snorted and nodded; storm clouds receded. "Why sealant, not a simple dressing? This burn isn't deep, no open wound here."

"Working in the kitchens now, sir. Figured it would be easier to keep clean than a regular dressing."

"Relegated to kitchen duty, hmm? Must have pissed somebody off. But you're right. It's not a standard prescribed use, but probably a better choice for that kind of duty. You realize under that kind of treatment you'll have to clean it off and reapply after each shift?"

"I just need it to keep the crap out and the oozing stuff in, sir."

With a final nod, he led the way into the dispensary. Shayla scanned the labels on the shelf and the multicolored racks of medical pens. She made a beeline for the sealant and glanced back at the nurse for approval before picking up a standard quick-setting mix.

He handed her an antiseptic medipen, then reached for a standard analgesic.

Shayla pointed to an applicator on the next shelf. "I find the natural opiate-based formulation kicks in quicker."

He gave her a sidelong glance, then rolled his eyes. "You holding out for the good stuff, eh? Okay, but not the industrial strength one." He picked up a pen next to the one Shayla had indicated. "Deal?"

"Deal!" Shayla grinned and pocketed the pens.

———————

In the kitchens, Shayla worked with a will. The misfortune that pursued PO Isobel Mullin throughout her navy career seemed to stop at the kitchen door. There were no slip-ups, no spills. She kept her head down and didn't antagonize anyone.

Even the chief cook, a skeletal sour-faced man in his sixties, had trouble faulting her work. That didn't stop him trying, of course. In between fusillades of barked orders and armor-piercing insults his head bobbed, slack-jawed and vacant-eyed as though his mind had wandered a million miles distant. But the apparent trance vanished at the slightest misdemeanor.

"Hammond, you snot-sucking sniveler! Fries! Servery! Yesterday!" and, "Van Brite, you modeling those meatballs on the contents of your fucking scrotum? I can't serve those deformed wartfaggots in the fucking wardroom!"

Shayla kept her head down and mopped and polished her steel worktop clean of lunchtime preparations.

"Cho! You're *stirring* that sauce, not flogging it into submission." This to an unfortunate two counters away and thirty feet behind him. "Mullin ... well bugger me sideways, Mullin, I forgot the fucking counter-top was meant to be *this* color!"

Shayla could have easily attracted fire from her colleagues, but alongside her own duties she helped van Brite finish his herculean task molding and frying vast pans of meatballs, shuttled heavy steaming trays of food to the canteen, and brushed scraps from neighboring work stations to speed up the cleaning effort.

Once, she glanced up in time to catch the chief cook gazing at her across the bustling kitchen, eyes narrowed. His brow creased slightly as he turned away, head bobbing, and retired to his office.

Towards the end of her shift, Shayla found a quiet corner away from unwanted scrutiny. With deft movements she whipped up a concoction of her own. A few spoonfuls of vegetable oil dissolved a generous squirt of skin sealant before it had time to gel in contact with air. A couple of squirts from her analgesic pen, and a pinch of sugar to mask the flavor. She decanted the mix into an empty vinegar shaker which she secreted out of sight at the back of a spice cupboard. All the while, she kept up peripheral surveillance, but she'd spent the whole watch busying herself helpfully, ranging far from her station, and nobody now paid her any attention.

On the evening shift, Shayla busied herself as before. She completed every menial task assigned to her with quiet efficiency and without complaint. As before, she went out of her way to help those around her. She was never idle for a moment, and nobody was surprised to see her appear, unasked, wherever help was most needed.

The routine here followed the pattern she'd known from her early years in the navy. Together with her sponge-like absorption of standard working procedures across all the major navies—such mundane intelligence could make the difference between invisibility and exposure when working under cover—she knew how this kitchen operated better than the men and women working here.

With a careful eye on the clock, Shayla surreptitiously positioned herself near the door that led to the freight elevator used to ferry food aft to the senior officers' wardroom.

Near the end of the shift the liveried serving staff returned from the wardroom. They paraded past the kitchen drudges with scarcely a glance, talking amongst themselves with exaggerated groans and sighs of relief as they unbuttoned crisp jackets, loosened starched collars and massaged necks where the collars chafed.

As they retired to the nearby stewards' mess, trays of food were already being laid out for them. In the moments of commotion, Shayla retrieved her preparation and bustled past the worktop. In between pressing bodies and the confusion of arms depositing dishes onto trays for the porters to take, it took a fraction of a second to decant the bottle's contents into the nearest pungent sauce dish. By the time the trays were taken through, Shayla was at the far end of the kitchen wiping down worktops, clearing dishes, and disposing of the evidence of her impromptu chemistry.

———•———

And here it comes, thought Brin, as he stared at the tactical plot. After another wearing day of inaction, the clamoring alarms came as a welcome release. "What are they bringing in this time?"

"They're slow," said Opscom, scratching the side of her nose thoughtfully. "Any readings off those plots, Weapons?"

The young weapons tech studied her screen. "Hard to say at this range, but from readings of mass and emissions signatures I'd say we're looking at gunships. And that looks like a flight of troop transports behind them."

The gunships lumbered closer and hovered, seeming to thumb their noses at the defenders, just on the edge of their weapons' range. Not quite close enough to tempt the automated systems into action.

"They learned some measure of our capabilities then," Brin muttered. On his orders, the weapons tech overrode the pre-programmed directives and let loose a concentrated blast at one of the gunships. Shields shrugged off the assault with contempt.

"Analysis?" Brin asked.

"I know it's at extreme range, sir, but we barely warmed them up to a few percent. Those things are shielded to the hilt."

"So they could probably ride right up to us before we cracked them." Brin mused. "They have something else in mind."

"As before," Opscom announced to the room, "this may be a feint. Keep eyes three-sixty and skywards."

"Keep a watch," Brin agreed, "but I don't think this is a decoy this time. Look. They're concentrated on our northern coast. They're out to break through."

They didn't have long to wait. The last of the gunships took up position then, without any preamble, they opened fire.

The tactical plot seemed to fog up with the number of active contacts. "Micro missiles," the weapons tech yelled. The weapons boards leaped into life as the defensive systems identified the threat. Too fast for the human eye to follow, beams targeted and flashed, but the tiny missiles were fast and hard to hit, dodging and weaving as they closed in on their targets.

Electromagnetic shields were useless against physical ordnance. Only the physical structure of the weapons bunkers protected them, and the emission domes were, of necessity, vulnerable. The missiles didn't pack large warheads, it would take many direct hits to breach the bunkers, but they rolled in in overwhelming numbers too fast for the beams to pick them off.

Status boards showed damage accumulating. Here and there a lucky hit took out the snouts of individual weapons and dark patches appeared in the defensive circle as the weight of numbers made itself felt. And the assault showed no signs of diminishing.

"Looks like they've found our weakness." Brin shook his head. "Better assemble the garrison, then. I think they'll be storming the surface bunkers within the hour. From there it will be hand-to-hand in the tunnels."

"You don't think we can hold them on the surface?"

"No point. Once they break through the defensive rings they'll have the advantage up there. It'll be a different matter once they're bottlenecked too far underground for the gunships to help." His voice turned grim. "Then we pray they run out of time before we run out of soldiers."

The payoff for Shayla's minor act of sabotage came early in the next shift. The chief steward, a heavily-built woman sporting a blonde buzz cut whose normally-cheerful manner was a welcome foil to the chief cook's acidity, stormed through the kitchen. There was no cheer in her face today. She entered the cook's office without preamble and launched into a low but heated discussion.

Shayla found something interesting to clean a bit closer to the action. She avoided the rookie mistake of sneaking up quietly, instead choosing the cover of plain sight. She joined the normal racket of the kitchen, busily scraping food scraps from a stack of serving trays then rinsing them off. All the while, appearing wholly intent on her job, her real focus was on the voices issuing from the nearby office. She set to wiping down the long countertop, a job she could do on autopilot, while her mind went into a near trance.

With practiced concentration, she systematically screened out extraneous noise. Gradually the words became clearer, one side of the conversation at least. The higher-pitched outrage of the steward carried clearly, but most of the cook's words were lost.

"Almost the whole team. It must have been something they ate."

Incoherent mumble.

"I know nothing like this has ever happened before. These kitchens are the envy of the fleet, but that's the only thing that makes sense."

Volcanic rumble.

"... Not suggesting any lack of care. I don't know. Supplies in storage can sometimes get contaminated."

An abrupt hush. Shayla pictured the cook absorbing the implications of this possibility. She finished sterilizing the countertop and heaved a steaming tray of pans and utensils from the nearby washer. A slightly paranoid compartment at the back of her mind quickly inventoried the items she'd used to concoct her debilitating brew. She reassured herself that all traces had been thoroughly cleaned up, and the ingredients would by now be broken down in the victims' bodies and not show up on any routine screening.

"Any word of illness elsewhere? Oh sweet Unity, have we started an epidemic?" That was the chef. Belatedly, Shayla realized that most activity in the kitchen had died away. Cooks and porters worked half-heartedly, movements hushed, eyes turned towards the open door.

As if noticing the argument for the first time, Shayla joined a growing press of bodies encircling the office.

"I'll get a hold of sick bay and see if there were any other cases," the steward said, hovering on the threshold.

The chief cook joined her. "And I'll get a crew checking through the supplies, whatever we used yesterday. Not much chance of tracing the source otherwise, everything's long since been cleaned up." He looked around the circle of curious faces, lips pursed, head wobbling on his long neck.

"That still leaves the problem of the wardroom." The steward herself was looking a little off-color, Shayla noticed. "Some of your staff have filled in before, who can you let me have?"

The cook reeled off a short list of names.

The steward mopped her forehead. "We're still way too short, and tonight of all nights. All my most *senior* staff ill, too."

Bingo! That made sense. Shayla had heard about the rigid hierarchy among the snooty wardroom staff, and the senior members would be sure to have first go at the prime cuts of meat and the richest sauces. They'd probably taken more than their fair share, too, and not left enough to go around. Sympathy was in short supply.

"What about you, Mullin?" The cook's voice snapped Shayla back to the here-and-now. "You seem to know your way around a working kitchen, any table service in your background?"

"Who, me, sir?" Shayla's heart pounded. She wiped her hands on the cloth hanging at her waist and stood to attention. "I mean, yes, sir. I have some experience in that department, including formal service if that's what's required, sir."

Someone off to one side flung a dish cloth at Shayla's head and yelled, "Suck-up!" Shayla caught the cloth without blinking, reflexes kicking in before she knew it. She caught herself from retaliating and simply tucked the cloth into her waistband. The call held no real animosity.

"Mullin?" The steward gave her a sour look. "New recruit? Same Mullin the chief engineer sent here?"

"I'm no engineer, sir. I think that much was evident." Shayla risked speaking out of turn. "I've heard no complaints since starting here. My experience is landside, not navy, so I guess there'll be traditions I'm not familiar with, but on one occasion, many years ago, I had the pleasure of serving at My Lord Scipio's table."

The steward frowned. "Didn't spill soup in his lap by any chance?"

"I strongly suspect, sir, that anyone so unfortunate would no longer have the full use of his hands. As you can see, sir, mine remain intact."

A few suppressed murmurs of knowing laughter sounded behind her. It seemed that Scipio's reputation was well known here even among the rank and file, and even after all these years out of the public eye. Interesting.

The chief steward and the chief cook exchanged glances. At last the cook shrugged. "She's been no trouble while she's been here. In fact I'd be sorry to lose her." It must have been a genuine compliment. The cook looked like he was chewing nettles. "And you're too short to serve the wardroom properly otherwise."

The steward sighed. "I hope I'm not going to regret this."

———⋅•⋅———

Anger and frustration seemed to have become a resident feature of Jared Tindall's existence.

Things had taken a nosedive when the bloody Imperials took control of the planet. Martial law, in the name of the Emperor, but they had to be renegades of some sort. For all his faults, the Emperor would never have sanctioned such a move.

Worse, Wolf suspected Imperial security was behind the Insurrection's recent setbacks on the surface. Acting fucking Governor ap Silessi had to be getting off-planet help from *somewhere*.

Communications with Wolf were now cut to a minimum and they had to be more careful than ever, so information was hard to come by. Rumors, dismissed at first but increasingly credible, said that Lady Carver was dead. Jared swallowed the bitterness at his thwarted vengeance and looked instead for ways to complete his primary mission goal, but even that now seemed beyond reach.

Wolf reported mayhem in the forestry camps. Military police, curfews, unheard of on this planet. He squashed a glimmer of sympathy for the incoming soldiers. They had no idea what kind of population they were dealing with.

"Lucky you ducked for cover when you did," Wolf said. "Looks like there's now a full-scale offensive going on over there and it's only a matter of time before the prison is overrun."

Jared swore. "Have the planners projected what will happen if those prisoners get rescued?"

"There's always been speculation, but that's old history now. The landscape's changed and there's too many variables up in the air."

"It can't be that fucking difficult!" Jared raged. "The plan was to kill them leaving a whole bunch of people with big battleships in their back pockets angry but leaderless. Events would be easy to steer our way. But a fleet of ships against the Emperor with strong and popular leadership? We're out of the driving seat and when the dust settles we'll have just swapped one tyranny for another."

He paused, sensing something important left unsaid, a telltale wariness in Wolf's choice of words. "Any orders from above?"

There was a long silence before Wolf said, "Communications off-planet have been cut. I can't raise any of our leadership. We're on our own."

Now it was Jared's turn to let the silence drag as he processed this new setback. He took a deep breath and quelled the despair crowding out his mind. He needed to be objective.

No communications meant no outside resources, no intel, but also no interference. They still had a resourceful team on the ground and feelers into some of the planet's administration. He had the equipment he needed for the original plan at least, and for a few creative alternatives if necessary. He reached a decision. "Even if the Imperials mount a jailbreak, they'll probably kill Scipio and do half our job for us, but they've got to break Ivan out of there somehow. I might still get a crack at him."

"You do realize you're talking about a suicide mission." Wolf's tone was matter-of-fact.

"Given the situation out there, how do you rate our chances of getting off this rock alive?"

"Right now, if we stay quiet and blend in, pretty good actually," Wolf said. "But how do you rate our chances of surviving the debriefing, if it turns out we missed a once-a-lifetime opportunity?"

"Yeah, that's the trick isn't it?" Jared felt almost cheerful. "So, we stay in place. We look for opportunities. We improvise."

Down in the clothing store once more, Shayla breathed in the scent of bleach and hot linen. She'd hacked the ship's watch rota and sought out the CPO who helped her last time.

"Hey!" the CPO called when Shayla stepped over the sill into the issue room. "It's Petty Officer Mullin. I thought you were supposed to stay away from anything breakable." She grinned. "Heard you had a rough time of it up in engineering."

Shayla shrugged. "Didn't break anything *important*, honest."

"But busted down to kitchen duty? That's harsh. I know one of the shift engineers ..."

"Thanks, but no need. I was the new girl there, of course they'll push to see if I'll break. You need to know who you can trust on that job. It's nothing I can't handle. Besides, I think I'm better placed where I am."

"You were sent to the kitchens as a punishment, and you're *happy*?"

Shayla flashed a small smile. "Don't tell anyone."

"Respect!" The CPO whistled through her teeth when she saw the uniform requisition. "Landed on your feet this time!"

"It's only temporary. Some of the regulars fell ill last night. Chief steward's in a panic."

"Listen, sailor, this will take a while to sort out and you'll need to be properly fitted, too. This is formal dress, not yer regular one-size-fits-all."

———•◆•———

"I don't believe it!" Opscom voiced what was on all their minds as they gazed at the tactical screen dominating the operations center. "They're pulling out."

"Looks so," Brin muttered. It made no sense. Another few minutes and the prison's northern border would have lain defenseless. "Must be a trap, but Spaced if I can see how."

"I think I can see why," called a communications tech from across the room. "We have incoming upstairs, or rather, *Hammer* has incoming."

"Tactical!" Opscom yelled. She didn't have to finish the order. The tactical plot was already shifting from the close-in view of the island and its surroundings, to show the whole solar system.

There was *Hammer of War*, menacingly close to Eloon, and the smaller *Vanquisher* that Brin suspected also stood behind Ivan. They'd made no objection to Captain Scorf's actions. With *Merciless* gone at Brin's request, hoping to bypass the communications blockade with messages for Magentis, these two ships were on their own.

A few light minutes away, but screaming in like an avenging angel, was a cluster of ships glowing on the plot in Firenzi red.

"Do we have any IDs?"

"Coming through ..." The comms tech gasped. "Space alive, that big fucker in the middle's an *Enforcer*." He studied his screen. "Putting out the call sign of *General Giotti Trincomali*."

Brin took in details from both the close-up and the wide view. "My guess is they're none too happy about an Imperial captain trying to take our prisoners." He pointed to the wall display. "Those transports are hightailing it back to mother."

Opscom looked puzzled. "Do you mean they're on our side?"

"Not a hope in hell," Brin spat. "They'll be Scipio's supporters, just as keen as Scorf to stage a jailbreak. The only bright side is that neither one will want to allow the other exclusive access."

"They could team up, couldn't they?" Opscom whispered.

Brin paused and thought for a moment. "Welcome to my worst nightmare."

That evening, Shayla noted a gray pallor in the steward's face and a subdued manner, as if she was holding herself under rigid control. Had Shayla's concoction hit her, too? It would make sense. The steward had been present the night before, but maybe had arrived late to the midnight feast and so missed most of Shayla's special ingredients. But not all, she guessed.

As the most junior member of the steward's contingent, Shayla helped load a mountain of food onto a series of carts. They would be serving sixty senior officers—the top one percent of the ship's company—and this was a full-on formal affair, hence the steward's anxiety.

Laden trays of meat, rice, soup, fish, vegetables, accompanying sauces ... some dishes fully prepared and ready to serve, some cooked or prepared raw in their component parts ready to be assembled at the last minute. A heady mix of aromas washed over her, the greatest burden of this duty Shayla had inveigled her way into. Maintaining her disguise, on top of the extra-curricular efforts she'd taken on, drained her. It was only two hours since she'd last visited the canteen and already she could easily tackle another full meal.

They wheeled the train of heavy carts into the freight elevator at the back of the kitchen area, and up two levels. Down a long passage and through a series of open blast doors, each resounding with a series of thunks and clicks as the carts' wheel mechanisms automatically tripped and stepped over the four-inch lips of the armored doorways.

A hundred yards aft of the kitchens, in the midships stack of decks that was firmly officer country and not an area Shayla was familiar with, they delivered the carts to a cramped kitchen and servery where a small contingent of cooks stood ready to bring each course to a state of perfection at the right time.

In the adjacent wardroom the steward, looking increasingly queasy, inspected the table arrangements and the steaming soup tureens standing ready on a counter to one side. The rest of the serving staff, including Shayla, lined up in front of the counter, all crisp whites and ironed creases and carefully neutral expressions.

While helping lay the table settings earlier, and in between a crash course in naval etiquette from the more experienced hands, Shayla had taken the opportunity to survey her surroundings. She badly needed information, or at least a few clues, as to where this ship's company stood in the rat's nest of factions that made up the Firenzi organization.

With a minimal sop to comfort amidst the warship's austerity, the gloss gray paint of the wardroom's walls was partly concealed by plush blue curtains and framed pictures. Two long tables down the center of the room were laid with white linen, china bearing the ship's crest, and gleaming silver and glass. There was little room to maneuver between the straight-backed chairs and the surrounding walls and sideboards at either end. This was going to be a crush, Shayla realized, with little opportunity to eavesdrop on conversations.

Worse, the serving staff did not fraternize with the officers. She'd expected nothing different given her past experience in the naval service, but the steward had been at great pains to emphasize that she was not to initiate a conversation other than required for her duties. In fact, she would not even be waiting at table, but would ferry dishes to and from the servery to the sideboards ready to be served up by more experienced staff.

Preparations complete, they stood ready while the steward kept an eye on an antique clock adorning the wall at one end of the room. A sideboard beneath the clock held a ceremonial nargile in pride of place, flanked by trophy cabinets displaying memorabilia from past campaigns.

With a nod, the steward signaled a fresh-faced sergeant-at-arms who threw open a door and invited the officers waiting in the lounge beyond to take their places.

The expectant silence in the wardroom was filled with dozens of loud and earnest conversations as the senior members of the company filed in.

Men and women in full dress uniform squeezed past and stood behind their assigned seats. While Shayla mentally checked off insignia identifying ranks and trades—medical, navigation, security (remember that face), pursar, chaplain, and no rank less than lieutenant—she only recognized one face in the retinue. The chief engineer stared at Shayla as he took his place opposite her. "Well, well. Have I punished you with a promotion then?"

"Sir, I think I am more at home in catering than in engineering."

"I hope my silverware is cleaner than my toolkit." He made a show of picking up a fork and inspecting it.

"Be careful, sir. I think I *did* eat my lunch with that."

He gazed blankly at Shayla, then his eyes flicked back and forth between his colleagues, who seemed to be pretending not to notice the exchange. His mouth twitched. "I guess I asked for that, but no more free passes, Petty Officer."

The captain, a slight man in his fifties, came last. He seemed too undistinguished to capture the attention of a barmaid in an empty pub let alone a roomful of chattering officers, in fact Shayla hardly noticed him enter the room, but all conversation stopped abruptly as he crossed the threshold.

Shayla assessed him as he approached his seat in the center of the near table. He looked weak and powerless, watery eyes fixed ahead, ruddy cheeks, trim gray goatee. He paused as he passed Shayla, then half turned. "You're new." His voice, soft as silk, felt like the caress of a garroting wire.

Shayla snapped to attention. "Sir!"

The bizarre tableau froze in place for uncomfortably long seconds. Shayla's mind went into overdrive. The silence begged to be filled with additional information but a hint of self-preservation from her training days asserted itself. *He had not asked her a question.*

At last, the lines around his mouth and eyes hardened a fraction. "Hmm." He gave the slightest of nods and continued on his way.

Struggling to conceal her relief, Shayla stood easy. She caught the eye of the steward, who also favored her with a barely-perceptible nod of approval.

The meal progressed with quiet ceremony, rituals as formal as any she'd seen in Court circles. With the special preparation she'd undergone for her undercover mission in the Imperial palace years ago, and the duties of a planetary governor since, she recognized most of the niceties. Throw in her own early experience in the Firenzi navy and she could have bluffed her way through most of the intricacies.

As it was, it would raise suspicions to be *too* good. She allowed herself a few harmless gaffes, especially ones that would mark her as a dirt-thumper, like clearing the soup dishes from the right rather than the eccentric navy quirk of left-handed clearance.

All the while, most of her attention was on the conversations that passed within earshot as she ferried dishes back and forth.

With the last of the dishes, glasses, and toasts out of the way, servers made their way around the table with small cups of poisonously-strong coffee and trays of cheeses, olives, and salted nuts.

The captain announced, "I believe a smoke is in order."

The chief steward nodded to one of her regular staff, the most senior one present Shayla guessed, before excusing herself and strutting for the exit in a manner that suggested she was barely hanging on to her bowels. At that moment, Shayla felt a pang of remorse. As far as she could tell, the chief steward was a decent person and had done nothing to earn this indignity.

The youngster she'd left in charge—Shayla wracked her memory for a name, Saul, she thought, from shreds of kitchen conversations—swallowed. He was a petty officer, like Isobel Mullin, and far too junior for this kind of company. He rallied gamely, but his face blanched and his hands trembled as he turned to the sideboard holding the wardroom's ceremonial water pipe.

"You okay?" Shayla murmured, edging a foot closer. She'd just spotted another weakness of overly-rigid hierarchies: knowledge was power.

"I'll manage," he whispered back. "Seen this done before."

"So ... you know the blend the Captain prefers?" The question was innocent, the tone pitched just right to induce doubt, with unspoken hints of the consequences of a wrong choice. In the last two hours Shayla had studied the balance of power in the top ranks of this ship. The captain was a martinet, a rigid disciplinarian. On top of that, he was likely a remote and fear-inspiring figure to anyone outside this elite. She realized she'd not heard him referred to elsewhere on the ship in anything other than stiff and formal terms.

Saul hesitated, and lifted the carved ebony lid of the chest next to the nargile. Ranks of cut glass jars faced him, multicolored labels announced leaves, syrups, and flavorings from a dozen worlds. A row of silver spoons of various sizes nestled in a velvet-lined tray along the front of the display. "The senior servers keep that kind of thing to themselves," he murmured.

"Is there a problem, son?" the captain asked.

"Sir," Saul stammered, "the steward-lieutenant left no record of the wardroom's accustomed blend of leaf for the nargile."

"Well then, improvise. Impress me." Though soft, the words had the cutting power of a shimmerblade.

Shayla glanced at the captain, who raised a bushy eyebrow. "If I may, sir, I know some blends favored by the Family in times past, particularly Lord Scipio." The lie came easily, and Shayla was certain none of those here would have been entertained at the Family's table to know the difference.

Without waiting for a response, she discreetly elbowed aside the flustering server. "Watch carefully for next time," she whispered out of the corner of her mouth. "Nothing more than showmanship and a bit of simple cookery." She dismantled the nargile, lifting each piece cradled reverently in two hands and setting it down on the sideboard. The base, a translucent ruby crystal antique bearing the Firenzi family crest and the ship's name on a silver plaque, she filled from a glass jug.

"Just remember the order, leaf then syrup then flavor ..." She selected jars, recalling a blend favored by her Firenzi medic, and spooned ingredients into the bowl as she spoke. "If in doubt, keep it simple and stick to the overall proportions nine to three to one and you can't go far wrong."

She lit the heater on top and waited for vapor to start forming, then she took a tentative puff. Satisfied, she handed the pipe to the captain. "Sir, may I present Lord Scipio's *Tropical Court Mystique*." The name of the recipe was entirely fictitious. She was equally sure no one here would know any different.

The captain puffed, and, without a word, passed the pipe around. Shayla took her cue and stepped back to the side of the room.

As the pipe circled the table, conversation flowed ever more freely, but to Shayla's frustration, nothing of any great secrecy was discussed openly. Not that she expected it to be that easy. The Firenzi navy she remembered was a hotbed of intrigue at these senior levels and paranoid secrecy, the jealous hoarding of knowledge, came as second nature. There were a few whispered exchanges, but never when any of the serving staff were nearby. Even compartmentalizing her attention to the best of her ability, Shayla couldn't afford the deep focus and near-meditation it would have taken to pick a low-murmured thread out from the ambient noise. It would take time and patience to piece together any worthwhile intelligence.

All the same, she left the wardroom that evening with one priceless nugget of certainty around which to plan her next moves. Distilled from a dozen half-heard snippets of conversation she deduced one fact that had not yet been generally announced. They were heading to Eloon.

Chapter 25

A greater reward for Shayla's preparations came unexpectedly. Along with the chief steward—who'd rejoined them, her cheeks now tinged with a measure of color—and the rest of the serving staff, Shayla trooped through the kitchens loosening her collar with a sigh.

She was about to remove her jacket and make for the main canteen, when the steward called her over. "Good work back there, Mullin. You temps get to chow with us when you stand in." She gestured to the open door of the stewards' mess. It seemed the other kitchen hands knew the drill. They'd already gone ahead.

Kitchen staff wheeled in steaming platters, accompanied by the chief cook himself, head bobbling on top of his thin neck. He held a low but intense discussion with the steward. Shayla could only make out snatches above the hubbub in the confined space but she caught the gist. They'd spent the day examining the contents of the larders and had found nothing suspicious. The steward didn't look happy. Everything used to prepare today's meals had been double-checked for contaminants, the cook assured her, and no one else on board had reported in sick so it must have been a one-off.

Shayla joined the rest of the serving staff attacking the heaped platters with vigor. Tuning into the conversation around her, she noticed how the gossip flowed freely behind closed doors, with little regard for rank. She decided to risk a direct approach with the steward. "I must be mistaken, sir, but back there I thought I heard we were heading for Eloon. I thought that wasn't part of Firenzi space any more."

"Mullin," the steward snapped. "What you hear in the wardroom doesn't get discussed outside." A sly look crept across her face. "But I heard the same thing elsewhere, so we can talk about *that*."

"Why would we be heading there, though? It *is* outside our jurisdiction, isn't it?"

The steward stretched her legs out and clasped her hands behind her head. "The Governor there is missing, presumed dead. No secret there, I guess."

When Shayla gave her a blank look, the steward rolled her eyes. "You should keep up with regional news, you know."

"Okay." Shayla shrugged. "So they appoint a new governor then? What's that got to do with us?"

Voice grim, the steward said, "You'd think, wouldn't you? But the Imperial commander on some fuck-off big battleship in orbit went and declared martial law in the meantime."

The bottom fell out of Shayla's world. It took every scrap of her professional training to keep the shock from showing in her face. She hoped nobody present could read micro-expressions because she must have given herself away. She masked her dismay under the pretense of puzzlement. "So, that means ..."

"It means," growled one of the kitchen porters, "they're effectively holding Lord Scipio, a Firenzi noble mind you, directly under Imperial guard now."

"That goes against every rule in the Trown Plains Accord," the steward added, somewhat superfluously. From the anger and disgust on every face around the table, it didn't take a genius to deduce where this ship's loyalties lay.

———◆———

Fine needle sprays tingled Shayla's skin, reviving flagging energy. Steam moistened her throat. Voices and laughter echoed through the tiled walkway outside her shower stall. You were never truly alone on a ship of war but these few moments of relaxation and solitude gave her the downtime needed to process what she'd learned.

So *Hammer of War* had revealed her hand back on Eloon. She wondered how Brin was faring. The Inspection team was now a side issue, the targets were clearly Ivan and Scipio. The prison was surrounded by a formidable ring of shields and armaments but those ships had forces enough to take them, given time.

That luxury of time was something the Firenzi didn't intend to allow them. How would an *Enforcer* fare against a *Sword* in an even fight? And what other forces were even now converging on her planet?

Determination settled in Shayla's mind as she left the shower room. She changed into workout gear and hung her serving whites in her locker on her way to her bunk. Whether *George Leonard* intended to fight or form an alliance with the Imperials, she could not allow the fight to be a fair one. She had to do something to reduce the forces arrayed against Eloon.

Now that she had a useable account, Shayla could access the battleship's systems from her scroll. She lounged in her curtained bunk, no more skulking in empty offices with the ever-present danger of discovery.

Once she'd opened a doorway into the system, the limited set of tools Simone had assembled allowed her to conceal her real activities and prevent them being traced back to PO Isobel Mullin. Once again, as she'd done every day for the last seven years, she briefly mourned the loss of her brother. The tools he'd given her on her old notepad, long since destroyed, would have let her walk past Firenzi security like a ghost. Her limited resources now only served to remind her of him.

She gritted her teeth. If wishes were fishes we'd give up on meat. Right now she had a battleship-sized goose to cook before they reached Eloon.

A few minutes' work located what she needed from the engineering stores. As an afterthought, her lips curled in a sly smile, she made the requisition out to PO Christy van Belling.

She snapped the scroll closed, emerged from her bunk and grabbed a pair of heavy overalls.

It was the quietest hour in the middle of the night watch. Despite a good meal and the enervation of a scalding shower, fatigue dragged at her. Ears and eyes strained to stay alert for any signs of suspicion as she slunk through the ear-splitting machine whine of the engineering and maintenance deck. She grabbed a small cargo cart and headed for the nearest freight elevator. Right now she had no intention of running up eight flights of steep stairs.

Up in the brightly lit storage deck that ran the length of the ship she faked a casual swagger and a cheerful whistle as she pushed her cart. Even at this hour, one-man cars beeped and clattered with small trains of wagons in tow, some laden, some empty. They had the right of way down the main corridor. Shayla kept well to the side, pausing now and then to consult her scroll, checking corridor and compartment numbers against her forged requisition.

She found the intersection she needed, and the door to the electrical cable store. She punched the requisition number into the keypad alongside, and the door swung open. Lights flickered on inside, and her scroll gave her directions to the relevant aisle and shelf.

She loaded her cart with several lengths of heavy duty, insulated high-tension jumper cables. Each was about eight feet long and half an inch thick, with spring-loaded clamps at each end.

A couple more stops procured her the tools she'd need.

Shopping complete, Shayla gave a surreptitious glance up and down the main hall and disappeared down a side corridor. Tucked behind the store rooms, a steep ladder beckoned. Her ears strained for any sounds of footsteps above the all-pervasive hum of the ship. If caught, she had no excuse for being this far off the beaten track.

She draped the cables over her shoulder and scurried up the ladder, depositing her load on the floor of the maintenance corridor above. She returned for her tools and hid the cart in the nearest compartment.

The maintenance corridor ran near the outer skin of the ship. In compartments alongside, electromagnetic shield generators lay dormant ready to protect this flank of the ship in combat. Thick doors at intervals down the narrow passage gave access to the shield machinery. Vivid signs on each door warned of deadly levels of radiation and electrical discharges.

Shayla cracked open the nearest door and slipped inside. She stopped a few minutes to study the layout of cables and machinery. The shields may be dormant but the circuits would still be hot, ready to come to life at a moment's notice. She might not be an engineer, but she knew engineering, especially anything to do with weapons and defense systems—how to use the former, and how to disable the latter.

A ship's shields worked by deflecting the energy from charged particle weapons—beams and plasma. Most incoming offense was deflected straight back out into space, but the shields caught and channeled a significant amount of run-off. Shield machinery also contained a large quantity of delicate electronics. The two were not meant to mix.

Shayla stood between two green-painted electrical cabinets. Massive bus bars along the far wall linked the shield coils to banks of cells, reservoirs to contain the leakage. Florescent hazard lines on the floor warned against straying too far into the room. She eyed a run of white-painted pipes along the ceiling, picking her target. She cracked open the near cabinet and fed one of her jumper cables through a conduit at the back. One end she attached to the cabinet chassis inside. She closed the door and hoisted herself up into the mess of pipes tangling the ceiling. She carefully scraped paint from her chosen pipe, exposing bare metal to ensure a good connection, and attached the other end of the cable.

Tracing the pipe through the tangle, she stepped over the hazard lines and attached a second jumper cable to the far end of the pipe, working it as far out of sight as possible between the machinery before finally clipping it to the nearest bus bar. There was no connection to trip any alarms. As far as anyone down below could tell, the shields were functional and they'd show a working status right up to the point where they took a hit. The run-off from a direct hit would probably melt the pipe and jumpers in an instant, but not before it fried the vital innards of that cabinet.

She worked quickly but unhurriedly. That one compartment took twenty minutes to rig, then she moved on to another, then another.

Shayla had chosen her targets after some thought. On a vast ship like the *Admiral George Leonard* there was no way to sabotage all the shields. The design was modular, with banks of generators shielding different quarters of the ship. With all this effort, she'd opened up a vulnerability, nothing more. She dropped back down the ladder with the remaining jumper cables and slipped, ghost-like, across the stores level to the other side to continue her work.

Shayla returned to the crew's mess, limbs heavy, eyes drooping. She might get an hour's sleep, if she was lucky, before the start of her next watch back in the kitchens. Damn! She meant to drop off her serving uniform for laundering before she started her nocturnal sabotage but she'd been too preoccupied. The chief steward had asked her to be ready to serve in the wardroom again that evening in case some of the regulars were still sick. That suited Shayla, it might give her the chance to glean more information, but the detour would eat into her badly-needed recovery time.

She debated the pros and cons a moment before catching herself. What the heck had got into her head? She really had gone soft in these past years. Her mission, such as it was, demanded intel. The best she'd got so far was from hanging around the wardroom and the steward's mess, ergo that was where she needed to be. That needed a clean uniform or she risked blowing this opportunity in true Isobel Mullin style. She was Shayla Carver, master assassin, who'd gone days without sleep without batting an eyelid. There was no debate and no hesitation in which took priority.

As she diverted away from her bunk and towards the locker area, the undercover agent once more, hairs on her neck prickled. In her fatigued state, focused on her bunk and sleep, she'd missed small signals that should have put her on high alert. It was near the end of the night watch, the mess areas were normally quiet but there was always someone, a few small knots of people, eating, playing cards, gossiping in low murmurs. The mess tables around here were suspiciously empty. Instead, a few unfamiliar figures lurked at corners between bulkheads and lockers, feigning innocence. The stake out was obvious. Casual onlookers had been warned away. Casting back through her memory, Shayla pictured who was stationed where as she'd entered the labyrinth of the mess deck. In her mind's eye she mapped the outline of the quarantined area, aware of a slow drift of people closing in behind her. The epicenter lay ahead, where her locker was.

She rounded the corner. Ahead, Petty Officer Christy van Belling held Shayla's serving uniform at arm's length, admiring it. She looked up as Shayla came into view. "Seems I gave you a leg up in the world. You really should be careful, with your record for carelessness. You know, don't you, that white linen and machine oil really don't mix?" A tiny can nestled in the palm of her other hand.

"Hmm." Shayla's eyes narrowed. "I see you have a desperate wish to be sucking your food through a straw for the next six weeks." She started towards van Belling, hand outstretched. "Hand it over and I might let you keep your teeth, this time."

This was clearly not the reaction van Belling was expecting. She backed off a few steps, and held the can over the uniform jacket. "Stop." To her credit, she managed to keep her voice steady. "I mean it!"

Shayla kept moving. "You're trying to provoke me into a fight. You must have read my service record because you should know I have no qualms about throwing the first punch." Ten feet separated them. Van Belling's eyes darted nervously to either side. "And you should also know that when I take someone down they stay down."

A movement, nothing more than the hint of a shadow in her peripheral vision. Fighting reflex took over. A jab. Buckled windpipe. That would need attention in the next minute if she was to avoid serious charges. A kick to the other side and another crewman doubled up with a wheeze.

Someone tried to rush Shayla from behind. Bad mistake. A heavy-set woman crashed head first into the near bank of lockers and lay, dazed, on the deck.

Two quick paces closed the remaining gap between Shayla and van Belling. The uniform dropped to the ground, the oil can still clenched, forgotten in her hand. A solar plexus jab stunned her.

Shalya paused and glanced around, feeling her surroundings with all her honed senses. The rest of the pack had melted into the night. Boots with an altogether more official sound clattered closer.

Oh, heck. This mission was toast anyway. She opened her locker and wound her clenched fist into van Belling's hair. "A promise is a promise," she murmured. With studied care, and rather more satisfaction than Shayla would like to admit to, she smashed van Belling's mouth into the corner of the locker door.

Chapter 26

Perhaps, Shayla thought, she should write a comparative treatise on life in prison. She seemed to have spent a large part of her time inside a cell of one sort or another recently. Maybe she could award grades.

The fight with van Belling and cronies was over in seconds, but those seconds were enough to raise the alarm. Military police swarmed the mess deck just in time to find Shayla, emergency medical kit by her side, inserting a tube into her first assailant's neck. As he drew a long, whistling breath, a rifle butt smashed Shayla to the ground.

She woke, head pounding, on a hard metal bench and thought for a moment that she was still on Eloon. Her surroundings came back into focus: white-painted metal walls, a steel toilet and basin in one corner, a sliding metal grille for a door. The door and floor were painted a fetching blood red. The heavy omnipresent thrum of the warship enveloped her. The air was warm and dry, but pricked with a whiff of disinfectant.

She took stock of her circumstances. Her days on the steward's crew were doubtless at an end, but they could hardly bust her ass any further down than kitchen porter, could they? Kitchen duty was always regarded as the most demeaning of punishments, lower even than swabbing decks.

At least the lapse was in keeping with Petty Officer Isobel Mullin's record. As long as they didn't keep her locked up she should still be able to act effectively when the time came. Whiling away time in her cell, she tried to assess the severity of her situation. Fighting. A brawl, not a premeditated assault, shouldn't warrant anything more than extra duties and restrictions on privileges. She hoped.

Unless it got dressed up as something more.

She had hurt some of them pretty badly. She was provoked by a well-organized ring of bullies, but could she count on anyone to support that side of the story? Van Belling's gang clearly held the mess deck in thrall. She couldn't count on anyone there speaking out. The chief engineer obviously knew more about van Belling than he admitted but Shayla doubted an appeal in that direction would bear fruit. Exposing that kind of hazing going on under the chief's nose would reflect badly on him, and she had no solid evidence to back up her version of events. Best not go there unless she had to. She could take any punishment they chose, as long as she kept her freedom.

Her mind painted pictures of *Admiral George Leonard* going up against *Hammer of War*. Despite the difference in size and age they were fairly matched. The big offensive weapon of *Swords* made them terrifying ground assault ships, but that formidable firepower came at a cost. As general purpose battle platforms they weren't as invulnerable as the propaganda made them out to be. All the same, it would be a dirty slugging match. Not something she wanted to ride out helpless in a steel cell.

Then, of course, there was the matter of the sabotaged shields. Her plan had been to force a quick end to hostilities. The captain here would either surrender when it became clear how vulnerable he was, or the ship would be destroyed. She hadn't planned on being aboard when that moment of choice arrived.

Captain Scorf's face, larger than life on the conference room's wall screen, flushed red. "Dammit, ap Silessi, you have complete anarchy down there!"

Brin studied his fingernails. "No, Scorf, I don't. *You* do." He had to keep his words even briefer than usual, and his refusal to look direct at the screen wasn't a deliberate snub. He was having unaccustomed trouble keeping a straight face while Captain Scorf launched into another breathless rant.

He'd already read the reports fed to him covertly by Bard. Yes, things were getting out of hand in the camps.

The news of Lady Carver's arrest, nearly a month ago now, had been received with a depth of indignation that took Brin by surprise. He understood the psychology of propaganda well enough, and he admired the subtle skills Frank Wu and Yamen Kondosa's teams had used in the immigration center, but for all that he never expected the fierce loyalty and sense of purpose that had developed in many of the work camps. People had come here from one end of human space to the other to rebuild *something*, free from the authoritarian crap and violence that had displaced them. Here was a body of tough survivors. They'd already been through some of the worst the galaxy could throw at them, and they'd had enough. It was ironic that the rule on Eloon was probably as harsh as anywhere else, but at least it was even handed. And survival on this charred planet was precarious, but it was more than mere survival. People could see themselves making a difference.

Then, he mused, if ever there was an anti-authoritarian figure of authority, it was Lady Carver herself. She had grown this planet into a massive cult of personality. On reflection, it was no surprise that Imperial forces marching in and placing her under arrest would not be taken lightly, but at least there had been the faint hope that her arrest would be exposed for the evident nonsense they all knew it to be. Take that hope away and bring on martial law, and people would either curl up in despair or fight back.

Nobody on Eloon was the curling-up type.

In the past few days the work camps had degenerated into open rebellion against the Imperial soldiers trying to impose a kind of law that was neither needed nor wanted here. Very few fatalities, Brin was relieved to hear, but widespread passive resistance along with sabotage, ranging from minor inconvenience to the grounding of an entire squadron of fighters due to contaminated lubricant.

Brin waited for a pause in Captain Scorf's vehement tirade. "You felt the need to impose martial law," he said at last, "to counter what you saw as lawlessness, but when will you recognize that things have only gotten worse under your rule?"

"If your staff helped instead of trying to obstruct us—"

"Don't bring my staff into the argument. They're confined to barracks under *your* orders." A familiar, heady recklessness filled Brin's mind, too fast to resist.

"Dammit, ap Silessi, I need some co-operation from your people."

"That's not how your lackey, Lekk, put it." Brin bared his teeth in a feral grin. "His exact words were, 'We'll show you mud grubbers how to lick a bunch of gardeners into line.' Just let me know when you've had enough licking on the ground. Besides, it seems you have your hands full enough in orbit."

Over the last day, the space around Eloon was indeed getting crowded. *Hammer of War* had been joined by *Wrath of Empire*, another *Sword*-class battleship staunchly behind Ivan. Brin wondered at the timing. They'd arrived on the scene remarkably swiftly. They must have been patrolling the borders nearby. Fortuitous? Or in anticipation of events here?

Loyal *Merciless* had returned with orders from Magentis, much to Captain Scorf's displeasure. She was now transmitting the Imperial seal, elevated on the Emperor's orders to her ancient role of flagship. Much good it was likely to do them against hostile battleships already tainted with treason. It might keep them alive for a little while, but that was about it.

The real force holding Scorf in check wasn't the Emperor's pitifully weak presence. Arrayed against him were the Firenzi forces now numbering two *Enforcers* and numerous heavy cruisers and frigates. It wouldn't take much more for them to overwhelm even two *Swords*, but for now they were just holding the Imperials to a stand off.

"Rescind your laughable attempt at enforcing law on the surface, where you do not belong." With a savage snarl, Brin cut the connection.

The detention area consisted of a row of cells either side of a long and narrow corridor, with a small communal mess room overlooked by a guardhouse at one end. Shayla was escorted to an interview room behind the guardhouse.

She recognized the security officer from last night, a fresh-faced, and incongruously cheerful man who looked far too young for his seniority. His name tag identified him as Commander Brookingham.

Shayla stood to attention until he looked up from his notepad and jerked his head towards a chair opposite him. She sat, and he returned his attention to the notepad, lost in thought.

She wondered if this was a test. If a prisoner was going to get violent, this would be the time for it. He seemed unconcerned. Shayla guessed he could handle himself in a fight and she could feel the weight of unseen stares through the blank wall to her left that divided this room from the guardhouse. She flicked her gaze around as much of the walls and ceiling as she could without obviously rubbernecking. The compartments in the detention area were remarkably clean-lined for a warship, lacking the usual mess of trunks and pipes overhead, but this ceiling was criss-crossed by narrow I-beams that afforded any number of hiding places for cameras and weapons. There were probably several needle guns trained on her right now, with watchful eyes and twitchy trigger fingers beyond that wall.

"Well," Commander Brookingham said at last. " 'Petty Officer Isobel Mullin' it says on the file here, but we both know that's crap."

Shayla said nothing, but looked him in the eye and raised an eyebrow.

"I wondered what kind of a person we had on board, who could incapacitate four strong and healthy sailors in ... how many seconds?"

"I was off my game," Shayla said. "Tired after a long watch and a workout."

"And yet you still managed to perform life-saving field surgery in the remaining seconds before security arrived on the scene."

"Yeah. How is he, by the way?"

The commander's eyes narrowed. "I notice you didn't ask after PO van Belling's health."

Shayla shrugged. "She had it coming. Arranged little accidents to run me out of engineering, then couldn't stand to hear I'd landed on my feet. Of course, if you were even half-way competent you'd know all about her."

His face flushed briefly. "Don't make the mistake of thinking I'm blind to what happens on this ship."

"In which case you'll already know I was set up and acting in self defense. Are you going to tell the captain, or shall I?"

"Doesn't work like that, Mullin."

With a flash of insight, Shayla pictured the kind of spies and information network van Belling must have established. "So you turn a blind eye to systematic abuse as long as she keeps you fed with enough easy catches to make you look good."

He flinched. Bingo!

"I wonder how long you'd measure her life expectancy if word got out that she was one of your snitches."

He hesitated, then smiled. "Nice try, but no more deflecting. Let's bring ourselves back to the question of who *you* are. Your record is pretty flimsy. Enough to get by but nothing in here stands any close scrutiny." He gestured to the notepad. "Places, people, events ... none of this is backed up by any cross checks. It's a facade."

Shayla tried to mask her reactions as he spoke. They could well have remote sensors monitoring breathing, temperature, and pulse, but her dismay threatened to overwhelm her. There was no way this man would let her go free now he'd exposed her hasty cover.

Her mind flashed back to the original reason she was here. The intercepting of an Imperial warship and her planned abduction. If anyone here suspected who she really was, life would quickly take a turn for the worse.

"Biometrics in general didn't show up anything, which only proves my point. And then we come to your impressive and quite distinctive catalogue of injuries old and new."

A cold sensation spread from Shayla's navel, around the still-throbbing wound from her air-cruiser's control stick, and tickled her spine. Rational thought failed her for a moment. She fought to regain mastery over the pit of terror that beckoned. She'd always made sure injuries and treatments stayed off any medical records. Distinctive, yes, but surely nothing he could access would link her back to her true identity. That was a small blessing, though. The very absence of records raised more than enough suspicions.

"If there ever was such a person as PO Mullin then you aren't her. There is *nobody* in the Firenzi service, or lists of persons of interest, that matches your physical metrics. So I tried running a genetic match. Guess what? You are on file after all, but that file is locked to a security level even I can't reach."

Shayla kept silent. This one was the chatty type, and his own deductions might lead him astray. Maybe he was hoping the weight of evidence alone would persuade her to break silence. On the other hand, maybe, if he kept talking, he'd let something slip. She cast around for plausible cover stories that might persuade him to give her at least some limited freedom of movement.

"So I'm left with a real puzzle. You're no lowly PO, that's clear. Who are you? One of Jai Marx's spies?" He paused, musing. "If so, the old guy's slipping. That was a shoddy background story. Not his normal work. It sometimes takes years to sniff out his stooges."

The resentment in his voice said that claiming to be sent by Jai would not be a career-enhancing move either. In fact, she fancied her chances better as Shayla Carver than as one of Jai's henchmen. Okay then. Let's give him something to feed his imagination. "And I'm guessing those same stooges take years to put in place, too."

He blinked. "This was a rush job, wasn't it." Color drained from his face. "Why would Jai, *anyone* in fact, need to get eyes on board in such a hurry? This is a short term assignment, not deep cover."

"My presence here is closely linked to your current flight to Eloon." Oh! That got a reaction. She wondered if he had some truthsense skill. Anyone in his position would have received training, though few could use it. But her words rang with truth, even the slowest of students could have heard it. "But not in the way you are thinking." If he heard the harmonics in her voice, that should give him pause.

He was sweating now. Before he could respond, a soft voice sounded over the intercom, a voice like goose down over razor wire. "I think I will speak with our mystery guest up here, Commander."

Chapter 27

A squad of guards escorted Shayla out of the detention area and through the ship. Fleeting gazes followed the procession as they brushed past bustling crew in crowded corridors. She supposed she should be used to this by now, and maybe honored by the attention, but these escorts were sharp and wary and left little opportunity for escape. Her hands were manacled in front of her, but at least she was temporarily away from barred cells and locked doors.

Hairs on her neck stood erect like a static charge as her attention was belatedly drawn to the activity around her. There was no flicker of recognition in those gazes. Word of her escapade in the crew's mess must have got out, but few people in this huge ship knew of PO Mullin, and of those only a handful could put a face to the name. She was just an anonymous miscreant under escort from who-knows-where to who-gives-a-fuck.

They were all too preoccupied to be curious.

Then it hit her. She'd seen this intensity before in another life. *Admiral George Leonard* was preparing for war.

Shayla stumbled as blackness edged her vision. She took a deep breath and regained her balance, aware of suddenly-leveled weapons relaxing slightly. She longed for the practiced ease with which, in her younger years, she could kick her mind into hyperdrive, ready to analyze every threat and opportunity around her. She felt so sluggish these days. Out of practice, and so fucking *old*.

She plodded through her situation, desperately hoping to kick start the lightning flashes of thought that she would need to come out of this alive.

She was going to meet the captain. Maybe she'd get more clues as to what was happening in the world outside. Most especially, what was happening on Eloon.

More immediately, she tried to picture how she might appear to the captain and to the security chief. They certainly wouldn't welcome spies on board, but that was simply a part of life on a large warship. The ruling Family needed to ensure such potent weapons stayed loyal. Given the intestinal power-brokering that riddled the military, the aristocracy, the judiciary, any number of trading guilds and the Family itself, a company of six thousand might contain covert presences from many quarters. On top of that, many ships of this size had their own ingrained loyalties, their own culture, established over time. When power from the center weakened, captains might see opportunities to further their own favored agendas. And the vacillating Giovanni Firenzi, lackluster son of the bitterly-mourned patriarch, Josef, was the epitome of weak.

The squad leader brought them to a halt at an elevator door. He eyed Shayla coldly, but her heart fluttered with a brief glimmer of hope as the four guards took up positions around her. Her unconscious mind had recognized their two-in-front-two-behind routine and predicted where they would place themselves. These guards were alert, but working to rote. They bundled her into the elevator and she focused once more on her impending interview with the soft-spoken captain.

As a matter of course the Family's security service had its own official representatives on board, and as many unofficial agents as it could place without arousing suspicions. The service itself, a vast and secretive organization with many branches and ancient rivalries, might be pursuing multiple and sometimes conflicting agendas. Usually with the Family's interests at heart, though not necessarily favoring the *individuals* currently in power.

In such an environment, 'loyal enough' was the best anyone could hope for.

That she was still walking and breathing told Shayla the captain had no clue who he held, but what would he assume?

The command center of Shayla's old *Martha Sandover* had been strictly off limits to lowly grunts like her. A shiver of excitement ran up her spine as she crossed the threshold into this holy of holies.

The noise struck her first, or rather the lack of it. She remembered her first experience of an Imperial capital ship's command deck and the cacophony of sound that pervaded the space. Here, the air was heavy with a hundred murmured conversations that seemed muted and distant in comparison.

The captain stood, feet apart and hands clasped in the small of his back, behind a ten-foot-wide tactical display set into a central well in the floor. His white uniform jacket seemed to glow in the twilight world, lit by rank on rank of screens. In front and around him control stations radiated away into multi-hued corridors. A quick survey of insignia confirmed Shayla's assumption that the most senior officers manned the inner circle of stations, with their underlings seated in decreasing order of rank towards the outer reaches of the wide, low-ceilinged room.

Her guard led her to a clear space near the back of the room. She caught the eye of the squad leader, who hissed, "Stand to attention, sailor."

She sneered at him, then casually turned her back on him and slouched. Let him assume she was an undisciplined lout. Isobel Mullin's record for minor misdemeanors probably preceded her, and she might as well maintain that pretense as long as possible. She wondered again what news of the fight had circulated the lower decks. There had been few eye witnesses, van Belling had seen to that, so most accounts would be little more than rumor. Van Belling's crew would not be keen for details of their beating to gain too much traction. With luck, these guards behind her would assume the accounts had been wildly exaggerated. Such combat prowess was just not in Isobel Mullin's profile.

As if reading her mind, the captain turned and regarded her. "So, what's in a name? We can call you 'Mullin' for now, I suppose, until we know better, but Commander Brookingham informs me that you are a spy. What say you?"

Shayla pondered. "I suppose he is correct, in a way."

"That was a load of bullshit in the wardroom last night. *Tropical Court Mystique* indeed," he spat.

Shayla drooped her head, appearing to gaze at the deck but studying the captain from the corner of her eye. "That ..." She paused. His watery eyes had lost focus, but Shayla knew full well that a dimmed sense of vision could allow other senses to the fore. "Was a fiction," she admitted. "I couldn't remember a specific recipe, but I *have* served My Lord Scipio."

As she spoke Shayla focused on a memory of a time years ago, in her brief undercover role on Magentis, when she had indeed catered to Scipio as Emperor Julian's guest. With a sinking feeling she hoped her words had been close enough to the truth. She suspected that this man was a truthsenser, maybe even adept. She hadn't spotted the signs of a trained adept, but what if this captain was one of those rarest of humans, born with raw and natural skill? He may not even realize his sensitivity, but it would certainly explain how someone so superficially weak could keep control of a powerful company of ruthless and ambitious officers.

"Are you working for Jai Marx?"

The directness of the question threw Shayla off balance. "No, sir." The truth. She looked him in the eye, studying his reaction. Tangential questions out of the blue like that were a standard technique, but this man didn't seem to be following any of the regular patterns of inquiry she'd seen in practiced truthsensers. The signals he gave off were maddeningly inconclusive. Damn! She had to know how vulnerable she might be here.

He couldn't be allowed to lead the questioning anywhere close to the truth. Whatever plans had been laid for Shayla Carver's abduction, this ship had been sent to rendezvous with the defunct scout. This captain had to be complicit in the plans she'd managed to scupper. An oblique attack was needed to draw him away, and at this stage of the game something of a gamble seemed in order. "I don't report to Jai, but clearly Commander Brookingham *did* manage to bloody his snoop's nose on a sealed Special Service file."

His insipid gaze seemed to slide away from her eyes and flit around the room. "Hmm."

"Sir." An ensign approached and saluted. "We're entering Eloon space, ready to go sublight and match velocity."

"Thank you, Ensign." He turned to his navigator. "Take us sublight two light hours out from Chevin Chenga. Match Eloon's orbital velocity and collect readings before we close in and make ourselves known."

He turned back to Shayla and speared her with a remarkably clear look. Water turned to ice. "I listened in on your interview with Commander Brookingham. He mentioned nothing to you about *which* repository contained that locked file."

Shayla raised an eyebrow. The fact that he'd not immediately called the guards down on her suggested she'd guessed right. Not that it was a difficult guess. If the chief security officer had covert access to Imperial files and tracked her genetic profile *there* she would surely not be standing here now. Let the captain stew on the possibility that she was a secret squirrel who did not owe allegiance to the head of that most secretive of services. The best lies were those built and owned by the recipient.

———•••———

The ancient frame of the ship creaked and shuddered around them as the secondary drive strained to match their velocity to distant Eloon's. Slow rhythmic pulses of sound, felt rather than heard, thrummed from the engineering compartments fore and aft of the command center. The balls of Shayla's feet tingled in time to waves of vibrations running through the deck. She never remembered *Martha Sandover* feeling so decrepit, but then she never remembered maneuvers pushing her to the limits like this. The captain was in a hurry to adjust the huge ship's velocity and close in on the planet before they could be spotted.

He seemed to have forgotten about Shayla, standing quietly at the back of the control room, but she was not so naive as to imagine that to be true. The old guy was sharper than he made out to be. She puzzled over her status in his eyes. He'd given up his half-hearted attempts at questioning but she sensed he was looking for something from her, some sign as to her intentions. Here was a prime opportunity to fabricate whatever story she thought he wanted to hear. Therein lay the danger. The cunning old goat was giving her enough rope to hang herself.

His attention might be on the command of his ship, but the guards he'd assigned had not let up their vigilance for a moment.

Meanwhile, arrays of sensors assembled a two-hour-old view of the space around the planet.

From where she stood, Shayla studied the tactical display and icy fingers crawled across her scalp. She couldn't read the names from here, but the colors and coded symbols were clear enough. There were two *Swords* and two *Implacables* on the Imperial side, ranged against two— now three—*Enforcers* and numerous smaller craft. The Firenzi forces up to now were outgunned, but the arrival of *Admiral George Leonard* might tempt them into chancing direct action.

She was suddenly aware of the captain studying her. Her hasty cover was well and truly demolished. If she was going to replace it with something convincing that didn't lead to a quick appointment with the wrong end of a beam rifle she needed to show more depth than a mere petty officer.

What was their game? They'd snatched her from an Imperial warship. That was not something anyone would do lightly, so the stakes must be high. She herself was not the target, just a means to an end. Many people wanted her dead, she knew that, but she was also realistic enough to know that on her own she wasn't important enough. A welcome piece of collateral damage maybe, certainly not the end game.

The two prisoners. That was the only prize of any value in this system. Everything that had happened recently came back to them. Half the population in Imperial and Firenzi space had an interest in either their freedom or their deaths, with opposing forces held at bay only by her vigilance in granting them neither. And she'd felt the depth of passion on board this ship. There was only one thing they could be seeking here.

She stepped closer to the captain, aware of the sudden tightening of hands on weapons behind her. "The rumor is the Governor here is dead," she murmured, for his ears only. "The planet is vulnerable. Do you really think you have enough force in place to stage a jailbreak?"

"Where do you stand on Lord Scipio's incarceration?" His soft voice was hardly audible above the background hum of the warship.

Shayla thought for a moment. Some hesitation in answering would be understandable, given that he was asking her to voice treason against the Emperor's rule. She had no hesitation on that score; she was more concerned about giving an answer that would ring true. "He should not be in prison," she declared with quiet and entirely honest intensity.

"And what about the Grand Duke?"

Now, there was a good question indeed. Ivan and Scipio had conspired together and, in their past actions against the Emperor, had planned on a joint rule. But Shayla knew many of the factions behind them individually did not share any such collaborative ambitions. She was now close enough to the tactical display to discern the ships' designations. One *Sword* was *Hammer of War*. No surprise there, but the other name filled her with dread. *Wrath of Empire*. Traitor ship. Fully behind Ivan. And yet, by the maneuvering visible on the plot, the forces were faced off against each other. She could see no signs of collaboration here. It was time for another gamble. She allowed her true feelings to leak through. "For my part, sir, I wish him dead."

"Hmm."

Shayla remained silent, allowing him to process what she'd just said and, more importantly, how she'd said it.

"So, Petty Office Mullin, what *are* you doing on board my ship?"

Time to raise the stakes. "Intelligence is recent and patchy, but there is someone on this ship who wishes to see your present mission fail. That is why I'm here. You have a saboteur on board."

He raised an eyebrow and favored her with a bleary squint. "And you think to mention this only now?"

"I don't know who on this ship I can trust so I couldn't afford any hint of my identity to be revealed." She returned his squint with an icy glare. "To *anyone*. However I fear this ship's effectiveness as a fighting unit has already been compromised. I have nothing concrete to add. I ran into trouble before I could glean information of any substance and your own security officer blew my cover."

All perfectly true statements, yet so misleading. Let him stew on *that* for a while.

"Sir," the ensign announced, "we've matched velocity with Eloon. Ready to proceed."

The captain acknowledged. "Navigation, Weapons, Tactical, you have your orders. Sound general quarters. We're going in."

He turned to Shayla. "You've been hiding far more than you're telling. If you really were here in support of our cause you'd have known to confide in me or the chief engineer. You did neither." He signaled the guards. "Return her to the secure interview room." To Shayla he said, "I have a pair of *Swords* to distract while our party takes that prison. I'm going to be busy, but Commander Brookingham is fully skilled in the more persuasive questioning techniques. He'll soon loosen your tongue."

Chapter 28

Was it the effects of his illness, Brin wondered, or was it just his imagination? Or was he getting paranoid second-guessing every waking thought these days? Whatever, he used to be able to multitask, to flit effortlessly from one security threat to another during the course of his duties, and pick up where he left off. Details, lines of inquiry, complex chains of evidence and deduction used to settle back in the forefront of his mind like resuming a videoed report that he'd paused.

Not any more.

All his focus had been on keeping the Lords Ivan and Scipio safe from marauding forces. Then, even with the temporary stalemate in orbit, it had taken Captain Scorf's angry tirade to return Brin's attention to the situation on the planet's surface. Even during the airborne assaults on his refuge, the old Brin would never have lost sight of other dangers threatening his demesne.

The lawlessness on the ground was not what troubled Brin. It was a natural enough reaction to martial law and anything that distracted Captain Scorf from his main goal was welcome.

But there was still the matter of Cobra, the Insurrection's snake who'd gone to ground. And that same lawlessness, together with the constraints of martial law, were hampering Brin's own team as much as Scorf's.

Slumped in an unyielding chair, too exhausted to sit straight, Brin struggled to recollect the myriad investigations he'd set in motion, and to absorb the news the Imperial undercover agent was trying to relay.

Brin squinted at the grainy image on the wall screen in the same conference room where he'd confronted Scorf. With each side upstairs trying to dominate the other both in physical space and over the airwaves, communications across the planet had to battle through the fringes of sporadic interference.

"This surveyor, the Insurrection assassin, is the one who met with Cobra in Scale?"

The Imperial agent scowled. "From the descriptions provided, I believe so."

"And she was responsible for Commander ap Terlion's death?"

"I'm certain of that." The man's eyes glittered under a fringe of unkempt hair.

"Your orders were to take her alive. At all costs."

"Shit happens." His tone was neutral, but Brin detected a hint of satisfaction in his response. Brin needed to find Cobra. The visiting agents nominally shared that goal but the murder of their own commanding officer would have adjusted their personal priorities, regardless of professional obligations.

Brin's fists clenched in helpless fury. He'd just lost his one definite connection to Cobra and it was clear these borrowed agents had become liabilities more than assets. He should have seen this sooner.

"Gather what's left of your team and return to your ship."

The man looked on the verge of protesting, but he must have caught something in Brin's eyes. His expression hardened and he cut the connection.

He was a professional. He knew the score.

Brin's next call was to the lead agent of his own team. His message was brief and simple. No room for misunderstanding in the garbled ether. "Execute cuckoo."

When the screen was clear once more, Brin sighed and rested his forehead a moment on arms folded across the table. Under Commander ap Terlion, the Imperial team had offered his only realistic chance of tracking Cobra, but it was time to cut his losses. They wouldn't be prevented from leaving, but any of them staying on the surface would now be marked men. No longer welcome.

His one crumb of comfort was that all traffic to and from the prison was suspended. For now, there was no way for Cobra to reach the island.

⎯⎯⎯•◆•⎯⎯⎯

As the guards led Shayla away, she caught one last glimpse of the tactical plot spread out at the captain's feet. The view jumped abruptly as the primary drive re-engaged and closed the last billion or so miles in a matter of seconds. The last thing she saw as the door to the control room banged shut was the outline of a *Sword* growing at frightening speed.

They clattered up a companionway—at general quarters the ship's elevators were all grounded and their hatches sealed. Still taking no chances, two guards went ahead and covered her with their weapons before Shayla was allowed to start up the steps.

The detention block lay a hundred yards ahead, past the forward engineering compartment. Shayla swallowed a terrifying uprush of acid and hastily buried all thoughts of what awaited her there. She couldn't afford to let herself be returned to the cells, but neither could she afford the luxury of fear. Keeping paralyzing emotions in check, something that used to come so naturally, was getting harder with each passing year.

Their path took them through paired blast doors, forming airlocks between one section and the next, and along a long and narrow corridor. They were coming to the end, and Shayla was casting about for avenues of escape, when the ship shuddered violently. The lights dimmed and Shayla's ears popped at a sudden drop in pressure.

Galvanized by the distraction, she was already in motion before her conscious mind caught up. A pace backward took the guards behind her by surprise. A roundhouse kick drove up into the diaphragm of one. Shayla continued the motion ending up behind the second. She threw her bound hands over his head before he had time to react. Using his body as a shield she leveled his weapon and shot the three guards ahead in an indiscriminate spray of fire, before releasing her grip and breaking his neck.

Shayla's surroundings came back into normal focus after the accelerated awareness of those two seconds of violence. Alarms blared in the distance. The air pressure was already stabilizing, but for anything like that to be felt through the series of automated seals in the network of decks and bulkheads a major compartment must have been breached. A stench of burnt plastic leaked through the vents overhead.

Speakers at intervals down the corridor directed damage control crews to the hangars at the rear of the ship.

The deck bucked again and jarred Shayla almost off her feet. She had genuinely tried to warn the captain of sabotage. A hit on the rigged shields would have blown their circuitry, and the kind of strike a *Sword* could deliver may well have fried a battery of critical systems on its errant path through the ship's fabric. *Admiral George Leonard* was defenseless.

Shayla divested a guard of his weapon, oriented herself, and scurried up a nearby companionway. The overhead hatch had slammed shut at the first drop in pressure and wouldn't open. She cursed, and headed forward through a blast door into another long corridor. Another companionway. Another locked hatch. Forward again. This, she knew, was the last section of corridor before she reached the warren of compartments lying in between the forward beam batteries. That area would be crawling with crew. She could hardly expect her bindings to go unnoticed. She climbed the steep steps and breathed a sigh as the hatch above her popped open. Up another level and she raised the hatch leading into the corridor that serviced one bank of escape pods.

This corridor was guarded. Until an order was given to abandon ship, anyone trying to use a pod would be shot as a deserter. Head and shoulders out of the hatch, Shayla called to the nearest guards, keeping her stolen rifle out of sight. "Over here! I have wounded down here and the hatch for'ard is sealed." As they lowered their guard, uncertain but not yet suspicious, Shayla took a quick head count. Two forward and one aft.

She vaulted clear of the hatch, aiming the rifle with one hand, and picked off the two guards ahead. A bolt sizzled off the bulkhead alongside her and she ducked behind a bank of lockers. Feeling beside her, she fumbled a locker open. Emergency equipment. An oxygen cylinder. She loosened it, silently cursing her hampered movements and listening to footsteps approaching. She tossed the cylinder out into the corridor and loosed off a bolt. The cylinder exploded as she ducked back under cover. She emerged a fraction of a second later and shot the stunned guard.

With a quick glance up and down the corridor to confirm it really was empty, Shayla gathered the downed guards' rifles and slapped the hatch release on the nearest escape pod.

The double doors of the airlock hissed closed behind her as she sprinted towards the nose of the simple craft. Two banks of inward-facing seats on either side of a narrow central walkway reminded Shayla that she was depriving sixty crew of a means of escape. She brushed the thought aside as she vaulted into the pilot's seat and awkwardly strapped in. Realizing his shields were inoperable, the captain would by now have surrendered and the opposing captains would surely have no cause to press the attack. These two forces were jostling for power but they were not at war.

Ready for emergencies, the pod's systems had automatically come to life the instant she'd opened the rear hatch. Engines were already warming up for launch. The outer hatch—little more than a shield against orbital debris—split like a seed pod to reveal a black disc of space. With only a moment's hesitation, Shayla punched the release.

The white disk of Chevin Chenga, Eloon's sun, blinded Shayla as the pod spat into space. Even brighter bolts flashed past the forward canopy, but they were not aimed at her. *George Leonard* was still desperately fighting off an attacker which the comms screen identified as *Hammer of War*.

The Firenzi ship's vulnerability was clear to see. Finding a rear-facing video feed Shayla was horrified to see the damage already inflicted. The ship's hind quarters trailed wreckage. Great slashes in the hull armor looked like she'd been mauled by a gargantuan predator. Shayla's sabotage had worked all too well.

One of the forward beams was still hurling futile bolts at the menacing *Sword*. The others were either out of action or unable to bring their aim to bear.

She opened a channel on the comms screen and hailed the stricken battleship. All channels were dead. From her vantage point, with the upper surface coming into view, Shayla could see the midships communications array, a tangled and useless mess. There were secondary arrays, though. Surely *someone* could hear her? She switched to a general broadcast. "*Admiral George Leonard!* Anyone on board. Your defenses are down and you lack the firepower to take on a battleship. Cease fire and lower your remaining shields."

No reply. She repeated her message, all the while watching *Hammer of War* line up on the Firenzi ship's unprotected stern.

Frustrated, she hailed *Hammer* on an open channel and demanded to speak with the captain. A bored comms tech answered. "The captain is busy dealing with a hostile threat in a system under Imperial military rule."

"Firenzi battleship *Admiral George Leonard* is crippled and without effective command, otherwise she would have surrendered by now."

"I will happily convey her surrender when her captain or a surviving officer makes contact." She could hear the sneer in his voice as he continued, "They'd better make it fast, and you will turn yourself over as a prisoner of war if you want to keep breathing."

The implied threat to herself incensed Shayla, not from fear for her own life, but it violated all interstellar rules of engagement to fire on an unarmed escape pod. "Look, you supercilious little prick, her communications are down. There is physically no way to comply." She moderated her outraged tone. "She is no threat to you! Please stand down."

"Not my decision, Firenzi."

"Please put me through to the captain, immediately."

"Or what?" he scoffed.

"There are six thousand people on board. For the love of Unity, leave them be!"

With almost leisurely movements, *Hammer* rolled away from *George Leonard*. With a sick feeling in her gut Shayla knew this was no act of submission. The *Sword's* primary weapon, her city-wrecking plasma cannon, occupied the full two-thousand-foot height of the battleship from the bulbous upper pod containing hangars and the main battle platform down through the height of the hull to project from her underbelly. She was taking up an attack posture, lining up a kill shot.

Fully aware that she was painting a target on her back, Shayla keyed a series of secure identification codes onto the comms screen. She struggled to keep a quaver out of her voice as she announced, with as much cold authority as she could muster, "This is Lady Shayla Carver, Governor of Eloon. You are operating in a volume of space under my jurisdiction. I order you to stand down immediately." For good measure she added, "Any further hostility will be tried as an act of treason under the Trown Plains Accord."

A pause. That must have got their attention. Her codes would have triggered an automatic and immediate alert to the commanding officer. After an agonizing wait, a different voice, oily and contemptuous, whispered back. "Lady Carver was relieved of her Governorship. You have no authority here."

The plasma cannon belched lilac fire.

The remains of the once-proud *Admiral George Leonard* exploded as her atmosphere superheated. A fraction of a second later, the gutted shell erupted in a detonation that seemed to rend the fabric of space as her towering banks of power plants turned traitor. Whirling debris flickered briefly, then evaporated into component atoms in that hellish flame.

"Noooo!" Shayla screamed, careless of who might overhear. Tears blurred her sight even as her body, on some instinct of self-preservation, grabbed the pod's controls and flung her sideways as fast as the escape craft's pitiful drive could manage.

Too slow. It was like steering a cow. She was a sitting target.

Shayla's chin snapped down and connected with her sternum as the shock front from the battleship's demise flung the escape pod like a toy boat on a tsunami.

Liquid lightning stabbed through the space she'd just vacated.

More bolts followed, but she was closing fast on the hulking battleship and the *Sword's* prodigious secondary weapons were having trouble getting a firm lock.

Icy fury flooded Shayla. She blinked her eyes clear and brought herself even closer in. From past experience she knew these ships had many blind spots up close, the most extensive being right on top of that upper pod.

Hammer maneuvered away. Her captain was also aware of those blind spots and determined to bring his weapons to bear.

Shayla pushed the tiny pod as fast as it would go, knowing that this was a losing battle. The battleship may be massive, but it had proportionally powerful drives and could out-accelerate her. She was also conscious that if she pushed hard to regain safety she could easily overshoot if the captain below reversed course.

Her life was likely measured in seconds.

She cast around for other options. The pod had external grapples. If she could get close enough to make contact she might be able to latch on out of reach. That would buy herself a few minutes at least.

A shadow above blotted out the stars.

"Lady Carver, this is Imperial cruiser *Merciless*. Please hand over control and allow yourself to be docked in the forward hangar. You are to surrender yourself to our custody."

The cruiser positioned itself in between Shayla and *Hammer of War*. In the circumstances, accepting a hasty surrender to a captain not hellbent on blowing her up seemed the least-worst option.

This could easily be a trap. Good cop, bad cop routine. Placing her craft under remote control they could hold her steady while they picked her off. But, she reasoned, *Merciless* had ample opportunity to kill her while she played cat-and-mouse with *Hammer*. They hadn't. Praying to a pantheon of gods she had no faith in, Shayla turned control over.

This act brought back memories of her flight with the Emperor, seven years ago, docking with this very same craft. The same hangar doors yawned open.

While the craft maneuvered, other similarities came to Shayla's mind. Then, as now, her flight was accompanied by senseless atrocities leading to thousands of pointless deaths. In both cases, Shayla had been instrumental in those deaths but there was one crucial difference. Seven years ago, she herself had set those events in motion, a responsibility she accepted and a misguided crime she'd feel keenly for the rest of her life. Devoting her energy and passion to rebuilding Eloon, to giving hopeless people hope, seemed only fitting. But the callous destruction of a helpless ship chilled her. She felt dead and empty inside as the awful destruction replayed in her imagination. She'd only been aboard a few days, but regardless of the company's political leanings and traitorous intent she'd grown to appreciate the close-knit community on board. A ship like that was a living, breathing entity, with a life of its own and a weight of history and tradition beyond imagining.

And *she* had left them helpless and exposed to that vicious assault. She felt small and shriveled, an empty skin.

The docking controller brought the pod expertly into place and snugged a pressurized tunnel against the rear hatch. The brief vibration running through the deck jolted Shayla like an electric spark. Here we go, she thought. She climbed the companionway and entered the white-painted airlock at the top. In the corridor beyond was the expected honor guard, weapons drawn and leveled. She caught one familiar face at the back of the small crowd in the cramped space. "Joseph Herrin!" She noted the insignia. "*Captain* Herrin now, I see."

"Do I know you?"

She laughed, a wild and slightly manic laugh. "You do. You just don't know it yet. It's been seven years, but you must recall my flair for disguise."

"Lady Carver?" His voice was puzzled. Unbelieving.

"The same." She pushed the feelings of emptiness to the back of her mind. There was work to do and six thousand murders to avenge. "For now you'll have to trust in my security credentials until I can return my appearance to normal. It will take time, and some equipment. And enough food for a battalion, but I assure you it is me under this face."

He grunted and signaled two guards to search the escape pod. "The right codes were transmitted, but that doesn't mean a thing until you can repeat the feat in front of my communications chief. And even then I won't believe it until I see someone I recognize."

Shayla chewed her lip. "Fair enough. I will need privacy. The application and removal of my disguise is ... invasive."

He nodded.

"But what is happening out there? Your forces and the Firenzi were headed to all-out war."

He barked a laugh. "Nice try. You'll have no contact with anyone and no information until I'm satisfied. Let's just say, if you are who you say you are, you're safe enough with us ... for the time being."

Chapter 29

The march through the single main deck of *Merciless*, with its ice blue walls and checkerboard flooring in red and gray, brought back poignant memories. On this ship, Shayla had drugged and held the Emperor helpless while her brother's security routines fooled a pair of *Swords* into attacking the Imperial home world. In these corridors and compartments she'd been shot, imprisoned, pleaded for her life in return for helping the Emperor free his hostage family, seen those hopes dashed then rekindled, and finally vindicated.

Her actions here had led to her combined punishment and reward, exiled to govern a dead world—her childhood home—and coax it back to life.

Ghosts followed her with every step.

As she expected, they led her aft through the crew's dining hall and into officer country. Ushered into a narrow two-man cabin, she requested some supplies to help her with her disguise. The true capability of her biological implants was still a secret she wished to preserve. She reeled off a random list of solvents and skin treatments and a stack of medical wipes and towels, along with a food order with enough calories to choke a horse.

The hold-up frustrated her but she could understand Joseph Herrin's caution. Physically, she was not the person he remembered and security codes could be stolen. Until she could convince him of her identity, she would be kept under guard and kept in the dark. Simone's words from a lifetime ago haunted her. Such a good disguise was indeed a two-edged sword.

Simone! The one person in all these years that Shayla had felt truly able to confide in. A knock at the door drew Shayla back from the depths of sorrow. Now was not the time. The knock paid nothing more than lip service to courtesy; the door opened a fraction of a second later. An orderly brought in a tray with the supplies Shayla had ordered.

Another followed with a heavy tray of food. They barely had room to turn in the cramped space as they set their burdens down on the table bolted to the wall.

They left and another familiar face appeared in the doorway. The heavy-set woman clutching a notepad looked expectantly at Shayla.

"Stevie Molk," Shayla said. She glanced at the insignia on the comms tech's shoulder. "Communications chief now. Where's Frances?"

"Promoted and spreading cheer on board *Dagger of Fate* when I last heard." She grunted. "Well, you pass the first test anyway, but you might just have good intel." She handed over the notepad.

"You'll want my identification codes," Shayla said, scribbling on the surface of the notepad.

When Stevie held her hand out for the notepad, Shayla hesitated. "I wonder if I can remember this one. Here's something I doubt any intel could have dug up." She closed her eyes and reached back into her memory. Anguish flooded her. The code she was trying to recall was one which she and Brandt had used as a signature, and which unlocked the back door into their stealthy ship-corrupting routines. She'd disclosed it to Stevie back then, as a means of tracking and finally infiltrating a renegade *Sword*. This code was the key that finally cracked Ivan's defenses and led to his capture.

It was a code built on deeply personal and painful memories from their childhood. Memories etched in fire on their young minds.

Tears streamed freely down Shayla's cheeks as she reconstructed those memories in her mind.

Then the stylus in her hand, seemingly of its own accord, started to sketch the outlines of her childhood home.

When she finished, Shayla looked up to find Stevie regarding her with wide eyes.

"Standard Boor-Skam," Shayla murmured, referring to the algorithm needed to convert the raw topological content of the picture into a numerical code. She looked at the stylus in sudden surprise. "And I see you've stopped chewing these."

Stevie's face turned white. "It really is you," she breathed. "I don't know how you disguised yourself so completely, but *nobody* else could have done this."

Shayla gave a half-hearted shrug. She'd been working on her implants ever since the pod docked and after the efforts of the past few days it was already taking its toll. She managed a weak smile. "I'm sure if the real Shayla Carver was locked up somewhere and tortured, they could have dragged even this out of her."

"But I remember the pain in your eyes last time you drew this picture," Stevie said. "There was no faking that."

———

Another knock at the door, more respectful this time. Bleary-eyed, Shayla ran a hand through tangles in her hair. She'd spent the past six hours in ferocious, unremitting concentration.

She knew she was a long way yet from properly completing the transformation. An extra dimension to her senses, one that had taken years to develop, gave her precise awareness of the state of her implants. It had taken a long time to get used to the idea of *feeling* the color of her skin. What she felt now didn't comfort her, but at least she'd worked first on the shape and texture of her features. The face that stared back from the tiny mirror above the wash basin was pale, puffy, blotchy, but recognizable once more as Shayla Carver.

She opened the door. Her guard detail had changed some time in the past hours. She'd been so focused, her usually-sharp hearing had failed to alert her to the movement in the corridor. Captain Herrin stood patiently. He peered close, examining her up and down. Shayla looked for any flicker of recognition, of a brief friendship rekindled, but he simply pressed his lips tight and nodded. His grim expression cut through Shayla's fatigue.

"Am I still under suspicion then?"

"I'm satisfied, especially with what Lieutenant Molk reported. If this is what you go through every time you go under cover then I pity you. You look like shit, but we're pressed for time."

He gestured back to the cabin. Shayla took the hint and made room for him, sitting on the lower bunk while he closed the door and took the only chair next to the fixed table.

"Your announcement over an open comms channel stirred them up like a pack of hokloks scenting blood. If they really believed you we'd have been grappled and boarded by now, but I managed to persuade them your codes had been compromised and faked by a Firenzi officer trying to distract them."

Shayla gave him a skeptical look.

"I'm not sure how much they bought it, but I sent them security footage of you, looking nothing like Governor Carver, leaving the pod. For now they're satisfied that I've got you in irons and will turn you over in due course."

"Thanks Space for disguise."

Captain Herrin grimaced. "Meanwhile they have more urgent mischief to concoct. You asked about the situation on Eloon. We *had* it under control ..." He paused. "No, it was never under control but at least it was balanced with neither Firenzi nor renegade Skamensis forces able to take command. That third *Enforcer* tipped the balance and the Firenzis were ready to risk a move. With that ship gone, we were back to a stalemate."

"Neither side trusts the other and neither was prepared to let the other take a lead storming the prison."

"That's what we've been banking on, but time is running out. There are more ships due any hour now, loyal to the Emperor and to that wastrel Firenzi, that will send the renegades packing. They're getting desperate."

"They're banding together." Shayla's heart sank.

His shoulders slumped. His gray complexion told Shayla he'd been as busy over the past hours as she had. "We can't crack their encryption, but the pattern of comms traffic between ships tells me they're setting aside their differences. I fear an all-out invasion is imminent. We are just one medium-sized cruiser. We can't hold off those battleships."

Shayla stared at Captain Herrin, then her expression hardened. "So, we'll have to pre-empt them." She thought furiously. "What is the situation with the Inspectorate?"

"Why? What have they got to do with anything right now?"

"They were hit by a combination poison. A rare specialty of the Firenzi."

"How did you ..." Captain Herrin's jaw dropped. His eyes glinted. "The medical team here got help from the Firenzi. You tipped them off. How did you know?"

"I puzzled it out." Shayla shrugged. "I had time to kill while wondering what fate was in store for me. A long story for another time. Did they isolate the poison and the trigger?"

"I assume so. They were able to concoct an antidote. I know nothing more than that."

"They survived?"

The captain grimaced. "Most of them."

"And they have an antidote," Shayla breathed, mind racing. The fact they'd produced an antidote meant they also managed to find the poison in the team's bodies. Maybe nothing more than a trace, but that would do. "Right! I'll need a craft, something fast, with shields." Shayla stood abruptly, then staggered back onto the bed.

"And a pilot, I think," the captain said.

Shayla almost argued, then relented as the room swayed and settled in front of her eyes. "But time is of the essence. Do you have contact with the surface? Can you take us in low and fast? Are they imposing any kind of blockade? What about comms interference?"

Captain Herrin stemmed the flood of questions as he stood to activate the comms panel in the room. He issued a stream of orders, in between answering Shayla's questions.

They decamped to the operations room next door to the main control deck, to brief the ship's senior officers. Captain Herrin introduced Shayla to the pilot he'd chosen, a skeletally-thin woman with dark leathery skin and ice blue eyes. She looked frail, but she held herself with poise and a glacial calm. When Shayla was last on board, Joseph Herrin had been the senior operations controller, guiding pilots and platoons of marines on hazardous landing missions. If he recommended this woman, that was good enough for Shayla.

"Coming up over Torremis in fifteen seconds," the current operations controller announced. "You'll only have a minute to get your message across."

The loyal cruiser *Merciless*, the captain explained, had been playing a game of tag with the other warships congregating around Eloon. It was a delicate balance. The Imperial warships wouldn't open fire on another Imperial craft, not until they had Ivan free and in charge. That would change things dramatically, and *Merciless* would have to flee or be destroyed, but until then she enjoyed relative safety. By the same token, the Imperial goliaths wouldn't allow a foreign power to harm her either. Not yet.

And so, *Merciless* had roamed freely, guarding the planet and warning off any craft from either side that strayed too close.

At unpredictable intervals she also closed in and used a direct line tight beam to contact forces on the surface and check on conditions dirtside. As a matter of course, they used secure encryption so the besieging forces couldn't eavesdrop. This, both Imperial and Firenzi captains discouraged and it was never long before communications got cut off in a blanket of interference.

Shayla closed her eyes and rehearsed her message. When the comms tech told her the link was live she announced in a clear, calm voice, "Message for Sam Kattergee. Eagle mother returning to nest. Imperative to get all samples of isolated poison, trigger compound, and antidote to the prison site within an hour. Message also for Felicity Marr from eagle mother, report to the prison site. Use extreme caution, hawks in the air."

She repeated the message again, and once more before the comms tech placed an arm on her sleeve and shook his head. "They were quick that time. They're getting sharp."

Shayla hoped the codes embedded in the message would convince them it was legitimate. Her medic, Sam, would surely have been the one to work on treating the inspection team. The code word 'eagle' was to be used only in extreme circumstances—a 'do it and don't ask questions' imperative.

She stood and nodded to the pilot.

Captain Herrin gave Shayla a brief salute. "Luck." He turned back to his operations team and gave the order to bring the ship up to a higher orbit and try to evade the lurking forces. This was in keeping with their normal behavior, and they hoped to lull the wary forces around them and give time for Shayla's message to be received and understood.

Shayla and the pilot hurried aft to the rear hangar, where four heavily-armored troop transports lay, fired up and ready to drop.

They boarded and strapped in. Minutes ticked by. Now they'd completed their pass over the planet's capital and were no longer trying to talk to the ground forces, the blanket of interference lifted. The ships aloft were equally blinded by it, and they were keen to resume their own seditious chatter.

They had no way of knowing what was happening on the ground. Shayla knew the captain was taking them into a high loop around the far side of the planet, hoping to keep hostile eyes on them and away from the movements dirtside that she desperately hoped were now taking place.

At last, a voice on the intercom announced that they were going in. There was no sensation of movement cloaked in the ship's enveloping grav field, but a sustained tremor through the frame of the ship and transmitted through the docking clamps told Shayla the secondary drive was pushing them through tight maneuvers at a crushing acceleration to shake off their chaperones.

The hangar lights dimmed and the rear hatches opened. A ghostly radiance of planetlight reflected off the hangar ceiling. Within seconds, the order came and the four transports hurled themselves backward into space. Together they plunged towards the surface in a sickening arc.

Tattered banks of high cloud shrouded the lines of the continent below. The transports screamed through thickening air, streamers of plasma heated by their dash clawing at the magnetic shields.

Vicious bolts of fire flicked past. A near miss rocked their craft.

Shayla studied the small tactical screen. One *Sword* and a smaller Firenzi craft roamed high above loosing off a few badly-aimed shots. But the main strength of *Swords* lay in wholesale destruction, or battle in open space. They were unwieldy platforms against small craft near a planet's surface. The smaller frigate was more accurate, but less powerful.

The flight of transports split up and started tracing criss-crossing paths across the sky, concealing their true destination until the last minute. The space-bound warships struggled to obtain a decent lock on them, and now found themselves under fire from *Merciless* running brave interference for them.

Their assault had taken the surrounding forces by surprise. They would need to launch smaller atmospheric craft of their own to intercept Shayla and her companions. By the time they could scramble their forces it would be too late.

As the surface drew near, Shayla saw *Merciless* break off and retreat, her job done. The three companion transports peeled off and scattered.

Their orders were to distract intercepting forces if possible, then land at Torremis.

Her own craft plunged on, over the coast and out to sea.

Rear-facing sensors alerted her to squadrons of craft emerging from the battleship lurking a hundred miles above.

The island of Sherrin loomed dark on the horizon. Shayla readied herself to enter the code to grant herself safe passage through the coastal defenses.

Instead of the customary warning, blue-white bolts of energy zipped at them, zinging off the shields at this extreme range.

"What the fuck!" Shayla yelped. "We're nowhere near the ... Oh crap! Pull around. Back off."

The pilot responded. "Orders?" she asked, calmly.

"They've switched to assume all craft are hostile. I need a minute."

"I'll give you what I can. We have company."

"Circle the island to the north. Keep your distance." No time for pleasantries or explanations, but the pilot was professional and acted without hesitation. Meanwhile Shayla opened a channel on the Eloon security frequency and keyed an identification code.

Immediately a voice, remote and tinny, replied. "Approaching craft, this is a secure zone. State your business."

"I've given you my identity codes. This is Shayla Carver. Eagle, eagle, eagle! Switch defenses back to standard operation so I can approach and authenticate myself for safe passage."

Shayla traced a route on the navigation screen for the pilot. The transport bucked and its shields sparked. The approaching fighters were coming into range. "Follow this path precisely. You won't have much room to take evasive action. The safe corridor is only a mile wide. Stray outside it and you won't get a warning."

"With these jerks on our tail I can't land without getting toasted." The tone was uncomplaining, matter of fact.

And she was right. "They won't be able to follow us in, but they'll have a long range shot at us." Shayla was already out of her seat and rummaging through the transport's standard kit lockers. "You'll have to drop me." She shrugged into a suit of body armor and strapped on a heavy personal grav unit, checking the charge on the power pack.

"Three hundred feet do?"

Space! This girl was all business. Shayla nodded in approval. "And as fast as you can go without breaking limbs."

"Reckon they've opened the door for us?"

"We'll soon find out."

The transport banked sharply and headed for the northern coast. Incoming fire rocked them from behind but the island's batteries stayed quiet. The comms screen spat the familiar challenge. Shayla keyed in the response. "The door is open."

The pilot jerked her thumb behind her, and Shayla hurried through the transport to where the rear hatch was opening. Her breath fogged in the sudden chill and pressure drop. She staggered as the transport weaved an evasive dance then shuddered to more hits from their distant pursuers. Beam discharges crackled through the fabric of the ship and Shayla's hair stood on end. Oily smoke and ozone hung in the air.

From the corner of her eye she watched the ready light above the gaping door. The familiar coastline disappeared fast into the distance, contours and landmarks unrolling behind them. A searing flash directly astern blinded her. She peered through the afterimage of a fighter's death, caught in the crossfire from heavy ground batteries. Her world revolved around that ready light and the landscape below.

When the light turned green she was already breaking into a run for the rear-facing ramp. She launched herself and curled into a loose tuck position.

The slipstream hit Shayla like a trip hammer. Her armor absorbed the worst of the impact. After taking the brunt of the shock she reversed her posture, arms and legs splayed so the rush of air flipped her forwards and downwards. With no instruments to guide her she judged the approaching ground by dead reckoning.

Blinding bolts cracked the air above her head. They felt close, but were aimed at the fleeing transport. Shayla gave the brave pilot a brief salute, which no one could see, and prayed to gods she didn't believe in for her safe return. She blinked away tears in the whistling wind and focused all her attention on the baked earth rushing towards her.

The low buildings of an entrance complex lay half a mile ahead.

At a hundred feet she smacked the bulky grav unit on her belt. There was a sickening delay, less than a second but it felt like forever, before the field kicked in. She thumbed the unit to maximum strength, willing the downward plunge to slacken off.

"Ah, fuck it!" Her feet hit, far too fast, and her forward momentum flipped her into an involuntary roll. She tucked her head in and once again the armor on her back saved her. Then she was ten feet in the air and gliding. Her hand fumbled for the grav unit's controls and cut the field back.

Her second landing was more graceful. But not much. "I'm too old for this shit," she gasped as the ground steadied beneath her feet. She glanced around, self-conscious, hoping no one had seen that royal fuck-up of a low-level insertion. Her old drill sergeant would have had a fit.

The transport had already disappeared over the horizon along the southerly exit corridor she'd marked. A few scintillating clouds to the north marked the demise of those pursuers who'd tried to follow them in too closely. The rest had abandoned the chase.

She took her bearings and shucked off the armor and grav unit, leaving them where they lay. The Empire could sue her for the equipment for all she cared.

Chapter 30

From his vantage point overlooking one of the prison's northern entrances two miles away, Jared adjusted the focus on his visor in disbelief.

Ever wary of the battle sporadically flaring on the edge of his vision, he'd been keeping close watch on developments on the surface. The military action had put his plans on hold, and there was no predicting the eventual outcome.

On top of that, Wolf's disappearance, caught in the noose still tightening around the Insurrection's local operations, left an uncharacteristic emptiness inside. His chosen career was notorious for its abbreviated life expectancy. Anyone still on active service after the number of years Jared had clocked up was hardened to death. And yet Wolf was one of those rare characters, a long-timer like Jared, who exuded a solid permanence despite the odds.

She was dead. He was sure of it. There had been precious little reliable information on what had happened, but no-one had escaped from the compromised safe house and she would never have allowed herself to be taken alive.

Brindis ap Silessi would be held to account, so Jared watched for any opportunity to turn events back on track. At the same time, he subconsciously calculated and recalculated the risks, ready to bolt like a rabbit into the transit tunnel if things got too hot.

He removed his visor and rubbed sweat from his eyes before replacing it and steadying his chin on a boulder. White sun hazed the air across desiccated soil. The landscape sloping down to the bunker entrance was broken by ochre rocks and decades-dry runnels. He strained once more at maximum magnification, trying to get a clear view of the figure blurred in the distance.

The approach of that transport had startled him. He'd been used to the fighting happening far off on the horizon as fighters and gunships pounded the formidable ring of weapons batteries, but this one had come tearing unchallenged through the invisible boundary of death and had crossed the island.

He'd instinctively ducked for cover before more rational thought took hold. The defenses were still active, so this craft had been *allowed* to approach. This assessment was confirmed when he realized that the transport was under fire. Maybe it had planned to land, but that would have been suicide under the remote but hostile fire from the fighters still challenging from a safe distance. The pilot must have realized that and aborted the landing, but Jared's sharp eyes spotted a tiny speck left in the transport's wake. The speck resolved into a falling person, making a late and risky landing.

The figure stood. For a moment it seemed to be looking straight at him and Jared's heart thudded.

There was no mistaking the face of his old enemy. Somehow the bitch had survived. Shayla Carver was back, and Jared Tindall was back in business.

Safely inside the bunker's entrance, Shayla breathed the blessed cool of filtered air and paused to brush the worst of the dust and ash from her clothing. It had been a long time since she'd worn an Imperial navy service uniform—all they had to offer her on board *Merciless*—and she hoped the visitors quarters in the main base accommodation held something more suitable for what she needed to do.

The express elevator whisked her down to the prison level in seconds, and decanted her into the labyrinth of tunnels that honeycombed the bedrock far below ground. There she was met by a major of the prison guard, a remotely familiar face though Shayla couldn't quite attach a name to it, breathless from a hasty dash along the transit tunnel.

"Acting Governor ap Silessi sends his regards, My Lady. He wants a positive identification before letting you proceed any further." The major offered Shayla a notepad. She accepted it without a word, both anxious at the delay yet pleased that her staff were taking sensible precautions, and wrote a series of recognition codes.

"I understand you've been in a state of siege these past days. Your caution is commendable."

"And you were reported dead, My Lady. Your appearance has caused quite a stir and no small measure of disbelief." The hint of a smile softened his stern features. "But you have a reputation for surprises."

Shayla bit back impatience at the hold-up. "That I do."

The major cocked his head to one side, listening to some private chat on his helmet comms. "I concur," he said into the lapel microphone. He gave a brief bow. "Follow me, My Lady. You'll have to excuse the walk, we're keeping vehicles well back behind our lines of defense."

As they hurried down the transit tunnel, Shayla checked the armored blinds at intervals next to heavy blast doors that could be dropped in seconds. Armed and armored soldiers manned the defenses. A small force could keep an army at bay down here, and she knew there were miles more tunnels to traverse, equally defensible. The coastal batteries had held the attackers off so far but they would fall to a determined onslaught. When that happened, the ground above would be untenable and the prison entrances would be overrun. Brin had chosen his stand well.

A ground car drove them at breakneck speed through the labyrinth, past more defensive positions and, Shayla knew, sections of tunnel that were rigged with demolition charges if the onslaught proved too much.

Her mind raced, too. They could hold out here long enough against any ordinary attack, she was confident of that, but those captains in orbit were getting desperate. And they had enormous resources at their disposal to take drastic and ruthless measures if they combined forces and put their minds to it. The death throes of *George Leonard* preyed on her. She couldn't allow them the luxury of time to think things through.

* * *

The walls of the conference room around Brindis ap Silessi blurred in and out of focus. A deep draught of nicodyne hardly seemed to dent the fog of fatigue that pressed on his mind. He barely had the strength left to fend off the reckless madness that lurked, ready to take over in an unguarded moment. He'd lost count of the times he'd felt the hot feelers of enraged joy take hold, compelling him to insane and pointless action. More than once he'd caught himself, beam rifle clutched in trembling hands, ready to storm up to the surface to threaten the orbiting battleships.

He took a deep breath and steeled himself, locking down roiling emotions. He needed his judgment and logic intact for a little while longer. Surely he could manage that.

His fists clenched and unclenched at his sides. Sweat trickled down his back under the stiff uniform jacket. He glanced to one side to see if either of his companions had noticed his discomfort. Relieved to see that neither Doctor Sam Kattergee, nor Felicity Marr were paying him any attention he returned his gaze to the door.

Hope and suspicion battled in equal measure. He'd seen the reports from the wrecked *Vixen*. Lady Carver's body had never been found, but then again many of the crew were also unaccounted for. The damage had been so extensive that the network of airtight doors and bulkheads proved futile. Barely a compartment had survived intact and many bodies were swept into the depths of interstellar space on a rush of air through the shattered hull. It seemed impossible that she should simply turn up here, back on Eloon, and yet all the identity tests proved positive.

All the same, she herself had proved the best tests could be faked. The forces upstairs had formidable resources and intelligence. This could yet be a trap, honeyed with the lure of false hope.

It was a paradox he was too weary to untangle.

The door opened. She entered, and closed the door behind her.

"Brindis ap Silessi, what the hell have you been doing to my planet?"

Giddy relief flooded him. There was no mistaking that acid tone, the quirk of her mouth that drew the sting from the words, those eyes piercing his mind with unstoppable resolve. She was at once teasing and deadly serious. If this was an imposter, he deserved to be taken in.

"My Lady, I'm unbelievably glad to see you back with us. I'm ready to—"

"Say nothing further." The sharpness of her voice halted him dead. He stood, confused. She elaborated in a more moderate tone, "There will be a proper time and place for what you were about to say, and appropriate witnesses. I need the forces upstairs to have no illusions as to who's in charge."

Brin swallowed and nodded. "I'm afraid my lapses have become more frequent and potentially more damaging recently." He cursed himself for not thinking things through. Returning control of the planet to its rightful governance was not like passing a baton in a relay. Of course it would take more than a brief exchange of words in this room to make that stick.

Lady Carver eyed him. Sadness and sympathy filled her face. Brin didn't know which was worse. "Then we'll not prolong your ordeal any more than necessary."

She turned to Felicity, the legal brains of the planetary government, such as it was. Felicity was studying the two of them, eyes narrowed, glancing from one to the other. Deep creases in her forehead told Brin that last exchange had made no sense to her. Lady Carver had kept his confidence, he realized, and was keeping it still. She ignored the glaring question marks in Felicity's expression and instead said, "I will ask you to oversee the transition of power back to me. You'll know the proper forms to make sure it's legally binding, and we'll transmit the exchange on an open channel back to Magentis."

Felicity gave her one last 'this isn't over' glare, then was all business. "An open channel means our babysitters will eavesdrop."

"I'm counting on it."

Brin's heart sank. "There may be a problem there." He exchanged a worried look with Felicity in the sudden silence, then met Lady Carver's frosty gaze. "The Firenzi have cut off all communications out of this region."

Lady Carver's sharp intake of breath tore at his conscience. Rational thought told him this was beyond his sphere of control, yet he still felt personally responsible for delivering the news. Felicity quickly recounted what they knew of the blockade leading up to the hasty assaults by the Imperial captain. The communications techs back in Torremis had reached the same conclusions.

After that momentary betrayal of her disappointment, Lady Carver hugged her arms tight around her chest, deep in thought. The minutes lengthened. At last she turned back to face them. "Has anyone given thought to how they might have imposed the blockade?"

Without waiting for an answer she strode to the door and called a senior comms tech from the operations room. "Do you think they would have actually destroyed the nodes, or are simply filtering the traffic through them?"

The tech frowned. "If I were a gambling man I'd say filtered. The nodes are tens of light years apart, for one thing. It would take days to do the rounds, otherwise do they have enough warships to spare to send to each one? Plus"—his face brightened—"any physical attack on a node would have broadcast alarms right across the network."

Lady Carver nodded. "I plan on transmitting under the Imperial seal. That should override any blocks they might have been able to impose."

She cocked an eyebrow at Felicity, who blanched and glanced in turn at the comms tech. He pursed his lips. "If you have the necessary authority, that should be unstoppable by any regular means. Nothing can get through a brute-force blanket, though."

"That would only come from ships in orbit locally. Another wild card altogether." Lady Carver became brisk, the unstoppable force Brin had always known. "We have no choice. We'll proceed on the assumption that the transmission will get through."

Still pale, Felicity said, "I'll talk to the base commander about rigging up a temporary studio. Don't know what they've got lying around but should be able to find some props to make it look official."

"I'll make sure Lieutenant Colonel Bertoia gives you every co-operation." Brin struggled to get the words out. "When do you want to do this, My Lady?"

"How active are things upstairs?"

"Since your arrival I've been expecting some backlash, but until a few minutes ago it was still quiet."

"Do you think we've got two hours grace?"

Brin thought about it. The urge to hasten into action threatened to overwhelm him.

Lady Carver interrupted his thoughts. "Do you think they even realized I landed? They were more focused on chasing the transport, they may not have noticed me eject."

"It's possible, My Lady." The heat passed, leaving an icy calm that Brin knew wouldn't last. "I think we can afford to wait two hours."

"So be it." She nodded to the two of them. "Make the arrangements. I need to discuss some arrangements of my own regarding our prisoners. And, Brin, make sure no word of my arrival reaches their ears. Vet the staff on duty if necessary to make sure you can count on discretion."

Chapter 31

Shayla masked her profound relief at seeing both Sam and Felicity waiting for her with Brin. After her reception out at sea she'd feared they might have fallen foul of the trigger-happy defenses. But they'd have had the luxury of communicating their intent ahead of time, and of not having to fight off a fleet of swarming fighters at the same time.

Brin was another matter. His appearance came as a shock to her, and he was visibly losing control to that insidious illness eating at his mind. The pressures of the last few weeks couldn't have helped his condition. If she could have done anything differently ... but that was pointless thinking. And, she forced back the rage that burned in the back of her mind, this whole sorry mess was never of her making. That, she lay firmly at the feet of the two insufferably smug traitors gracing her hospitality.

The thought made what she was about to do all the easier.

Outside the conference room, while Brin and Felicity went to make arrangements for the upcoming ceremony and broadcast, she took Sam Kattergee to one side. "You have what I asked you to bring?"

He nodded, looking troubled. "Back in my quarters. But how did you—"

"I guessed the nature of the poison while I was traveling, and pulled some strings with my old Firenzi colleagues."

He made a face, and shrugged.

"Do you have samples of the poison isolated?"

"Not as such. We never needed to isolate and purify the poison, the Firenzi scientists directed us to perform a series of reactions and tests and were able to work out what they needed to know from that."

"Not as such?" Shayla felt the edges of despair creep into her mind.

"I have infected tissue samples. I should have destroyed them. They are dangerous."

Shayla hid her delight at this. Meat could be mixed in with food, and dangerous was good. "And the trigger?"

"Eloon sumac."

She smacked her forehead with the palm of her hand. "That bloody fish dish their chef asked for specifically."

"He poisoned himself?"

"He didn't know. Someone must have planted the idea that this would be a fitting dish for the feast." She looked sharply. "Did you bring some?" That was a rare spice that would not be found in the usual prison stocks.

Sam nodded again, looking even more troubled. "Though I don't understand what you could possibly want with them, I brought everything as instructed. And doses of the antidote."

"Evidence," Shayla said grimly. "I plan to conduct an experiment to flush out the guilty party."

"Aah!" Relief flooded Sam's face. Shayla felt a wrench deep inside at duping her trusting medic, but his hands needed to be clean. What she was about to do would be on her head alone.

She instructed him to fetch the samples, then went in search of the base commander.

—————•—•———————

Under Felicity's direction, the base staff had done a good job of transforming the conference room into a makeshift broadcast studio. Unnecessary furniture had been removed. Someone had found a stern portrait of Emperor Julian Skamensis to hang on the wall, and draped the hard plastic table with cloth in Imperial green. Felicity had borrowed a weighty oldworld book from the library in the prison's well-equipped recreation area—living in confined quarters so far underground, small comforts could make the difference between peace and riot. It lay open on the table, its title hidden and irrelevant, nothing more than a symbol of legal writ.

Next to the door, a comms tech sat at a smaller table with a scroll in front of him and a tiny camera on a stand at his side. The wall behind him showed both a live feed from the camera and the edited signal being broadcast. Right now, the latter showed nothing more than the Imperial crest superimposed on the seal of the Freeworld of Eloon. This announced to the waiting galaxy that this was an official transmission in the name of the Emperor himself.

Misuse of the Imperial device was tantamount to treason, punishable by death. After recovering from her initial shock, Felicity had given the question the benefit of her incisive intellect and assured Shayla that she was on moderately solid ground under the circumstances. Of course, when lawyers got involved nothing was certain.

Equally, nobody in orbit should dare try to blanket the broadcast under that seal, also a treasonable offence. Given that they were already on a treasonable course, that protection was far less certain. Shayla was banking more on curiosity to keep the channel open.

Felicity stood behind the green-covered table in formal-looking robes that she must have somehow found time to gather. She was sharp, and it would hardly have been a stretch to deduce that Shayla's cryptic summons pertained to official business.

Brin paced the room in a borrowed dress uniform. Traces of sweat already stained his armpits in that short time. Sam Kattergee hovered beside the door. He had no part to play here, but Shayla had insisted on his presence.

A squad of soldiers also in dress uniform lined the walls to either side, weapons gleaming and very functional. Nobody questioned their presence here as being anything other than to add a small measure of pomp to this meager gathering.

Cleaned and freshened as best she could in the time available, Shayla herself had found a simple tunic and leggings. Her formal robes of office would have been more fitting, but they were all in Torremis.

Everyone was in place. Impatient to get this over with, and conscious of the volatile situation around them, Shayla gestured to Felicity.

Felicity cleared her throat and made one last circuit of the room, manhandling Shayla and Brin to adjust their position and stance until she was satisfied. She assumed her station once more behind the table, and checked the view through the monitor on the opposite wall.

Satisfied, she gazed down at the open book and held up an open hand to the comms tech. Fingers counted down seconds. On two, her hand joined the other, clasped in front of her.

Shayla counted the last couple of seconds in her mind, knowing they were now being broadcast to the outside world.

Utter silence ruled.

Neither Brin nor Shayla moved a muscle.

Felicity held the pose for seconds that seemed to stretch to hours before she slowly raised her head and pierced the camera with a look of regal arrogance. When she spoke, her voice rang clear across light years with unstoppable authority.

"I am Felicity Marr, Honorary Prandis Orator in Residence, Associate Juris Doctor of the Trown Association, and appointed by His Excellency Imperator Julian Flavio Skamensis as General Counsel to the Freeworld of Eloon,"

There were none of the waspish undertones that normally infected her speech. The razor wire teasing was absent. This was a high-ranking legal force, not to be questioned by anyone less than her intellectual equal.

This was a side of Felicity that Shayla had never seen before. In that moment, she understood the commitment the Emperor had made in staffing this venture. So many of her senior team had been Imperial appointments, not hers. She'd tolerated the interference, having little choice in the matter, but had assumed in the early years they'd been placed simply to keep tabs on her. But seeing the depth of competence they'd brought with them she knew these appointments had not been made lightly.

Brin, she'd long known to be a superlative security chief, though she also suspected he held hidden agendas close to his secretive mind. Frank Wu was another, an invaluable asset with his astute planning.

But Felicity! Shalya had always known her to be a sharp lawyer, always ready with interpretations and arguments and loopholes in times of need. But seeing her here and now, she was in her true element.

"Governor-in-waiting Shayla Carver, do you pretend to the Seat of Governance of the Freeworld of Eloon?"

Straight to business! "I do so pretend." The formal wording felt awkward on her tongue. This was Felicity's world. She wielded words with the same precision that Shayla used a blade.

"Acting Governor Brindis ap Silessi, do you recognize and confirm the identity of Governor-in-waiting Shayla Carver?"

"I do."

"On what grounds did you assume the role of Acting Governor?"

Brin swallowed and flicked a glance at Shayla. She desperately wanted to give him some reassurance. How the man had suffered on her account. His mental disintegration had probably gone unnoticed by those around him, or ascribed to the pressures of the intolerable situation they found themselves in, but she was comparing him now to the immovable granite-faced warrior she'd last seen three weeks ago. How long did he have to live? How long before the rot in his neurons hollowed him out completely? She willed him to hang together for just a few more minutes.

He seemed to have trouble recalling. He struggled to form the words. "In the circumstances prevailing ..." He tailed off, then collected himself with a deep breath. His voice continued strong and firm. "I judged that Governor Carver's confinement rendered her unable to execute the duties of her position."

He looked like he might say more, but Felicity smoothly steered the course of the dialogue. "Do you judge that the Lady Shayla Carver has returned in good health, in sound mind, and with freedom of action to execute the duties of Governorship?"

"I do."

"Do you acknowledge her as the rightful Governor of Eloon?"

"I do."

"Do you relinquish the role of Acting Governor?"

A long pause. Shayla wondered about those hidden agendas. What would become of them when he could no longer act as he used to?

"I do." Brin gave a formal bow. "Welcome back, my Lady."

Shayla released the breath she'd been holding and bowed in return, then both turned and bowed to Felicity.

"As duly appointed representative of His Imperial Majesty, I relieve Brindis ap Silessi of his acting role, and confirm the resumption of Lady Shayla Carver as Governor of Eloon until such a time as it pleases His Imperial Majesty. Let the court records show this entitlement effective Magentis day two hundred and twenty three, in the year eight-one-oh-one Dynastic Calendar."

Shayla waited three heartbeats, then turned to the camera. What needed to be done next she wanted to do quickly. A barely-perceptible signal to the comms tech, and the official broadcast ceased. All that remained now were two encrypted tight-beam signals to the Imperial

Hammer of War and the Firenzi *General Giotti Trincomali*. "Now, down to business."

The signals carried respectively Imperial and Special Service recognition codes that Shayla knew would attract the highest level attention.

Two faces appeared on the wall across from her. Captain Arrand Scorf of *Hammer* she recognized, his face flushed with outrage. The woman alongside she knew from her intelligence sources to be Captain Mariota Ferdinand. A mountain of black hair cascaded to her shoulders in a feminine style that was utterly at odds with the brutal lines of her square jaw. Dark eyes glittered malice from deep sockets.

Captain Scorf fired the opening salvo. "That little show just now means nothing. My marines still run the planet and we'll drag you from your hiding place to a very slow death."

"You're welcome to try. My position remains that I am the legal authority on this planet and all military forces, both Imperial and Firenzi, are to remove themselves from Eloon space."

Captain Ferdinand spat a curse in a remote Firenzi dialect.

"I see you had the pleasure of meeting my mother," Shayla said, unfazed. "And I see you are both still bent on self-destruction. I expected no less."

She didn't give them a chance to devise suitably scathing rejoinders. Instead she snapped her fingers and the squad of guards leveled their weapons at her companions.

In the shocked silence she said, "I am placing chief of security, Brindis ap Silessi, legal counsel Felicity Marr, and Doctor Sam Kattergee under protective custody for the duration of the current illegal occupation." She nodded to the squad leader, whom she'd briefed beforehand. The looks of shock and betrayal on her three friends' faces pained her beyond bearing, but those looks were genuine and exactly what she needed her audience to see.

While they were escorted from the room, Shayla addressed the watching captains. "I want you to be under no illusions as to who is in charge at this facility, and I fear these three will not approve of my next actions." That was an understatement. "I will stand no further interference, from *any* quarter."

She had their full attention. Jaws hung slack at this abrupt turn of events.

"As you know, the Imperial Inspectorate was struck down by a mystery illness. Of course that was no mystery to you conspirators."

Before they had a chance to protest innocence, she stepped closer to the camera. "Don't bother to confirm or deny. I'm not asking you to incriminate yourselves, but you *do* know what this poison will do."

She nodded to the tech handling her communications, and two new feeds joined the patchwork of images on the wall. Ivan and Scipio down in their comfortably-appointed quarters were both visibly suffering. Their faces sheened with sweat, skin gray, breathing fast and shallow. Even as they watched, Scipio heaved himself from his bunk and staggered into the adjacent bathroom.

"I personally helped prepare Lord Scipio's and Grand Duke Ivan's last meal a little over an hour ago. That one meal contained both poison and trigger in successive courses."

"What nonsense is this?" Captain Scorf blustered.

"Yellow Snapper Margerite, prepared with local Eloon sumac. Quite a treat for our high ranking prisoners. I'm told they ate with relish."

Captain Scorf looked confused, but Shayla had the satisfaction of seeing fleeting panic cross Captain Ferdinand's rough face.

Ferdinand rallied quickly. "Whatever ailed the inspectors, they survived for days without any effective medical intervention. You don't have days. We will be on the ground and you will be overrun. I'll take great personal satisfaction in overseeing your questioning and punishment."

Shayla pursed her lips. "You might want to revisit your assumptions. The combination poison was administered to the inspectors long before they set out for Eloon. It had weeks to work its way deep into their tissues, waiting for the trigger to bring about a slow illness and protracted death." She gestured to the two prisoners. Ivan reached feebly for a pitcher of water. His weakened finger fumbled on the heavy crystal and it crashed to the floor. "With the poison still spreading freely in their bloodstream mingled with the trigger, its release and action will be a lot quicker. By my estimation, these two have less than six hours to live."

"This is outrageous!" Scorf fumed. "You wouldn't dare! The Emperor will burn you for this. It might be worth letting you live just to hand you over."

Captain Ferdinand remained silent—Shayla judged she was the brains of the coalition—but her eyes blazed hatred.

"Oh, we'll make them as comfortable as we can, but here"—Shayla held up a medical applicator—"is the last remaining stock of the antidote."

She looked each of the captains in the eye. Their attention was fixed on the tiny medipen in her hand.

"Unfortunately, there's only one dose left."

Chapter 32

Base commander Lieutenant Colonel Hale Bertoia stood at ease next to Shayla, studying the tactical plot of Eloon's orbital space. Opscom had the control room staff on high alert. Everything that could be done in readiness had been. The tension in the room crackled like an approaching thunderstorm.

"Placing your senior staff under arrest was a noble gesture," Hale whispered, "but it can't honestly protect them if either of the prisoners die."

"The prisoners are in no danger. No more than the rest of us."

He gave her a sidelong glance.

"Yes." She sighed. "I lied. I have more shots of the antidote. Did you really think I'd commit such open murder? I'll let them suffer a little longer in case we need to remind our friends upstairs of the stakes, but they'll receive the cure before any permanent damage occurs."

"So everything back there was a staged production. It was convincing, but what if they call your bluff?"

"Firstly, I've since briefed my staff on the situation although it makes it no less painful. Even though they understand my reasoning they will find my actions hard to accept, and their ongoing confinement under guard is very real. Until this crisis is over, there is no question of them interfering, and there will be no accusation that they could have done anything to turn events."

She kept her gaze on the colored tokens drifting lazily across the plot. "And as for calling my bluff," she murmured, "I'm counting on it."

Hale turned to face her, mouth open. Comprehension lit his eyes. "The simple thing would have been a straightforward hostage threat. Back off and I'll let them live. But knowing that one side or the other is about to lose its figurehead there's no way they'll back off. You've provoked them into an all-out attack."

Shayla pointed back to the plot. "And here they come."

On the wide tactical screen, *Swords* and *Enforcers* wheeled like circling vultures. In a matter of seconds the green and red symbols were obscured by clouds of smaller points of light as they emptied their hangars of ground-capable war craft.

Unhurried, Shayla strolled to the comms desk. "It's time to turn out the lights."

"Are you talking about a communications blanket, My Lady?" the tech asked. "That's controlled from the operations center in Torremis, still under Imperial control."

Shayla grinned a savage grin. "So they think." She wrote a long series of authentication codes on the screen. "I am the planetary governor. My word is law."

The comms tech grinned back.

Shayla gave a theatrical bow with a flourish. "Cloak the planet, if you please."

"With pleasure, My Lady!"

As the impenetrable blanket of interference jammed all communications for thousands of miles out from the surface, the tactical screen adjusted. No longer able to use more sophisticated tracking and identification, it showed simple points of light, intelligence gleaned by cruder sensors not affected by the jamming. Although the information was patchy and uncertain, the overall picture was clear. An angry swarm of craft descended on their previously weakened northern front.

There was no more testing, no probing, no attempt at stealth or subterfuge. This was all out and desperate fury.

The view switched to cameras scattered across the miles of coastline and prison grounds as the front of the assault rolled in. Heavily shielded gunships formed the vanguard, loosing wave after wave of micro missiles.

Despite the ferocity of the battle above, a thousand feet below ground the response was orchestrated with surreal calm.

Status dashboards showed the effects of the attack. Traffic light colors glowed amber, red, and growing patches of emptiness as the defenses crumbled.

Sensing victory, the hovering forces swept in, widening the gap. Another wave of gunships rolled over the coast. Armed with heavy beam weapons this time they blanketed the prison perimeter, overwhelming the inner rings of air and ground defenses.

Barracks and other surface structures burned fiercely in the intensity of the attack. Thankfully everyone on the surface had long ago been brought down to the safety of the underground barracks. With all the construction workers and temporary guards still on site, conditions below ground were cramped but manageable.

The bombardment, Shayla noted, was carefully targeted. Everything that could pose a threat to infantry had been obliterated, but they were careful to leave the prison entrances intact.

Lumbering transports now took the lead, bellies pregnant with their deadly spawn. One by one they landed and disgorged platoons of soldiers who took up positions, securing a beachhead against forces that had already abandoned this particular battlefield.

"They're coming in at shafts 'A' and 'B'," Opscom announced calmly into her microphone.

"Hold them off at the foot of the shafts as long as you can," Shayla said, "but don't squander lives. Be ready to fall back as soon as things get heavy."

Opscom acknowledged. "They have a serious bottleneck to get past. Unless they spring some surprise we should be able to keep them holed up in that shaft indefinitely."

Shayla chewed her lip. "Don't underestimate them. Be alert, and keep a lookout on the rest of our perimeter, too. This could be a distraction."

"Sir," called one of the surveillance analysts from the far side of the room. "It's not really a combined force. Two distinct groups, Firenzi at the main 'A' entrance, and Imperials at 'B'."

The analyst added information manually to the short range plot.

Hale cocked an eyebrow at Shayla, who relaxed slightly with a low chuckle. "I was worried about a joint attack. They've got the numbers, but they're competing, not co-operating." On an impulse she counted the craft. "Nine landers at each site. Equal forces. They don't trust each other."

Opscom called out, "Do you have eyes on them?"

More ground-based camera feeds joined the collage of images on the operations room wall. "Nothing closer," the analyst said. "Their bombardment took out most of our outside cameras. We should get a better look at them when they breach the bunkers."

They didn't have long to wait. Meeting no ground resistance, the invading forces quickly gained access.

If, as Shayla surmised, this was a race between the two groups, it was currently neck-and-neck. The Imperial forces had a few miles further to travel to 'B' bunker but made up for lost time with brute force on entry. Their transports mounted heavy projectile weapons and simply blew the armored doors off their hinges.

It didn't surprise Shayla that they clearly had detailed intelligence on the layout of the bunkers. Their heavy-handed approach could have blocked the access shafts but their shots were angled carefully to avoid collapsing the ceiling. Once inside, the first wave of troops checked for resistance then systematically took out the cameras.

The Firenzi attack was more cautious. Shaped thermal charges opened the doors with minimal interior damage. Firenzi troops flooded in and quickly broke open the elevator doors. The elevators had all been immobilized at the start of the invasion, but this would hardly slow them. Teams of sappers tramped in with tripods slung between them, which they deposited unceremoniously in the middle of the floor. Two seconds later the feet were anchored into the stone by pitons fired from single-use launchers. These were well-drilled teams. Even as the footings were secured, the first wave of shock troops clipped lines to the tripods and flung themselves over the edge, rappelling down the shaft.

"Wait!" Shayla called. She pointed to one view from inside the main entrance. "Back that up a few seconds."

The analyst complied.

"There." The image froze. Shayla inspected it closely. "Opscom, pull back our forces at 'A' and seal the blast doors."

Without waiting for an explanation, Opscom caught the urgency in Shayla's voice and relayed the order. Meanwhile, Shayla approached the screen and pointed to one of the soldiers whose face had momentarily turned full on to the camera.

In the shadow of his helmet the lines of his mouth and nose looked subtly wrong.

"Nose plugs and breathing unit," Shayla said. "They're going to gas the tunnel."

"Obviously something inhaled," Opscom said. "They're not worried about skin contact."

Something like peritax, Shayla thought. Could they be carrying enough of the drug to pollute that whole stretch of tunnel?

Opscom sent instructions to the issuing room to break out face masks and breathing units to send to the defenders. She also ordered ventilation to be shut down in the approach tunnels. "No point sucking in whatever they've got there."

Good thinking. Shayla mentally kicked herself. The fight could have been very brief if they really did have enough peritax to flood the whole complex. Then again, they had the resources. They managed to cripple a small warship.

"Meanwhile, the Imperials are going for brute force," Hale muttered. "Typical."

It was impossible to make out details at the range of the nearest surviving cameras, but it was nevertheless clear that teams of soldiers were manhandling heavy equipment out of the transports' loading hatches.

"Enough force to take out our blast doors?"

He sniffed. "Enough to take out any soft targets stupid enough to stay the wrong side of those doors, then it's just a matter of time."

"Opscom," Shayla called, "get someone with good tactical judgment on the ground at 'B' tunnel. Give them discretion to direct local operations. If the Imperials bring down enough heavy ordnance to threaten the doors, they have permission to fall back and collapse the tunnel."

Opscom acknowledged, and Shayla turned to Hale. "I need some ordnance of my own, some transport, and a volunteer for a sortie above ground. It's time to test their new-found friendship."

Shayla had no shortage of volunteers, but she needed someone with very specific skills. Her guide, a scrawny youngster in his early twenties, had seen combat and, Hale assured her, would stay calm under pressure. Most importantly, he knew the surface intimately. Every hill and valley, every fold of the terrain, hiding places, and lines of sight.

The hundreds of square miles of the prison site looked flat from the air but that was deceptive. It was easy terrain, offering few hiding places if any more transports flew over. That was a risk they had to take. For

Shayla's purposes the gently undulating landscape would allow them to approach unseen from the ground.

They emerged from 'C' complex on lightweight, fat-tired ground bikes just small enough to fit into the elevator. Her guide took them in a wide arc north then north-east, following a shallow valley that circled lazily between the bunkers where the transports had landed. Greasy coils of black smoke obscured the sun high overhead, bringing an unaccustomed cool to the desert landscape. The acrid stench of destruction caught at Shayla's throat.

Their powerful bikes swallowed the miles, raising only the faintest trail of dust from the baked earth. As they neared a direct line between 'A' and 'B' entrances, invisible in the distance on either side of them, they slowed and weaved their way closer to the Firenzi position. Shayla had briefed her guide carefully on her requirements. He slowed further, then signaled a halt. Shayla pulled up alongside.

"Fifty yards up that slope and you'll have a clear view of 'A' bunker," he said. "I'll move a bit further along. I should be able to get a view while staying low."

Shayla turned her bike around to face the way they'd come, and dismounted. She unshipped the three disposable missile launchers strapped to her back and scurried up the slope, dropping lower as she neared the top. She finished with a belly crawl, inching forward with her burden until the outline of the bunker appeared in the distance. They were half a mile away, as requested. She counted the transports clustered around the entrance to confirm none of them had taken to the air.

With a quick glance around her, she assessed her position. She would need a fast retreat and her back would be exposed for a dangerous few seconds before the hill covered her. Speed versus cover, that was the compromise. She let her subconscious mull over that question knowing that when the time came it would provide the answer.

She readied her launchers and waited patiently. Her guide, having further to go to get into position, would take the first shot. That would be the signal for the fun to begin.

A minute later, a thin vapor trail traced a silent line through the air. The nearest transport took the hit on its weak rear armor and exploded. Shayla already had a shot lined up on the next craft, and squeezed the trigger before the first missile hit. Her shot sped right into the opened ramp.

Another round flashed across the intervening ground as she reached for her next launcher. That shot exploded on side armor, impossible to tell how badly the craft was damaged.

They had the Firenzi's attention now. Distant troops scurried like ants away from the stricken craft.

Shayla kneeled and sent her second round at the bunker itself, hoping to collapse the entrance and slow their incursion.

Her guide's third shot demolished the transport he'd weakened.

Shayla stood now, careless of the scattered fire peppering the ground to one side where that last missile had come from. There would be eyes on this slope now, she knew, and she'd changed back into her borrowed Imperial uniform. She meant to be seen.

She hit the bunker entrance again, then ducked down as a furious barrage toasted the face of the slope.

Cover was the priority, her subconscious advised. She grabbed the straps of the spent launchers and wriggled backwards until she could turn and scamper in a crouch, with beam rifle discharges crackling furiously overhead.

She covered the remaining ground back to her bike in loping strides, strapping the launchers onto her back as she went. They hoped to leave no trace of their presence or true nature. Her guide was already approaching along the valley as she leaped onto her bike, and they took off at full speed, angling away from their line of attack.

It took a minute for the surviving Firenzi transports to clear their loading ramps and take to the air.

The roar of their engines thundered across the undulating ground, sounding far closer than the two miles back they should be. By now Shayla and her guide were out of sight of their attack position. The ground all around had been beaten down by countless works vehicles over the years. There should be no tracks that anyone could follow.

They put more distance behind them, and the sound of engines diminished. The Firenzi would figure out soon enough that they'd been ambushed by a small and mobile strike force, but Shayla hoped that was the only correct conclusion they drew.

They regained the safety of 'C' bunker, and Shayla punched in the codes to admit them.

Back in the operations room, Hale Bertoia brought Shayla up to date with developments. The incensed Firenzi had, as Shayla hoped, assumed the attack was an act of Imperial treachery and had launched an all-out counter attack on the transports at 'B' entrance. In doing so, they must have destroyed much of the Imperial equipment.

The Imperial forces had lowered heavy armor and a shield generator down the elevator shaft, but had failed to follow up with the semi-portable beam weapons that Shayla had feared. Their troops were protected at the foot of the shaft behind their shields but pinned down by the relatively light defending forces. They were unable either to advance, or to bring enough firepower to bear to threaten the equally well-shielded defensive positions.

Meanwhile, the Firenzi attackers at 'A' shaft had indeed released large quantities of aerosol drugs into the tunnel, but the defenders there were prepared and held their ground. Both assaults were at a temporary stalemate.

To add to the confusion, neither side could communicate through the interference Shayla had ordered. Neither side could summon help, but many ships aloft must have had eyes on the ground because fresh waves of craft flooded the upper atmosphere.

Now, all pretense at co-operation was gone. Gunships from both sides scoured the island's perimeter, silencing the remaining weapons batteries on the ground and giving themselves clear air in which to maneuver. Both sides brought in transports with troops and equipment, and each side was harried by gunships and fighters from the other.

They threw themselves in with careless desperation, each trying to land its own forces while trying to stop the other from gaining the upper hand.

Conflicting emotions tore at Shayla. On a professional level, she felt fierce joy at the conflict above. Those few rockets had fanned the already-simmering fires of suspicion. She could hardly have hoped for a better outcome from her brief excursion topside. But the tragic waste of life grieved her. No matter that these people were ready to plunge a hundred worlds into a bloodbath in pursuit of their leaders' ambitions, the carnage above was insane.

She closed her eyes for a moment and prayed, truly prayed to the Essence of Unity herself to bring an end to the mayhem once and for all. She'd abandoned prayer when her world burned thirty years ago. Now it burned again.

Opscom stiffened, studying the tactical plot intensely. "Eyes!" she called. "What's happening up there?"

"Capital ships maneuvering, sir," the surveillance analyst drawled.

"Purpose? Are they lining up an orbital attack? Are they taking up attack positions against each other?"

The silence lengthened, maddening. Shayla knew better than to hurry things along. The techs and analysts were well aware of the urgency and they knew their jobs. It took time to decipher the ponderous movements of forces hovering at the edge of visibility.

"Neither, sir," the analyst said at last. "One of the *Swords* is breaking orbit. So's that *Enforcer*. Looks like the party's breaking up."

"Drop the blanket," Shayla said. "Enough for a quick peek at what's out there. I want a deep scan."

"Okay," said the surveillance analyst. "Comms? Two second window, on my mark."

He studied his screen, mouth opening in disbelief. "This is either good news or very, very bad. I have two ... no, three more *Swords* incoming."

Silence fell on the operations room. All eyes turned to the analyst.

"Call signs?" Shayla asked.

"*Dagger of Fate*," he read off, "*Mace of Terror*, *Spear of Retribution*."

Shayla's legs failed her. She slumped into a nearby seat. "*Mace of Terror*," she breathed. "I know that name." A broad smile spread across her face. "Loyal to the Emperor. The cavalry's here."

Chapter 33

Jared Tindall whistled as he punched the starter codes on the excavator he'd been assigned to. In the confused aftermath of the battle, the clean-up was in full swing and it was easy to insert himself with his assumed identity back into the work crews.

Careless gossip between crew and guards confirmed his astounded observation that Milady Carver had indeed returned. Rumors ran rife. The most conservative stories told how she'd single-handedly decimated the orbiting forces with nothing but a troop transport and a few smart bombs. Accounts got more fanciful from there on. Any other time and the evident adulation would have turned Jared's stomach, but even this couldn't dampen his good mood.

He was in position, with an increasingly solid and trusted identity. The island may have lost its automated defenses but security landing and leaving was stricter than ever, enforced by squadrons of circling fighters and platoons of grim-faced soldiers from the battleships loyal to the Emperor, Unity damn him! But that may yet work to his advantage. Once on the ground, there were few checks on movements on the surface. It would have been impossible to keep a tight rein on the thousands of workers now swarming the site making good the damage.

His hideout had survived with its precious stash of equipment, gear that he'd have had no hope of smuggling in by any regular means.

And his targets were all here.

His few remaining sources told him that Carver was fully occupied overseeing the rebuilding. She'd not yet made plans to visit the prisoners down below but it was only a matter of time.

She'd ordered that news of events in the prison should be kept from the prisoners. Only a select few most trusted guards and staff interacted with them. As far as the Lords Ivan and Scipio were concerned she was still safely dead. The Insurrection's sources confirmed they'd concocted the plot to abduct Carver, and given the orders to trusted henchmen.

They were likely now on edge expecting their followers to free them. So far underground, no sign or sound of the fierce battle could reach them. They were in the dark, except for what dribbles of misinformation Carver chose to feed them.

Jared and others of the Insurrection had studied her closely over the years. He felt he knew her mind better than she did herself. She would confront them in person, but that would not be a hasty move. She'd want to prepare for it. She'd wait until she could turn her full attention to crushing their hopes. She would want a clear mind to savor the moment, and it would be done with full pomp and ceremony.

All of that would take time to arrange, and could not be hidden from Jared's spies.

The sun and clear skies above mirrored Jared's mood as he lowered the giant excavator's shovel and leveled a shattered gun emplacement.

Shayla piloted a borrowed *Lance* fighter, venturing at random across the two hundred and fifty square miles of the prison site proper before turning away for a leisurely circuit of the island's coast.

After ingrained habit, it felt strange to be flying so freely, not confined to jealously-policed safe corridors. She kept checking the navigation screen, with an involuntary clenching of her fist every time she saw her position so far out of bounds.

But the island's defenses were dormant now, those that had survived the onslaught. Construction crews below her worked their way slowly around the broken perimeter. Orange machinery, massive up close, looked like crawling insects in the morning sun.

Anger blazed once more in her chest, soon overtaken by a profound sadness. So much work laid waste, so much investment that could have been put to better use elsewhere on Eloon. All for what? Keeping in check two charismatic old men who held the balance of power over far too many worlds?

The Firenzi stance she could understand. The death of old Josef years ago had hit the Family hard. His son and heir, the weak and vacillating Giovanni, hardly had the presence to command a kindergarten let alone dozens of fiercely proud worlds. If Shayla had still been part of the Firenzi machinery she'd be tempted to support moves to replace him with Scipio, despite the latter's brutal philosophies. Strong leadership, even of his style, was better than no leadership. The Firenzi people longed to hold their heads high once more.

But Scipio was nothing more than a pawn to Ivan, the real political power. His attraction was less easy to condone. It was not about leadership, it was about wealth. Far too many influential people had fared well under the old regimes, which Ivan represented, and would take their bitterness at Julian's reforms to their graves.

The mountainous and inhospitable south coast of Sherrin looked entirely untouched. The low-lying north was another matter. Every few miles, dark scorch marks plowed the earth around smoking concrete shells. Thankfully all the installations above ground were automated. None of her own people lost their live here. The attackers were another matter, but—she gritted her teeth—they'd brought the destruction with them, uninvited.

Sweeping along the soot-smudged coast, she felt herself drawn inland. This was a pilgrimage she'd studiously avoided in all her time here, but there was no denying the grim compulsion now.

Forty miles from the prison site, her ancestral home was unrecognizable. From the air, faint lines marked the outlines of buildings. When she landed and climbed down, the hand of man was all but impossible to discern. Here and out to the horizon new life greened the land and hid the decades-old scars.

Shayla climbed to the top of a hill that she recognized from her childhood. From the summit she knew she'd have a panoramic view across her father's lands. She slowly turned a full circle, mouth hanging open.

Outside of the hand-planted forests and farms, she'd grown so accustomed to endless tan and gray and niggardly stands of desert-hardened plants that she'd forgotten about the resilience of life left to its own devices.

When her first pioneer teams had surveyed the planet, a few patches of scrubby grass and thorny bushes struggled to retake the glassed and ash-choked landscape. They'd given those struggling plants little thought, little hope for survival. And yet right under her nose an ecosystem had re-established itself. How many more pockets of resistance now thrived across the globe?

She ran back to the *Lance*, fired with new determination. Pointless or not, the fate of the prisoners was in the Emperor's hands. They were still in her charge, and until that changed she'd fulfill her duty to the best of her ability. The rebuilding would soak up precious resources but they'd managed before and still worked wonders in their planting projects. Now Shayla wondered what could be done to encourage the natural revitalization alongside the more planned efforts.

Now, with the heat of battle cooled, she tried to fathom why she'd kept events hidden from Ivan and Scipio. She wanted to deliver the news in person, that much was clear, but her motives remained clouded. She had never been one for gloating. Maybe she felt she owed them the courtesy of speaking in person. But why had she delayed? She'd been busy, but that was hardly an excuse. Was she waiting for the right time? When would that be?

There would be no further delay. This was her duty to perform.

Then there was work to be done.

It took all of Jared's professional training to remain calm and detached. The day was here. She was going to confront her prisoners and show them the depth of their defeat.

Jared had a list of names to choose from, guards who'd been detailed to form the honor guard later that day. The list agreed well with a much longer list of likely candidates he'd compiled and whose movements he'd studied over the last two days.

Several names he discarded quickly. They were all somewhere below ground, inaccessible. He turned his attention to the last few.

Surreptitious inquiries located his mark, a guard who would shortly be leaving his post at the ravaged main entrance—the one they called 'A' bunker. He would return to his barracks below to clean and change into his ceremonial uniform.

Jared's excavator trundled into view of the bunker entrance, and stuttered to a halt. He dropped the front shovel with a bang and leaped from the cab.

An unnatural hush fell on the ashen plain surrounding the bunker. The shattered hulks of transports and equipment had long since been removed, along with the bodies. The entrance itself, half demolished,

had been cleared of debris yesterday and work was now focused on dev-
astated perimeter defenses miles away. This area was quiet. The lonely
guard posted here was little more than a formality. Jared gave him a brief
wave as he strode around the far side of the machine.

He waited a few seconds, surveying his surroundings to make sure
there were no unwanted observers, then lifted a side hatch and let it fall
with a loud clang and a shouted curse.

He peered around the back of the machine, wincing and rubbing
the back of his head, and beckoned to the guard who'd already started
strolling in his direction, curiosity piqued. "Hey! Give us a hand 'ere,
mate. Third time today this fucker's done this."

"Problem?"

"Loose connection. Easy fix, but the hatch keeps slamming shut on
me. Can yer 'old it up while I fix it? Won't take a jiffy."

The guard slung his rifle over his shoulder and lifted the hatch.
"Odd," he said, "the latch looks fine from here—"

He never finished the thought. Jared clapped him on the shoulder.
To any distant observer it would look like a comradely gesture but the
assassin's needle he'd palmed delivered a fast-acting paralyzing agent.

The guard froze in place, and the hatch slipped from nerveless
fingers.

"Told you," Jared said. "It keeps banging shut."

In a matter of seconds, Jared reached around, unclipped the rifle's
power pack and replaced it with an identical-looking unit. Next, he
reached up and tinkered with the guard's combat visor. When he took
up his next duty down below he'd exchange his utilitarian field helmet
for an elaborate ceremonial headdress, but the visor worn underneath
was as personal to a soldier as his toothbrush and would go with him
everywhere. The standard comms unit attached to the microphone and
camera looked just as it had before, but it now concealed an extra sliver
of electronics.

All the while, Jared counted the seconds in the back of his mind.
The paralysis would wear off quickly and the shock and impotent rage
in the guard's eyes promised swift action the moment he regained the
use of his muscles.

Jared readied another needle and watched closely. At the first
muscle twitch he pressed the point into the skin just below the guard's

ear. The expression slackened, rage replaced by confusion as the short term memory block took effect.

"You alright, mate?" Jared snapped his fingers in front of the guard's eyes. "Looks like you took a bit of a turn just then."

"Huh? What?" the guard mumbled, bringing a hand up to his temple.

"They must have 'ad you standin' out in the sun too long."

"Um, yeah, I guess." The guard shook his head and absent-mindedly rubbed the back of his neck.

"Anyway, thanks for the help, mate." Jared swung himself back up into the cab and started the excavator. As the engine roared to life he gave the confused guard a broad grin and two thumbs up.

Chapter 34

The squad of guards trooped into the antechamber deep underground, and took up positions around the walls. Brindis ap Silessi, restored to his role as chief of security after his brief imprisonment, stood silently to one side, every muscle tense. By rights he ought to feel safe with a thousand feet of bedrock above him, despite the lack of other defenses. Even *Swords* couldn't wreak havoc this deep down. The best they could do was turn the ground above into a sea of glass and seal them in. They had supplies down here to last a year, and a cavern beneath still held the drilling equipment used to hollow out this secure prison. The worst that could happen was they had to wait until it was safe and drill themselves a new exit.

He should feel safe.

His nerves said otherwise.

Maybe he was jittery after Lady Carver's stunt with the poison. He understood her logic, and her reasons for secrecy. She was right. He would have done everything in his power to stop her if he'd guessed her intent. But he hadn't so he was on edge now, painfully aware that threats could appear unannounced from the unlikeliest of quarters.

Brin still hadn't decided how to feel about that treachery. He ought to feel betrayed, and yet she'd acted the only way she could see to bring them through an impossible situation with as little damage as she could. As ever, her motivation was positively saintly, and effective. She'd turned the full attention of the besieging forces to the ground and to each other. When the loyal *Swords* appeared, the attackers were unprepared. If they'd been allowed to join forces and mount a defense the battle in orbit would have been long and bloody. Instead they retreated in disarray.

The visible threat had gone, so what was he missing?

There was still the matter of Cobra, whose trail remained stubbornly cold somewhere south of Scale. But an impassable strait lay between the prison and the mainland. Even though the island's formidable batteries were little more than smoking ruins, they still had state of the art sensors scanning air and sea. On top of that, he'd assembled a trusted team of hand-picked guards to screen all incomers. Security and background checks now rivaled those in place around Magentis, the Emperor's home planet.

The memory of Lady Carver's barely-concealed frustration at the resulting delays in bringing in repair crews and supplies almost brought a smile to Brin's lips.

Almost.

In his unguarded moments he found her simmering helplessness comical to watch, but the very efforts she made to control herself always brought him back to reality. They proved to him that his judgment, in this matter at least, was sound. She understood the reasons for the slow movement of people. Cobra could not be allowed near this site.

Still, the nagging unease raised goosebumps along Brin's arms.

He forced himself to calm and reviewed his surroundings again for anything out of place. Compared with the polar prison, this installation was a palace. Ivan and Scipio had held an entire family under cruelly spare and cramped conditions for over two decades. Of course, they'd been working within limited means and in deathly secrecy which restricted the scale of building they could manage, whereas Brin and Frank had been dealt an almost free hand. They hadn't been willfully extravagant, but neither had they been stingy. This chamber was typical of the accommodation down here.

A midnight blue carpet bore the Imperial crest in the center, a reminder of whose authority held sway in this corner of the planet, Freeworld or not. Soft hangings masked the armored plastic of the walls, abstract swirls in warm colors. Overhead, the ceiling glowed the natural light of a hazy summer afternoon giving an overwhelming impression that the semi-circular chamber was open to the sky.

The overall impression of warmth and coziness did nothing to dispel the chill down Brin's back.

Keep them locked up, and keep them alive. That had been Brin's task from the Emperor in person and he treated it, as he treated all things in life, seriously.

The squad of a dozen guards lined the curved wall of the chamber. The flat wall, currently semi-transparent, looked into the empty interview room where all meetings with the prisoners would be held.

Like its counterpart in the abandoned northern prison, that half of the circle was screened to offer utmost privacy. Brin had used Firenzi contacts on his staff, with, ironically, a good word from Scipio, to get hold of stocks of the holographic screening material used in the old prison that would alert them to any electronic activity in the vicinity. Ivan, and especially the paranoid Scipio, could meet with lawyers and the occasional dignitary knowing that no form of intrusion or eavesdropping could take place. The exorbitant cost of that material had raised eyebrows amongst the Imperial accountants. Fuck 'em.

Keep them locked up, keep them alive, and keep them *sane*. High ranking prisoners they may be, but they still had contacts, pulled hidden strings, and could still bring on the bloodbath so recently averted if they felt all hope was lost.

Hmm. About that. Although no direct evidence linked them to the poisoning of the inspection team and Lady Carver's arrest and kidnapping, they had to be at the back of it somehow. He wondered how they would receive the news that the plot had failed. Brin had personally overseen all contacts with the prisoners since then, to make sure no hints or rumors reached them ahead of time. Lady Carver was preparing to deliver the news in person, hence the unprecedented preparations down here. Between them, they hoped to learn much from the prisoners' reactions both to Lady Carver's continued existence and to the news from the world outside.

If anyone wanted to make mischief, now would be the time.

A technician entered the room and strode over to Brin, whispered briefly in his ear.

Unnatural calm washed over Brin. As long as everything appeared normal he was on edge, waiting for the blow to fall. Waiting for an anticipated but invisible opponent to make a move. That was always the worst part, the waiting. Now the game was afoot.

Brin stepped forward and addressed Captain Bard Jovin. "It appears there will be a delay. The prisoners are refusing to move until they've finished an unusually leisurely supper. Pecking daintily like starlings, I understand." He left the room and walked a little way up the hall led by the technician, who ushered him into a darkened office nearby. Bard followed. Good, he'd clued in to the keyword.

Lady Carver was there too, pacing the floor like a caged tiger, glowering occasionally over the shoulder of another comms technician, a petite woman with a colonel's insignia on her shoulders.

"Can we talk safely here?" Brin asked. Lady Carver nodded.

"This has nothing to do with supper, has it?" Bard growled. "What's going on?"

Lady Carver gestured to the comms tech seated at a screen showing a schematic of the prison level and a ream of technical readouts alongside.

"There's a very weak directional signal being sent from outside the interview room to somewhere on the surface," the tech said. "It showed up when the guard detail entered the outer zone."

Brin closed his eyes and breathed deep through his nostrils. This was why the sensitive smart material had cost the Imperial coffers so dearly, and he thanked Space he'd stood firm on this matter. The rock above and around the interview room, antechamber and surrounding corridors had been honeycombed and screened also, with monitoring devices set to alert this office of any anomalies. It seemed this extravagance had paid off.

The tech continued reporting. "I've got a contingent camped out in the crawl space placing passive detectors into the line of sight. We should get more data shortly, but right now I'm treating this as suspicious."

Brin glanced at Bard. "Presumably none of the guards in there is actively transmitting?" Hurt anger crossed Bard's face and Brin hastened to add, "Of course they all know the protocols down here, but I just want to eliminate the bleeding obvious."

Before Bard could answer, the tech shook her head. "Not a regular comms signal, I can tell you that right now. Had to hunt around for the frequency and it's nothing we ever use."

"Without that outer shell you insisted on, we'd never have spotted anything amiss." Lady Carver's voice was barely a whisper. Her face was ashen.

"Got something, sir," the comms tech said. "There are two distinct signals. One is a low grade audio-visual feed. Outbound only. The other,

I didn't notice it at first. It looks like a simple heartbeat, two-way. I don't know what to make of it."

Lady Carver exchanged looks with Brin. "Trigger signal?" she said.

Brin pursed his lips. "A simple trigger signal wouldn't need to be present at all until you wanted to trigger the device. A heartbeat, though ..."

"Continuous presence. Dead man switch. If the signal cuts out that would also be a trigger."

"So we can't just jam the signal."

"And ..." She tapped her teeth deep in thought. "If someone's pulling strings from the surface we can't afford to spook them. We need to find and deal with whatever's in that room without arousing suspicion."

Brin's pulse hammered in his throat. "Can you get a lock on either signal?" Right now they were dealing with too many unknowns by way of means, motives, and ultimate goals. And just how did you search a room and a dozen guards without tipping off anyone in the room or the unknown watcher on the other end of that signal? Brin was not a superstitious man, no belief in the paranormal, but this ghostly pulsing on the comms screen made his skin crawl.

"Not precisely. Both are coming from inside the room, but"—the tech squinted at the screen—"not quite the same point. Must be at least a foot apart given the resolution I've got to work with, maybe two or three, no more."

"I'm presuming a bomb, or a gas grenade." Lady Carver was still deep in thought, externalized as a running monologue. "Something to be set off when Ivan and Scipio are in the room. Must be on one of the guards. Where would you hide a device like that? Those dress uniforms don't leave much leeway."

"Bard, could there be a traitor in our ranks?" Brin voiced the unwelcome question.

"We need to identify the carrier," Lady Carver added.

"Leave it to me," said Bard. He strode back into the corridor. The tech brought up a screen showing the antechamber from a position high on the dividing wall just in time to see Bard enter and bellow, "Squad! Squaaad ... present ... *arms!*"

The soldiers snapped to attention, weapons held in front.

"The heartbeat shifted a fraction," the comms tech said. "Would have to have moved at least a foot to be noticeable. Must be in one of the weapons."

"That was a fucking *shambles*," Bard bawled. "Call yourselves soldiers? Hold that position for inspection and Space help you if I find a speck of dirt or a single fucking *wrinkle* on those uniforms."

He worked around the circle, inspecting each soldier in turn, straightening a rifle here, adjusting a collar there. When he was done, he stood the soldiers at ease. "I don't want to have to inform Her Ladyship that you bunch of barfbrains are in no fit state to escort my fucking *grandmother*, let alone royalty on their first official audience in their new fucking palace. So, we will do this again until you can get it *right!*"

He marched to the end of the line. "Sar'nt Major! I leave these asswipes in your tender care. Drills until they can perform a full tattoo in their sleep." As he stalked out of the room he muttered under his breath, not troubling to hide his disgust, "And let's find out what the fucking holdup is."

Nice touch, Brin thought.

"It's Collins," Bard announced without preamble as he strode through the office door.

Brin's attention turned back to the screen, and the heavy-set Wala near one end of the line. "How sure?" He reached past the comms tech and pulled up a personnel file.

"Fairly. The power pack on his weapon carries the wrong serial mark. My money says that's the device."

"Traitor? Or unwitting mule?"

Bard sucked his teeth. "This contingent was all screened and psych-profiled for any signs of instability, and contact with radical organizations. And I've known Collins for two years. I don't see it in him."

"They had more than the usual screening for this duty," Brin added, for Lady Carver's benefit. "People can be coerced into working for organizations they have no clear sympathy for. We looked for any family history, friends, contacts, any point of leverage that a group like the Insurrection could hold against them. Never any guarantees, but we were more than usually thorough this time around. How did he seem to you?" This last was addressed to Bard.

"No sign of nerves, any more than the usual after getting chewed out on parade. Someone about to do something this big would be keyed like a battleship's mooring line, and that inspection should have rattled him. He'd have needed years of deep training to avoid showing some signs ..."

"There was no gap in his history that would allow such a training regime."

"I don't think he knows he's carrying a bomb."

Some of the tension eased out of Brin's shoulders.

"And," Lady Carver said, "if he was a knowing assassin there'd be no need for an outside agent or a remote control. No signal to risk giving the game away."

"It was a pretty small risk," the comms tech said. "The signals are so weak, so directional, and on way-out frequencies. We had no chance of spotting anything through regular means."

To one of the soldiers at the door, Brin said, "Get the word out to evacuate everyone from the habitat core. Word of mouth only. Everyone from this side outwards. Assemble them in one of the far exit tunnels but no movement onto the surface." He glanced at Lady Carver. "That room is the only way into the prisoners' quarters. We can't bring anyone through without being seen. For now we can't do anything about the squad in that room, and we need a skeleton crew of techs in here and monitoring that signal. I want to know about any change in status."

She chewed her lip and nodded. Damage limitation first. In theory they could abandon the meeting, disperse the guard and isolate Collins somewhere he couldn't do any harm. Instead he was buying time to turn the trap onto the trapper. To Brin's mind, the next step was obvious. "We need to get that rifle off him."

"Without being seen on that spy signal?" Lady Carver's question was rhetorical. Brin could see her mental gears working on solutions.

They both turned to Bard. "On it." His face was pale, but he grinned. He re-entered the anteroom where the sergeant major was putting the squad through ever more complex drills, and called the sergeant to one side. They conferred in low voices. Bard pointed to the center of the room. "Fall in! Present arms!" From one end of the line he squinted. "Better," he growled. "Let's see if you're finally fit to welcome royalty to our shiny new Palais-sous-Terre."

Another detailed inspection followed. The sergeant major stalked behind the line, keeping step with Bard. When he reached Collins, Bard took his rifle off him and made a show of inspecting the muzzle. "Sar'nt Major! My eyesight is only half what it once was. Does this weapon look like it's ever been fired?" He handed the rifle past Collins.

"Doesn't look like it to me, sir," the sergeant major replied, handing the rifle back.

"Collins!"

"Sir!"

"Ever shot a man, Collins?"

Collins swallowed. "No, sir."

"These are valuable guests we host here, Collins. We need to protect them. If it came to it, could you shoot to kill?"

"Yes, sir."

"Collins! Say it like you *mean* it! I can't have any doubts here. Could you kill a man if ordered to do so?"

"Sir! Yes, sir!"

Lady Carver exchanged looks with Brin. "Did you see that?"

Brin nodded. "At least I think so. It was so damned quick." He gestured to the one guard remaining in the room. "Get ready to trade weapons with the sergeant major, but outside in the corridor. Stay out of sight of the room."

"That's better," Bard was saying. "Sar'nt Major! With me."

The two of them left. The sergeant major reappeared a moment later and took up his position at the end of the line.

"Hand that over, Captain," Brin said quietly when Bard joined them. He examined the weapon with care. "Definitely something odd about the power unit." He hefted the weapon and balanced it in his palm. "Heavier than it should be, too. Not that you'd notice in ordinary carrying, but the balance is a fraction off."

The comms tech eyed them warily, subconsciously edging away in her seat. "That's where the heartbeat's coming from. I could see the signal shift as you left the room. The audio-visual feed is still coming from inside."

Brin scrutinized the power unit once more. "That unit could hide a thermal grenade big enough to slag this whole level. Probably still be a small power pack too, so the rifle will still operate, for a while. And what's the betting it's rigged to blow if you try to remove it?"

Lady Carver held her hand out.

"Oh, no!" Brin said. "You're needed here. Stall for another ten minutes while I get this somewhere it won't do any harm, then let the ceremonies begin." He turned to the comms tech. "Any chance of a fix on the other end of that transmission?"

Huddled in the ruined basement, Jared used every meditation technique he knew but nothing stilled the hammering in his chest. His visor showed the view, dim and grainy, from deep underground where his Trojan soldier stood in line.

Palms slick, Jared's fingers trembled on the remote trigger. He forced himself to place it gently on the ground in front of him and wiped both hands on his tunic. He'd sat on long watches and stakeouts, many times felt the pangs of anticipation in the hours before a critical mission, knowing that all possible preparations had been made and they were committed come what may. Nothing in his long and dangerous experience matched this.

He was about to enact the single most shattering event in living history. Get this right, and aristocracies would crumble.

His earlier conversations with Wolf haunted him. He was about to plunge the Empire into all-out war. Although he understood that on an intellectual level, the true implications had never felt real until he witnessed the fury with which renegade units had launched their assault on this island. He tried to imagine that chaos multiplied up a few orders of magnitude. His mind blanked at the effort.

He reverted to more immediate concerns. Those invading forces, taken by surprise with all their attention focused on the ground, had fled in full-scale retreat to lick their wounds. That troubled him. Had they been too badly beaten to rise up in outrage when their figureheads, their hopes, were destroyed? Milady Carver's abduction and the subsequent fighting had never been part of the plan. This assassination was meant to be a bombshell dropped into an otherwise calm scene. Would it now have the same impact? He'd leave that for the political analysts to ponder. No one had instructed him differently so right now he had a job to do.

Piano-wire taut nerves screamed as his mind ran through all the ways this could still go sideways. The transmitted image was low quality. They'd made sacrifices in order to keep the signal down to a barely-perceptible whisper in the ether, relying on sophisticated enhancement and de-cluttering at his end to sift a useable image from the quantum noise. But he still had to be sure the right people were in the room. Could he make out enough detail to be sure they were all present and positively identified?

And these interminable delays preyed on his imagination. What if this whole event fell through? Intelligence reports said that Lady Carver had arranged this meeting with her favorite guests. That alone should be enough to guarantee it would happen. The lady had a will of iron and it would take a supernova to deflect her. But intelligence reports had been known to be wrong.

Something was going on, for sure, but what if the whole thing was an elaborate hoax, or a last-minute no-show? And nothing could ever account for those unexpected outside forces that could derail the best laid plans.

The soldiers had been in position for over an hour now, and they were still waiting. Drills and inspections. That scarred half-faced captain betrayed the jitters with his endless fussing.

Brooding in the background Jared had recognized Carver's head of security, Brindis ap Silessi. Stone-faced and humorless, according to Jared's briefing notes, he could discern no useful facial expression on the blurred image. His breathing grew ragged at the sight. Another welcome piece of collateral damage to avenge Wolf and all the other agents killed on this shithole rock.

If this operation was delayed or aborted, would he get another chance? The bomb was in place, but Jared wondered how long it might go undetected. The tampered weapon would pass a casual inspection but every day's delay was a risk. And there was no guarantee that his chosen guard would be on escort detail next time around.

Jared forced himself to calm. Nothing in anyone's actions suggested anything out of place, just those damned prisoners playing mind games with their captors.

The sergeant called the squad to attention. A moment of queasiness as his vantage point wobbled, then movement on the far side of the room glimpsed on the edge of his field of view. The door that had up to now remained closed, opened. At last! This was no longer a drill.

Unnatural stillness descended on Jared. Moving with care, he picked up the trigger. Now the target was near, he was all professional focus once more.

Shadowy figures moved into the edge of his view. He kept willing the viewpoint to shift to give him a better look, forced down frustration when he realized the subconscious futility. The guard was motionless, facing front and center. They'd have to pass in front to enter the private interview room. He had to exercise patience.

The first to appear were servants, escorting their charges. Two figures followed, robed and hooded. Jared cursed.

One of the servants turned at a muttered instruction from the sergeant, then turned back to the robed figures. The nearest shrugged and removed his cloak. Only the back of his head was visible as he handed it to a servant. From behind it looked like Ivan, but the picture quality was too poor for a confident recognition. The other slouched and hesitated before removing his robe.

Jared poured all his awareness into that grainy feed and willed at least one of them to present a partial profile. He might have no more than a glimpse to confirm he had the right people in his sights. Once missed, the opportunity might never reappear.

Yes, Jared was sure that was Scipio, dragging his heels like a sulky child.

"Well, well."

Jared jumped at the unexpected voice behind him. He turned, trigger clutched in fingers that had suddenly lost all sensation. His pulse hammering in his throat. Twenty paces away, face expressionless as ever, Brindis ap Silessi leveled a rifle at Jared's chest.

Hardly able to control the shaking in his limbs, Jared thumbed the trigger to the 'armed' position. "This trigger has a dead switch. I don't need to elaborate." He surprised himself with how calm his voice sounded even through the constriction in his throat. Now that the trap was armed, icy calm washed through him. He'd had little hope of escaping alive. His evacuation plans went as far as retracing his path to the mainland, but in the aftermath of this multiple assassination he'd always known his chances of getting off-planet would be slim. But with the dead switch armed, Lady Carver's forces had no way to stop the destruction. "Shoot me and you will only hasten the deaths you're trying to avoid."

"So," said ap Silessi. "Now what?"

They stood, surreal statues in the gloom of the ruins. The sour-faced head of security bared his teeth in a feral grin. For a moment, Jared thought he was going to shoot.

In the corner of his eye, Jared saw the unmistakable profile of Lady Carver sweep regally into the room far below ground. Escape or not, he would not be taken alive and his mission was now complete. With a fierce joy burning in his chest, he squeezed the trigger.

A moment's confusion, as a high-pitched whine cut through the air from the rifle in ap Silessi's hands ...

———————

Unforgiving sun burned the back of Shayla's neck. She was well used to near-meditative trances, but always with a purpose in mind: to exercise patience on a long and eventless watch, or to focus her faculties on senses other than the dominant visual. Her daily vigils here near the edge of her prison domain were something else altogether. Something foreign to her experience. Introspection.

When Brin disappeared with the booby-trapped rifle she'd assumed he would simply take it up to the surface, somewhere it could do no harm, and send a squad of guards to capture the assassin. He'd been so calm and rational up to that point, she hadn't figured on him taking a self-destructive course.

She should have.

The thought tormented her.

She'd lost count of how often she'd run variations on the same scenario through her mind since that day. Could she have done any differently? Of course she could. Was it reasonable to expect her to have foreseen this in the heat of the moment? Debatable. Nevertheless it was her duty. Reasonable or not, the responsibility ultimately rested with her.

Her mouth twisted as she recalled the same logic used against her by the Governor of the Inspectorate, so long ago.

A cough behind startled her. She turned. Frank Wu and Felicity Marr stood at a respectful—read *safe*, Shayla thought wryly—distance. It was Felicity who'd broken the silence. "It's time."

Shayla closed her eyes briefly and suppressed the urge to turn back once more to the simple grave marker standing on the lip of the blackened crater. "Then let's go."

A mile away, a shuttle sat on the landing field waiting to take her up to *Merciless* and then on to Magentis. She hadn't even heard it land.

Shayla squinted against mid-morning sunlight glinting off the shuttle's polished skin. She'd grown so used to stark practicality without adornment or luxury, the sleek craft looked out of place among the dusty, sturdy workhorses on the landing field. The Imperial acacia emblazoned in green and black on its burnished copper flank announced the shuttle's exalted status among its scarred and battered brethren. This was a craft for royalty. At the far end of her journey it would convey her without pause past the orbiting security around Magentis, using clearance codes reserved exclusively for military and high state matters.

The privilege did nothing to dispel Shayla's growing state of anxiety. The Emperor might be honoring her, or simply eager to bring her before him to wreak new punishment on his wayward governor-assassin.

After their poisoning, most of the Inspectorate still lay recovering in their quarters. Lady Josephine bin Mellion, weak but steely-eyed, made it clear to Shayla that the inspection was over. She'd lodged her report, such as it was, for the Emperor's eyes only. She and her team would quit the planet as soon as they were fit to travel.

The eagerness for them to be gone was mutual.

Whatever Lady bin Mellion had chosen to report, matters were out of Shayla's hands. Memories from weeks ago reminded Shayla that the inspection was rigged against her from the start. Its abrupt curtailment could hardly have made things worse.

As they neared the shuttle, Felicity asked, "Are you sure you don't want me to accompany you?"

Shayla was sure that efficient Felicity would have bags packed and ready in case she changed her mind. She was equally sure her own mind was made up. Not that she wouldn't appreciate the company over the coming days in flight, but this was too close to a similar voyage she'd embarked on recently. Shayla wasn't superstitious, but it didn't feel auspicious to leave for the Imperial home world with another close friend and colleague in tow. The chain of events that followed her voyage in *Vixen* were still too raw in her mind.

She forced a quaver out of her voice. "I am at the Emperor's mercy. Whatever he has in mind, I don't think legal arguments will help. Besides, Eloon needs her sharpest and most capable minds right here."

If Shayla felt the weight of the last seven years of exile, at least the relentless activity out in the field all the while dodging beams and blades had kept her fit. The years had not been so kind to Emperor Julian Flavio Skamensis. The lingering excess of too many state banquets clung to his once-lean frame.

The Emperor sat at his desk in the Office of Deliberation. Shayla stood in front of him as she'd stood once before in another life. The murderous rage she'd struggled to rein in back then had long since evaporated. She felt a moment of vertigo, as she'd felt many times in recent years, at the memory of what she'd come so close to doing. This man, who she thought had ordered the attack on Eloon three decades ago, had been her target for so long it was a hard habit to shake. But he was one of the good guys. Heck, he was her cousin. That had taken some getting used to. Her own father, exiled brother of Ivan and of the old Emperor Paul, had been this man's uncle. She was a full-blooded cousin of royalty. She'd absorbed the fact on an intellectual level but with all the busyness of the past seven years she'd never absorbed it emotionally.

Until now, standing here, in the heart of the Mosaic Palace.

She'd last stood here as an assassin infiltrating the enemy stronghold. Now she was back, not as an equal, but certainly as a formidable part of the establishment. For how much longer, she had yet to learn.

The lands around the Imperial capital were hot desert, yet they harbored an abundance of life. The city bustled. After the bleak emptiness of Eloon it was overwhelming. At the same time, the stark contrast reminded her what she had yet to accomplish. They'd made a start. *All* the planets of the Imperium had started out barren and lifeless and yet now teemed with people. True, Eloon had hardly been sterilized, just cleansed of its troublesome population. It still had soil, life-bearing oceans, a breathable atmosphere, advantages not found when the early pioneers had settled. So they were hardly starting from nothing, in fact most of the work that faced those early settlers was still in place. Shayla was embarking on the last one percent of the journey.

A journey, she realized with growing dread, she desperately wanted to finish.

The Emperor seemed in no hurry. He'd acknowledged Shayla with little more than a nod when she'd been announced. Guards, ever vigilant, stood at a respectful distance at doors and stationed around the edge of the room. Behind the Emperor, the fountains and rose beds of the Fountain Court glowed in impeccable color through the windows in the fading rays of the evening sun.

Even in this desert climate, growing things was so *easy*. The hundreds of square miles they'd planted on Eloon represented a long and exhausting slog, and still so fragile. Until they could coax rain from the sky and nurse into existence full cycles of water, of carbon, of nitrogen, ecosystems of predator and prey, of spreader and pollinator, it would all return to dust the moment they left it unattended.

At last the Emperor swept aside the reams of documents he'd been studying. Their images skittered across the desk's surface and vanished before they reached the edge. Just one page was left in front of him. Shayla resumed her study of the scene outside. He glanced up, catching her unawares. He followed the direction of her gaze and nodded. "The new head gardener is most ably filling the shoes of his predecessor. I've rarely seen the gardens looking so good this late in the season."

He looked back down at his desk, at the one page remaining. From here, Shayla could make out text and the Imperial crest and seal, but even the heading was too small to read at this distance. For no apparent reason her heart thudded hard in her chest and goosebumps pricked her arms.

With no pause for ceremony, the Emperor picked up a stylus and scrawled his signature at the bottom of the page. "There." He looked up. "That was the proclamation to re-affirm you as Governor of Eloon and to renew its provisional Freeworld charter for another five years. Formalities over, Governor Carver."

Shayla took an involuntary step back. She forced herself to silence, realizing, in the flurry of thought and emotions swirling through her, that her first, second, and even third choices of words were likely to be inane and inappropriate.

That's it? she wanted to scream. *No investigation? No questions? No lectures or speeches? Just a quick flick of a stylus and we're done here?* Somehow, it seemed that something this important, something that would confirm or condemn her fate and the fate of a whole planet, should be accompanied by a bit more ceremony. Instead, she simply composed herself and said, "I thank you, My Lord."

He pushed himself away from the desk and stood. "You're probably thinking that this is a bit anticlimactic after all the formality of the Inspectorate. I'm sure the Office of the Master of Circuses"—Shayla flinched at the mention of the administrative post she'd co-opted in her vengeful infiltration of Palace life—"will arrange some more fitting pomp for public consumption on your return to Eloon. You know yourself the importance of the face we present to the public. But regardless of any amount of public spectacle this act here, this signature, is what really counts. I wanted you here to witness it in person. This is a private act, between Emperor and Governor."

Shayla took a deep breath. The knots between her shoulders and the clench in her gut relaxed.

The Emperor approached Shayla around the desk. He paced, footsteps muffled in the softness of the rug that spanned most of the width of the office, hands clasped behind his back. "More than this, I owe you my thanks for giving the medics the clue they needed to isolate that poison."

"I should have recognized the technique sooner." She wondered at the sudden change in his demeanor. She felt he was skirting something, unsure how best to broach a subject.

"My medics wouldn't have recognized it at all," he retorted. "And those few in the Firenzi camp who might have had a suspicion were not motivated to betray Family secrets."

"It did take some persuasion." Her mouth twisted. "And the deaths could have been avoided if I'd been quicker." *If I'd been free to investigate properly*, she restrained herself from adding. She was certain her imprisonment hadn't been the Emperor's doing.

"On the other hand, we could have lost the whole team."

Shayla inclined her head in acknowledgment.

"Of course it's clear who was behind this plot. It needed an unprecedented level of co-operation between Imperial and Firenzi factions, but the trail of evidence is too faint to follow. The poison itself could have been administered months ago for all we know."

"We believe we know the motive," Shayla said, "but the ultimate beneficiaries may genuinely have known nothing about the details."

"True. I would like to think that." A pause. "Tell me how my uncle fares."

"He ..." Shayla was about to give the expected bland nonsense about being in good health, well fed and cared for. He was in her care, after all.

But Ivan's face haunted her, his expression when she entered the interview room back on Eloon. Brin had done his job well. News from the world outside hadn't penetrated the prisoners' suite. Not even rumors, though she was sure they'd begged, bribed, and threatened for any snippet of information. With all the secrecy and renewed security maybe Ivan had expected, or at least hoped, that the Emperor might be there in person to end their isolation. Whether freedom, a trial, or swift execution, anything would be better than the limbo they'd endured up to now.

Before entering the interview room, Shayla had steeled herself and reminded herself that these two had held five members of Julian's family in worse conditions for far longer. But her mental preparations came to nothing.

Anger, she could have coped with easily enough. Shock, betrayal, hatred ... all these were there for a fleeting instant. Then Grand Duke Ivan Skamensis seemed to fold in on himself. His physical presence remained, but the essence that moved him fled.

This man, thirty years ago, had ordered Shayla's father killed and her home world burned. She'd spent most of her life seeking revenge— on the wrong target, admittedly, thinking the Emperor to blame, but she'd seen her error before *too* much damage had been done. For a while, after she'd helped the Emperor break Ivan's power by finding and releasing his Imperial hostages, acting as Ivan's jailor had seemed fitting.

Here was a man she could never forgive, but now it seemed he'd sidestepped that stage. She could no longer bear him the same poisonous malice she'd once felt. She hadn't forgiven him, no, but the whole question of forgiveness now seemed irrelevant. This was simply not the same man.

Shayla had killed many times in her life, sometimes in the heat of a fight, sometimes the cold quiet of a prepared assassination, sometimes at a distance and sometimes up close and intimate. She knew death. She knew killing. But nothing had ever appalled her so much as seeing a proud man die in front of her leaving his still-breathing shell behind.

She gazed at the rug and clasped her hands tight in front of her to calm the trembling that had suddenly gripped her. When she spoke, it was little more than a whisper. "His body is well, but his spirit is ailing. He is a broken man. I believe he's finally given up hope."

The Emperor led Shayla to a circle of deeply-cushioned easy chairs set around a carved cherrywood coffee table. He sat, and gestured to Shayla to do likewise. "I had heard as much, but I wanted to hear it from you in person. Does it distress you?"

Shayla nodded. It took a couple of tries before she could speak past the sudden blockage in her throat. "If you'd asked me years ago I'd have said this was nothing more than he deserved, but it was a terrible thing to witness. I feel nothing but a deep sadness. It's weighed on me throughout the flight here."

"More so than my judgment on your Governorship?" His voice was sharp, his eyes wide and questioning.

Maybe he was right to be offended. In theory, *nothing* should be more important than an Emperor's mind, but he was only a man, at the end of it, and by now Shayla was heartily sick of politics. She met his gaze. "Even so."

He sat back, eyes still wide but now she looked more closely Shayla could see no censure in his expression. He sighed. "You *have* grown. Maybe you *can* help me after all. I had my reservations but you've come a long way from the hot-headed murderess I last knew."

"Flatterer."

He huffed. "You haven't yet been cured of speaking out of turn. That's good." He leaned forward, suddenly earnest. "I need your honesty above all else. It saddens me, too, to hear how far my uncle has fallen. More importantly, I fear to think what might fill the vacuum his leadership will leave behind." Gray eyes regarded her. "For how much longer do you think you could keep the pair of them safe in your custody?"

Shayla snorted. "You know as well as I do that this imprisonment could only ever be a temporary measure. Every day is a roll of the dice.

Recent events proved that beyond all doubt. Even with the new prison and all the security around it, sooner or later someone will break through. If not that, something will befall one or other of them. Illness, maybe, or eventually old age. Even an Emperor can't stop the march of time."

"I can't just free them. They are guilty of high treason and that can't go unpunished. But I can't bring them to trial. The only conclusion would be execution, and that would set the Empire warring with itself and with the Firenzi. We've already seen how close we are to that unthinkable outcome."

"This isn't news. That's why you dumped them on me in the first place. You've had seven years now to think of a solution."

"Tell me, Governor Carver, what would *you* have me do?"

"It seems like an insoluble conundrum." She shook her head, and a snap of irritation crept into her voice. "They are yours to deal with. I don't have an answer but I do know the time is long past for you to face the issue."

"May I remind you whom you address?"

"You asked for honesty, and I know damned well *whom* I address. The friggin' *Emperor*. That's my point!"

Julian's face twitched. At first Shayla wondered if she'd pushed too far, if he was controlling an outburst of rage. Then she realized he was struggling to keep a straight face. First his mouth curled into a barely-concealed grin, then his shoulders shook. He sagged back into the depths of the cushions stifling laughter that came out in a series of grunts. A worried sergeant at arms hastened forwards from his station near the Emperor's desk. Julian waved him away.

"I do believe," he said at last, "that only you could get away with such frankness." He sobered and sighed. "It's refreshing. And you do make a valid point, damn you. So what *do* you think I should do with them?"

Shayla regarded him long and hard. "Dammit. You're messing with me, aren't you? You've already decided."

Julian held up his hands in surrender. "I faced a similar conundrum once before, as I recall."

"And produced a uniquely elegant solution, as *I* recall."

A faint smile briefly smoothed out folds of skin sagging at the corners of his mouth. "Personally, I think the solution has worked out very well."

"At one stroke, both a gift of life and the cruelest punishment."

"But it kept you out of trouble ... sort of. And I look back to that conundrum for inspiration in solving this new one."

"A gift wrapped in cruelty?"

"If you insist on looking at it that way, yes. The principle is the same, but the specifics have taken the past seven years to occur to me and, once again, I have you to thank for my inspiration."

Shayla gave him a puzzled look, but curbed her impatience.

"People need a frontier. Something to push against. Something to expend their energy on, or all that energy is trapped and turns in on itself."

Shayla wondered at this unexpected tangent to the conversation.

"Your Eloon has become a new frontier. People flock there out of desperation, but they find new hope there. I know it's rough. Conditions are primitive and the labor is brutal, but there's purpose like nowhere else in the Empire."

This was true enough. Shayla repeatedly surprised herself at the renewed energy she gleaned from each new challenge faced and surmounted.

"The Empire has stagnated. Do you know how many millennia it is since we last opened up a new world? Made a barren rock habitable?"

Space alive! A history lesson now? Shayla shook her head. "We've built orbiting habitats and hollowed out moons and asteroids, but if you're talking about a proper terraforming, then not for thousands of years. Five? Six?"

"Close enough." He leaned forward, watching Shayla intently. "You will be pleased to hear that Ivan and Scipio will shortly be taken off your hands."

"You're bringing them to trial?" Shayla could hardly believe it. "Or imprisoning them somewhere else?"

"Far worse." The Emperor grinned, and for a moment the years washed from his face. "I'm putting them to work."

———•◦•———

For a moment, Shayla saw echoes of her own father in the Emperor's face. The memory, the likeness, hung in front of her eyes as she hastened through the long halls of the Mosaic Palace to her next and final appointment before she boarded a shuttle and returned to her exile.

She was still officially confined to Eloon, both reward and punishment for her actions seven years ago, but that didn't trouble her. What else would she do? Her life as an assassin was long gone. Her skills remained sharp, true enough, but only in pursuit of survival for herself and her new world.

Maybe those skills would be put to the test less often now that she'd no longer have her unwelcome house guests to protect. Her face split into an involuntary grin, frightening a clutch of fawning servants as she hurried past. She wondered if the troublesome twosome knew yet what the Emperor had planned for them.

A new frontier.

Yes, it had been thousands of years since humanity had opened up new worlds. The science had lain dormant, the technology and practical know-how virtually forgotten. The current stock of habitable worlds had mostly been given life before the collapse into war, ten thousand years ago, that had all but destroyed the human race. Creating those worlds must have drained the resources of those long-dead civilizations to the point where the expansion slowed and stopped, and useable worlds became precious territory to fight over. Why invest the immense effort in the centuries-long process of terraforming a ball of rock when you could steal a ready-made ecosystem from your neighbor?

So, the terraforming came to a halt. Ironically, Eloon was one of the last worlds to be made habitable, part of a last effort on the margins of Firenzi space. Now the re-seeding of Eloon was the inspiration for a new push into virgin territory.

A new frontier.

The Emperor was right. Humanity was stagnating. It had taken thousands of years to rebuild a true starfaring civilization and reconnect most of those worlds they'd almost lost. Renewing the ravaged population was slow, but they were starting to get crowded. People needed a frontier to push against.

And Ivan and Scipio, willing or otherwise, were going to seek it out.

Shayla chuckled again at the thought. A fleet was already assembling, a joint venture with the Firenzi and Wala Families, to explore way out to the north of the galactic plane in a currently unpopulated direction. The fleet would leave repeater buoys every few hundred light years to allow them to communicate their findings, but for all practical purposes they would be on their own, dependent on their own resources.

This was an exile more complete than Shayla's. They would be gone years, maybe decades, charting and exploring. The astronomers and a few scouts over the centuries had compiled a long list of possibilities, worlds that may be fit for habitation, but they would need to travel to each to survey for conditions and essential resources.

Between them, Ivan and Scipio were nominally in charge. An exile, but also a great honor and responsibility. They would have many of their supporters with them—a great clearing-out of the most troublesome factions—but the balance of power would lie with loyal crews whose duty it was to keep them on the straight and narrow.

In some ways, Shayla envied them. Then she thought of Eloon and the mountain still to climb there. She was lucky. She might see results in her lifetime.

If she survived.

———◆———

Shayla accepted a dash of honey to sweeten her strong black tea. She really needed something far stronger, but the time was not yet.

After the harrowing events of the last few weeks, the anxious waiting and the Emperor's report, she felt drained of emotion. No, the emotions were there, but like warring factions on a distant field their clamor belonged to another world.

The servant withdrew, joining a disproportionate and attentive retinue of liveried staff and guards ranged around the perimeter of the drawing room, one of many surrounding the Fountain Court. Shayla returned her attention to the only other seated occupant of the room.

Magister Chalwen ap Gwynodd, Commander in Chief of Imperial Security, stirred in the depths of her chair. "Missy, you have much to learn about the ways of planetary rule." She set her own tea, unsweetened, on the delicately-inlaid table between them. "What did you think was the purpose of the Imperial Inspectorate?"

"To assess our progress on the path to full Freeworld status." There was the merest hint of a questioning rise in Shayla's voice. She hated the way Chalwen's most obvious questions turned out to be traps for the unwary. She was too spent to fret, and waited for the inevitable correction.

Chalwen's sides shook with mirth. "The cynic in me says they are nothing more than a public show. A circus. But that's not entirely fair. They serve a purpose but assessment is not it."

Shayla raised an eyebrow but chose not to rise to the bait.

"By the five-year mark, new colonies are well-established and in danger of complacency. The inspections, especially the early ones, are intended to shake things up before people have a chance to settle in a rut."

"They find fault to remind us how far we still have to go?"

"Indeed. The real report was delivered long before the inspectors even landed."

"I know many of my staff are Imperial agents"—Shayla felt a rush of giddiness at being able to talk about them once more in the present tense—"but I assumed they were there only as spies, not as assessors and auditors."

Her mood crashed as her words recalled memories of recent loss, and the true purpose of this appointment. The well of sorrow threatened to leak out. She pushed it firmly aside and came straight to the point. "I know Brin worked for you."

Chalwen's expression settled into a blank mask. Shayla paused. Was she not supposed to know about that? It was hardly a secret that Brin was an Imperial appointee, and hardly a stretch to deduce his origins in the Imperial hierarchy. She fingered the cloth-wrapped package in her lap. "I have trusted staff packing his personal effects for shipment, but I brought something of value with me that I wanted to convey in person."

Chalwen accepted the proffered package and undid the silk ties. Shayla noticed the implacable, oft-times brutal, Chief of Security's fingers tremble. The cloth unfolded to reveal the two framed plaques from Brin's office. The Imperial Order of Merit shone proud in Chalwen's lap, but it was the other that drew her attention. Very few people would know the significance of this featureless black plaque. It was a secretive thing, something of an 'in' joke within the security services, awarded only for deeds of the greatest valor. Deeds which could never be openly acknowledged.

This was only the second such award that Shayla had seen. The other hung in Chalwen's own office. She took a sip of tea to moisten a suddenly dry mouth, and felt a need to fill the lengthening silence. "I was never aware of any next of kin. Brin was always guarded about his personal life"—well, most of it—"I trust you'll know who these should go to."

Chalwen fingered the plain surface of the plaque and nodded, blinking back tears. "This is a heavy co-incidence. I had a surprise of my own to spring. I think you should meet the *real* head of the Inspectorate." She signaled to a guard at a side door. He saluted and opened the door, talking briefly to someone outside.

That someone entered the room, and stopped a few paces from Shayla and Chalwen.

The world around her, the drawing room with its plush rugs, hanging tapestries, and antique furniture, faded to an ethereal dream. With an effort, Shayla placed her cup down intact and struggled to her feet. At last, she caught her breath. She glared down at Chalwen. "So, Simone was one of yours, too."

"Always."

Shalya turned to Simone, tears welling from the onrush of long-suppressed grief. "I saw *Vixen* explode. I didn't imagine I'd see you again."

Hazel eyes bored deep into Shayla's, then Simone's gaze drifted to the plaque in Chalwen's hands. "This should have been a happy reunion, but I see you've brought dark reminders with you." Her fingers twitched, clasping and unclasping in front of her. "Trovor Scarth was a communications technician, not a weapons specialist. He didn't manage to override all the safety mechanisms on the warheads."

"But the ship blew up."

"Only the arming charges actually went off, and the escape pod protected me. Yes, they set off a chain reaction in all the other warheads in the weapons bay, but all you saw was a chemical explosion. There was no secondary fusion. The plasma never ignited, otherwise neither of us would be here now."

Chalwen stood and held out the two plaques. "Brindis ap Silessi left no recorded family. I believe you'd be the closest thing to next of kin."

Simone straightened her posture and accepted the plaques with a brief formal bow. "I thank you." To Shayla she said, "I mentored Brin for many years. I'm sure you know the regime, how we never let ourselves get too close to anyone, how we harden ourselves to loss, but he was like a younger brother to me."

Shayla squeezed hot tears from the corners of her eyes. Memories of her own brother still etched on her mind. "We can never be hardened to loss."

The room grew still. The three of them stood for many long minutes, each lost in their own thoughts. At last Shayla cleared her throat, dreading to ask the next question. In some ways, dreading the answer, whichever way it went. "Will you be coming back with me to Eloon?"

The corners of Simone's mouth drooped. "With my cover blown? I could hardly perform the duties for which I've been trained, could I?"

"I rather valued you for your service to me, and for your friendship. But I see your point."

"I believe it's best all round. In your service I found my loyalties impossibly divided. My duties now lie elsewhere."

"Outside of this room," Chalwen growled, "Lady Laskenza's identity in my service remains intact."

Shayla looked sharply at Chalwen. "You're entrusting me with classified information?"

"I am deferring to Lady Laskenza's judgment in this matter." Chalwen looked like she was chewing nettles.

"All the same, what secrets of mine have you passed on, I wonder?"

"Not ... *everything*." Simone gave Shayla a pointed look. "As I said, my loyalties were divided and I judge there are some *intrusive* matters that you are entitled to keep private. And I persuaded Magister ap Gwynodd that my secret would remain safe while I held an equal bargaining counter."

Shayla nodded, feeling suddenly empty. The palace, the city around her teeming with millions of lives, pressed in on her, overwhelming her senses. The rich luxury, the softness, offended her senses long grown used to simple subsistence. She longed for empty spaces and bare horizons, for the daily struggles that made each breath of clean air, each morsel of home-grown food, a treasure to be savored.

Without a backward glance, Shayla strode from the room. She had a shuttle to catch, and work to do.

Epilogue

Shayla fumed at the unexpected delay. The hapless clerk at the landing field office looked ready to faint. Not surprising. Shayla was ready to lash out at the nearest obstacle, and the clerk, three assistants and five ... no six ... armed guards stationed near the exits might just provide a suitable workout for her frustrations.

And it looked like the clerk knew it. Shayla's reputation on this planet was legend, even more so after her recent exploits.

But she was no longer the old Shayla Carver. She was a planetary governor and would act accordingly.

Except even that wasn't quite right. Most governors in her experience would by now be ordering the guards to skin the clerk alive before turning his family out into the street for such temerity.

The poor kid was only doing his job and had clearly drawn the short straw on this occasion. Even so, ashen faced, he held his ground. Her anger shifted subtly, directed now at his unseen bosses and colleagues who'd left him in the line of fire.

She took a steadying breath. "I believe you said Magister ap Gwynodd had a message for me."

He swallowed, and handed Shayla a secure and encrypted message capsule. "Magister ap Gwynodd sends her apologies, but *Merciless* was called away on urgent business right after you landed. I understand alternate travel is being arranged and in the meantime you are being offered quarters in the State Apartments at the Mosaic Palace. And"— his forehead crinkled—"Magister ap Gwynodd suggested you might find time to do some ... some *shopping* during your stay."

Shayla had suppressed a groan at the thought of more days in the oppressive opulence of the palace, but her ears pricked up at that last stammered sentence. What the heck was that about? And she had not long ago been drinking tea with Chalwen ap Gwynodd. If she had something to say, why not simply say it there? Puzzled, Shayla turned the message capsule over in her hands. The security keys were unusually thorough. This felt like something to be viewed in private. "And do you have any details of transport back to Eloon?"

"They must involve fleet movements I'm not privy to. The message might contain instructions." He spread his hands in desperate helplessness. "I only wish I could be of more assistance, My Lady."

———•◆•———

Alone at last in a lavish apartment fit for heads of state, and biting back her impatience, Shayla turned once more to the message capsule. One by one, the locks opened to her identity and access codes until the brief contents lay bare. Only for a few minutes, though. The capsule included hard-wired mechanisms to erase the message once read.

Hammer of War had been captured and was being escorted back to Magentis. The renegade battleship would be supplemented with reliable crew and would eventually join the exploratory fleet assembling near the Imperial/Firenzi border. It would also be her ride back to Eloon.

Shayla frowned. The sinking in the pit of her stomach eased as she read on. She hurriedly committed the remaining instructions to memory, including a dangerously classified package of security codes, the merest possession of which would merit summary execution.

She paused to savor the irony. The all-powerful Imperial Chief of Security begging a favor from the governor-assassin. A loose end to be tidied up. One of those difficulties that couldn't be addressed through normal, legal, means. Chalwen demanded stealth, discretion, and total deniability. But Chalwen guessed, correctly, that this was one assignment that Shayla would be happy to undertake.

Her lips twisted in the merest hint of a smile. She did indeed have some shopping to do.

———•◆•———

Commander Haalv Lekk thumbed the code to his private quarters. He entered, and leaned against the door as it closed behind him, allowing his weariness to show now he was away from snooping eyes. As an expert in security matters, he'd always succeeded in keeping his quarters free from unwanted surveillance.

With some difficulty he'd swallowed his gall at best-laid plans lying in ruins around him. It could, he reflected, have been a lot worse. That buffoon Scorf and many senior officers had taken their own lives when they'd finally been cornered, rather than be returned to Magentis to face charges of treason. But they could hardly execute *everyone* sympathetic to the Emperor's uncle or there would be no one left to run the empire. And he'd always been careful to cover his tracks. Nothing of the joint plot with those damnable Firenzi could be traced back to him.

The original plan to force Carver to free her prisoners had evaporated when her abduction from Imperial custody went so badly wrong. The backup plan to act with force dissolved in mutual suspicion when the asinine Scorf chose to seize what he saw as an opportunity for pre-emptive action.

At that moment Lekk had realized the truth, blindly denied by the assembled captains, that it was time to abandon a hopeless position and retrench for a future chance. Long before that final battle, he'd already set in motion measures to tidy any loose ends that could lead back to him.

The most dangerous witness to his treasonous thinking had been dealt with most fortuitously. It hadn't been hard to manipulate Scorf into showing no mercy to that battleship. In Scorf's eyes, *Admiral George Leonard's* sudden arrival had represented a fatal shift in the balance of power. Scorf might have wavered in the end if he'd been allowed to realize their true helplessness, so intercepting the pleas of that Carver woman had been a worthwhile risk.

That he was still alive, relatively free, and even promoted, proved his precautions had been effective. True, he was a watched man for his political sympathies and consigned to an unwanted voyage of discovery, but Grand Duke Ivan would soon also be freer than he had any right to be. Between them, they'd turn this situation to their advantage. Eventually. They'd waited and plotted for years. They could wait and plot a few more.

He sniffed. Something felt off. A strange scent in his cabin, barely detectable, but there. A cold sting in his neck startled him. He turned to face his attacker. Instant agony burned him to the core and blinded him. All his senses froze, succumbing to the unimaginable pain that scored his mind.

Vision returned in patches, and hearing. A low voice was guiding him across the room. His feet moved of their own volition, powerless to resist the instructions.

He recognized the voice. Carver! Panic gripped him. How did she get into his cabin? He'd set those locks himself. Again he tried to look around and was rewarded by another stab like icicles through his mind. This time a hastily-learned reflex relinquished all thought of voluntary movement and the pain receded as rapidly as it had come. Trylex. The control drug. How in Space had she gotten hold of that rare concoction?

"Chalwen ap Gwynodd sends her regards. She knows much of what you've done, but only by gut and inference. She has nothing to hold against you in any court of law."

The voice behind him whispered on. The icicles had now moved from his mind to his stomach. The words that technically put him in the clear nonetheless filled him with dread. She would hardly have broken into the cabin and drugged the security chief of an Imperial capital ship just for a chat.

"She knows you orchestrated the poisoning that you tried to pin on me. It galls her that she can't prove it, but sometimes we just have to do what's right, not what we can prove. All off the record and utterly deniable, of course."

The bottom dropped out of Lekk's world. This was an assassination.

"Good boy. Sit on the edge of the bunk, facing me."

Helpless, his mind recoiling all the while, his body meekly complied.

"But I know what you did. I remember your voice mocking me and condemning a fine ship to a needless death."

She approached him with a long needle. Despite himself, he tried to follow her movements with his eyes, and to draw back as the needle slid gently up one nostril. The inner pain this time was joined by molten fire as the tip of the needle drove on up into his skull.

When his vision cleared, Carver was wrapping the needle carefully back in its cloth packaging.

"By my estimation," she said, "your life is now measured in months. There won't even be a lucky accident to arouse the suspicions of the habitually paranoid. The fleet will be well on its way and far from help by the time symptoms start to show, then your mind will rot from the inside."

She slipped the packaging inside her robe and pulled out another, smaller, bundle.

"My greatest sadness is that when you finally die, you'll have no idea who did this to you, or why. But let's enjoy a few minutes of realization before I sedate you and wipe your memories of the last half hour."

So they sat, she smiling, he mute but reeling inside in mindless terror. Finally she sighed and picked up two gleaming medipens. She patted his cheek, gently, sisterly. "Pleasant dreams."

The end

Afterword

If you've enjoyed reading a book — any book, not just this one — please consider leaving a review where other readers can find it.

One of the greatest challenges Indie authors face is gaining visibility in the immense marketplace of online publishing. Indies can't hope to compete with big publishers for shelf space or advertising copy or magazine column-inches. Our visibility to readers, our ability to be found, rests on ranking algorithms at online stores. Those algorithms rank books on sales and reviews.

You've got this book in your hands. You've already made me happy. The best way to make me even happier is to leave an honest review wherever you bought the book, or on a readers' forum where you hang out.

Thank you!